DEMON'S TEAR

About the Author

R.E. Sanders was born in England and moved to Wales to study archaeology. He has published the novella *Tann's Last Stand* and the novel *A Path of Blades* both set in the same world. He lives in Cardiff.

Visit https://resanderswrites.wixsite.com/r-e--sanderswrites for more information about R.E. Sanders.

THE JANTAKAI SAGA

BOOK ONE

DEMON'S TEAR

R.E. SANDERS

This novel is entirely a work of fiction. The names, characters and incidents portrayed in it are the work of the author's imagination. Any resemblance to actual persons, living or dead, events or localities is entirely coincidental.

No generative AI was used in the production of any of the text or images that are included in this book.

Copyright © 2024 by R.E. Sanders
Cover by getcovers
Maps by Inkarnate
All other artwork by P.A.Bennett

All rights reserved. No part of this publication may be reproduced, stored in a retrieval system, or transmitted, in any form or by any means, electronic, mechanical, photocopying, recording or otherwise, without the prior permission of the copyright owner.

First edition May 2024
ISBN: 9798880395637

https://resanderswrites.wixsite.com/r-e--sanderswrites

Sing, muses of life and death, of war and peace. Of betrayal and hope, of two brothers and of the forging of the Swords.

- Prathin Pra Mithrin

CONTENTS

Map	*viii - ix*
PROLOGUE	1
PART ONE	5
PART TWO	87
PART THREE	157
PART FOUR	251
PART FIVE	331
PART SIX	403
EPILOGUE	527
GLOSSARY	535
AUTHOR'S STATEMENT	539
THANK YOU	540

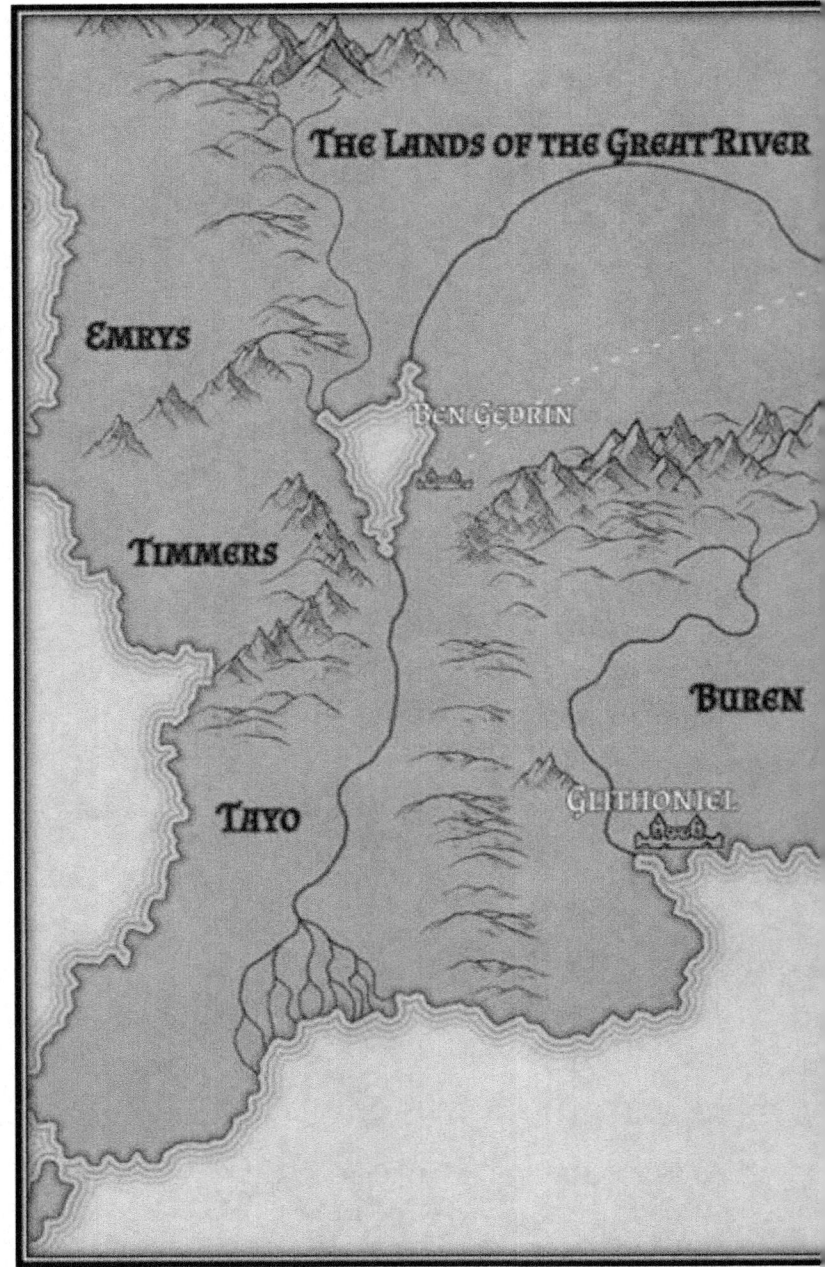

The Jantakai
The Lands of the Twin Swords

PROLOGUE

The power of the final blow had been terrific.

The warrior knelt on the edge of the high escarpment, as he did not have the strength to stand. His eyes were heavy with fatigue and grief as he gazed down into the abyss, trying to comprehend what he had done.

The war had threatened his people's very existence. Hordes of beasts with terrifying, inhuman strength had poured down from the hills. They sought nothing but destruction, and were relentless.

Outlying villages had fallen, one by one, the good people torn to pieces by the creatures' cruel claws. The thought of their pain alone was enough to make him weep, even after everything else he had endured.

He and his eleven brothers had fought desperately, alongside their mighty father, the King Leowrac. Yet, they had not slowed the advance and soon the enemy was at the gates of the capital Ostrebrost.

Fire, death, terror. The creatures attacked in unceasing waves and the fall of the city, and then the country, seemed inevitable. That was when his father had been forced into his terrible decision.

Kell, for that was his famous name, closed his eyes and let out a small sob at the memory. He knew that there had been no other choice. His father could not abide his people's suffering.

So, he had unlocked the ancient chest, that should have remained locked. He drew forth the sacred, historic swords, that should not have been drawn. He looked into his sons' faces, staring deep into their eyes. At last, as if bearing a heavy weight, he had raised the Twin Swords and gone out through the city gates.

The deeds of that night would be woven into sagas to be sung through the ages. Blood, and courage. Fear and triumph. And everywhere, death. At the centre of it all, his famous father and the power of the Twin Swords.

He had shattered the enemy ranks and driven them back. His twelve sons had followed on his heels; hounds on the scent of a lone wolf. Soon, the other brothers fell behind, looking after the survivors as Kell and his father surged ahead.

Kell still felt the exultation, and the agony. Mixed emotions warred within him as he recalled ferocious charge through the night. It had surely saved their country, but doomed their father.

For the power of the Swords was wild, and malicious. It was too much for a man to bear for long without being corrupted. It coursed through his father throughout that long night, warping his mind and changing him irreversibly as they chased their foe.

The pursuit of the beasts brought them here, into the northern mountains and to the brink of a deep, forbidding chasm. The cliff fell away, sheer as a sword, to a dark and ancient forest below.

Leowrac had turned and Kell knew immediately that he was lost. His eyes were not his own. His hands were twisted into claws around the well-worn hilts of the Swords.

One sword gleamed with the cool, calm power of flowing water; the other writhed and rippled like the coils of a serpent. Using both together had taken all the strength that Leowrac possessed.

Now, the Swords would possess him.

Leowrac attacked. With murderous intent he swung the Swords at his youngest son. Kell brandished his own blade, *Myrkybriardmest*, and blocked the strike. Leowrac lashed out again and Kell was resolute in defence. Their skills were evenly matched, both powerful men, and as the King attacked savagely Kell countered every blow.

Their duel had lasted a day and night, atop that high, barren place. Kell's exhaustion grew as his father seemed to gain strength. The end was near.

Kell knew what he must do but dreaded to do it.

As dawn broke, he stumbled and Leowrac was on him, quick as a falcon's stoop. He lifted the Serpentsword to end his son's life, but Kell's trip was feigned.

He leapt up, surprising the beast that had once been his beloved father. His first strike stole one of the Twin Swords from his father's hand. The Riversword. As he grasped it, a calming force flowed through his body. It whispered to him in the bubbling tones of a mountain stream, speaking of peace and urging him to stay his hand.

A roar came from once-was-Leowrac. Now the evil power of the Serpentsword was possessing him completely. Now, he was more monster than man.

Kell had but a bare moment to gather all his resolve, all his courage, and all his remaining strength. Then he struck with the Riversword. The blow hit with the force of a bursting dam, as if the power of the ancestors themselves drove it home. It echoed to the tips of the mountains. It would echo down the ages.

Leowrac fell. The final blow from his youngest son had defeated him. His legs gave way and he tumbled backwards.

Kell staggered forward and fell to his knees as his father, the King of Banahgar, fell from the high cliff. His body tumbled like a broken doll and was lost in the trees below. The tangled branches swallowed his limp form, and he was gone. Lost forever.

Kell knelt there for a long time. One by one, his eleven brothers joined him and he felt the judgement of their eyes pierce him like a hundred spears.

He had killed their father. He had killed the King. Nothing would be the same, ever again.

So sing the skalds. From that day to this, the braided Sjonacaidhan travelled the land, telling the tales to ensure that those deeds were not forgotten.

With Leowrac's fall the Serpentsword was lost. Kell struggled with his grief and guilt for many years, until he too vanished. He had taken the Riversword with him, wherever it was that he went.

The Swords were both gone from Banahgar, and their power waned. The exploits of Twelve Brothers were celebrated in legend as Sjonacaidh told the stories again and again, until all knew them by heart. The tale of the Twin Swords faded to a cautionary parable.

But, although they were lost they were not destroyed. Their power waned but a spark endured. The story of the Swords became myth but was not forgotten.

The Twin Swords slept through many years of history, their potency and danger no more than a memory.

Soon, they will wake.

PART ONE

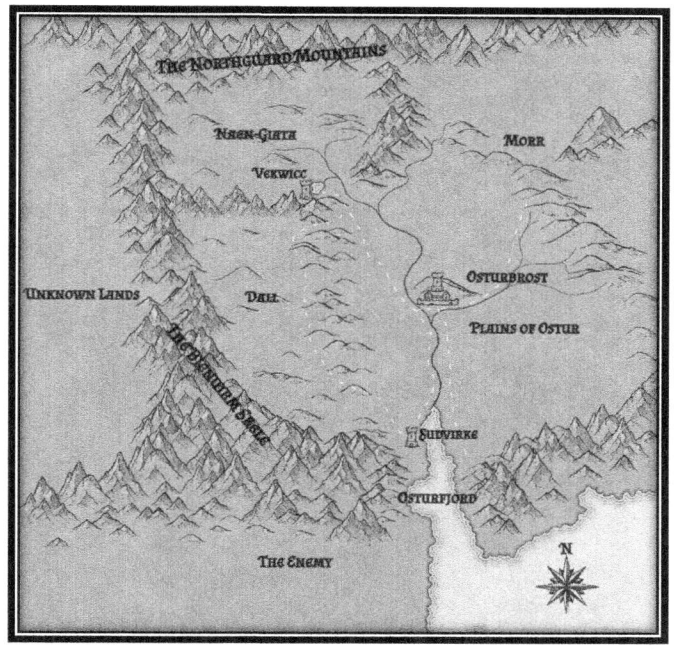

BANAGHAR

ONE

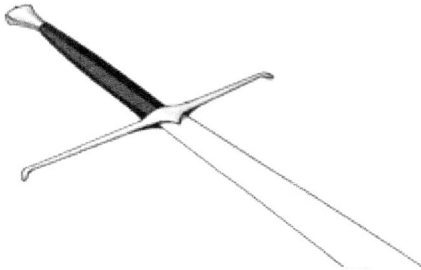

The earth moved.

Rock cracked, soil heaved and the ground shifted in shuddering, shaking convulsions. It boomed like thunder. Gaping fissures opened, like hungry mouths. Farmhouses, forests and their unfortunate inhabitants were swallowed, sinking into the black depths in those destructive moments.

Then, all was still again. The hillsides ceased their restless rolling and the dust settled.

But, somewhere deep underground, in a silent, forgotten void…something stirred.

Eain Connow ran.

He ran in warm afternoon sunshine, but dark clouds gathered over the mountains. Dusk would soon close in. The clatter of a distant rockfall broke the still of the afternoon as house-sized boulders tumbled down the ragged slopes behind him. He ignored it. His mind was on the path ahead.

Time was running out.

He paused and turned, teeth bared in a grimace of doubt. The small group of trainees he led were spread out down the hillside, jogging steadily up to his position. Should he nag them to move faster?

Towering mountains filled his eyeline, running north to south in broken, jagged ridges. Even in the summer, the very highest were crowned with gleaming hoods of white snow. The road they had used to get here ran away into the distance, skirting their feet to vanish into the northeast.

He already felt that he had pushed them too hard this day. Actions could be better motivation than words. If he was calm, impassive and appeared unfatigued, then the ten youngsters that followed him would mirror his attitude. He hoped.

He had promised that the Masters' messages would be delivered by sundown of this day. He could feel them, a solid, leather wrapped bundle inside his coat. To fail would be to shame himself, letting down the Masters who had scratched their runes onto the linen parchment.

'We could be in Osturbrost now if it wasn't for the rest of them slowing us down.' Eain looked up at the speaker, as she reached the crest of the climb and joined him.

Cerla was a tall and long-legged girl a few years younger than him. She was always one of the fastest and most resilient runners, although he wondered whether her speed and endurance were strengthened by the motivation of keeping the others behind her.

She was breathing deeply but evenly, a slight pinkness in her cheeks the only sign of exertion. She was right, too. Eain could have run this distance easily alone and cut hours off the time.

This was not just a messenger mission, though. It was a test. For them, a test of their speed and endurance and for him, a trial of his ability to lead. Could he motivate this group of younger soldiers to keep running when they were tired, keep moving when all they wanted was to rest? That was his challenge.

The others were just starting to lag. Eain had outpaced all of them on this short climb apart from Cerla and the tousle haired Edich Iansson, who was also looking back down the track with his hands on his hips. Eain masked his worry as he replied to Cerla.

'We will get there together,' he replied. 'Or not at all. Train together, run together, win or lose together. You know that, Cerla.' She rolled her eyes but said nothing. Edich nodded. Eain had grown up alongside the younger man and knew he could rely on him.

Despite his words, which came easily, Eain fretted. To arrive at the fortress at Osturbrost after dusk was to fail. Failure could not be tolerated. He would have to answer for it, but they would all be punished.

He was a Claihedehlar, the second highest rank in the army of the Claihed and below only the red-shirted men of the Claihedehmore. He was responsible for the younger trainees of the Sverlaeggare beneath him, a duty which pressed on his shoulders like a shirt of iron.

The others began to arrive in ones and twos. Eain watched as they strode the last few yards to where he stood in the heathery ground beside the road, but held his tongue.

'Time for a rest, eh?' said Haefrad as he flung himself down. Eain groaned inwardly as Foinn, with his long, lanky frame and straggly fair hair, joined Haefrad where he lay in the heather. It was always the same with this group. They tired towards the end of the run and resorted to jests and banter to keep their spirits up. Eain wished he could join their easy camaraderie, but he was a rank apart and always felt like an outsider.

'Sweating cobs, boss,' chuckled Kater, as he sat, a grin on his face as always. 'Not too far now, is it? Time for a breather. I saw you, Haef!' He turned to his friend. 'Saw you looking over your shoulder! Didn't want me to catch you, eh?'

'Just a quick rest,' announced Eain as the rest arrived, pitching his voice so all ten could hear. 'There is still a way to go before dusk. If we get there late, we might find the gates locked already. And you know what that will mean.'

It would mean punishment for all of them, and Eain did not want them to have to endure that again. The boys bore their punishment, often extra runs or extended sessions of weightlifting, with a resigned stoicism, but it was the shame that he felt that stung worse. He did not want to be the one who always failed.

He turned to stare out to the west. It was early summer, and the days were long. It was late afternoon already though, with many miles still ahead.

The sun glowed like an ember through the hazy, wispy clouds that stretched away to the distant horizon. Blurred by distance, Eain could just make out the jagged black smudge that was Banahgar's mountainous western border.

'I'm ready to keep going,' said a quiet voice at his elbow. Aidtha stood beside him, her chest rising and falling deeply but a steely look in her dark eyes.

She was short and wiry, with the typical dark hair and complexion of a lowlander. Aidtha had told Eain that she had four older brothers, and her whole family were aurochs herders. It showed. She had the stubborn temperament of the huge cows that roamed the plains of Ostur in belligerent herds and would drive herself hard to keep up with the others.

A cool breeze stroked Eain's face. The wind surged through the gap between two green hills that rose to either side of this pass. The road down to the lowlands took the low point on its way from the high mountains of the north. The well-worn trail snaked back, winding through valleys and around the bases of peaks that reared towards the sky.

He closed his eyes for a moment, seeking calm. Five years of training had taught him much about discipline and self-reliance. He drew on it now, thinking how best to inspire these youngsters to move faster. Cerla spoke first.

'You lot are so lazy,' she said, voice dripping with contempt. Her fair hair, long at the back of her head and shorn at the sides, shook in waves as she stood over the sprawled figures of the boys. She radiated the typical aggression of a highlander, those sturdy tribes that dwelled in isolated villages amid the northern peaks.

'No, we're just smart,' retorted Kater. 'I'm recovering, isn't it? Watch me now, I'll outrun all of you girls.'

Cerla scoffed, putting her hands on her hips. 'In your dreams, maybe. You boys spend too much time swinging swords. You can't run.' Aidtha and the other girls stepped forward to stand beside Cerla in solidarity.

Eain seized his chance. 'A race? Loser on boot cleaning duty? Let's go then!'

'Perfect, Kater does a lovely job cleaning boots!' added Edich, grinning. Kater grimaced at his words. Eain was pleased to hear Edich speak up.

He was the younger brother of one of Eain's oldest childhood friends, Arin Iansson. Edich had been devastated when the older boys had gone away to join the Claihed, but his chance soon came. And he had taken it well. A weedy, hapless child, he had transformed in his time with the Claihed and was turning into a tall, broad-shouldered man. In this group, Eain looked to him as a natural second in command and he had proved dependable and loyal so far.

The little group scrambled eagerly to their feet and set off down the track.

The hard-beaten path turned to contour along the steep slopes. This undulating range of hills, green with tussocky grass and short, springy heather marched away southwards as far as the eye could see. Where they fell away the smooth, flat fields and grasslands of the lowlands formed a natural border; the rolling hills of the Dall above, the plain of Ostur below.

Eain had to pump his legs hard to catch up with the group as they sprang away. The men and boys of the Claihed, and the women and girls of the Skjilde shared a common aim in the pursuit of speed and fitness. On foot, they all strove to travel further and faster.

Boys who were able to meet the strenuous physical demands of Claihed training could rise to the highest rank and join the elite warriors of the full Claihedehmore. This was Banahgar's professional army, and the country's pride and joy.

The Skjilde provided similar training but did not send its members to battle. They became messengers, camp wardens and were occasionally called upon as archers. Eain had met plenty of women he would not wish to face in battle, but accepted that there were reasons for the way things were.

This was why the Claihed trainees carried a greatsword across their backs, a mighty weapon around five feet in length and a symbol of Banahgar's historic skill-at-arms. Eain's slapped against his back as he ran.

Just up ahead, the track turned a tight switchback. The hillside was so steep here that the road had been built in zigzags to enable the passage of ox-drawn wagons, laden with quarried stone or piled with crops, to make the difficult journey.

A large boulder sat beside the bend and atop this was a tall and improbable figure. Twenty feet high and shaped like a tall, regal man, it was a statue made of stripped pine logs. The materials were simple, but the skill of the woodworker gave the figure an imposing realism. It held a carved wooden greatsword, almost as long as the sculpture was tall, and to Eain the figure looked ready to strike.

This was a tribute to Bran, one of the twelve sons of Leowrac, the last King of Banahgar. The carved lines on its noble face stared out impassively towards Osturbrost. Eain reached out to touch the towering figure's wooden toe as he ran past. A patch on the foot had been worn to a polished sheen by generations of hands doing likewise, hoping to obtain some of the strength and prowess of the Brothers.

The rest of the group copied the action as they rounded the bend, and they all ran on again to the next switchback. His hopes rose. If he could keep them moving at this pace, then they might make it to Osturbrost before dusk.

As he jogged easily around the next bend, the ground hard and gritty beneath the soles of his boots, an excited shout from behind made him turn.

'Cloudberries!'

Kater had darted off the path and was striding purposefully into the heather.

Just beyond where he stood, a green cleft in the hillside marked the path of a small stream. It babbled noisily as the foaming water flowed across the polished stones of the stream bed. Kater stopped at the crest of the bank and even from this distance Eain could see the clusters of red-orange berries that grew thickly on the bushes at his feet.

Kater straightened, scooping a handful into his mouth, a wide grin across his face. As most of the others surged off the path to join him, Haefrad and Foinn among them, Eain's heart sank.

Cloudberries were a rare treat, prized by all Banahgarians, but he did not have time for any further delays. He could imagine their reactions if he tried to drag them away, though. He hesitated.

'Look over there, boys!' Kater was pointing out more clumps of the unevenly shaped berries growing further over the bank, his mouth full as he chewed gleefully. 'There's loads of them!'

Aidtha and Cerla stayed beside Eain, but the rest of the group milled around in the heather. Haefrad's arm went back, then snapped forward and a small red mark bloomed on Foinn's face. There was a moment of silence, then the tall Sverlaegga bent his lanky frame and hurled a handful of berries back in the opposite direction.

In a heartbeat, cloudberries were flying everywhere. The creamy white linen of their shirts was spotted with bright red marks where the fruits found their target. Even Edich was giggling and joining in with the battle.

Eain despaired. He knew he was losing control. They would be late, and they would face punishment. He would be shamed and who he was, and what his family had done, would be rubbed in his face once more. His young charges would suffer, because of his weakness.

'Blood! Blood!' laughed Kater. His hands were slick with the deep red juice from the berries, and he pressed them to his face. The crimson palm-prints stood out lividly. With the others also splattered with the juice, the whole scene resembled a battlefield.

When Eain was much younger, his mother had sent him out to gather berries. It had been autumn and the brambly bushes near the village had been heavy with fruit. He had reached deep into the thorny thickets to find the plumpest, piling his woven wicker basket high. His hands had been dyed with the thick, red juice.

It was only then that he had noticed the pain. His hands and wrists suddenly throbbed like fire. He held them out and stared down, watching as blood oozed from scores of tiny cuts that crisscrossed his skin. As it dribbled down to his fingertips and mingled with the berry juice, he felt a sob of fear and worry grow irrepressibly in his chest.

He had run all the way home, his harvest forgotten.

'Ow!' Eain's attention was wrenched back to the present by a loud cry beside him. Aidtha was wiping reddish residue from her face.

Raucous laughter rang out as Haefrad and Kater clutched at each other, wracked with mirth. Foinn was staring across to where Aidtha was wiping the mess from her dark skin, guilt writ plain across his face.

Something inside Eain snapped. This behaviour was disrespectful and dishonourable, and he knew it was up to him to stop it.

'Enough!' he roared. Laughter stilled immediately to silence. He felt his cheeks flush as his pulse pounded in his ears. 'You forget yourselves!' You are representing Banahgar, and your country deserves better behaviour than this. The Ancestor's curse you!'

The group shifted awkwardly in the face of Eain's frustration. 'We have a task that is not yet complete,' he continued, his voice quieter and calmer now. 'Unless you do not remember? We must get these messages to Osturbrost, and I intend to see it done if I have to drag you the rest of the way. Back on the road and get running. Now.'

He stepped forward to stand before Haefrad and Kater. Haefrad was broad, and as tall as Eain, while Kater was a little shorter. Eain drew himself up.

'You two will run at the front. You will not pause or walk until I give you permission. Do you understand?'

'Yes, Master,' they mumbled, before moving off and breaking into a run as the track continued steeply downhill. Eain tapped Edich on the shoulder as the rest of the group followed.

'You're to count for me,' he said to the younger Sverlaegga. 'I want them running for a thousand paces, walking half that.' Edich would count in his head as they ran to keep track of the time. One by one they saluted and set off along the road.

Eain breathed deeply as he ran, pleased to be finally making progress and trying to suppress the guilt he felt for his angry outburst. It had been needed, though. He told himself that and tried not to worry about being late.

He noticed the boys glancing at each other as they ran, discontent on their faces. But they remained silent. That was probably for the best.

He hated to lose his temper. He knew that the best leaders were capable of always remaining calm, but sometimes his frustration became overwhelming. This group knew him well and were used to his fleeting fury. He hoped that they also knew that it was a sign they had pushed him too far.

The hillside spread out before them, soft and green with swaying grass and tufty heather. Here and there stunted oaks or the odd rowan stood a lonely watch over the lowlands below. The day was still bright, but Eain kept glancing towards the distant western horizon. The sun, glowing a washed-out yellow through a haze of clouds, seemed a hair's breadth from setting. The day was almost done.

The isolated humpback ridge of the Konnarstyrie stood out clearly from the plains, even in the fading light. This range of hills was revered through Banahgar as a place of legends. The kings had dwelled here in ancient times and battles had been fought on and around the steep slopes. So much history had been laid down there, never to be forgotten.

The town of Osturbrost huddled around the southern extent of the range. Through the still evening light, Eain could pick out the line of the road, the long span of the Osturbridge, and the city wall beyond.

Would the gate in that wall still be open as they hurried across the bridge? Or would they be shut out as night fell?

TWO

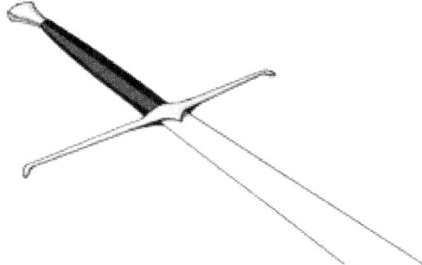

The group had run in near silence, Eain hoping he had said the right things and with enough authority to keep them moving quickly. So, it proved.

He had set Edich to count the turns, as they jogged a thousand paces then walked five hundred. They repeated this, heedless of fatigue and the oncoming night, and the miles passed swiftly beneath their boots.

'Last push for the gates now!' called Eain as they jogged along the flat, straight road that led to the bridge. The fields to either side were high with growing crops, green leaves swaying and swathes of tall wheat rippling in the evening breeze.

He upped his pace, moving easily to the front of the column. 'We can make it in time!' He spoke as much for himself as for the others. His voice was even but his insides were roiling. He could not bear to be late again. To have an example made of him, again.

He squinted into the distance. The bridge was a dark line across the deep-cut channel of the river Ostur, and the solid grey bulk of the city wall rose beyond. The gateway was a dark, indistinct void in the wall. Was it open, or shut? The light was fading, the sun had set.

Eain grimaced as he ran. He had to hope.

His hope was dashed moments later. Even as his boots clattered on the worn planks of the ancient bridge, he could see that the gates had been closed.

'Sorry, Master,' said Edich between deep breaths as he slowed to a walk beside Eain. He smiled grimly in response. It was too late for apologies.

'Eain Connow and Sverlaeggare arriving!' Eain raised his voice to be heard beyond the tall, aged oak planks of the gate. He waited a few heartbeats and then thumped on the gate with his fist.

There was a pause.

They would be let in, Eain knew, even if they were made to wait. Even though they faced reprimand and punishment. The tightly wrapped strips of linen in Eain's pack would guarantee that the gates were opened.

'I bear messages from Vekwicc,' he continued, projecting his voice. 'Messages for the Masters.'

'Latecomers!' rang out a voice, muffled and indistinct through an inch of solid oak. A small hatch in the gate folded back. A single, glowering eye peered out at them. 'Name yourself, latecomers!' The voice was clearer with the hatch open, and Eain recognised it immediately.

'Callan?' he asked, relief flooding through him. This might mean he would escape punishment. 'Open the gate, you big ox. We're starving!'

'Connow?' There was a slight laugh in that voice. 'I should've known. Late again? This will go down as well as ever.' His voice dripped with sarcasm but was punctuated by a solid thumping as the bar behind was lifted. The gate inched open.

Eain rushed through to be confronted by the imposing figure of Callan Fraevar. Several inches taller, Callan looked wiry but Eain knew from painful experience that there was terrifying strength in those long limbs.

'Where've you been?' asked Eain, reaching out to grasp his old friend's wrist in a warriors' handshake. 'Not seen you in months. It's been great.'

Callan grinned. 'Just got back from a stint at Sudvirke. The Seekers brought in a bunch of new Hniffare. Wanted them to be put through their paces with a bit of unarmed.'

Hniffare were the very lowest rank of the Claihed, teenage boys just past the age of majority who had been recruited by the Seekers. The Seekers were experienced Claihedehmore who travelled the land, visiting isolated villages to find fifteen-year-old lads with the aptitude to train with the Claihed. To be selected by the Seekers was a huge honour for the boy and his family, although few of those selected made it all the way to becoming full Claihedehmore.

Eain glanced down. Callan's knuckles were bruised. He was a fearsome boxer. The Hniffare he had been sent to train would have had a very tough initiation.

'If I'm allowed to stay here a few days I'll come and find you. With luck, I'll escape another messenger job. Now, if I get a move on, then they might not notice I was late arriving.'

Callan's grin faltered. 'Too late! I saw your group on the bridge and sent a lad to the fortress. One of the Claihedehmore will be waiting for you.'

Eain swore. He beckoned to his group, who were milling around uncertainly in the gateway.

'Let's not make it worse,' he called, raising his voice. 'Let's move, and quickly.' He started forward along the street that led from the west gate into the centre of the town.

'Hey, Connow,' called Callan as Eain moved off. 'If you don't want to keep getting in trouble for being late…' Eain paused, half-turning towards his friend.

'...Stop being late!' Callan finished, laughing to himself. Eain grinned and turned away, but the grin became a grimace as he broke into a run.

This was exactly the sort of thing Callan found very amusing; other people getting in trouble. It had always been easier for him. His resilience and natural physicality meant that he had taken the challenge of the Claihed in his long stride.

Cal had arrived with a blank slate. He had never had to deal with the judgement, the expectation and the pressure that Eain had faced purely because of his name. His family name.

Eain had needed to prove himself every single day, to everyone he met. He had to show everyone that he would not be the same as his grandfather.

Haefrad and Kater turned left onto a cobbled street that rose steeply. Eain increased his pace and the rest of the group followed.

Raising his eyes, he beheld once more the solid, squat fortress of Osturbrost. This functioned as a garrison, a school, and the headquarters of the Claihed in the lowlands. Dusk deepened and the torches illuminating the gateway sent flickering, orange-edged shadows climbing up the rough, sheer walls.

Set on the flanks of the southernmost hill of the Konnarstyrie, it loomed reassuringly over the town, and afforded a grand view over the wide, flat river plans that spread out east, west and south. No enemy could approach Osturbrost by land or up the river without being observed from many miles distant.

'Roast beef for supper, Master?' asked Cerla, hopefully. She unconsciously touched her hand to her belly. It was a long time since any of the group had eaten.

'We are late,' replied Eain. 'We'll get brawn and bread, if we're lucky.' Then the gateway was before them, and all eyes turned upwards.

Set on a stone-built plinth beside the gate was another tall sculpture built from tree trunks. This one was, if anything, more imposing and impressive than the representation of Bran on the sloping borders of the Dall.

For this was Bran's brother, Kell. Although he had been the youngest of the Twelve Brothers, he was reckoned to be the best swordsman and had become their leader after the passing of the last king, Leowrac.

More, he had designed the first Banahgarian greatsword and achieved mastery of the formidable weapon before founding the Claihed to unite Banahgar's warrior clans. After laying down the foundations of the Claihed and the Rules of the greatsword, he had vanished.

The sages told how he had been bowed by grief and guilt after the death of his father, but even so was still revered throughout the land. The group filed past and each touched Kell's carved foot. The statue's rough surface was lined and darkened with age but still held power and nobility.

Eain bowed his head as he pressed his fingers to the smooth, polished wood. He felt the sculpture's ancient gaze looking down on him. Looking through him, judging him. Was he worthy?

Then he was through the gateway and Kell was left behind. His immediate worries, about the dressing down he was about to receive, returned like a heavy weight on his shoulders.

Beyond the gateway was a wide, flat courtyard; the *claidah*. Walls bounded it on four sides, pierced by many gateways leading to various other parts of the fortress. The main bulk of the fortification rose directly opposite the main entrance. Despite the late hour, with the light fading from the indigo sky and the shadows lengthening, it buzzed with activity.

Individuals scurried to and fro, on errands or just heading to their barracks for the night, while here and there small knots of young men were finishing their day's training. Some sparred with wooden weapons and others performed exercises; lifting carved stone *holters* or long, heavy wooden *cabers* to build strength.

Grunts of exertion and the percussive clatter of strike and parry resounded between the ancient stone walls that surrounded the area.

'Dismissed,' said Eain abruptly. They all knew who he was talking to, and the girls of the Skjilde turned aside to head to their own separate area within the fortress. They would answer for their late arrival to their own Masters.

'You ran well today,' he added, although he felt self-conscious at offering the praise. 'You can all be proud of your efforts.'

Aidtha turned, giving him a brief nod before striding away. It was time for him to report in and face the consequences. He steeled himself.

At the northern end of the courtyard, beneath the higher wall of the inner fortress, a short flight of blocky steps led to a pair of open doors. A bulky figure stood in the doorway, arms folded over a deep chest as he observed the young soldiers practicing with a sour expression on his face.

He was one of the Claihedehmore. A dyed red jerkin showed beneath his thick, crossed arms. It would have a golden crown and sword emblem embroidered upon it to show his rank. These men were professional, career soldiers. Most had seen battle many times and were all expert swordsmen. They were, almost to a man, hard as old oak and entirely lacking in sympathy.

He turned to watch Eain's approach and smiled grimly, eyes gleaming. This man was Arall Rathvedd, also known by his Sword-Name, The Hound's Tooth. Eain knew him all too well.

'*Master* Connow,' he sneered, suffusing the honorific with heavy sarcasm. 'Wonderful that you and friends have finally chosen to join us. I hope you enjoyed your relaxing stroll through the countryside together.'

Eain saluted, the back of his right fist pressed to his left shoulder. 'Master Rathvedd,' he said briskly. 'I apologise for our late arrival. I take full responsibility. I bear messages for the Masters.'

'Give them to me,' replied Rathvedd curtly. His feigned pleasant manner had gone completely. Eain grasped the roll of hide that held the messages and passed them up to Rathvedd. 'The responsibility *is* yours, Connow. Your lateness is disrespectful to your brothers. You will answer for it, but later. First, you will do your drills.'

The Claihedehme gestured a dismissal, his attention already elsewhere. 'Poles against swords,' muttered Rathvedd, as he waved Eain away. 'Get on with it.'

Eain nodded to his younger charges. They knew what to do.

A rack set against one of the walls held bundles of carved wooden swords as well as an equal number of long, straight staffs. Haefrad, Kater and Foinn rushed over and quickly seized swords. The other three; Edich, Guther and Offha lined up against them holding staffs.

Edich and the other two stood shoulder to shoulder, holding the staffs as though they were spears. The other three stepped quickly towards them, swords raised. Eain stood to one side to observe, arms folded.

This was one of the rules that the Claihed applied strictly to the lower ranks. After a day out on an exercise, a session of weapons training was required before they would be allowed a meal.

'The enemy won't wait for you to eat before they attack,' said Eain, reminding them of the reason for the drill. They managed not to groan, although they had heard it all before. 'And most battles are fought on tired legs. The fittest, wins. I want to see full focus now, full effort.'

Most of the Claihed's battles were fought against the Stobyvar, a wild clan of dwarves who raided from Banahgar's northern mountains. They were ferocious but fought with little organisation and sought only to kill and steal. Their attacks were easily repelled by the Claihed.

The enemy that was truly feared was the neighbouring nation of Kotev.

Everyone in Banahgar still talked of the time that Kotev had sailed ships up Osturfjord and invaded. It was forty years ago but there were plenty of elders who had lived through that dark time.

The war had raged for half a year as the mighty Kotevari army advanced steadily across the land. It had taken a heroic and desperate raid by Claihed Masters to turn the tide. The success of this raid had enabled the Claihed to muster and drive the invading Kotevari army back to their boats, but the cost in Banahgarian blood had been heartbreakingly high.

So, the Claihed now trained with another invasion in mind. The entire country was determined that they would never be taken off guard again. A constant watch was held over Osturfjord from the southern fortress of Sudvirke. Meanwhile, the soldiers drilled endlessly with greatswords. The younger ones had to be constantly reminded of the threat. It was just too remote, and distant in history for them to be truly afraid.

Kater was at the forefront as the three swordsmen attacked the short rank of makeshift spearmen. The spearmen thrust their poles forward and Kater knocked them aside with a wide sweep of his sword. Foin moved quickly, slashing his own wooden blade downwards in a powerful stroke that could cut a spear haft, were the sword sharpened steel, but in this case it pinned the staves to the ground.

The spearmen were helpless as Haefrad dashed past the now-useless weapons and tapped his sword to the left and right.

'Dead,' he said in a flat tone. 'Dead, dead.'

Eain felt a small surge of satisfaction. They had at least listened to something he had told them. They were still young, and they could improve their skills further yet.

'Good,' barked Eain. 'Now swap and go again. Spearmen, keep tight. Don't make it easy for them.'

He watched impassively as the teams swapped weapons a few more times. He could almost feel their hunger and fatigue as the light faded from the sky and torches were lit around the perimeter of the *claidah*.

'Enough!' Rathvedd's voice rang out. 'Enough for today. You have practised well.'

He came down the steps towards them. 'Commitment to practice is an admission of the need to improve. Admitting the need to improve reveals a humble spirit. A humble spirit will learn and grow. When you seek to learn and grow is when you find your best self.'

The gentle, wise words sounded jarring spoken by the brutish, granite hewn Claihedehmore.

'Now,' he continued. 'It's your Master's turn. Three swords facing Connow together. Don't pull your strikes. Go.'

Eain had expected this and took a deep breath as he slipped the baldric from his shoulder and leaned his greatsword against the wall of the *claidah*. Facing three swordsmen was difficult, regardless of individual skill. He knew too that Rathvedd would love to see him fail. The thought hardened his resolve, and he clenched his fists in a tight grip around the handle of the wooden practice sword.

Even as he stepped into the space in the middle of the *claidah*, the three sword-bearing Sverlaeggare moved to surround him. Edich and Foinn stood in front, spreading apart to his left and right while Kater stepped around to stand directly behind. Their brows were furrowed, faces serious. There was no joking around now. All three had seen Eain fight before and knew of his skill.

The weight of the long blade in his hands felt familiar, and comforting. The stress of the day was forgotten. Slowly and smoothly, he raised both hands above his head and adopted a stance like that of Kell's statue, but with the blade pointing down his back and towards the ground behind him.

For a heartbeat, all was still. Then he moved decisively. He stabbed backwards, and as the point of the wooden sword extended, he pivoted rapidly on the balls of his feet. Kater was just raising his own blade as Eain's point caught him full in the chest. Eain had known that Kater would try to attack first, thinking to catch him by surprise while out of sight.

It was too obvious. Kater grunted in surprise and pain, staggering back. In the same motion Eain swept the sword back and let the point circle his own head as he took a stride to the right, and then to the left.

Foinn and Edich had been moving forward, but they danced back out of range as the tip of Eain's wooden sword hissed past their noses. They spread further apart, sensibly, threatening him from opposing directions.

Eain set his feet a stride apart, knees slightly bent, and raised the hilt to his right eye. For a moment his blade was horizontal, pointing directly at Edich. The starting pose of the fifth Rule of the Sword, as set down by Kell himself.

His feet moved. He took a rapid stride in Edich's direction, extending his arms to drive his point forward in a rapid thrust. Edich was a good swordsman himself, and fast, and spun his own blade to block and counter.

His riposte found only empty air. Eain's thrust had been a feint, and his true target was Foinn. At the extent of his lunge, he let the point drop and as he pivoted his body, he turned it into a savage downwards cut in the opposite direction.

Foinn was surprised, and got his body out of the way, but not his blade. The two wooden swords collided with a jarring crack, and Foinn's was beaten to the ground. Without moving his feet, Eain followed up with an identical diagonal cut, slanting towards Foinn's right shoulder.

The tall youngster dodged desperately but before he could regain balance or raise his sword, Eain's next blow thumped into his ribs.

Eain finished the technique, Kell's sixth Rule of greatsword combat, and his last stroke came to rest lightly at Foinn's throat. He tapped gently then spun to face his last opponent, and his main threat of defeat; Edich Ianssøn.

Edich had talent, and a couple of years of Claihed training had transformed him from a timid, scrawny child into a confident, powerfully built young man. Not everyone could cope with the physical intensity of the training – it had been too much for Edich's older brother Arin – but Edich himself revelled in it. The greatsword looked at home in his strong hands.

Eain could not let him win. He could not face any more shame this day.

Edich set himself in a balanced guard, legs spread and his blade extended forwards. Njall's guard. Eain could have mirrored that stance. It would have made sense.

Instead, he thrust his left shoulder forward and set himself with his sword trailing backwards and down towards the ground; the stance named after Bran himself.

As he paused, he thought quickly. What would Edich do? He clearly respected Eain's skill, and his guard was set to defend against his first attack and offer a quick riposte. Edich shuffled his feet slightly and Eain made up his mind.

Two quick steps, left and right, closed the distance. His sword whipped up, the point travelling towards Edich's midriff with ferocious speed. As the blade started moving from behind Eain's body, Edich saw it, but too late. He blocked, but the pure brutal power of Eain's strike knocked his blade aside, and left Edich out of balance.

Eain's next strike, another uppercut from the other direction, thumped into Edich's guts and the younger boy doubled over, winded.

Eain spun and saluted towards Rathvedd, fist to chest with his sword pointing down. He would not be criticised for failing to show respect. Only then did he turn back to check on his young charges.

'Are you alright?' he asked quietly, looking around towards the three defeated Sverlaeggare. They were all gingerly rubbing bruises but did not seem badly hurt. Eain looked away, moving towards the steps.

'Three cheers for *Master* Connow,' sneered Rathvedd. 'Bravely beating up a bunch of kids.' Eain set his jaw and held his tongue. He was used to this.

Before the Claihedehme could try to provoke Eain further, the sound of rapid footsteps rang out. All heads turned as a young, dark-haired man sprinted across the *claidah*.

'Message!' he gasped. In the flickering torchlight his face shone slickly with sweat and his breathing came in ragged gasps. He had clearly run far and fast. 'Urgent message! For the Masters!'

The lad brandished a roll of linen. The dark, black "M" rune was clearly visible, drawn on the linen in charcoal. This message was for the eyes of one of the Masters alone. Arall Rathvedd pursed his lips, deciding what to do, but at that moment there was movement in the doorway behind him.

As the figure emerged, the gathered ranks saluted as one. The slender, bald-headed man that moved out into the orange torchlight was Skyle Burns, one of the twelve Masters of the Claihed.

While Rathvedd projected aggression, power and a capacity for brutal violence, Burns was different. Eain had never heard him raise his voice, or act without calm consideration. He was respected as one of the oldest members of the Claihed and yet his skill with a greatsword was unmatched, his prowess near to legendary.

The hilt of his unusual, single-edged greatsword that shared his Sword-Name, The Centre, loomed over his left shoulder.

'Show me,' he said. His voice was quiet but all in the *claidah* heard his words. The messenger passed the folded linen up to the Master, bowing his head deeply as he did. Burns unfolded the message with a casual attitude that bordered on disinterest. He read. After a moment, he passed the small square of linen across to Rathvedd.

Eain looked between the two men, similar in height but where Rathvedd was dark and broad, Burns was pale and slender. They shared glances. There was something wrong. Burns remained cold and emotionless, but Rathvedd was suddenly tense. His forearms bulged with tight cords as he gripped the message.

'Tell them,' said Burns, coldly.

'But…' Rathvedd was hesitant. 'The Masters…'

'All must know,' cut in Burns. 'Tell them.'

Rathvedd took a deep breath and reluctantly turned to face the *claidah*. Eain's heart hammered in his chest. The stolid Claihedehme's unease was clear, and for such a man to hint at an emotion meant that he was truly rattled.

'This message has come from Sudvirke,' he announced, eyes darting. He paused. He licked his lips. 'Ships have been seen sailing up Osturfjord. Kotevari ships.'

A murmur went around. They all knew what this meant.

'Kotev are attacking again,' he continued. 'Banahgar is under attack. We are at war.'

THREE

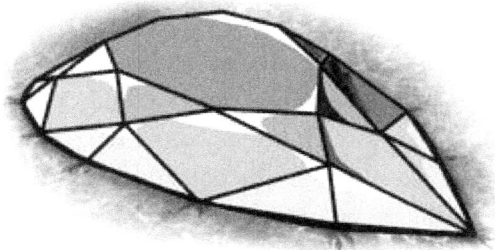

Clayton Moore licked his lips. The carved stone all around him glowed, lit an unearthly red by the fire below.

A bead of sweat rolled down his brow and he tried not to let the weight of it disrupt his concentration. He was so close. So close to victory.

He calmed his breathing. His inhalations and exhalations barely disturbed the still, stagnant air. It had not been easy to get this far, and there was no reason to expect the final steps to be any more straightforward.

Concentrate on the trap.

He studied every detail of the scene before him, considering every angle. The walls and columns around him held a heavy permanence in their carved planes and angles but hid many moving parts. Many secrets.

Breathe. Take your time.

He stood before a portal. Formed of two uprights and a lintel hewn from the same smooth black stone, the open doorway gaped invitingly before him. This was it. Beyond the threshold was his goal. Passing through the doorway would kill him, if he made a mistake now.

He had passed many dangers to reach this forbidding doorway, this cube of carved stone hidden deep within a dark and labyrinthine underland. He had overcome them all, needing every ounce of his skill and persistence. He had found what many others had not, and had succeeded where many had failed, where many had died.

Because he was the best.

He had entered through the half-buried doorway of the forgotten, ancient temple as the light of both moons shone brightly into the interior. The silvery glow traced a clear path deeper into the sunken, ruined structure but either side remained shrouded in darkness so profound as to feel like a living, malicious presence.

Gathering his courage and opening his dark eyes as wide as he could, he stepped forward; toward the darkness and away from the light.

Moore had descended a flight of cracked stone steps from the entrance hall into a lower level of the building with cat-like stealth. The soft soles of his shoes still caused rasping echoes though he moved in near-silence. The floor tilted and the walls leaned inward as if frozen in the process of collapsing.

It felt like the ground had opened up and swallowed the temple, a hungry mouth formed by the earth in times long past.

The stories of the lost temple had circulated for years, but the rumours of secrets or treasure were laughed away. The few who had found it told that beyond the first few passageways, the rock and earth had collapsed in on the lower levels. There was nothing there but cold stone. It was a dead end.

Or, it had been.

Moore had been awake to the potential when the first hints reached his ears of tremors in the ground on the border between Anish and Kotev. Demons beneath the earth stirring in their sleep, or merely the earth shifting.

What if what was lost could now be found?

What if those closed passageways were once again open?

He gathered his resolve and moved forward. The passages wound through the earth like a creature's underground burrow, or the web of a spider. Confusing, winding tunnels that twisted and turned, crossed and recrossed.

The crunch of bones beneath his shoes broke the silence. It was easy to get lost down here, easy to forget the way out. Were the bones animal, or human? Another hunter? He did not stop to find out. He knew where he was going, what he was looking for.

And, as he moved forward, the darkness closing around him like a clawed hand, he found it.

The faintest stirring in the dead air warned him before his reaching hands found the void. There was an opening ahead.

His night vision was good, for a human, and he could make out the rent in the side wall of the passageway, a slightly lighter square of darkness in the resolute black of the stone. He squeezed through to sit on the edge, and his breath caught in his throat.

Before him was a cavern. He shook his head slightly. The word "cavern" was inadequate. This was a gallery. A vast void, formed by a gaping, subterranean ravine. Deep below, many fathoms down, he could see the sullen orange glow of *earthfire*. The warmth of it rose to meet him.

Beneath his dangling feet was a sheer drop down to a rocky platform. His sharp eyes could make out several dark shapes sprawled lifelessly on the rocks. He was not the first to find this place, it seemed. But, he would be the first to navigate to the centre.

Turning, he climbed deftly down the underground cliff. His strong fingers found edges and pockets to cling to as he worked ever downwards, the toes of his soft, tight shoes wriggling onto the smallest ledges.

Jumping down the last few feet and landing silently, he ignored the broken bodies on the rocks to either side and stepped forward. The *earthfire* bubbled and hissed, pulsing as if the very earth was living and it was its lifeblood. The air was thick with fumes, and he pulled his woollen scarf up over his mouth. Keeping his breathing shallow required an effort of will, but he did not want to disturb the silence with a cough.

Like stepping stones in a river, black rocks rose from the oozing liquid fire. Chunks of stone which had fallen from above, but could provide a way across. He looked up. Another sheer, black cliff rose on the other side and almost directly above him a broken-off spur of overhanging stone showed where a walkway had been before this gorge had swallowed it.

A less skilled adventurer might have struggled with the crossing, but he moved cautiously and lightly, leaping from rock to rock as the fiery warmth rose beneath him. He would not let his concentration drop now. A six-foot leap took him across the last gap to the opposing cliff and his fingers grasped for holds.

His foot fell, a rocky ledge breaking and dropping into the *earthfire* to be gulped down with a serpentine hiss. His fingers clutched the sharp black rock. He held on. Just.

Calming his breathing, he began to climb. The structure at the end of the walkway was calling out to him.

He pulled over onto the walkway at the top and regarded it carefully. It must be a remnant of the ancient temple; a crypt or cellar that been isolated in this unearthly place in the same upheaval that had buried the upper levels and destroyed the walkway. His goal was what lay beyond the portal, inside the final chamber. The door rose before him, and he drew a breath.

He reached out to the right-hand pillar. The carved stone, marked with *pentangs*, felt unsettlingly smooth and cold beneath his fingertips. Unmoving, forgotten and dead. Quickly, he found the invisible panels in the stone and pushed them in a specific order, with precise timing. One wrong press meant death. He had passed such traps many times before in his long career.

A soft click and thud told him that the trap was disarmed. He stepped forwards into the final chamber. A pedestal stood in the centre of the room, bearing the ultimate prize. Its value was many times more than mere gold. It would allow him to escape. It would allow him to become someone…new.

The culmination of all his work stood before him as he approached the pedestal, an ornate plinth carved from smooth, black marble. Midnight-dark stone flecked with silver and gold and polished to an entrancing sheen, the plinth alone was worth a king's ransom.

Moore barely glanced at it. His attention was entirely held by what rested atop the pedestal. He was transfixed.

A thin beam of crimson light lanced onto the plinth. Channelled to the interior by a crack in the wall, a bright column of fiery light picked out gleaming veins in the dark stone.

As Moore watched the thin red beam, it shifted slightly to shine upon the top of the pedestal. This was the prize. This was what so many others had sought but never found. This was what he alone had the skills to acquire.

The ruby. The almost-mythical Demon's Tear gemstone. Believed lost, but rumoured to exist somewhere and now, here it was within his reach. Moore's eyes glittered even as crimson fire blazed in the very heart of the jewel. It throbbed like a living thing. His breathing quickened.

The deep red, translucent stone was roughly the size of his fist, or a man's heart. It was heart-shaped, with intricate and finely cut facets that split the dim light into a multitude of flashing beams. They flickered on the dark walls as though the thief stood in the centre of a constellation of blood-red stars.

Moore's heart hammered in his chest, and he blinked as for a moment it seemed as if the light at the core of the gem pulsed in time. His hand twitched, summoned to grab at the glassy surface.

TAKE ME.

He shook his head to clear the fancy, and concentrated. He would take the jewel, but in the same manner he had got this far; with professional care and caution.

Don't get attached. It's not for keeping. It's for selling on. Think of the gold!

The shaft of light crept over the surface of the gem, bursting into scarlet lightning within. The glow washed over Moore like eldritch fire, and he bathed in it as he waited for the right moment.

In mute awe, he forced himself to breathe calmly. The glow dimmed, and the life faded from its heart. The fire died and it became as a simple jewel. Dormant, but not extinct.

Only then did the pain from his cramping muscles hit him. He had been staring at the stone, totally motionless, for at least an hour. The time had passed like a couple of heartbeats.

Now. Do what you came to do, now, and get out of here.

Reaching into a pouch at his belt, he selected a replica stone and held it carefully. Legend said that the Demon's Tear was a ruby the size of a man's heart. Moore had spent some time making several replica jewels from paste. The one he had chosen should be an almost exact match for the size and weight of the true ruby.

A weighted trap within the plinth, rigged to go off if the stone was lifted, was a near-certainty. Such a mechanism may have failed after all this time, but he could not take that risk. The world and a badger would drop onto his head if he got this wrong, and the trap was sprung.

Calming himself again with an effort of will, he leaned closer to the pedestal. He poised his hand over the Demon's Tear and held the fake as close as possible with the other.

Breathe. Calm. Breathe.

His hands moved. It was done. All was still. He remained alive.

His heartbeat thudded crazily in his ears as his senses expanded to take in the surroundings, alert for anything different. Any movement or shifting that might signal doom.

There was nothing. The fake rested on the plinth as though it belonged there, and the smooth planes and angles of the famous jewel rested thrillingly against his palm. Allowing himself a small smile he turned, ready to reset all the traps and escape without a trace.

He frowned. His hand felt warm. Red light shone upwards, and he looked down to see the gem glowing once more, its light shining between his fingers. The heat grew as crimson fire raged in the very heart of the stone.

He cried out as the heat began to sear his palm, even through his glove, but he could not let go. His hand was locked around the ruby like an iron claw. Blistering heat roiled up his arm and began to burn within the very core of his being.

The smell of burning flesh filled the room as the glowing ember at the end of his hand seemed to burst into flame. He opened his mouth to scream but no sound escaped his desperate lips. Scarlet flames lit the room, centred on the jewel.

His eyes rolled back in his head as his knees collapsed and he dropped to the hard, stony floor in mute agony. The heat seemed to flay the skin and muscle from his bones, but still he could not let go.

As the torture intensified, he wished fervently for death. Prayed for it. But death would provide no release for Clayton Moore.

Shre Evane Claes, High Priest of the Veil, woke with a scream.

Pain gripped her skull like a clawed fist, and she tumbled from her narrow cot onto the flagstone floor of her cell. She raised her hands to her head and curled her knees into her chest, bracing herself for what she knew was about to come.

A sensation of falling away from her body. Searing agony, lashing through her entire being. Then, silence, absolute darkness and the humbling impression of being within a vast and empty space.

'Desya, I serve,' she said, speaking into the echoing darkness. 'My faith is strong.'

She willed her body into a kneeling position on the ground, feeling cold and jagged rocks beneath her. In the back of her mind she knew that her body was still lying curled up on the floor of her cell, but bitter experience had told her that did not make what happened in this place, this version of reality, any less vivid or painful.

The dark air underground surrounding her moved, almost imperceptibly. Then, a sudden fresh wave of agony washed over her. She gritted her teeth and remained still. He approached.

It has been found.

The voice roared through her mind, loud and harsh. It sounded like the growl of a huge bear, if such a creature could form words. He spoke in a monotonous rumble that seemed to fill the dark, cavernous space.

Claes did not move but inside she exulted, even through her pain and fear. He could only be talking about one thing. The one item that she had devoted the last year of her life to locating.

The Demon's Tear.

'This news is good,' she said to the darkness. 'Mighty Desya.' She bowed her head respectfully. Pain crawled across her skin like biting ants.

The demon rumbled once more.

The jewel remains where it was found, with the finder.

You must summon it. You know how.

It was not a question.

'Yes, master,' she replied quickly. 'I will use the power you graciously grant me. I will possess the jewel soon.' She was delighted. The ruby had been lost, in ages past and its mere existence was still considered a myth by some. Yet, she had baited a trap and it had been sprung.

You must.

The demon's growled reply was ominous. Desya did not tolerate failure.

Claes felt more movement in the dank air, and the surging pain eased slightly. The demon had moved away. A metallic scraping and rattling echoed for a moment, vibrating through her knees. The chains.

Desya was restrained, trapped down here, deep below the earth. Thousands of years had passed since The Others had banished the demon, chaining it away.

Only now had he regained enough strength to wake, and to communicate. He had reached out, searching for a receptive mind. Claes had also been searching, looking for truth, desperately seeking answers.

Their minds had met and in that moment Claes had found her truth. She had committed her soul in service to the demon without hesitation. She had always known she was marked for greatness.

Desya required a conduit that could act on the surface. In return, Claes had been granted knowledge and power that exceeded any other mortal. She bought that power with servitude, and with physical pain. But it was worth it.

'I will labour ceaselessly for you, mighty Desya.'

A wordless, snarling grunt was the only response, and then Claes felt the familiar sensation of rapid movement. The dark, terrifying pit was left behind as she ascended back to her physical body.

She cried out aloud as she felt herself lying on the cold stones of her meagre cell once more. Hot knives stabbed her as pain gripped her whole body. She curled into a ball and whimpered.

As the pain ebbed away, she grasped the edge of her cot and pulled herself to her knees. She had plans to make and work to do.

Using the dark power granted by Desya, she could locate the ruby and use its own magic to control the finder. Even though they no longer truly lived, they could still be used.

In the meantime, she had to use more prosaic power to command his other, lesser followers. The secret cult that she had founded would be able to guard the jewel until she could come to it in person.

She glanced around at the stark, empty cell. This was what her commitment to the Veil had earned her so far; nothing. Her new master would give her so much more, and when this plan came to fruition she would rise higher than any other mortal since the Diminishing.

Closing her eyes, she began the difficult process of drawing power, magical power, from deep in the earth.

FOUR

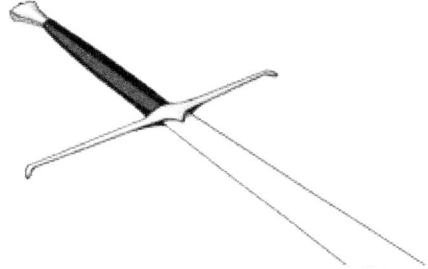

Eain ran.

The inky fist of night closed tightly around him, and aside from the regular, repeating sound of footfalls, all was still. Inside, however, his thoughts tumbled in turmoil.

There would be war. He struggled to believe it.

He had been brought up on stories of the last Kotevari invasion. Hushed voices had spoken of the terror, the uncertainty and terrible bloodshed of that time. Some of the older men's hands still shook and they cried out in the night thanks to the things they had seen. The things they had done.

And yet, this was what all his training in the Claihed had been for. He could fight, and fight well. He would be able to stand alongside his brothers in the Claihed and defend his country, and would be proud to do so. It would be his chance to finally prove himself.

'We won't be stuck at Sudvirke, will we?' Kater jogged up alongside Eain at the front of the running column. His brows were furrowed. 'You know, if the Kotevari are really attacking? They won't leave us there.'

'No,' replied Eain, with confidence he did not entirely feel. 'I expect you and the other Hniffare and Sverlaeggare will be sent back north once these messages are delivered.'

As he mentioned the messages, the rolled strips of linen in the knapsack he carried seemed to grow in weight. He knew that they must be significant.

'Messages must be sent to Sudvirke, immediately.'

Skyle Burns had turned to Rathvedd while the assembled group had been digesting the news of the Kotevari invasion. Rathvedd raised his eyes to stare at Eain, and smiled; a twisted, knowing wolf's smile. Eain felt a thrill in his heart and an ache in his heavy, tired legs. He knew what was coming.

'*Bhienn* Connow is ready to go,' he said, the formal Banahgarian title dripping with sarcasm. 'Think you can handle another little jog, big man?' Eain forced down his anger at Rathvedd's tone, and nodded silently.

Burns had disappeared inside to call the other Masters together, and to prepare the return messages. Rathvedd pointed to Edich, then beckoned him with a curling finger.

'Go to the kitchens,' he barked. Edich listened impassively. 'Fetch marching rations for six. Go.' Edich saluted and hurried off. Six? Why rations for six?

'Your exercise has not finished,' Rathvedd went on, turning to face Eain. 'You are still responsible for these Sverlaeggare, Connow. Where you go, they go.'

Eain nodded, then saluted briskly. 'Yes, Master.'

A stab of guilt shot through him. As he had feared, those he led were sharing his punishment for bringing them in late. So, now he would have to lead them through the night, toward the danger, and on the verge of exhaustion.

Yet, on they all ran.

If they blamed him, they stayed silent, and if they felt any fear then only Kater showed it. The only voice to be heard as the small group jogged through the night was the lyrical bubbling song of the River Ostur beside them.

The path was slightly downhill here and the riverbanks, invisible in the darkness, narrowed closer together. The flow of the broad Ostur sped up and the waters foamed white as they tumbled and gurgled noisily over the boulders and pebbles of the riverbed.

Eain had run this path countless times and the familiar sound of the river was a comforting presence this night. He had never felt the same confusion of emotions before, though. He was running a path where the final destination was unknown.

All he could do was to keep running.

They had made good progress through the night and Eain had ordered a hasty camp in the silent, grey hours just before dawn. They had huddled together among the roots of a small grove of young oak trees and got what rest and sleep they could.

As first light filled the sky they had risen, and the expressions on the younger soldiers' faces reflected Eain's mood. They were exhausted, and reluctant to start another day's travel. Yet, they must.

'This is a run of heroes, boys,' he had said, trying to encourage them as they stumbled along the road once more. 'They will sing of us in the days to come.' Edich met his eye unsmilingly.

They arrived in Sudvirke in the gathering gloom of the following evening. Guttering rushlights showed the outline of the main gates, but aside from the greasy flames the fort was a silent silhouette looming in the darkness. Unfamiliar. Unhomely.

Their welcome was perfunctory.

'Messages?' A short, bow-shouldered northerner with a thin, tail-like beard stood as night sentry. He wore the insignia of the

Claihedehlar but Eain did not know him. There were many soldiers who held that rank. 'You have messages? I will take them.'

After that they had been left alone in the broad, empty entryway. Few others moved around the fortress as the evening wore on but nevertheless there was an atmosphere of tension that seemed to inhabit the very stones of the building.

Sudvirke was a truly ancient fortification. Built as a simple stone watchtower within a fortress of earth and wood, it stood sentinel over a narrow strip of flat land that bounded the western shore of the Osturfjord. The expanse of shimmering water, and its shoreline, was the only weakness in the towering bulk of the Beinuirm Skele, the bounding southern mountains.

These dark, white-tipped peaks defended Banahgar's southern borders more effectively than any man-made rampart or palisade. Like the mountains that encircled much of Banahgar, these mountains were formed of jagged, sheer-sided black rocks that were completely impassable.

Sudvirke sat in this low-lying space beside the broad waters like a squat, stubborn warrior. Rebuilt in grey stone that surrounded the fort like battle-scarred armour, it would defend Banahgar indefatigably.

They had climbed the stairs and tumbled straight into bed without being able to see much of the fort or the dramatic surroundings, utterly exhausted.

Shutters clattered back against stone walls. Unwelcome light streamed into the bunk room, shining harshly into Eain's bleary eyes. He blinked owlishly, raising his head. It felt far too early for the sun to be up.

'Wakey, wakey laddies!' a loud voice rang out. One of the Claihedehmore, in full fighting leathers, was striding along the length of the room. 'The enemy is at the gates and you lot are lazing in bed! Up! Dress! Move!'

Eain sighed and swung his aching legs onto the floor. His day clothes were roughly folded beside the low bunk, and he grabbed them. Waiting for one of the Claihedehmore to issue an order twice was unwise, in Eain's experience.

Eain looked out of the window as he hurried to dress. A brisk wind blew and ragged grey clouds swirled relentlessly across the sky. Small patches of blue appeared and vanished again as if the sky itself was indecisive. Looking into the distance he saw them; dark triangles, standing out starkly against the shining blue-green of the fjord. Sails.

He shivered. It was real. What would this day bring?

'Edich,' he called across the room. There were twenty bunks and all had been occupied overnight. Now, the occupants who were mostly Sverlaeggare and Hniffare, were all hurrying to pack up and head down to the main hall for breakfast. Eain did not want to lose his younger charges in the crowds. 'Find the others and bring them to me.'

Sudvirke swarmed like an ant's nest that had been kicked. Younger warriors streamed from the bunk rooms on the upper floors, flooding like a wave down the steep wooden staircases towards the main hall.

At the base of the stairs, Eain stopped abruptly, flinging out a hand to stop those behind. A fist of full Claihedehmore, ten or fifteen men with greatswords on their backs, strode past towards the main gate. They moved with efficient, muscular purpose.

Eain watched them pass. To a man they were hard-faced and broad-shouldered. The pommels of their greatswords, each sword unique and bearing the Sword-Name of the soldier that wielded it, loomed behind their heads. Each wore a long, leather greatcoat with pockets that bulged. They would need to move too quickly for armour.

They marched to war. The Kotevari would land in great numbers, so the Claihedehmore would use the land to set ambushes and hinder their progress. It was a mission that held incredible danger and Eain wished he was marching with them. Wished he was one of them.

'Makes you realise,' Edich had leaned in close to speak. 'This is serious. The Kotevari are coming, and we will have to fight them.'

Eain shook his head. 'Not you, not yet. You'll all be somewhere safe. It will be for the Claihedehmore and Claihedehlar to drive them back.' Edich nodded in understanding, although his shoulders sagged a little.

And I will be stood with them, thought Eain.

The main hall hummed with conversation as Eain and his six Sverlaeggare filled their breakfast plates and found a bench. Eain helped himself to a big scoop of thick, salted porridge from a black iron pot and a few rounds of dark, freshly baked bread. There was an edge to the chatter. Men and boys talked in anxious whispers, brows furrowed. The occasional stab of laughter seemed too loud, too shrill. The room was full of nervous energy.

The main hall lay at the very heart of the fortress. The same solid, square shape of the exterior was mirrored in the grey, dressed stone of this huge room. Light filtered in from high, slitted windows above and clusters of rushlights guttered and spat in alcoves in the lower walls.

Long tables were spread in angled lines across the floor, like the spokes of a great wheel. Eain took a seat and the others sat nearby. His stomach growled as he spooned lukewarm porridge into his mouth. The hub of the wheel was a raised circular dais, and movement there caught Eain's eye as he ate.

A tall, imposing figure strode across the hall and up onto the dais. Eain saw who it was, and his blood ran cold.

Scanning the room with his cold, hawklike eyes was Morgan Blane. Often known by his Sword-Name, The River in Flood, the man was the youngest Master of the Claihed. A man, who, rumour said, had marched up to the front gate of Vekwicc fort as a youth and demanded to be accepted into the Claihed.

A ragged orphan, he had been laughed at and turned away but had challenged one of the Sverlaeggare guards to a fist fight. And knocked him down. A fully grown soldier, defeated by a scrawny fifteen-year-old lad.

Blane never spoke of it, but Eain believed the tale. The man was tough as old leather and hard as oak.

Eain had first met him when he was about thirteen years old, a couple of years short of the age of majority. A couple of years away from being allowed to join the Claihed. It had been his dream since he could remember, and to have a Seeker come to Keldfirth had been exciting for all the boys of Keldfirth.

Morgan Blane had seemed huge to Eain at that age. He was a tall, lean man with the typical dark hair and eyes of a lowlander. Towering over the boys who clustered around him, he was inscrutable as they clamoured to be part of his test.

Eain remembered the thrill he had felt when Blane had singled him out. He pointed, then beckoned.

'You, bairn,' he had said. 'Come out here.'

Eain had stepped confidently out into the forming circle, the use of the diminutive word for "child" not acting as a warning. If the test were to be of swordsmanship he knew he had nothing to fear. He was already the best sword fighter of the boys of Keldfirth, and had even beaten Haemma, the blacksmith's son, a boy several years older.

Yet Blane had held no blade.

He held a simple stick from the nearby forest.

'I'm going to pretend I don't know your family name,' said Blane. 'Pretend I don't know who your grandfather was.'

That is when a chill hit him that was nothing to do with the autumn wind.

Eain had always tried to avoid thinking of his grandfather.

He knew that his father's father, Cerle Connow, had been one of the Claihedehmore. He was known as a hard and uncompromising man, and highly regarded as both a warrior and a teacher.

But his reputation was tarnished.

On the eve of the last war against Kotev, forty years ago, Cerle had vanished. Even as the enemy ships turned the placid waters of Osturfjord to white foam beneath their bows, Cerle and his wife Indaella had packed their bags and left Osturbrost. They had taken their son, Eain's father Reid, with them.

Some said that Cerle had lost his mind and forced his wife to flee with him. A more pervasive rumour had it that it was his wife that was mad; that she was an enchantress and she had put a curse on him and commanded him to abandon his duty to the Claihed.

The same words were thrown at Cerle in every version of the tale, though; traitor, coward…deserter.

Eain could not bear the thought of this tall, impressive man of the Claihed looking at him and associating him with his grandfather's actions. Including him in that shame.

'This is a lesson, not a test,' continued Blane, projecting his voice so that all the gathered youths could hear. 'The task is simple. Get this stick out of my hand.'

With that, he lifted his arm and held the plain, dull brown stick out toward Eain.

It should have been simple, but Eain realised quickly that Blane had set him up to fail. Eain had lunged at the stick, grappled for it, and struggled until his breath came in ragged gasps, but the man was just too quick, too strong. The stick darted from his grasp, again and again, and with deft flicks of his hips and wrists he flung Eain to the floor. The shame reddened Eain's cheeks. Laughter filled the air.

'Do you understand the lesson yet?' asked Blane, staring down to where Eain lay panting among the dirt and dead leaves.

Eain had not. The humiliation of that day had stayed with him ever since.

'Men of the Claihed!' Blane's harsh, clipped tones rang out around the hall, disrupting Eain's thoughts. 'And women of the Skjilde!' Eain glanced around and saw that a number of Skjilde-maidens had entered the hall and were standing in neat ranks around the walls. They were all in this together. For Banahgar.

'War comes,' Blane went on. 'The army of Kotev sails into Osturfjord as we sit here, just like they did last time. Your fathers have told you the tales of that invasion. We have not forgotten the lessons we were taught. Last time they caught us by surprise. This time they will not! Last time they advanced their lines almost to Osturbrost. This time they will not!'

He paused. All knew the story of the last war. The shock assault from the river, the desperate, retreating rearguard that the Claihed fought to slow the advance. Then, at the last, when all was nearly lost, a do or die attack on the Kotevari royal camp. Overconfident, the High King of Kotev had come to watch Osturbrost fall.

It had been his undoing. He had not counted on the skill of Banahgar's best warriors, and the daring bravery of a handful of men who risked everything to win the war. The High King had been killed in his bed and the army routed back to their boats. It had cost many Banahgarian lives. The sadness endured.

'We have long planned for this moment,' Morgan Blane was still talking, 'which we thought would come one day. Plans are in place. The Claihedehmore are already moving into position, even as I speak to you now. The army of Kotev will find no easy landing place this time. No safe harbour.

'Together, we will support our soldiers. The Skjilde – you know what you must do. Deliver messages, carry supplies, treat the injured. The Claihedehlar – you will be our reserves. You must be ready to fight, ready to fill gaps in our lines. You will need all of your courage.'

Eain thrilled inside. This was it. He would be given his chance to march to war. He would show what he could do, and what he had learned.

'Sverlaeggare, Hniffare. You will be kept away from battle, for now. The time may yet come for you to show your skill, and your heart, but for now you will man the defences at Osturbrost and Vekwicc. You will practise, train and be ready when your country calls you.'

A slight groan resounded around the hall. The significance of Blane's words was clear to the younger warriors; they were being sent away.

'You will leave immediately. Each group will be assigned a Claihedehlar commander to lead you.' Eain's eyes widened and he turned to stare in Blane's direction.

No. Please no.

He could guess what was coming next.

'Half will be led by Kiarden Letheyt,' Blane spoke quickly, dismissively. Eain picked out Letheyt's disappointed face across the hall. His heavy shoulders had slumped slightly. 'They will go to Osturbrost by the river road. The other half will run north to Vekwicc by the Dall road. They will be led by Eain Connow.'

Eain was on his feet before he knew what he was doing. Every eye in the room burned into him. His heart hammered in his ears, almost deafening in the silence.

'Problem, Master Connow?' Blane's voice was cold.

Eain flushed. He knew that objecting to his orders would get him nowhere. Yet, now he was up, he might as well speak. He squared his shoulders. 'I can fight. You know I can. Send me out with the other Claihedehlar. Please, Master, let Edich Iansson lead the group in my stead. He is to be trusted, and he is ready.'

'My trust in Edich Iansson is not in question,' replied Blane, raising an eyebrow. 'The question is why you would object to a direct order. You were told, not asked.'

Eain clamped his lips together. He forced down the childish outburst about the unfairness of the order, that had been on the tip of his tongue. He could not give Blane a reason to belittle him further.

'I'm ready to face the enemy,' he said, voice level. 'I'm ready to defend my country, not to run in the opposite direction. Whatever I have done wrong, I deserve this chance.' He spoke evenly but felt his face heating, colouring.

'But this is not a punishment, young Claihedehle,' rang out a new voice. Eain looked up in surprise. Helden Haradsson, Grandmaster of the Claihed, had stepped up onto the dais. His famous sword, Death's Face, was on his back. Eain had not even noticed that he was in the room. He bowed his head in respect.

'We trust you to lead these younger soldiers. It is why you have been given this task. We may all face danger soon enough, Eain. Do not hurry towards it.'

The Grandmaster moved forward to stand beside Blane. Haradsson was several inches shorter than the Master, and twice his age. His hair and moustache were white, contrasting starkly against skin like faded leather. Yet, his eyes were icy sharp and his shoulders remained broad and powerful.

'I only wish to serve Banahgar, Grandmaster,' muttered Eain, eyes on the ground. While the Claihedehmore strutted their strength and skill, Haradsson moved deftly and spoke quietly.

You would not know he was a warrior at all. He had no need to prove himself.

'And by doing what is asked of you,' he said, patiently, 'you will be serving. This is an important duty, Eain. Bear this burden with pride.'

Eain nodded and sat. He burned with disappointment and embarrassment. The Grandmaster's calm, measured words had shamed him even as Blane's order had frustrated him. He could say no more.

'I would have led them, Master,' said Edich as they filed out of the hall. They had been dismissed to their duties. Eain watched the other Claihedehlar enviously, knowing they would be marching towards the front lines, marching to support the Claihedehmore. Marching to glory.

'I know, Edich,' replied Eain as they moved towards the main gate of the fortress. 'Blane wouldn't let it happen though. He just loves rubbing my face in the dirt too much.' Edich grimaced, but said nothing more.

They passed through the gate and Eain looked up in surprise. Standing beside the path, his muscular arms folded across his chest as he watched the younger soldiers stream out, was Morgan Blane.

'Connow! Come!' Eain flinched at Blane's barked summons, but responded, bowing his head as he approached.

'Master,' he said, respectfully. Blane passed him a hide-wrapped bundle. More messages.

'Take these with you and deliver them to the Masters at Vekwicc. I should not need to tell you how important it is that these get through, and that they arrive swiftly. But, as you seem to have picked up a habit for dawdling, and see fit to publicly question my orders, I will.'

He leaned closer. 'Get these messages and the young soldiers safely to Vekwicc, and move quickly. If I hear that you let yourself be delayed then I will personally hunt you down and teach you a lesson about haste. Do you understand?'

Yes, but, came to Eain's lips, but he swallowed the words.

'Yes, Master,' he said.

'You stand on a blade's edge, Connow,' said Blane. 'You have potential but you let yourself down. There is a path before you that has you in the red of the Claihedehmore, and soon. You could serve your country well. There is another path that leads to more disgrace for your family name and a return to your farming village. Choose your path. Now go. Time is wasting.'

Eain turned wordlessly away from the grim Master and headed north. It was typical of Blane to be encouraging and belittling in the same breath. Inside he fumed, and worried. He hated Blane for speaking so, but feared that his words were true.

A group of Sverlaeggare and Hniffare had gathered, standing ready in the patchy sunshine. He put thoughts of Blane aside and concentrated on his task. He tapped two younger men on their shoulders. One was a russet-haired lad from the Dall, Banahgar's western region, and the other had coppery skin. He was probably from the eastern plains or the hilly Morr.

'You two will lead the run first,' he told them. 'Run for a count of two thousand, walk for the same. Be ready.'

The sun had not risen much higher over the distant eastern mountains by the time the whole group, around thirty boys and men, were jogging away from Sudvirke. Eain glared up at the sky suspiciously. There could be rain on the way.

A well-trodden trail led eastwards from the fortress. In days gone by it had been busy with heavy wagons carrying stone quarried in the Dall southwards and returning empty. These days, Banahgarians shrank from the remote edges of the country. Osturbrost and the farming villages of the plains grew, while isolated villages of the Dall in the west and the Morr in the east were abandoned, one by one.

The quarrymen's hammers were now silent, the old roads overgrown with weeds. Only the Claihed used them now.

Eain jogged easily at the back of the group. He did not feel like talking. The hills of the Dall rose ahead, soft green and heathery slopes steadily climbing to rounded ridges and peaks.

The road itself could be seen in the distance, climbing the nearest slope of the Dall escarpment in wide curves. Eain knew that many of the runners would be panting and gasping before they reached the top.

Beyond the green hills, far in the distance, the western peaks of the Beinuirm Skele soared to the sky. Clouds clustered around the highest summits, hiding the loftiest tips, but the dark mass that was visible below the cloud base still rose to dizzying heights.

These mountains formed the border of Banahgar to the west and south, and were known to be impassable. No one would even dare try. What lay beyond; none knew. The same mountain range ran from the very north-east of the country all the way down the western border, and wrapped around to the south until coming to an abrupt end at the gap of Osturfjord.

Eain turned his face north, concentrating on his onward mission. His obligated duty. He tried not to think about the approaching ships, the invading army. He could do nothing about it now.

Yet, the mountains hid dangers that Eain knew not. The invasion of Banahgar was just beginning, and the black hand of war would prove to have a longer reach than any had guessed.

FIVE

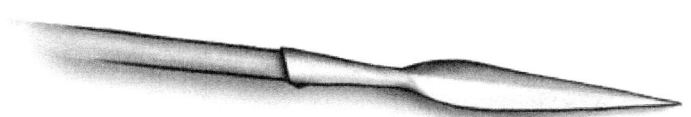

Arista Mara va Pushtu dug her heels into her horse's flanks. The animal was weary, but Mara could restrain her anticipation no longer. Not when they were so close. The final few yards of the steep, rocky trail passed beneath its hooves, and as she took in the view beyond the crest, her breath caught in her throat.

There could be no turning back now.

The landscape spread before her was beautiful. From this lofty viewpoint, high in the mountains, she could see beyond the dark mass of the nearest rocky foothills, across rolling hills with lush green grass and all the way to the plains of the river beyond.

She had been told that this was a rich land, and could already see that the stories were true. Fertile soil for the growing of crops spread from the feet of mountains full of minerals and metals. Rich, easy, and there for the taking. Some said that even small villages had hoards of gold and gems. All of Kohtef knew the stories.

'Husband mine!' she called, without turning her head. 'Hurry to me! Come and see what we have done together.'

The even tread of her husband's fine mount grew louder, then ceased as he reined in at her side. Aristo Besnik vo Pushto was an impressive sight. His hair, black as a raven's wing, was smoothed back over his scalp with oil, which also gleamed in his sideburns and thin moustache.

Like all the nobility of Kohtef, the *tecati*, he wore a red sash and his riding breeches were tucked into his bright, bright red socks. The gilded hilt of his curved sabre shone beside his hip, and he casually rested his hand on it as he surveyed the broad landscape for himself.

Mara ran her hand over her own hair, neatly trimmed and smoothed back with oil like her husband's. Hers, though, was dyed an opulent fiery red. No one could fail to recognise her as a high-blood noble, and she dreamed that this enterprise would elevate them to *duca* and *duco*. They and their children would be entitled to wear ceremonial red hats.

She copied her husband's stance, placing her hand on the hilt of her own rapier. He looked at her and smiled.

'This time,' he said, his voice throaty and full of meaning. 'This time we will take what we deserve. We will win glory for Kohtef.' She smiled back, full of pride.

'Your father would have been full of joy to see this,' she said, and his smile faltered.

Aristo Pushto vo Rruge had conceived of this plan, this endeavour. He alone had seen the potential that the rugged Giarprey Mountains offered. He had petitioned the ruling council for support, but they had dismissed his ideas.

To the council, the *hieraad*, Pushto vo Rruge was a delusional maverick with a head full of impractical ideas.

He had ignored them. He was a man of means and wealth, and did not enjoy being refused. He persuaded or coerced many other nobles to join his cause, and to pool their resources. Together they had set their peasant labourers, the *hafioh*, to work.

It had taken years.

When Mara had been summoned to the Pushto estate so that Besnik could commence courtship, his father had hardly ever been present.

He made frequent excursions deep into the northern mountains, the Giarprey, often staying away for weeks at a time. Even when he was home, he was often preoccupied and irritable.

In the north of Kohtef, far from the cities of the Inner Sea, scrubby foothills led toward the barren and forbidding peaks. Pushto had spent months exploring this area until he had found what he had been searching for. He found a pass.

He had traced a path up this vertiginous gap between two sheer peaks, and once he was sure of the route, he began to build. Under the shovels and picks of the *hafioh* labourers, the path became a wide track, and the pass became a route. Their labour though, was just beginning.

Pushto travelled deeper into the mountains, his growing workforce living in mobile towns of tents, as this new road extended further north. Soon, wagons trundled along the track and progress accelerated.

Two years ago, Aristo Pushto had fallen ill. The illness had consumed him until, in the end, he had been confined to his bed. Besnik had taken on responsibility for his father's project without hesitation. Mara had been at his side as he ordered the works to continue.

Pushto died that winter. Besnik had channelled his grief into the project, inspiring the *hafioh* to work even harder, exhorting the minor nobles to dip deeper into their purses. The rewards when the project was complete would pay them back handsomely, he assured them.

Mara had admired and respected her father-in-law, but Besnik had worshipped the man. She could see the emotions that churned within him to see his father's will done at last. From the high point of his father's endeavours, below the final steep ridge, Besnik had worked tirelessly to force the path all the way to the summit.

That is where they now stood.

On the trail behind them was an army. The convoy snaked back down the mountain for several miles. They had marched all the way from Kohtef's lowlands; thousands of *hafioh* foot soldiers bearing long spears, led by a host of mounted *tecati* knights. All were aware of the glory and wealth that would come with their success.

'Their redshirt warriors will be overwhelmed this time,' said Besnik, loudly enough for the front ranks to hear. 'We are stronger than they, and we are many. We need not fear their long swords.'

Mara put her hand to her husband's arm. The fighting skill of the enemy was near-legendary. Their army was filled with giants who wielded swords longer than a man was tall. She knew though, that this time the Kohtefar had the numbers to sweep them away.

'We will return to the king as heroes,' she said to her husband, to reassure him and to strengthen his resolve. They both knew the stakes.

When Besnik had finally been granted an audience with the king, Sulndimtat had immediately seen the value, and the potential. A new solution to an old problem. A route to somewhere that had always been inaccessible. A great opportunity to be the Kohtefer king who finally won this great victory.

The plan had come together quickly. A waterborne raid would be mounted, but as a feint, a mere distraction. From this new and unknown route was where the true assault would be launched; a spear flung toward the enemy's heart, while their attention was elsewhere.

At the end of the audience, Sulndimtat had made it clear what he expected in return for his trust, and support.

'Come back to me,' he had said, his voice echoing through the cavernous hall of his palace. 'With the riches of the country overflowing your hands. Or,' he fixed them with a watery stare, 'do not come back at all.'

They had understood clearly. Make this invasion a success, or die in the attempt.

Arista Mara va Pushto raised her hand, then looked to her husband. He nodded decisively, and she waved the army forward.

She smiled to herself as her horse began to pick its way easily down the shallow slope beyond the ridge. Conquest was in the air. Conquest, victory and glory with va Pushtu leading the way.

They would be remembered in history as the ones who had led the triumphant invasion of that rich, northern country. They would be remembered as the conquerors of Bannakar.

SIX

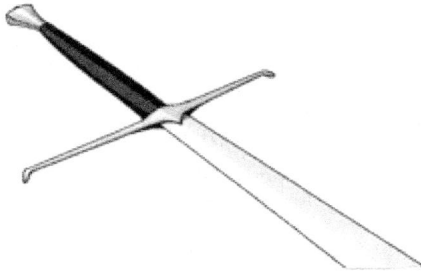

The Dall was a creased green blanket. Softly sloped hillsides led down into lushly wooded valleys from bare, rounded summits. Villages huddled comfortably in the broader vales, timber walls and roofs almost blending in with the surrounding woodland.

It was a quiet land, where the sound of the wind in rustling leaves and bubbling water in deep-cut streams provided an endless, soothing music.

For Eain, it had been home. He had been born and raised in a village just like the one that sprawled out beside the road they travelled.

Edich jogged beside him. 'We could be home in a few hours.' He pointed away toward the northwest, where Chaihfe Haed could just be seen as a flat-topped lump on the horizon. Keldfirth lay at the foot of that hill, in a sheltered, rounded vale.

Eain grimaced and replied with a grunt. It was not home any more. It seemed like a different life when he had lived there. Would he ever go back?

They had been running for a few hours already, and when the pale sun peeked out between the fleeting clouds it appeared high above the eastern mountains. Noon was much nearer than dawn.

Eain turned, glancing back down the line of runners. They were all still jogging easily. All the faces he could see were calm, and as yet there were no stragglers. He considered raising the pace, to see how they coped. It would be good training. Returning his gaze to the front again he scolded himself. Would it make him feel better to see the Hniffare gasping with the effort, the youngest soldiers struggling to keep up? Maybe. Would it be worthy of him?

Movement in the sky caught his attention, distracting him from the unwanted questions.

He shaded his eyes with a hand as he looked up.

A dark shape wheeled against the fleecy white of a drifting cloud. A bird in flight, and Eain knew that even though it was a mere speck in the heavens, the span of her broad wings far exceeded his own height.

It was a *korohnn-uirn*; a crowned eagle. It soared majestically over the land, its far-seeing eyes taking in every detail, lord of all the skies. As Eain watched, the eagle circled lower and he could make out five splayed feathers at the end of each wing, like feathers grasping at the air.

All eagles were descended from mighty Maneg, the ancient god of the skies. The crowned eagles were held to be closest in descent, nearest to the gods. Maneg herself was the foremost of the animal gods and was still revered as a totem of wisdom.

The worship of this animal pantheon stretched back into the distant past of Banahgar, many years before any recorded history. The primitive tribes of the young country had told stories of the gods who created the world before the age of heroes, before the founding and ending of the line of kings, and before the coming of the Twin Swords.

Eain hoped for a small measure of the wisdom of noble Maneg to help him bear this duty without resentment, and to be a good leader.

With a sudden flash, the eagle beat her vast wings and soared away northward. Something had startled the great bird. Something was wrong.

'Is it time for a rest?' asked Kater, trotting to a halt next to Eain. Eain had paused in the middle of the rough, overgrown track. 'I thought we'd give the greenies a bit more of a workout, boss.' He nodded back down the path to where the younger warriors were gradually slowing to a walk.

'Quiet. Everyone be quiet!' Eain snapped, raising his voice. The hairs on the nape of his neck had risen, prickling his collar. He felt suddenly uneasy, and not just because of the flight of the eagle. Was he being foolish? There was no danger here.

The Kotevari ships, even if they had landed yet, were fifty miles away to the east. The Claihedehmore and a wide expanse of open ground were between them. The Beinuirm Skele mountains to the south and west were impregnable as any fortification or rampart.

They could not be safer. So, why did Eain feel a thrill of danger? A sense of threat.

'Edich!' he called, and the younger man stepped forward. 'Keep them here. Make them eat something. Drink a little.'

Edich nodded confidently. 'What's wrong?'

'I'm not sure,' replied Eain. 'Probably nothing. But keep your eyes and ears open. Haefrad, come with me.'

Turning his back on the milling, uncertain group, Eain stepped off the track. Haefrad followed, looking uncertain. They set out west, where the land fell away from the road in shallow, heathery slopes. The ground was springy and yielding beneath his feet and he moved quickly and without a sound.

Isolated dwarf oaks and rowan trees dotted the open ground, but before his path the eaves of a thicker band of woodland rose imposingly. The higher boughs were heavy with lush greenery, and they rippled and danced in the erratic breeze.

All was quiet.

Eain had grown up playing games with his friends in forests just like this one. Hide and seek, tag, climbing trees and jumping out. At need, he could move silently and even though he strode quickly through the sparse undergrowth, not a twig snapped, not a leaf crackled. Patchy sunlight flashed through the dense, swaying canopy above and dappled about his feet.

The light was brighter up ahead. This band of trees was narrow and there must be a clearing beyond.

Eain stepped cautiously between a gnarled, twisted oak and a tall, smooth-skinned beech and found himself on a narrow walking trail. Haefrad paused behind him, leaning on one of the trees. Glancing right, Eain could see the path snaking away. It must join the main road somewhere beyond. A village must lie further along the leftward trail.

The sense of something amiss still lingered, and Eain took a deep breath to gather his courage before stepping out onto the path. Why did he feel afraid?

Then he saw the smoke.

It was rare that a Banahgarian village did not lie beneath a hazy pall of blue grey woodsmoke, or pungent peat smoke above the settlements of the rocky northern Naen-Giata.

This was not that. This was a sudden gout of blackish smoke, blooming into the sky like a miniature thunderhead cloud. A house was burning.

A scream split the air.

Eain reached out instinctively, grasping Haefrad's shoulder to hold him still. Shrill cries of alarm and pain were filtering through the trees from the same direction as the rising smoke. Fixing the younger man with a warning stare, Eain laid a finger across his lips to indicate silence, before beckoning him to follow.

With quick, quiet steps they darted across the path and between the trunks of the tall trees on the other side. The undergrowth beneath the canopy was thick and thorny, so the pair were forced to skirt the edge. Eain led them forward, one tree at a time.

He was suddenly back in his acceptance test for entry into the Claihedehlar. Several days survival in the forest while being hunted by soldiers of the Claihedehmore. To be caught was to fail, and to be seen or heard was to be caught. Those with the skills to able to pass the test became like ghosts, or woodland spirits, slipping through this dense vegetated landscape without leaving a trace.

Ahead, the path curved to the left and Eain caught a fleeting glimpse of the village. The houses were unremarkable. As with much of the Dall, the quarries that scarred the landscape had not served the local area. The stone was carted away by ox-drawn wagons and the villagers continued to build in wood.

The nearest buildings had lightweight walls of woven hazel rods between a frame of sturdy timber logs. Heavy thatch sat atop like an aurochs' shaggy hair, almost brushing the mossy ground.

It was thatch that burned. Eain could now see the reddish glow of the smouldering reeds and the black smoke that curled and billowed spoke of a damp, dirty fire.

If it were just a house fire, then his troop could help. A stream gurgled noisily through the village, and the villagers would have buckets and bowls to use. He should divert their journey to help. It was the right thing to do.

Eain was just about to turn to Haefrad to send him back to the others, when another scream rent the air. Figures moved through the smoky haze and Eain caught the flash of metal in a beam of sunlight. The glint of a sword.

There was fighting here. How could this be? Who could be fighting?

He felt the weight of responsibility pressing down on him like an invisible hand. He could not walk away from this. He could not just do nothing. The Claihed existed to protect all of Banahgar. Yet, he could not lead the younger warriors into danger. He had been given an order to protect them, and to march them straight to Vekwicc.

He thought very quickly, and with his heart hammering in his chest, he made a decision.

Crouching behind the nearest tree, he shrugged out of his knapsack straps and reached inside. His hand closed around the pouch of bound hide that contained the bundle of messages.

'Go back to the others,' he hissed, face close to Haefrad's. 'Tell the Sverlaeggare to come here to me, quickly and quietly.' Haefrad nodded. He took the bundle of messages from Eain's hand. 'Take these,' continued Eain,' and lead the Hniffare on.' Haefrad opened his mouth to argue, but Eain cut him off.

'There is no time!' he hissed. 'Lead them on up the road and we will catch you after we have dealt with this. You must keep the young ones safe, you must keep them moving. Got it?'

Haefrad nodded again. His eyes were wide.

'Go. Now.' Haefrad slipped silently away.

The wait for the others to arrive seemed to last a lifetime. Eain gritted his teeth, forcing himself to be patient. More shrieks and shouts came from the village, interspersed with the occasional metallic sounds of weapons clashing. His fingers twitched to draw his greatsword and hold it.

Not yet, he told himself. *Not yet*.

He crept forward, slowly easing between the twisted trunks and clinging undergrowth. A gap between two straight beech trees gave him a better view.

The course of the tumbling stream had left a flat space on either bank, and houses clustered along this shallow valley. The buildings rose higher towards the upstream end of the village, the settlement following the meandering line of the bubbling water.

A figure ran between two houses. Eain caught a momentary glimpse of a dark-haired man wearing pale, baggy breeches tucked into bright, bright red socks. He was holding a slightly curved sword in one hand, but that was not what made Eain draw and hold a shocked breath.

He was not Banahgarian. His hair, his clothes and his weapon were all unusual, alien.

What was going on?

Movement in the corner of his left eye caused him to turn his head. Edich was stood under the eaves of the wood on the opposite side of the path. Eain felt a surge of pride at how close they had approached without making a sound. He beckoned them over.

The group of twenty or so Sverlaeggare crossed the path with nervous stealth and melted into the forest. A moment later, Edich was beside him and Eain could see a host of worried faces peering in his direction from further away in the woods.

'Enemies,' he whispered to Edich. The word felt alien and bitter on his tongue. 'In the village. I don't know who they are, but we must protect the people.'

'Yes, Master.' Edich's voice was level and unafraid. 'We are with you.' He turned to pass the message down the line.

Eain moved on through the woods. The leafy shadows were reassuring as the sounds of struggle and fear grew louder. The screen of trees and the nearest buildings meant that as yet, they could see little.

Fear slowed Eain's steps, but then another shriek rang out. He sped up. The thought of innocent Banahgarians suffering was a spear in his heart. He moved closer to one of the houses. The smoke created an eerie, dreamlike atmosphere.

Close to the centre of the village a simple bridge of logs spanned the stream. A flat, grassy green had been left free of buildings at either end of the bridge. When Eain saw what was happening on the other side, he stopped dead.

A handful of figures were stood on the grass, dressed like the first he had seen, with colourful coats and the same baggy breeches. Gathered behind them, on the edge of the green, was a small herd of strange beasts, with halters on their long noses and saddles on their backs for riding.

Eain had heard stories of these creatures, and one thing he knew was that they carried the knights of Kotev into battle. The beasts themselves looked placid and unthreatening, like lightly built elk but without antlers.

A cry sounded, and Eain looked across the green to where two Kotevari men were holding a villager between them. The Banahgarian was head and shoulders taller than the men that roughly grasped his arms, but though he struggled desperately he could not get free.

His unbound grey hair shook across his face, pale and twisted with fear, as a third man stepped forward. This invader held a single-edged sword.

As Eain watched, barely daring to breathe, the Kotevari barked a short series of harsh syllables. It had the tone of a demand, or a question.

'I don't know what you want!' wailed the villager. 'I don't understand! Hurt me if you want, but please spare my wife.' A Banahgarian woman was standing by the open door of a nearby house, hands clamped to the sides of her face, a picture of anguish.

The Kotevari repeated the demand, the unfamiliar language ringing out loudly.

'I don't know.' The man was shaking his head. 'I don't know.'

There was a pause, then the knight stepped forward and thrust out his sword. Vivid crimson blood streamed down the villager's shirt as the cruel point pierced his throat. He collapsed to the ground with a forlorn, wet gurgle. His wife's cry of anguish was chilling.

Eain turned his head. Edich's eyes were wide, his face pale.

They had to act.

'Swords,' he said decisively, reaching over his shoulder to grasp the hilt of his greatsword.

They had to fight to defend Banahgar.

SEVEN

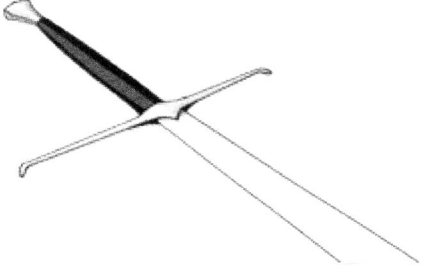

I am Eain Connow. I am Claihedehlar. I am Banahgar. I am alive.

Eain whispered the Claihed salute fiercely to himself, hoping to draw extra courage from the ancient words. He grasped his greatsword with both hands, holding the point upright as he stepped from the trees. The leather grip felt clammy.

When he wore the red as one of the Claihedehmore he would bear a sword that had been forged for him personally. He would name it with a title that captured his personality and fighting style. He could earn it this day.

The trees were left behind as he surged toward the bridge. The grass was soft beneath the soles of his boots, deadening the sound of his approach. He floated, as if in a dream.

A handful of Sverlaeggare followed and the rest went with Edich, fanning out upstream to prevent any of the enemy moving further into the village.

The Claihed are here now, thought Eain.

He strode onto the bridge, ignoring the quavering, fearful voice of doubt inside him. His boots rapped a strident rhythm on the worn oak logs and the eyes of all on the green snapped toward the sound.

'Begone!' Eain raised his voice and the Kotevari looked immediately uneasy. The leader, blood still staining his curved, short sword, advanced on Eain.

He barked an unintelligible sentence at the others, who moved hurriedly toward their tethered beasts. He raised his sword.

This was it. Real combat for the first time. Eain bent his knees and raised his sword to the horizontal, the blade extending forward like a single, straight aurochs' horn. His opponent did not look afraid. His expression was furious, dark brows furrowed and eyes narrowing. His oiled hair gleamed in the dappled noon sunlight that filtered through the trees.

For a moment, all was still.

The Kotevari lunged. His whole body twisted and the point of his sword stabbed forward, driven rapidly by the power in his broad shoulders.

Hurried, Eain dropped the point of his sword to meet the strike and guide it away. At the same time his body moved with pure instinct, stepping quickly to the right. Training and practice guided his movements as though he were a puppet with invisible strings.

In the same flowing motion, his sword came around his head in a wide circle and slashed down in a raking cut, right to left. His opponent danced back, his footwork precise and his sword held low.

The momentum of Eain's five-foot sword carried it around in another scything arc and he stepped forward into another diagonal cut.

This time the Kotevari invader darted to Eain's right, evading the strike and stabbing his shorter sword at Eain's body again.

Barely conscious of any thought process, mind floating as his body simply reacted, he swung his sword into a vertical position, point downward with his forearms crossed. His opponent's sword scraped along his blade as he guided it away from his body.

Eain locked eyes with the other man. They were dark, and wide with concentration. He saw them open wider still as he realised that he was overextended, blade caught on Eain's. Eain pushed the hilt of his sword forward, knocking the smaller man backward and off balance.

Unwinding his hands, he swept his blade out in a vicious horizontal cut. His opponent was fast and agile, and recovered his balance before dancing back.

Even as Eain raised his greatsword again, and made to follow, a barking command came from the Kotevari leader's lips.

'Master, look out!' shouted one of the nearby Sverlaeggare, and he turned to see one of the beasts bearing down on him. Seen up close it was much less benign. It was terrifyingly large, and powerful muscles ripped beneath its glossy brown hair.

One of the other nobles was astride the beast's back, and as he closed the distance he slashed down with his own sword. Eain desperately threw himself to the ground, and the beast and rider passed by, its hooves drumming like thunder.

He rolled over and jumped quickly to his feet, sword raised. The low pounding of the beasts' footfalls faded as the invaders spurred them away, toward the edge of the village.

'We chased them away, boss!' Kater's voice was jubilant as he slowed to a halt on the green. His face was pale and his hands were shaking. 'We won. Didn't we? They won't mess with us again.' Nobody replied.

Eain looked around. The other Sverlaeggare were jogging out onto the grass. He could not see that any bore injuries. The widowed villager was still bent over the body of her murdered husband and her shoulders shook as she wept. A crowd of other villagers were gathering, their faces pale with shock.

Downstream, in the direction that the raiders had gone, several plumes of damp black smoke were still rising into the air to drift into the canopy of the forest.

Eain could almost hear the villagers' thoughts.

You arrived too late. You let them escape. You failed us.

Would other villages suffer the same fate from this band of raiders?

'Edich, Kater,' Eain called out. 'We need to give chase. The Claihed cannot let this raid go unpunished. We can't let them attack any other villages as they flee. And maybe we can discover how they came to be here. It is important to know.' He reached across his shoulder and deftly sheathed his greatsword across his back. 'You two, guard the rear as we run. Keep everyone together.'

Moments later, they were running in pursuit. The great beasts had left deep hoofprints like upturned bowls pressed into the damp turf. Tracking their escape was easy.

The forest closed in over the stream at the downhill end of the village. The path they had originally followed came from the left and another well-used track continued to the right, winding away through the trees.

The wide, round hoofprints led clearly away down this trail, in a southward direction.

'We follow,' said Eain. The nagging worry about the punishment he might receive from disobeying his orders was pushed aside by his urgent need to catch the raiders. It was the right thing to do, even Morgan Blane must see that.

They filed quickly and silently along the path. Without a word, they split into two columns, one hugging each side of the path. They wanted to stay close to the treeline.

The centre of the path was humped, and there was a deep rut worn to either side, a sign that wagons had once been drawn this way. That time had passed, and the track was mostly overgrown now with long tufts of wispy grass, thistles and *sunblooms*.

They ran easily. Eain glanced back frequently at the group, concern creasing his brow, but if they were getting tired they gave no sign. Many faces were pale or blank with worry, though. Pursuing an enemy was one thing, but what about when that enemy was caught?

Eain passed a junction in the track. Ahead, the path curved sharply to the left, but another joined from the right. It looked rarely used, even was even more overgrown. The hoofprints were clear on the ground on the path ahead.

He continued running and rounded the bend. And then he stopped dead. And reversed his steps quickly, urgently and beckoning to the others to follow. He prayed to the Brothers that it was not too late.

He had only had time for a fleeting glimpse, but had seen enough. There was a broad clearing ahead, where the trees had been cut back in a wide semi-circle on either side of the track. The clearing was not empty. It was full of people.

The clearing contained an army. An army of Kotev. It must be thousands strong. He gasped to breathe. His mind worked frantically. How was it possible? What should he do?

Shouts came from the clearing, followed by the jangle and judder of those tall beasts being coaxed into motion. They had been seen.

'Turn!' he shouted. 'We must run. Run!'

He had made a terrible mistake. Why had he not just followed his orders? Blane had made himself very clear. He burned with the shame of it. Now, he and the young men he led were fleeing for their lives.

The foreboding sound of galloping hooves grew louder. He half-turned as he ran, seeing a cohort of mounted knights closing in as they pursued. Behind the cavalry, several ranks of spearmen marched in close formation.

He thought hard as he ran. Up ahead he saw the junction in the path. It gave him an idea.

'Turn left,' he panted to the lads ahead. 'Follow the other path.' To go straight on would be to lead the army directly back to the village. He could not do that. If they followed the smaller, more overgrown path then hopefully they could lead the pursuit away. Then, they could scatter into the trees and escape. They had to warn the Masters of this.

Eain kept at the rear as the group ran along this new path, ready to turn and fight if they were caught. But, the path quickly narrowed as it headed uphill. If it had been used for wagons, then it must have been many years ago. A wagon would struggle to fit along it now. The bordering trees overhung the path, boughs reach towards each other like grasping arms.

The Sverlaeggare behind him ran through a gloomy tunnel of branch and leaf, the heavy sounds of pursuit a malicious presence at their heels.

A pale circle of light shone through the trees ahead. The golden green tone of sunshine through leaves was bright against the surrounding shade. There must be another clearing ahead.

'Into the clearing,' shouted Eain between deep, ragged breaths. 'Spread out. Go in different directions. Hide in the trees.' His legs burned as he drove hard to climb the last yards of the incline. 'They will not know. Which of us. To chase.'

The younger soldiers around him were struggling. Their faces were flushed, twisted with exertion. This had to be their last effort. Maybe, if he led the chase straight on then the others could escape into the woods to either side. Eain felt confident that he could lead the Kotevari a merry dance up into the hills before vanishing.

They would all get away, and be able to warn the Masters of the Claihed that the Dall was overrun with enemies.

With a rush of footsteps, the leading runners burst through into the light. Eain took one last look over his shoulder and saw Kotevari riders ducking beneath low branches further down the track, before turning and following the Sverlaeggare out into the clearing.

He froze. His heart fell through the soles of his boots.

'Oh, shit,' moaned Kater. 'What now?'

Before them rose the stern grey wall of an abandoned quarry. Eain looked desperately left and right but only saw more sheer walls of hewn rock. The quarry penned them in on every side apart from the way they had come. They had run right into a trap.

There was nowhere to go.

EIGHT

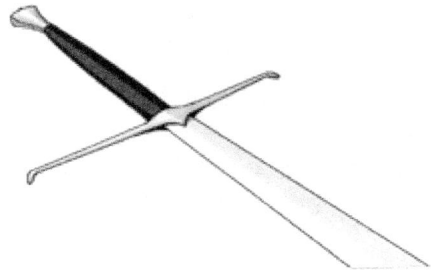

It was an old box quarry, a square-cut hole in the hillside. Sheer walls rose to the north, south and west. The only way in or out was the old wagon way they had just climbed, which was now full of the enemy.

'No, no, no...' Eain slowed to a walk, looking around at the steep, frowning walls in pure denial. This could not be. There must be another way out.

The sound of hoofbeats grew louder until he could feel the earth trembling beneath his feet. He dashed away from the head of the track and out into the centre of the quarry. The other Sverlaeggare had spread out, looking for a way to escape. There were none.

He had done this. He had doomed these young men. If he had done what he had been ordered to do, then they would be safely approaching the solid fortress of Vekwicc by now.

But, spoke another, calmer voice from his mind, *if he had obeyed orders then an army would be ranging through the west of Banahgar, unknown and unfought.* They would have to be fought now. There was no other choice.

'To me! To me!' he called, trying to fill his voice with a confidence that he did not feel. 'Claihed to me! Swords up, form ranks!'

He caught sight of the worried expressions on the faces of Edich and Kater as they scurried across the rough floor of the quarry to join him. He suppressed another twinge of deep guilt at what he had done.

'We will show them our hammered edges,' he called, as the line assembled. 'And drive them back to where they came from.' The Banahgarians clustered together, lining up with the main quarry wall at their backs as the Kotevari advanced.

The cavalry did not charge. Instead, they fanned out to either side, eyeing the thin line of swordsmen warily. The beasts they rode stepped forward in unison, hooves thudding heavily on the ground. Their weight and size was an intimidating presence.

A gentle breeze blew and the treetops swayed, leaves lifting and waving in elegant mockery of the scene below. The line of cavalry parted at the head of the trail and two figures rode forward, side by side.

The unnatural bright red of the woman's hair caught his eye first, but both were dressed in fine, expensive cloth and gold shone on the trappings. A curved, single-edged sword hung at the man's belt but Eain was surprised to see the decorated hilt of a slender rapier at the woman's hip. She rested one hand on it as they rode forward.

She moved her eyes across the line of Banahgarians dispassionately. For a heartbeat, Eain felt her cold, dark eyes looking into his, and saw only indifference. She turned her head and barked an order back down the track.

For a moment, nothing happened, but then Eain could see steady movement behind her. Foot soldiers bearing long spears marched into the quarry, blinking in the brighter light but moving forward in neat lines. They formed up facing the Banahgarians in several wide ranks.

The female noble now drew her sword. It was light and narrow-bladed, glittering coldly in the patchy sunlight. With a loud and strident cry, she gestured forward with the weapon, and the ranks of spearmen began to advance.

Eain raised his own sword, lifting the long, gleaming blade high above his head. His mouth was dry, but he had to do something to control his troops' fear.

'You know what to do!' he cried, trying to keep his voice even. 'You are the best swordsmen in the world! You have trained for this moment, and your time has come.'

He lowered his blade, dropping into a low guard with his sword horizontal. 'For the Claihed! And for Banahgar!' He advanced on the Kotevari line, and the others were beside him.

The men of Kotev strode forward to meet them. The front rank lowered their spears and those behind thrust their own into the gaps. It was a great, thorny hedge on marching feet.

When the lines were a handful of paces apart, the Banahgarians suddenly sped up. A few rapid strides and the Kotevari spear points were now very close. Greatswords swept out in unison; every third man used their swords' long blades to sweep a couple of spears aside. As if rehearsed, the next men in line stepped forward and repeated the action with the spears of the second rank.

Eain watched as his young charges calmly demonstrated the skills they had been taught. Before him was a writhing tangle of swords and spears. The shorter, slighter Kotevari soldiers tried to free their trapped spear-hafts and the Banahgarians used their strength to hold them down.

Now it was his turn.

With the spears bound up he was able to step forward and raise his sword. He risked a quick glance, left and right, and saw others doing likewise. His heart fluttered and his breathing was shallow. His arms did not feel like his own.

With an abruptness that startled him, he moved with a motion that he had practised until his arms ached. His hands moved left and right, the point of his greatsword arcing rapidly. There was a slight sensation of resistance after each strike.

And, just like that, it was done.

Two Kotevari spearmen clamped desperate hands to gaping wounds in their throats, where Eain's precise strikes had cut them with lethal force. As they fell, Eain knew that he had stepped across an invisible boundary. He had undergone a rite of passage.

He had killed his first men.

He felt sick.

Spearmen fell all along the line; either collapsing to the ground in a wordless welter of blood or falling back through the line, clutching injuries. Howls of pain filled the air.

The Banahgarians found their blades becoming free as the resistance of the spears was removed. They struck with their swords, and more Kotevari fell.

'Keep pressing!' Eain heard himself cry, shock and revulsion conflicting with a roaring sense of triumph. He thrust his greatsword forward and felt the resistance as it slid deeply into a spearman's body. There was a terrible cry of fear and agony, and Eain quickly withdrew his sword.

A moan came from his left and he turned. One of the Sverlaeggare was clutching the dark, wooden haft of a spear. The point was buried deep in his chest.

'Sorry…' he gasped as he fell. Eain could not remember his name.

The point was withdrawn, and the spearman thrust it desperately at Eain. He had dark hair that hung down around his ears, and was cut at that length in a severe line all around his head. His eyes were pits of terror.

Eain easily deflected the spear thrust and raised his sword. He caught the man's fear-filled eyes and knew nothing but pity. Then he remembered the dead Sverlaeggare beside him, and angrily lashed out with his greatsword. The Kotevari man did not have time to cry out.

The organised battle lines had descended into a brawl; a chaotic mess of men struggling with one another in every direction. Some of the Kotevari spearmen had tried to retreat, but the beast-riding nobles moved to cut them off and herd them back into the fray.

As Eain watched, Foinn swung his greatsword into the neck of an enemy. Blood spurted and gushed down the man's shoulder and along Foinn's blade. With his last breath, he drew a short knife from his belt, and thrust it into Foinn's chest.

Eain could do nothing as the boy fell back onto the scrubby ground, clutching at the hilt. His legs jerked for a moment and then he was still.

He turned and saw another Sverlaeggare surrounded by three spearmen. The boy slashed his greatsword in scything arcs but could not hold the Kotevari back. He went down moments later, stabbed again and again by the cruel spears.

They must not get isolated. They would be picked off.

'Claihed! To me!' shouted Eain, his head swivelling as he watched for threats. 'Circle on me!' Edich was quickly beside him. Their eyes met for a moment, and Edich's expression of stoic resignation shamed Eain anew.

The remaining Banahgarians backed away from the enemy and arranged themselves in a broad semi-circle, backing onto the main wall of the quarry. Eain felt sick to the stomach with horror at the death he had already seen and caused himself. They had to escape.

'At my command,' he said clearly. 'We charge at a weak point. We can break through and escape into the woods.' It was a desperate gambit. He knew it was unlikely to work, but he had to try. He had to be a leader in this moment. 'Follow my lead.'

The spearmen were regrouping and Eain knew that to give them too much time was to doom his plan to failure. It was now or never.

'For Banahgar!' he roared.

For survival, he thought.

He surged forward and sensed that the others were following. He drove ahead as the tip of the wedge. He was the point of the blade.

The Kotevari ranks were caught by surprise by this sudden charge, and recoiled slightly. It was all the hesitation that Eain needed, and in a few long strides he was on them.

The despairing thrusts of a couple of spears were beaten aside with ease, and then he was in amongst them. He acted without conscious thought, on instinct and a surging will to survive.

His sword swung left and right. More men died. His blade was painted red.

Grunts of effort and cries of pain filled the air. His eyes darted, looking for attacks and countering them as he forced his way forward. He had almost broken through the line.

A loud, damp exhalation blew air into his face. He looked up in alarm. One of the brown beasts stood in his path, and the mounted noble was raising his sword. A solid rank of cavalry now stood before Eain, a solid wall in the path of his escape.

He took a step back as a meaty thump beside him made him turn. Kater was raising hands to his face, which was streaming with blood. His nose was crushed and his cheek was torn open. His mouth was a red ruin.

The butt of a spear had struck him full in the face, smashing out his teeth and breaking his nose. His breath came in snoring, rasping groans as he collapsed to his knees. Eain stepped forward to guard him, or to offer some help, but at that moment a bright spear point burst from Kater's chest.

All Eain could do was retreat.

His last chance had been snuffed out like a guttering candle flame between damp fingertips.

Gripping his greatsword tight, he felt wetness between the warm leather grip and his sweaty palms. He looked down to see that his hands were scarlet, gleaming damply.

Red, like fresh cloudberry juice.

He backed away, watching in numb horror as the Kotevari cavalry advanced, swords sweeping down at the scattered Banahgarian survivors. The sky was still blue, the sun not far past noon. It had all happened so quickly.

So blue.

Edich was surrounded, but fighting like a demon. Eain wanted to help him, but he was too far away. The younger man's sword moved in blurring arcs, and the Kotevari around him could not get close.

But it was only a matter of time. Edich knew it. He swept his sword in a huge arc around his head, then darted away, heading toward where Eain was watching helplessly.

There was the rolling thunder of hooves once more, and a curved blade slashed down on Edich from above. A livid red slash appeared between his neck and his shoulder. It was deep, and Eain could see the flesh beneath for a moment before blood welled in the wound.

Edich's eyes glazed, his head lolling to one side as his legs faltered. He tumbled to the ground. His fair hair shone in contrast to the dark green of the grass where he had fallen.

Deep green grass.

Eain was the only one left. Everyone else was slain. The massed Kotevari army was closing in. It was over. He looked down at his hands once more.

So red.

The thorny bushes had pricked his hands. He could not tell the blood from berry juice. He should run home to his mother.

Red blood.

He staggered and the cold stone of the quarry wall was at his back. He was surprised to notice that he held a sword. It was very red.

So red.

Red blood. Green grass. Blue sky.

Red. Green. Blue.

Red.

Red.

Black.

PART TWO

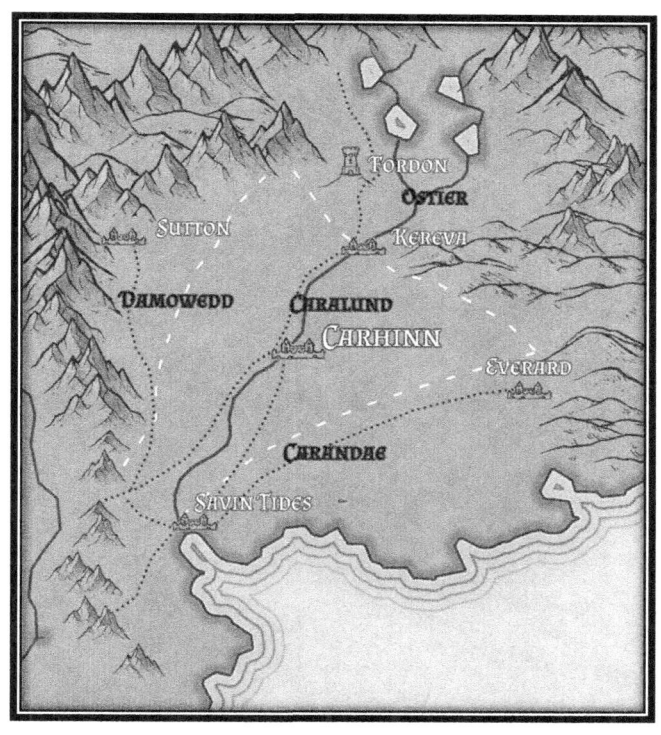

ANISH

NINE

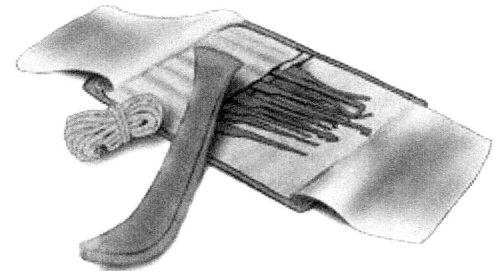

Ellyah froze. Two shrill whistles had just sounded from outside. The signal.

It was not unexpected, and she forced herself to calmly continue with the job in hand. She had a few moments, yet. Her hands were steady as she returned her picks to the tool roll around her waist, and reached forward for her prize.

The wooden box felt surprisingly heavy as she lifted it from the chest and closed the lid. She snapped the lock shut too.

Leave everything as you found it.

Her curiosity to open the box was intense. The fact that the Mackems had hidden this treasure away from their own gang members had made her wonder. Made her want it. The value must be high if the upper echelons of the gang wanted to keep it secret.

What was in the box?

The sound of footsteps on the stairs up to the room focused her mind away from the contents of the box, and onto escaping with it.

She listened. There were more than one pair of feet climbing the stairs. Maybe three.

'Shit,' she muttered to herself, her mind working as she adapted her plan.

The room was at the rear corner of the building, with the shop floor below and the shopkeeper's living space adjacent. The merchant must owe the Mackems for protection, for them to use her shop as secure storage. Information to be remembered for later.

A side window looked out onto the street below, and another at the rear gave a view over the mess that had once been communal gardens. Escape options, but both bad. The street was too public, and the gardens could turn into a trap…

The heavy tread of the shopkeeper's footsteps got closer, approaching the room's only door.

Think, Ellyah. Think!

A large crate stood in the corner next to the door. Ellyah had been mildly curious about such a tall, sturdy container when she entered the room but had been focused on the contents of the chest. Standing beside it now, she felt an unsettling presence within. She was still curious, but also felt strongly that she should not try to open it.

A key clattered in the lock. Ellyah looked toward the door.

She quickly ran through her escape options again. Through the window and down onto the street…no. Out of the window and up onto the roof…no. Hide behind the crate and try to sneak past…no.

All of these ended up with her being caught. The door handle began to turn. Her time had run out.

Ellyah reached into the pocket of her breeches, where she kept a throwing dagger and an egg. As her hands brushed these contrasting items, the door swung open and the merchant stepped into the room.

Their eyes locked. The merchant opened her mouth to shout. Ellyah threw the egg.

The egg arced through the air and into the merchant's face. It broke on impact and the doorway was suddenly filled with a burst of white. The egg had been filled with flour, and now it surrounded the merchant in a swirling cloud. Ellyah was already moving.

'Guards!' shouted the merchant, trying to wipe the flour from her eyes. She beat at the floating white specks with flailing hands and stepped further into the room. The shutters to the window above the street had been flung open, and were swaying in the slight breeze.

'Down on the street!' she bellowed back to the guards. 'They are out on the street! After them!'

Rapid footsteps receded from the room as the guards clattered back down the stairs. The merchant crossed quickly to the window and leaned out, scanning the street for a running figure.

Ellyah swung back into the room through the other window. She landed softly as a cat and her felt-soled shoes made no sound. Heart beating rapidly, she moved silently across the room in four long, careful strides. The merchant's head was still out of the window, swinging from side to side as she scanned the street below.

Ellyah smiled as she left the room. People could be so stupid.

She strolled casually down the stairs, footfalls deadened and silent on the wooden treads. The box was tucked under her arm and she shrugged her long grey cloak more closely around her body to cover it.

He shoulder-length brown hair was pinned back, out of the way and she pushed through the shop's doorway unhurriedly and stepped out onto the street. Her free hand darted into her pocket and a moment later she wore five slim rings on the first and second fingers of each hand. Most were of dull pewter apart from three on her left index finger, which were of yellow brass.

She strolled away, her hands declaring her a normal commoner, but one whose fortunes were on the rise. She smirked inwardly. Little did they know about the true fortune she carried beneath her arm.

It was drizzling. Small spots of rain prickled insistently across her face. Probably a good thing; the pursuit might be less rigorous in the rain, if she could avoid being caught for long enough.

Shouts rang out from the alleyway that ran beside the shop. Ellyah schooled her face to calmness and did not look around, but guessed that the guards had realised that she had not gone that way.

Walk, she reminded herself. *If you aren't running, then you won't be chased. Keep walking.*

There was a covered market at the end of the street. Tall poles had been hammered into the packed earth and broad sheets of coloured canvas had been stretched between them. The sheltered area beneath was busy with people browsing the stalls and barrows, which were laden with goods.

A man walking beside Ellyah, hooded against the misting drizzle, increased his pace to reach the cover of the canvas more quickly. Ellyah took the chance, lengthening her own strides to match.

Just a commoner, hurrying to get out of the rain. No one would be suspicious.

Rapid footsteps came from behind, growing louder. 'You, girl! What are you carrying?' She turned to see a stocky, bald-headed man pointing her direction. 'Stop. Stop!'

Seems that someone was suspicious, after all. Time for a different plan.

She ran. Clutching the box tightly, she broke into an easy, loping run. The angular edges of the box dug into her ribs, but she covered the distance to the market quickly, legs pumping.

Multiple sets of running feet slapped on the wet earth of the street behind. The chase was on. Ellyah swapped the box deftly to the other side to rest her arm, and ran beneath the eaves of the market.

The gloom surrounded her immediately as she slowed from her run to a sedate walk. She controlled her breathing, not allowing her shoulders to heave. It would make her stand out.

The market was busy. Fragrant steam billowed past as filled leek rolls bubbled in a black pot atop a glowing brazier.

'Nutmeg! Piment! Curcumin!' bellowed a hawker. 'Finest spice, imported from Kotev! Marjoram and tarragon from Tayo!'

Ellyah kept moving, aware that the pursuit was still behind her. Her eyes darted, alive for opportunities. A skinny man with a wide-brimmed hat pushed a barrow piled high with turnips across the aisle and behind her. She bent her knees and ducked low.

As she squatted down, she pulled at the cord that held her double-layered cloak together. When she stood again, the grey wool hung down from her waist as a green skirt. Dipping her hands in her pockets, six of her fingers, three on each hand, were now decked in brass and tin rings.

Walking on, she pulled out the pins that held her hair in place. She shook it loose and it fell down to her shoulders. Shouts and cries told her that the merchant and her guards were searching through the market.

Calming her breathing still further, she carried on.

'Find the thief!' they bellowed. 'Stand aside, a filthy thief be among you! Let us through. Show your face!'

Before a ramshackle stall with crates of parsnips and red yams, she paused. An empty basket lay on the ground before the stall. It was exactly where she had placed it earlier.

With a sleight of hand, she palmed the box down her body and dropped it into the basket without bending. An unseen hand reached through from behind the stall and placed a loaf of bread and a bunch of carrots into the basket, before drawing a square of thick cloth across the top.

Ellyah did not glance down.

'How much for three yams?' she asked the stallholder, putting on the accent of the city. She passed over a few copper sections, casual and unconcerned. Placing the roots in the basket, she hoisted it up onto her hip.

She turned and walked back the way she had come. With the basket resting on her hip, she walked with a more exaggerate sway and a slight stoop. An older woman who had birthed children.

The merchant was standing in the centre of one of the aisles, fists on hips and an expression of fury on her narrow face. Rings of bright metal on many of her fingers stood out starkly in the gloom. Ellyah could only read her anger as a victory, and lowered her face to hide her expression, a gesture to be read as respectful subservience.

Her guards were upturning stalls and rifling through crates as Ellyah strolled away from the market. The rain had eased and watery sunshine was filtering through the clouds.

Ellyah let a wry smile creep across her face as she strolled away, the basket and its valuable contents resting safely on her hip.

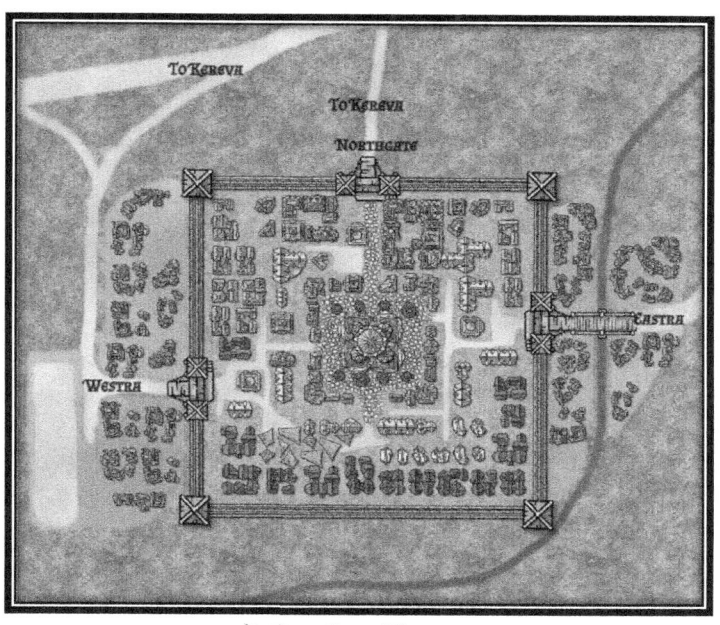

CARHINN

TEN

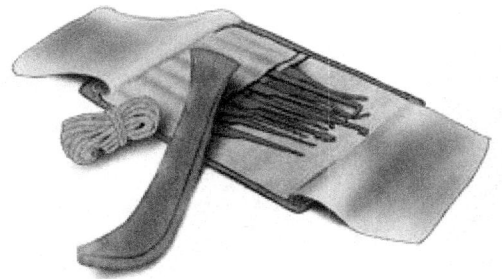

Carhinn at night was alive with shifting shadows.

Ellyah was one of them as she slunk through the dark streets. There were more people around than usual, despite the late hour. She had heard many voices shouting, and the patter and slap of running feet. Chasing feet. It made her uneasy, especially when she was so near her destination.

Although, she should not have been too surprised. Someone had just outwitted the most dangerous criminal gang in Carhinn and stolen a treasure that most of their members did not even know existed. She smiled to herself.

And the best part was, they had no idea where it had gone.

She had strolled casually away from the marketplace and past the shop itself, the basket held firmly under one arm. The sounds of the frantic search had faded into the distance as she turned and headed north, out of the merchants' district.

There were plenty of hours left in the day, and leading the Mackems to her hideout would be extremely stupid. And Ellyah despised stupidity. So, she walked in the opposite direction.

An inn, The Night Owl, stood before a small patch of scrubby grass, grazed half-heartedly by a couple of goats. Ellyah had once helped the cook out of a sticky situation, and he quickly ushered her in after she rapped on the kitchen door.

'What trouble are you in now?' asked Graghe Fuure, the cook of the Night Owl, as he shut the door firmly behind her. His dark eyes were sharp beneath his heavy brows.

'Trouble?' she arched an eyebrow. 'Why would you think that?'

He laughed. 'Trouble there be, my dear. Whether you be in it or whether you have caused it. However, I'm sure I don't want to know.'

She smiled sweetly. 'No, you really don't.'

'The eternal veil will judge you, I won't.' He invoked the judgement that waited after death, but he was laughing as he said the words. Ellyah rolled her eyes. She had done nothing wrong, and whoever or whatever judged her at the end of her life would see that, had they wit and sense.

A few short moments later, the bread and vegetables were on Fuure's kitchen table and the basket was discarded. Ellyah stepped out through the door in a long, smoothly woven robe and wearing a silken cap; a highborn woman on an afternoon errand. Her twenty rings, five on each first and second finger, were all of thin bronze.

A wicker case with a floral decoration hung from a strap around her shoulder.

Graghe Fuure had watched out of the corner of his eye as Ellyah had quickly transferred the wooden box from the basket to the wicker case. It really was better for him if he knew nothing. As she handled the box, it seemed as though it were slightly warm. As if there were something hot inside.

She shrugged. It was not important now. Maybe the sun had warmed the box. Within a basket. Beneath a heavy cloth.

As she walked north, the streets became wider and the houses were bigger. This was where the wealthy of Carhinn dwelled. She moved with a confident, purposeful gait. She belonged here, and had business to attend to.

Rounding a corner, she stepped into a broad street paved with cobbles. Up ahead rose the grandeur of the Royal Palace.

Carhinn was a new city, built to a grid plan. The streets ran in a strict cross-cross pattern within four sturdy walls. From the air, the city would appear a perfect square, with the palace in the centre.

It was a grand, ornate building and it dominated the centre of Carhinn. The lower levels were constructed of smooth blocks of well-dressed pale stone, in contrast to the rough-hewn rubble that was used for the lower walls of the surrounding buildings.

The stone rose two stories high, pierced in many places by dark, shuttered windows. It was above this level that the best Anise craftspeople had been allowed to show their skill and imagination.

Timber spires climbed dizzily into the afternoon sky. The gentle breeze caused the colourful pennants at their tips to wave and snap, some fifty feet above Ellyah's head. The structures were arranged with geometric precision and yet the effect was of something that had grown naturally, and with freedom.

Every timber beam and column was carved with intricate designs recalling leaves, vines and flowers, and even the wooden shingles covering the myriad of angled roofs were leaf shaped. Gardens were arrayed below, planted with trees from around the continent and flowers and shrubs that bloomed like a rainbow.

It was an impressive sight, one of the great feats of engineering of the modern world. Ellyah would have given a handful of silver rings for a quiet snoop around inside the palace. Preferably wearing a coat with very deep pockets. The wealth of the current royal family was well-known, but the reason that no one would even try to rob the palace stood in a loose, motionless ring around the perimeter of the gardens.

Ellyah spared the stern, upright figures a quick glance and hurried past. Catching the attention of the Royal Sentinels was not something that a sensible person did. Especially not someone escaping a criminal gang and carrying a rare, valuable artefact.

The Sentinels were famed throughout Anish and across Re'Emsser, the confederacy of the southern countries, although their origins were shrouded in mystery. They existed under oath to serve and protect the royal family of Anish, but their headquarters and garrison was in the far southeast of the country, in the duchy of Carandae.

It was their presence along the eastern border of Anish that deterred neighbouring Kotev from mounting more regular invasions.

Ellyah strolled past several as she took a route around the perimeter of the gardens. They were motionless, impassive, and she knew that they were undertaking a guard vigil that lasted from dawn to dusk. They were famed for their ability to stand absolutely still for hours at a time. Most of their members were elves, as few human men or women could cope with the intense physical demands.

The tips of their heavy-bladed polearms gleamed in the afternoon light, as did the gilded helms and plates of armour that covered their shoulders and chests. Ellyah tried to think innocent thoughts, and strolled on and out of the other side of the palace square.

Shadows were lengthening as she moved through the quietening streets. The upper floors of most of the buildings overhung the streets, making her path between them a gloomy tunnel. She knew every turn, every alley, and felt that she was far enough from where she had staged her theft to relax a little.

The darkness thickened before her. A square shape loomed in her path as she approached, black in the dusky light. The muffled, indistinct sounds of people chanting came from within, a ghostly sound in the evening air.

As she drew closer, the twelve stone columns that supported the Northgate temple appeared, harsh and angular in the gloom. Tradition held that you should not walk beneath the temple, between the columns. The gods were above, but the demons were below. Ellyah had no time for superstition and strolled confidently through the covered, empty space.

When she reached the north wall, she began to hurry. The gathering darkness hid her well. The alleys close to the city walls were shadowy and narrow, and dangerous at night. She, though, had no intention of loitering.

It was night by the time she neared her destination. As dusk fell, she had affected one more clothing change; stashing the fine robe and decorated box behind a loose stone in a wall, and skulking away into the gathering gloom in snug, dark-coloured breeches and shirt, her roll of tools a comforting presence against her back.

Pattering feet and urgent calls rang out through the streets. She was still being hunted.

She had transferred the wooden box into a leather sack, strapped securely across her back to leave her hands free for climbing. She would need them soon.

She was heading south, keeping close to the city's western wall. She made sure that she did not use any of the same streets that she had passed on the outward journey. To be recognised, or to be followed, would be a disaster.

At the corner of a large, dark house she paused. The stony lower walls rose up above head height. On top of the walls, beginning higher than she could reach by jumping, was the timber part of the house.

This was built out from the base in all directions, the upper floors overhanging on every side. She glanced up at the planks of the soffit above. Now, most of all, she must not be seen.

Wary as a raccoon, she reached up the rough, blocky wall until her fingers curled over a chiselled edge. A useful hand hold, invisible to passers-by. In moments, she had climbed up the wall to the overhang.

She reached back, above and behind, pressing the palm of one hand to the planks above and lifting. A small section rose; a hidden hatch, and she pushed it aside. With practised haste, she wriggled her shoulders through the small gap and climbed up.

Ellyah had happened to be inside this house some months ago, and had noticed that a large bookcase had been built against this wall. It covered the whole wall, floor to ceiling, but did not quite fit flush. There was a narrow void behind.

It was up this void that Ellyah now shimmied, hands and knees on one side and her back pressed against the other. She made very little noise, and in any case the owners of the house were old and seemed to sleep very soundly.

She had carefully cut another hole through the sturdy boards of the ceiling, and it was through this that she now climbed. This was her base, storeroom and hideout, up in the roof space of the house.

'Took your time,' came a voice from the other side of the attic. The soft glow of a single candle illuminated the space, heavy beams slanting down from either side of the roof's central ridge.

'Can't rush perfection,' replied Ellyah. She was half-joking. She slipped the bag off her shoulder and retrieved the box, before moving closer to the light. 'I thought I might run into the Mackems at every turn.'

'Yea,' the other replied. 'I saw plenty of them, rushing about. But they don't know I know you, so they dashed straight past.' She giggled softly.

The attic's other occupant was Luara Orsini. Her long, chestnut hair was loose, hanging down past her shoulders, and her pale skin gleamed in the candlelight. She was much older, Ellyah guessed at nearly forty, but her only real signs of age were some very fine crow's feet around her bright eyes, and a few strands of white in her hair.

'The Mackems don't know it was me, either,' said Ellyah. Luara twitched her lips in agreement. 'And it would be better to keep it so. Were you careful climbing up here? You made sure you were not seen?' She could not keep the anxiety from her voice.

Luara waved the concern away. 'Yes, yes! I'm not silly. You worry too much.' Ellyah grunted a non-committal response.

The two had met in Kereva, the second city of Anish. Luara had suddenly appeared on the scene, and had been desperate to get involved in anything that was going on. They had first bumped into one another at a shady bar near the river wharfs, and Ellyah realised instantly that for an older woman, she had an unusual and useful set of skills. Also, despite her outward cheer there was a secret sadness within her.

Ellyah had not asked, and Luara had not told.

They had found an immediate connection, and when Ellyah had been forced to flee Kereva, Luara had come along. They both vowed to look for opportunities in Carhinn. That time had come when Ellyah had picked up the rumour that the Mackems had obtained something rare, dangerous and valuable. Something mysterious. Something that they were trying desperately to hide.

This could be the big job. The one that set Ellyah up for life, and let her escape from all this. She had been unable to resist the temptation to try it, but had known that she could not do it alone.

As an unknown face, Luara had kept a careful watch on the Mackems in Carhinn and had located the shop. She had been the lookout earlier today, and Ellyah's backup in case things went wrong.

'I started the food already,' said Luara, indicating a half-eaten loaf lying near where she sat. 'Was hungry.'

'It was there for you to eat, hen,' replied Ellyah warmly. She reached out and tore herself a chunk of bread. Sitting down, she let out a long, deep breath of fatigue and relief.

It was done. Perfectly planned, perfectly executed, and a poke in the eye for the Mackems. Their leaders would be furious.

She did not understand the significance of the treasure, but the layers of secrecy suggested they considered it to be very important. Or, very valuable. And to Ellyah, the two were exactly the same thing.

As if reading her thoughts, Luara spoke. 'Can I see it?'

Ellyah shrugged. 'Why not?'

She reached out and pulled the box toward her. As she sat cross-legged on the floor, she set it down between her feet and felt for the catch. It was a simple hook and eye latch, and it flicked open at a touch.

For some reason, she felt suddenly wary. She glanced up at Luara, who was watching intently with her lips slightly parted.

'Let's have a look at it then, hen,' said Ellyah, gathering herself. She lifted the lid of the box.

The attic space was instantly lit by a fiery red glow. A fist-sized ruby sat within the tight confines of the simple wooden box. It was incongruously grand in the basic surroundings. Ellyah leaned closer. The ruby was cut with many complex facets and they shone ominously in the low light. They looked like knife edges.

Yet, the heart of the jewel...the more Ellyah studied it, the deeper she felt like she was falling into it. The candlelight reflected and refracted inside, but it also seemed to glow from within with a raging, coruscating inner fire.

The silhouettes of the two women were cast in sharp relief onto the slanting boards of the roof above, haloed by a crimson glow.

'Are you going to take it out of the box?'

Ellyah jumped at the sound of Luara's voice. She had been staring, rapt, into the centre of the ruby. She nodded, and lowered her hands slowly towards the jewel. She bit her lip.

Her instincts had been ringing like a warning bell since she had opened the lid of the box, but as her hands got closer to the glassy surface of the ruby they screamed an alarm. Ellyah had survived this long by paying close attention to her inner voice. Luara was watching.

'No,' she said abruptly, jerking her hands away. 'I think I'm just going to leave it in the box, for now.' She shut the lid, gratefully. They were plunged suddenly into darkness.

'I think that was a good decision,' said Luara. 'What do we do now?'

'We wait. The Mackems will get bored of searching before long. They will assume it's been taken out of the city. Then we find someone who can help us to fence it on.'

'We're not going to be able to sell that to just any jewel trader.' Luara's voice was doubtful.

'Oh no, hen. Of course not.' Ellyah smiled toward the older woman. But I know someone who can move nearly anything and not leave a trace.'

It was almost time to find Nastja.

Skane was a simple man.

He did what he was told, so long as what he was told made sense. And so long as they spoke loudly to him; his hearing was failing. He had never been afraid to put his head in the way of blows, so perhaps going deaf was the price he now had to pay.

The Mackems had seen his potential as his reputation as a backstreet brawler and part-time prize fighter. He had worked as a labourer, hefting heavy timber and stone, but fought in the evenings. He was good at it, and he enjoyed himself. Like many things, it seemed simple to Skane.

The offer to take employment as a gang member instead had also been a simple decision. They had used fancy words, of course. Security. Enforcements. Debt collection.

Skane's hearing might have been poor, but his eyes were wide open. He knew that the Mackems wanted him as muscle. Someone to be the heavy fist when needed. Someone to knock down doors and intimidate those behind them.

He also understood that the offer had not been a decision for him to make. You did not refuse the Mackems and walk away with your limbs still in the same places. So, he had shrugged his acceptance and flung himself into his new career with gusto. It was easier work than lifting and carrying. Better paid, too.

Skane was a simple man, but he was not stupid. He paid attention to what was going on around him and could tell which way the wind was blowing. A new wind was blowing through the ranks of the Mackems, and it was straight out of a midden. It stank.

The room was hushed. Usually the meetings were raucous, the long-time members chatting and sharing tales. Not today. Today, an atmosphere pervaded that kept voices low, eyes down.

'Something's gone wrong,' rumbled a deep voice near Skane's ear. He turned and looked up. Then further up.

'Something bad,' finished the towering figure. Dusky-skinned Jhari stood beside him, his head almost brushing the roof beams. The half-elf was seven feet tall if he were an inch, and huge in the shoulders too.

Skane nodded mutely. He could beat Jhari in a fistfight. Easy.

A space had been cleared in the centre of the room, upstairs in one of the city's roughest taverns. The gang members kept back wordlessly, huddling around the walls.

Without warning, there was a shimmer in the air. As if rising from cloudy water, a masked face appeared, floating five feet above the ground in the middle of the circle. Thick black stripes covered both of the figure's eyes, and silver-grey panels ran down each side of its face. Another thick strip went from the forehead down to the mask's pointed snout.

It spoke. 'Where is it?'

It was a human voice, but distorted by the mask. Skane strained to hear, unable to even tell if the speaker was male or female, without being able to see their lips move.

The crowd milling around near the walls shuffled their feet uneasily. The mask swung, side to side, as if searching for faces in the crowd. It stopped.

'You.' The voice spoke again, hard and abrupt. 'It was you. Step forward.'

Brin Gallit stepped reluctantly out of the crowd. Skane had seen this man cutting fingers off a man with a hatchet, joint by joint, to force him to confess the location of hidden gold. He had shown no hesitation or remorse. Now, he looked anxious. His hands writhed at his belt.

'We gave it to the merchant, Cenrys' he said, pleading in his rough, gravelly voice. 'She promised us it would be kept safe.'

The striped mask swung again. 'Cenrys! Show yourself!' A harassed-looking woman stepped forward. Her cloth was fine and her hair was neat. She looked respectable and out of place. Bright rings shone on her fingers.

'My strongroom is very secure,' she blustered. 'And nobody could know that the jewel was there! Or they should not have. Unless someone shot their mouth.' She directed a meaningful look at Gallit.

'I never said nothing!' replied Gallit, angrily. His face twisted, his recovering his usual belligerence.

'Silence!' the voice from the mask rang out with intense volume. The walls seem to shake with it, and some of the gathered crowd raised their hands to their ears. Skane did not need to, of course.

'The task was important. The safety of the item was important. The two of you, together, failed in this task.'

They opened their mouths as if to argue, but any words they might have said were drowned out by a new sound. The sound of intense buzzing.

It began as an indistinct hum, but rose in pitch and volume to become a saw-edged whine. Skane could not tell where it was coming from, and he could see others also glancing around the room in confusion.

He was looking directly at the merchant when she suddenly opened her mouth wide. His own mouth dropped open in horror as a swarm of fat, black flies buzzed out of her mouth and out into the room.

The same thing was happening to Gallit as he stood, head back, mouth open. Flies filled his mouth and were streaming out to form a dark cloud above both of their heads.

Gasps of disgust and fear came from around the room.

The intensity of the flies increased, now pouring from their noses and then, horribly, from out of their eyes. Their arms were limp at their sides and their knees began to sag. Skane was frozen to the spot with confusion and terror.

He could not tear his gaze away as a thin trail of black flies came from each of their ears. One by one, their legs gave way and they both collapsed to the floor. The dull thumps were final and chilling.

Skane had seen enough unpleasant things in his life to know that the merchant and Brin Gallit were both dead. The flies had stripped the life away from their bodies, from the inside out.

As abruptly as they had arrived, the swirling swam of flies funnelled down towards the floating figure in the striped mask, and were gone.

'A warning,' it said when the buzzing had faded away. 'Failure is not acceptable. Excuses are not acceptable. The jewel must be recovered. Who leads here, now?'

Cannis "Butcher" Flett stepped from the crowd. She was a broad woman with very close-cropped hair and thick forearms. Tattooed rings showed vividly on eight fingers.

'I will lead,' she said. Her voice sounded calm, despite what she had just witnessed. She was actually a butcher, so maybe she was used to it.

'At the merchant's shop there is a…tool,' the voice behind the mask continued. 'Go there when I command, and I will manifest to instruct you on how it can be used. It will help us recover the jewel.'

"Butcher" Flett nodded.

'Everyone else must continue the search in the meantime. Do not rest. Tear every hiding place in this city apart to find the thieves. Then bring them to me.'

'You heard him.' Flett's voice was harsh and commanding. 'Get to work. Out! Now!'

Skane sniffed the air. It stank even worse now. He did not know who had blabbed about the location of the jewel, but he knew it was not an inside job. He could only think of one thief with the skill and brass neck to pull off such a robbery.

Ellyah Jerim.

He just had to think of a way to find her.

ELEVEN

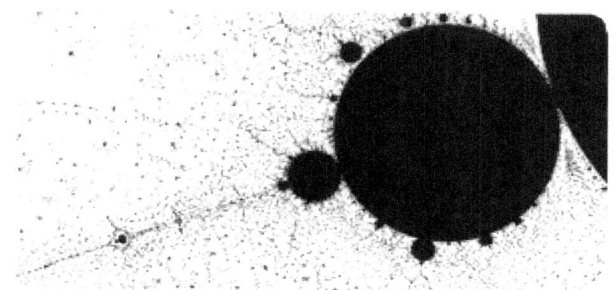

'Run, you knob-kneed sack of shit!'

Nastja leaned on the rough timber rail as similar shouts of exhortation filled the air. Her manner was one of engaged interest. The thunder of hooves shook the very ground as the riders passed, heads turning to follow their progress in hope and expectation.

The crowd moved to watch the dromedaries as they closed in on the finishing line. Nastja craned her neck as if watching, mirroring the actions of those around her, but in reality she was too short to see.

In any case, it mattered little. She was already confident in the outcome of the race.

The crowd erupted as the contest came to an exciting finish. The name of the winner was shouted, echoing into the evening sky.

'Judah! Judah!'

Nastja bowed her head in apparent disappointment. She had not picked the winner.

That was the last race of the day, and the crowd began to disperse. Nastja joined the queue filing slowly past the booths of the bookmakers.

The drom races took place outside Carhinn's city walls. A patch of cleared ground was reserved for the racing, within the ramshackle settlement that had sprung up outside the city's west gate. Most locals called the shanty town the Westra.

Nastja had been exploring the city for the last few weeks while she waited, and the races seemed a good place to spend some copper and pass some time. It had been a fine, dry evening after a warm day and she felt comfortable.

'When do you think we might get called up again?' Two burly men were ahead of her in the queue, and they had that solidity and balance that suggested that they were soldiers. They both wore a few bright steel rings on their fingers, each telling of a season of military service. The rest were dull tin or brass, typical of peasant labourers. One had just turned to the other, to ask the question.

'Could be soon,' answered his friend. Both were dressed in mid-length smocks of coarse wool. 'Mate of mine, Kefed, just came back from Ostier. Was serving hard on the eastern border. Said that the Kotevari walls were thick with spears. They are planning something.'

'Na, not sure mate,' said the other. He had been drinking, and was swaying slightly as he shuffled slowly along. 'Didn't they send a new emissary to the Sentinels, asking for peace? Made a load of promises.'

'Can't trust Kotev.' The first soldier was dismissive. 'Their king is under pressure. Needs a victory, see? He'd be daft to come against our border again with the Sentinels there in strength. But he might get desperate.'

'Maybe the spears are just for show.'

'Maybe,' he replied, hawking and spitting on the ground. Nastja stepped around it. 'Maybe they are up to something else. You heard the stories from the Teliyade? They tell that the Kotevari were building a new fleet.'

'Get out!' Can't believe anything those drunkard sailors say. They'd tell you that the Southern Ocean had frozen over for a slug of wine!'

They laughed to each other and moved forward to stand before the bookie. They had each won several scraps of copper, and took them with a few words before strolling off into the Westra.

'Slip,' called out the bookmaker, as Nastja moved to stand before her. Her tone was bored and abrupt. Natja handed over the small scrap of linen paper, and the woman read it with a scowl. She glanced down at Nastja's hands, noting her basic pewter finger rings before looking up at her face. 'You were a lucky one today,' she said, handing over a cluster of copper money rings.

'Yes,' replied Nastja, putting on a coy smile. 'It is my first time here. The gods must smile on me.' She slipped the rings onto her wrists and walked quickly away, smile vanishing as she turned.

No, Nastja had not picked a winner. Lucky fools or cheats bet on winners. Nastja had placed a wager on five different dromedaries, who had all finished second or third in their races. A very nice little earner, and much less likely to attract unwanted attention. Bookmakers did not like punters who won too much. It made them suspicious and inclined to ask tricky questions.

She had quickly established that the bookies were backed by the Mackams, and she did not like the way they went about their business one bit. Much better not to attract their eyes.

Her own flicked left and right, and she noticed a stall selling cider. Yes, a drink would go down nicely. She handed over a copper scrap, cut from a money ring, and wrapped her hands around the small wooden cup.

Small groups still stood near the racetrack, drinks in hands, making the most of the festival atmosphere. At the periphery of a group of laughing, chatting young men Nastja noticed one of them standing quietly to the side.

His face was smiling as he laughed at their jokes, but Nastja could see a certain stiffness in his posture, a blankness to his eyes as they flicked between his companions and the dry ground. His hands absently smoothed the sleeves of his mid-length robes. Where his copper and silver money rings should be.

He had lost it all on the races. His body language made it clear. He had got carried away in the excitement and risked too much. If he was lucky, he would just be made destitute. If he was unlucky then he would end up in debt to the Mackems. They would collect what was owed, one way or another.

Nastja had noticed the Mackems' broad shadow over much of the city since she had arrived here. Or at least, over the parts of the city that Nastja found interesting. The shadowy parts.

She had kept her nose clean, these past weeks, earning some copper but making sure to keep a low profile. Bartending, sweeping up, a little light labouring here and there. No one remembered a small, dark-skinned girl in a big city. Especially one who could easily pass for a boy. She had even found a bit of work mucking out the dromedary stables.

Knowledge gained, stored away and then used when she had found herself at the races this evening with some spare money. It had been well invested. She could take a week off now.

She had spent little, in any case. She did not need much food and she tended to take jobs which included meals and sometimes a bed for the night. She had saved some money by accepting invitations back to the rooms of a few men and women, who had been bold enough to ask.

The simple strategy of flashing a smile and listening to them talk could achieve much, especially if the timing was right. Especially if they were deep in drink. A pretty face could be enough to unfasten tightly tied purses. Although, Nastja conceded, her face was not even that pretty.

However, a woman who did have a symmetrical, fine-featured face had been watching her for several minutes now. Out of the corner of her eye, Nastja had seen the woman look her up and down several times, then nod to herself in confirmation.

She had been matching Nastja's appearance to a description she had been given, no doubt. Double-checking and then making a decision. So, this was who had been sent to fetch her. Finally. Nastja was relieved. She had just been starting to get bored.

Without staring, Nastja turned her head to watch the other woman approach. She was pale-skinned and had long, chestnut hair that was tied back neatly. Not a local. Probably from somewhere in the north. Her clothing suggested that too. She was dressed in rider's leathers rather than robes or a smock.

She walked with a balanced sway to her hips, and there was obvious strength in her body. Her shoulders were broad in contrast to the slimness of her waist. She could be a fighter, or an acrobat. Or both.

And yet…there was something in the width of her hips, in proportion to her waist. This woman had borne a child. Curious. Nastja shrugged the thought away. Knowledge gained and stored away.

'Yes, I am Nastja,' she said, jumping in before the other woman could speak. She pursed her lips, then opened her mouth again. Nastja interrupted once more. 'Ellyah has sent you to fetch me.'

The other woman scowled, but nodded. Her nose wrinkled and fine lines spidered across her forehead with the expression. Nastja guessed that she was about fifteen years older, in her mid to late thirties.

'I can see why Ellyah would want you around,' Nastja continued, wanting to say something nice at this first meeting. 'You look useful. Strong. I'm sure you are very muscular. Underneath your clothes, that is.'

The other woman's brows rose in surprise, mouth twitching in slight amusement.

'I would ask you your name,' continued Nastja, quickly, 'but I think for now it's better I don't know.'

'That's fine with me,' said the other woman, speaking for the first time. 'It's nice to finally meet you though. Ellyah talks about you a lot.' Nastja's face stayed blank, but something inside her fluttered excitedly. 'You know what you need to do?'

'Yes,' she replied, simply. The other woman's blue-eyed gaze bored into her, tightening with frustration. More was required. 'I've made a contact who should be able to…move things. I'll make the final arrangements, then find you two afterwards.'

The northern woman nodded. 'I'll give you directions for where we'll be.' She described how to find Ellyah's hideout, and Nastja memorised them.

'Fare you well,' said Nastja, and turned away. She returned the cup to the cider seller and strode away towards the west gate that pierced the looming city wall.

'Cease this profane din!' shouted the old man, one hand raised in warning. 'Heed not the uncouth voices within! Chant and song bring dishonour to the gods!'

Nastja stepped around the edge of the gathering crowd, eager to be on her way. The man was in full flow, although it was not clear whether he was preaching to the curious onlookers, or if he beseeched the singers in the temple above.

He was dressed in a long, fine robe of good cloth, and his silver hair and beard were well-tended. His colourful attire was in stark contrast to the simple, charcoal-dark outfits of the priests of the Veil. This preacher was clearly of noble, wealthy stock. There were piles of rolled linen paper scrolls in bound bundles around his feet, and he clutched a thick, wood-bound book in his spare hand.

'The word of the gods must be set down in writing! Immortalise the names and deeds of the sacred Five in ink, and their glory will be restored. These Chanterists pollute the heavens with their childish noise!'

Nastja walked by, pushing his fervent ranting out of her focus. The Westgate temple rose above her head on twelve broad, ornate stone columns. She glanced up, the ceiling of this colonnaded place forming the floor of the temple above; wide, aged hardwood planks spanning the space between the columns.

A harmony of chanting voices drowned out the scratchy voice of the Charterist preacher as Nastja strolled away.

It was an irrelevant argument. The Veil awaited beyond the pall of death to welcome all souls, whether they had chosen to revere the gods in life or not. The exact nature of the afterlife was impossible to know, unless the gods themselves awoke from their slumber and spoke. Worrying about it was a waste of time. She walked on.

Evening was closing in as she walked through Carhinn's narrow, overhung streets. She moved carefully through the lengthening shadows, and replayed the conversation with Ellyah's messenger in her head.

Had she said the right thing? It was usually hard to be sure. It was very frustrating when what people said was not what they meant.

Every interaction was transactional, whether the participants would admit to it or not. One party offered something, the other accepted or rejected the offer, and gave something in return.

A conversation contained the same transaction, just like any deal. No gold changed hands but inevitably each person felt like they offered something of themselves and expected something to be given back.

The problem was that most other people were not honest about what they were offering, why they were doing so, and what they thought it was worth in exchange. The rules were not written anywhere yet everyone else seemed to know them. It made Nastja extremely frustrated.

She headed north and east. This quarter of the city was where the traders of fine goods and commodities sold their wares. The streets were narrow, but clean, and bulky men and women with sturdy clubs stood prominently on the corners. The traders paid handsomely to keep the area safe.

Her mind drifted back to Ellyah as she walked. She would see her soon. That thought filled her with a mild but effervescent excitement.

Ellyah was one who was always honest in terms of her needs, and what she offered in return. Nastja had earned her praise before, when they had worked together in Kereva. When Ellyah had asked Nastja to come to Carhinn she had believed that she would really be needed.

Ellyah made her feel important, in terms of what she could offer with the skills she possessed. Nastja loved to be helpful, and relished sharing knowledge that others did not have. Maybe, if she helped Ellyah with this job then she would look on Nastja as more than just a colleague, more than just a friend. Excitement mixed with terror at the thought.

Her eyes darted. She was yanked immediately back to the here and now. Something was not right.

She was near the jeweller's shop, but the guards on the street corners ahead were not his hired heavies. Nastja knew exactly who they looked like.

She had spent the weeks she had been in Carhinn carefully making contacts and sounding people out. Ellyah had been able to tell her that she was hoping to obtain a jewel of significant size and worth. Not all jewellers would be willing or able to deal with such a high value stone, either to cut it up and sell it in pieces, or to fence it on to a single buyer.

Also, Nastja had quickly found that the Mackems' influence pervaded all the trading districts of Carhinn. Like a malignant spider perched in a complex web, little happened in the city without them feeling the tremors, and then rushing in for a bite of the juicy fly.

It had taken her time, effort and great delicacy to find a gem dealer who was not beholden to the Mackems and would agree to being party to moving the stolen jewel, albeit for a generous cut.

So, why were there Mackems gang heavies standing on the corner beside his shop? Whatever the reason, it was not a good sign.

Nastja turned the nearest corner, maintaining her strides as if she had intended to go in that direction all along. She had to think quickly. She needed to find out what was going on.

The street ran parallel to the front of the jeweller's shop. She knew that the blocks of buildings had been laid out with a shared yard or garden to the rear of each. If she could get into that, maybe she could get to the rear of the shop.

After walking another few steps, she saw what she needed. A tiny alley opened out onto the street. Barely wider than a drain run, it was no more than a narrow gap between two houses.

Why not build the houses joined, with a wall between? thought Nastja. No alleyway then. Much more secure.

She emerged at the other end, squeezing between the rough, blocky walls and edging out into an open cobbled space. Piles of rubbish lay in the corners, and a small grey cat raced away as she moved quietly across the open area. It had the feel of communal space, shared but with no particular purpose.

She slunk across to the opposite wall, catlike herself. If she was right, she should now be at the rear of the jeweller's shop. She was just trying to count rear doors to work out which one it must be, when she heard a raised voice, followed a moment later by a cry of pain.

It had come from the house just to her right. She moved across, silent on the tips of her toes. There were no windows in the inscrutable grey masonry, just a single, narrow wooden door. The upper floor overhung in timber, like most Carhinnen houses.

Nastja huddled beneath the dark soffit, examining the door with fingertips for cracks or chinks. She only needed a tiny gap to enable her to see what was happening inside.

There. Her searching fingers found a small split in a plank, and heartbeat later her eye was jammed against it. What she saw inside made her heart sink.

The jeweller, the narrow-faced, elegantly dressed man that Nastja had spoken with only yesterday, was being held down by two Mackems thugs. The rear of the building was his living quarters, and Nastja could make out the corner of a smoking hearth just beyond where the jeweller's face was being pressed to a table. His cap had been knocked to the ground and his face was full of fear.

'Grab his arm, Skane,' ordered a strident voice. A woman's voice. The jeweller struggled ineffectively as one of the thugs wrapped a meaty hand around his wrist and forced his hand down onto the table.

'Now,' continued the same voice, with forced patience. 'I'm going to ask you the same question again, and if you answer me properly, we can stop this unpleasantness and be reasonable. Understand?'

The jeweller made no response, but his breathing came in fearful sobs, his hand still pressed flat to the table.

'We know that someone came to you, and asked you about fencing on a rare jewel,' stated the woman, slowly and distinctly as though addressing a child. 'Who? Who was it? Name or description, just tell us enough so we can find them. You'll squeal in the end, so you may as well just tell us now.'

There was an anxious silence. The jeweller shook his head mutely. The female Mackem, still out of Nastja's view, sighed heavily.

'Skane...' she said, and Nastja could see the grip tightening on the jeweller's hand. There was a flash of movement, and a thump. The jeweller shrieked in pain. A hammer had smashed down onto his little finger.

His whole face twisted with pain and distress. These injuries threatened his livelihood, but he was being brave. He could have easily given up the fake name that Nastja had provided. Surely, he knew that she would not have given her real name when they met.

'Nothing to say?' the Mackems woman sneered. There was another thump. Another stinging, crushing blow from the hammer. Another cry of despairing agony from the jeweller.

'A name!' he croaked. 'A name! Marin Cretos! She approached me. Just a small-time thief! She offered me a big cut. I didn't know she was stealing from you. I had no idea. I swear it!'

'She?' The Mackems' questioner was interested, the tone of her voice curious. 'What she look like?'

'Uhh...' The jeweller was surprised by the question. The hammer rose. 'Short! She was short. Dark-skinned, bit like a *helf*, but short and plump. Fair hair. I'd never seen her before.'

There was silence, only disturbed by the deep breaths and groans of the jeweller. The Mackems shared looks.

'Don't sound like her,' said the broad, bulky man gripping the jeweller's hand. His voice was thick, nasal. Like a deaf man, thought Nastja.

'Na, you're right. It don't. But it's her style to send a lackey. She knows we know her, don't she? She disappeared sharpish after she ripped us off on that riverboat job.'

'Everyone knows Ellyah,' said the man. Nastja froze.

'Everyone knows Ellyah,' confirmed the woman. 'And after talking to this streak of piss, I'm more sure it was her what was behind the theft.' She turned to address the jeweller. 'It's your lucky day. You get to come with us and meet the boss. You'll tell her what you told us, and if you've got any sense you'll spill more quickly for her.'

The whole group began to move, the strong gangster pulling the jeweller upright and steering him away toward the front door.

'And then,' the female gang leader's voice carried back to Nastja as she strained to hear. 'We are going to hunt down Ellyah Jerim.'

TWELVE

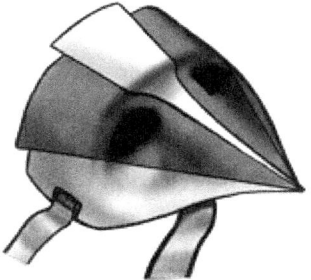

The cords tightened. Twelve sets of hands gripped the thin white rope firmly, and steadily lowered the body into the grave.

The priest stepped closer to the graveside, a large and intricately decorated ewer in her hands. Face serious, she tipped the jug and a stream of clear water poured from the spout and spattered down onto the white-wrapped bundle below.

She intoned:

> *Rise, rise from earthly chains,*
> *Soul will soar, unbound again,*
> *Towards the veil which ever shines,*
> *Beyond this place, beyond this time.*
>
> *Shining veil wash clean the cares,*
> *Pure and true, judgement fair*
> *The Five await, limitless and wise*
> *Eternal joy beneath their eyes.*

The mourners, all nobles dressed in fine white robes that almost brushed the ground, repeated the last two lines:

'The Five await, limitless and wise. Eternal joy beneath their eyes.'

They all bowed their heads, faces grave. She alone of the congregation knew for certain that the five gods of myth; Mordea, Kaled, Tureank, Conferan and Ome, were real beings that truly existed.

She just hoped that they continued to sleep for a good while longer. Her holy oaths would be forfeit if she ever voiced that wish aloud, however.

She schooled her face to sombre piety, trying to ignore the feeling that the mourners must all be staring at her, staring in horror at her face, and leaned over the grave.

'May you pass through the veil in radiant glory,' she intoned. 'May your judgement be fair and true. May your soul find peace in eternity.'

The mourners muttered the same words once more, and the twelve cord bearers cast the loose ends into the grave to lie with the body. An older woman, white-capped and olive-skinned, sniffed and sobbed. A group of younger folk, similarly well dressed, stood sadly beside her. The widow and her children, she supposed. They cried together but she was sure that the dead man had provided well for them.

Money would not be a problem.

The service complete, Shre Evane Claes led the congregation to the cemetery gates in a stately procession. At the gates, she stood aside and let the mourners pass by.

A gentle breeze stirred the coarse fabric of her dark, hooded vest and breeches as she stood waiting beside the low wall that bounded the ancient burial site. The cemetery lay on a green headland just outside the grand city of Glithoniel, and had been the final resting place for generations of nobles.

The mourners filed past slowly, ready to walk alongside the flat-bedded cart as it returned, now empty, to the city. Many of them subtly pressed metal scraps into Claes' palms as they passed. Sections of money rings, some copper, some silver. She barely glanced down.

'Your kindness humbles me,' she murmured. 'The blessings of the Five be upon your family.'

The metal glittered in her cupped hands like rays of sunshine reflecting off the rippled ocean below. Small fishing boats were as tiny insects as they bobbed on the gentle swells of Gojairse Bay.

The mourners moved away and Claes followed behind, at a respectful distance. The curving path led down the gentle slope toward the city. Only now did she let her face twist into the grimace of pain; searing pain that she had been suppressing all afternoon.

She looked up, beyond the sweep of the great bay, to the city itself. The warm sunshine that turned the peaceful waters of the bay a vivid turquoise gleamed on the towers and spires of the great city.

The First City. The Star City. Capital of Buren, and the jewel in the crown of the confederacy of Re'Emsser. From the height of the headland, every detail was laid out like a child's model.

Five ancient, conical towers surrounded the main bulk of the city. In later times, a high defensive wall had been built between the towers, encircling the city. Another vast and almost cylindrical tower rose from the very centre; the highest spire of the High King's palace. Even from this distance, the cascading water that ran down the side of the tower in a glittering, shining curtain twinkled and shone, although the viaduct that fed it was hidden from view to the north.

Lower Glithoniel sprawled out into the green countryside beyond the sheer, pale walls. Claes walked sedately through the twisting, ramshackle streets as the funeral procession disappeared into the distance, heading for the southeast gate.

The heat of the day beat down and sweat prickled beneath her rough vest. Her skin screamed as if rubbed raw.

She kept her eyes looking forward as she passed groups of commoners; labourers, traders and serfs. She felt like they must all be staring at her face. Even though she knew that it did not glow as if burned, it hurt as though it did.

Her vest and breeches were rough and of poor cloth, dyed a distinctive charcoal black. She wished for a robe or cloak that covered more of her, but as a priest of the Veil she was not allowed. The breeches were luxury enough. The commoners around her were mostly dressed in short smocks that left their dirty knees bare. She shuddered inwardly.

Then, the mighty arch of the gateway was above her head. She sighed with relief as she was engulfed by the cooling shade. The wall was many yards thick, formed from huge, polished blocks of pale stone, and it took her several moments to pass through to the other side.

Glithoniel rose before her, shining grandly in the bright afternoon sun. Houses and shops stood to either side of the well paved street that led from the gate; circular shapes that mirrored the five soaring towers, all built in black and yellow stone. Claes had no doubt that this was the finest city in the world.

When Desya rose, Claes planned to request that she be given Glithoniel as her seat of power. She could picture herself sat in the High King's palace, with all the comfort she desired, and deserved.

The central spire of the palace lay directly ahead, and the eternal cascade of fresh water down its steep, smooth sides sparkled in the afternoon sun. Some said that it was the shining Veil in physical form. Even for Claes, it remained a stirring sight.

To the north of the palace rose a long, arch-roofed building. The walls were made from the same bands of pale and dark stone and the curving roof was covered with thin, grey slates.

They had been brought to the city by the dwarves of the Severed City in the far north.

This was the temple and headquarters of the Priests of the Veil, and Claes hurried to the main doors. Eyes down, she swept inside the building and headed towards the living quarters at the rear. All she wanted was the cool solitude of her cell.

'Sister Claes,' called a voice from behind. She ground her teeth impatiently. She turned. 'Sister Claes, a moment, please!'

Claes schooled her face to blank receptiveness. She did not have time for this. Brother Hilass was approaching.

I am listening, she willed her face to say.

A tall, gangling priest in matching black clothing was approaching across the hall in long strides. His breeches flapped around his skinny ankles. His head was hairless and he had a prominent hooked nose that, in Claes' opinion, he thrust into too many matters.

'Ah, Sister Claes,' he sighed, coming to a halt. 'I'm glad to have caught you. How are preparations coming along?'

'Preparations?' The question wrong-footed Claes momentarily. The preparations she was fixated upon would have her thrown out of the order, and probably into chains, if they were to become known. Then she remembered, 'Ah, the preparations for the Veil-Flame?'

'Of course!' said Hilass, impatiently. 'What else would I mean?'

'The Veil-Flame,' confirmed Claes. 'I was momentarily distracted by thoughts of the Five, brother. Preparations are proceeding well. The city militia are recruiting irregulars to ensure that the streets are peaceful. We will not have the scenes that occurred last year.'

'Let us pray to fate that we are spared *that* again,' murmured Hilass.

'Indeed. I received a letter,' continued Claes, 'earlier this week. The Severed City is considering sending a dwarven choir to honour the occasion. It would add a rich gravitas to the ceremony if so, and would be a great boon, politically. The King's Moot would be well pleased.'

'Yes, I agree. The High King would smile on us, were that to be arranged. Do your utmost to make it so.'

Claes inclined her head. 'The only point of order that I cannot guarantee is that the gods will bless us with clear skies on the day.' She smiled broadly at her own attempted at a light-hearted jest.

'Hm,' Hilass grunted in vague amusement. He changed subject. 'And the funeral that you conducted this day?'

Claes shook her head sadly. 'Yes, Sir Arent will be missed by his family. A sad loss.'

'I imagine that the mourning party gave generously though...' Hilass gave Claes a meaningful look. 'To the order...'

Claes blinked. Hilass was hinting at something but in the moment, she could not think of what. Generous. Of course, Hilass was a stickler for the primacy of the order and the preservation of its edicts. He was as tight-fisted as any dwarf. There was only one thing he could mean.

'Generous, yes,' she said hastily, as her mind caught up. 'They filled my purse. I was just on my way to deposit the money in the coffers.' Her eyes shifted guiltily. She had clearly walked straight past the doorway to the small, chest-filled room. That she had forgotten about the bulk of metal scraps jangling at her belt would never be believed, so she kept the words behind her lips. 'I can give it to you, if you would prefer.'

'Thank you, sister,' said Hilass, sternly as he took the purse. 'May the Veil shine on your labours.'

'And yours, brother.'

Claes turned on her heel and walked quickly away.

The Veil-Flame would be celebrated as usual, which meant a cursory attempt at prayer and introspection as the sun set over the city's central pillar and the evening light was shattered into glimmering, fiery swords for a few moments. It only happened on the autumn equinox. In reality, the streets would fill with drinkers and revellers waiting to cheer the event with raucous, bawdy songs. Fights were more common than contemplation.

She passed through the small door in the northern wall of the main hall. A long, gloomy corridor led deeper into the building, with many doors opening from it on either side. These were the priests' cells.

She hurried to her own, pulling the door closed behind her before hastily pulling her vest off over her head. She flung it aside and dropped to her knees. The sensation of cold air hitting her skin was instantly soothing. It felt like she was scorched and blistered all over, but when she passed her hand across, the skin was smooth and undamaged.

As she removed her breeches and studied herself, she felt disbelief anew that the pain throbbing from her skin did not show in any scar or mark. She appeared as normal, but her whole body itched and burned.

Desya's fury when he learned of the theft of the jewel had been predictable, but explosive and violent.

When Brin Gallit had admitted that the Demon's Tear had been stolen, her initial reaction had also been rage, paired with anxiety about reporting it to the demon. Then, she had relaxed. A little. After all, the jewel had ensnared Moore. The new thief would also touch the jewel, before long. Another soul would be claimed, and the newly formed husk would lead the Mackems straight to the ruby's new location.

Yet, the new thief, or thieves, had not touched it. At least not yet. Either, they had not tried to move it, or felt no desire to handle it. Or worse, they knew something of what the jewel really was, of what it could do.

A thief who was aware that they held more than a quick route to riches was a danger to all her plans.

So, they must be found. And quickly. There was a way, but Claes would need to summon her strength and channel it in a spell. She hoped that she had recovered enough after the punishment she had been subjected to by Desya.

She had been burned and scoured by the force of the demon's rage. A creature of impulse and instinct, the anger had expressed itself as white-hot gouts of flame. Claes had summoned all of her will, and it had been enough to keep her alive. Just.

Although, she was still unsure that alive or dead, were concepts that had any true meaning in that dark, strange place where she was summoned to meet her demonic master.

In any case, when it was over, she existed still. She was wracked with incandescent pain, and sobbing as she was sent back with the strict instructions that she must not fail again.

She had lain on the floor of her cell, biting her lip to suppress the anguished screams that rose from her very core. When she glanced down, she was amazed that she was unmarked. Her skin screamed but the pain was somehow beneath the surface. A punishment for her alone, that she must suffer in lonely silence.

She had gone about her business over the days that followed unable to shake the feeling that her face must shine, a livid, sickly puce. Every time someone looked in her direction her fingers twitched to touch her cheeks, or cast her hood over the scars. Yet it was not so.

The pain had faded slightly over the last days, and she felt her inner strength begin to return. She recovered. She was as ready as she could be.

Gingerly shrugging her vest back over her narrow shoulders, she bent and recovered her mask from where it lay hidden in a box beneath the hard bed. The silver stripes were dull in the low light of his cell. She donned it. She closed her eyes.

Her faith in Desya was true. Her devotion to the demon was absolute. Desya was the only true god, unfairly imprisoned by devious forces. Desya would be restored to the world.

She recited these catechisms under her breath, pushing away all thoughts but those of the great demon. Her faith was anchored in that truth, and as she concentrated, she felt the power enter her body once more.

Raptures shook her. She felt like a vessel being filled, but rather than water it felt like a warm, effervescent liquid. Every sense fizzed. Desya granted this power in exchange for worship and service. The power would be used to glory the demon. She focused.

A small portal appeared in the air before her, formed of swirling purple light. With an effort of will, the portal shifted around her, and she became one with it. There was a rushing sensation, and then her view was no longer of her cell.

Through a shifting purple haze, she beheld the simple confines of the upper floor of an Anise house. The walls and floor were of plain, undecorated timber and a large, upright crate stood in one corner.

Before her stood a burly, hard-faced woman. Cannis Flett, current leader of the Mackems in Carhinn.

She wondered how long this one would last.

'My lord,' said Flett, the subservience forced and unnatural. She did not know Claes' name, and would not.

'Flett,' she replied, voice slightly muffled by the mask. She felt that using someone's name gave her more power over them. Made her dominant. 'You are prepared? You are ready?'

Flett brandished a long pry-bar, but appeared a little confused.

'The crate,' instructed Claes. 'Open it.'

She complied immediately. Gallit's fate was hopefully still fresh in her mind. That was to the good.

Inserting the bar into each nailed joint in turn, Flett forced the boards apart. The rough-cast nails squealed and groaned as they were dragged from the grainy planks. Claes waited impatiently.

Then, like a fortress lowering a drawbridge, the entire side of the crate tipped open. It thudded onto the floor of the room, as Flett stepped out of the way.

She glanced up at the contents of the crate and took a hurried step back. Her horrified intake of breath was sharp in the quiet of the room.

The weeks since he had seized the jewel had not been kind to Clayton Moore. First, he had been compelled to make his laborious way to Carhinn, directed by Claes' spell and powered by the Demon's Tear itself. Then, he had been forcibly parted from the jewel and hammered into this crate, away from prying eyes.

With the preserving properties of the gem removed, there was nothing left to hold back rot and decay.

He stood with a slumped, slack posture. His hands dangled uselessly next to his thighs. Previously snug and well-made clothing was torn and stained, and patches of discoloured skin showed through the rents in the fabric.

His face was a twisted ruin. Purplish, greyish skin was stretched tight over his skull and black patches added to the disfigurement. His mouth was pulled into a mocking, rictus grin. Milky eyes stared forwards, unfocussed and unseeing.

He looked exactly like a corpse, but one that stood upright. Judging by the way Flett gagged and retched, Moore's smell matched his ragged appearance.

'Our friend here is bound to the jewel,' explained Claes. 'With the right stimulation, it will summon him as a whistle summons a hound back to the master.'

It sounded simple, but in reality it was anything but. Her reading of the lore suggested that the jewel's pull on one whose soul it had ensnared worked best when it had lain in the same place for the long time. If the thieves had the sense, or the luck, to move it, then tracking it even across the city could be difficult.

Animating the corpse to enable it to walk required complex magic. Desya had shown her how, and she hoped that she had recovered enough strength. Even if she had, the spell was not one that she could sustain for long.

She prayed to the demon that it would be long enough.

Closing her eyes, she reached into the well of power that had been gifted by the demon, beginning to shape the spell. Red and pale blue threads swirled and mixed, forming a complex matrix. With a thought, she pushed it toward Moore and felt it spread out into a humanoid shape.

A crimson glow filled the room. The former thief's eyes were lit from within, a dull, smouldering red. Then it took a step. And another. With ponderous, heavy treads it moved forward. As once-was-Moore stepped out of the crate and into the room, Flett's lip curled in revulsion.

Claes concentrated on the jewel itself. She pictured it in her mind, formed an image of it, reached out for its mysterious power. Moore turned on the spot, staring at the wall. It faced almost directly due east. That is where the jewel must be.

Claes sagged with relief. There had been no hesitation. The pull of the jewel was strong. They would be able to recover it this night.

She continued to concentrate on the spell, jaw set determinedly. The thieves' souls would join Moore's in the jewel once it had been recovered. Their bodies could be left to rot.

Desya would be pleased with her.

THIRTEEN

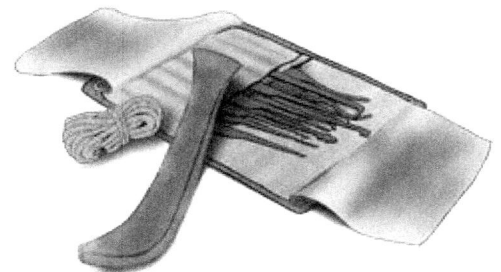

'Nastja! Will you just stop?'

Ellyah was frustrated. They had already agreed that tonight would be the night that they would attempt to leave Carhinn.

No. They would not just attempt, they *would* leave the city. To fail was almost certainly to end up dead. That was not good enough for Nastja, however.

'I was just saying,' continued Nastja, without a hint of contrition. 'If we really are going to go, we should go now. The Mackems could already be on their way.'

Ellyah bit her tongue. She had said that they would leave today, more than once, and Nastja's constant worrying was irritating. When they made their escape, everything had to be done right. If they rushed, they could be discovered. And if they were discovered, they would be found in a ditch in the Westra with their throats slit. Timing was crucial.

'Let's just run out into the street now then, shall we?' Ellyah's voice was dripping with sarcasm. 'I'd be delighted to introduce the two of you to the Mackems properly. I'm sure they'd be very welcoming.'

Nastja said nothing, but she pouted slightly.

Ellyah sighed. 'Come over here and tie a knot behind my back, if you want to be helpful.'

She turned, holding both ends of a strip of cloth in her hands. A final knot was needed to secure it in place. Nastja reached out sullenly to help.

They were donning disguises. It was the only way they would be able to get away. The Mackems knew her too well. They knew her face and had also been provided with Nastja's description. If they were not watching every gate for her, then they were even more stupid than she believed. Ellyah had more than one way to fool people, however.

Her disguise this time would be a pot-bellied, stoop-shouldered old man. Concealing her shape was the first part of the outfit. Nastja pulled the ends of the fabric tight and deftly knotted them behind Ellyah's back. The strips of cloth flattened her breasts, as much as possible, and she had also tied thicker fabric around her waist in several overlapping layers. These would disguise her hips and thicken her narrow waist.

Awkwardly, and with shallow breaths, she bent over and picked up a robe of a length appropriate for a merchant. She slipped it quickly over her head. It had a high collar which would cover her throat, the part of a disguise that amateurs often forgot. The lack of a man's apple gave them away.

She buttoned the robe to her chin and folded up the collar. She would be too warm in the evening heat, but she would be free and alive. Fate willing.

Nastja had bound her own chest too, although she had somewhat less to hide, and donned a child's robe. Her face remained petulant.

'This isn't going to work, I just know it,' she said, once more.

'It's never failed before,' replied Ellyah, wearily. 'And you know how often I've done it. People are stupid, they only see what they expect to see. You know I'm right.'

She reached into her bag of pigments and rubbed an ochre-coloured paint all over her face. It was a dark shade, and a good match for Nastja's skin tone. The idea of the disguise was that they would pose as grandfather and grandson. Just a pair of common traders heading back to the Westra after a day's work.

'It's not appropriate,' said Nastja, watching Ellyah with distaste as she coloured the skin of her face, hands and lower legs. 'My face is all wrong for a child. Any fool will be able to tell.'

Ellyah did not waste time replying. Frustrating as it was, naysaying and catastrophising were standard responses when Nastja was nervous. She set a straight-sided man's cap on her head as Nastja donned a small, round cap of a type that only a child would wear.

'It will work,' said Ellyah patiently. 'Normal people are very easy to fool. And when it works it will prove that it was exactly the right thing to do. The only thing that matters is getting out of the city and getting to Kereva with the jewel.'

Nastja rolled her eyes. 'Fine. But I warned you.'

Planning this escape had begun a week ago.

Ellyah had been bored. She had been confined to her hideout with just Luara for company for many days. Going outside was too big of a risk. The Mackems knew her face well, and would not let her walk by if they spotted her.

The knowledge that it was the right thing to do did not make it any less boring.

And then there was the jewel.

It sat in the corner, snug in its box. She made sure that the clasps were secure every now and again. Like a superstition. Did she think the jewel would open the box itself, climb out and then…what? She shook the thought away. Nevertheless, the slight red glow that leaked from the cracks around the box's lid was eerie and unsettling.

It was just a ruby. Just a lump of shiny stone. All that mattered was the gold that it was worth. The new life it could buy her, away from these crowded cities, and away from the life of crime.

She repeated this to herself, over and over, as she fretted the hours away.

Luara dealt with the confinement in her own way.

'They don't know me, do they?' she had said, while they were discussing strategy. 'I could go out.'

'They shouldn't know you, no...' said Ellyah thoughtfully. 'But what if someone saw you when you were my lookout for the jewel theft? If they made a link between us, or you and the jewel...they might follow you here.' Ellyah was thinking as she spoke. 'It's too risky. If there's a risk to you, there's a risk to me as well. I won't lose the jewel that way. You must stay here.'

She just could not bear it. The jewel, and the fortune it represented, was everything.

Luara had grudgingly agreed. She wanted to go out, but also seemed happy to comply with Ellyah's demands. She was clearly keen to be helpful. It could have been irritating but her company was pleasant, her conversation light. Ellyah got the impression, though, that there was a core of steel beneath her gentle exterior.

Ellyah decided early on that she would not want to fight the older woman.

As soon as the decision had been made, and they knew that all there was to do was wait for Nastja, Luara settled into a routine.

She stripped off her snug leather rider's coat, and began exercising in her trousers and the pale, tight vest she wore beneath. She lay on the rough, irregular floorboards and pushed herself up repeatedly with her arms. Ellyah could not help watching as the cordlike muscles of her shoulders and arms bunched and writhed. It was hypnotic.

After she had gone through a cycle of several different exercises, she put her coat back on and dug some food from her pack. She ate steadily, making idle conversation, then wrapped herself in a blanket and fell asleep.

She repeated that routine over and over as they whiled away the time. She never seemed to get bored. Ellyah wished she felt the same. Her eyes felt heavy and gritty, but she struggled to sleep. The jewel filled her waking and sleeping thoughts, and she ran over possible escape plans in her mind until she wanted to scream with the tension.

Ellyah was watching, days later, as Luara hung from a ceiling beam and swung her legs around. Her body bent into a tight angle, and she pointed her toes to all the corners of the poky attic space in turn. Ellyah envied her strength.

From somewhere beyond the cramped interior, a seahawk called. Once. Twice. Ellyah sat up.

'Quiet!' she hissed in Luara's direction. Luara pursed her lips sulkily, but dropped silently back down to the attic boards. The call came again, sharp and raking.

There were no seahawks anywhere near Carhinn.

'It's Nastja.' Ellyah was already moving. 'Quick.'

She strode across the floor of the attic room and lowered herself down the narrow gap behind the furniture of the floor below. Bracing herself against the opposing walls at the base of the void, she lifted the trap door and looked down.

The light streaming in was blinding after the perpetual gloom of the roof, and she blinked and winced for a few moments. As her eyes adjusted, she reckoned that it must be about dusk.

A figure strolled past the house. Hands in pockets. Just passing by. It was a small person, with a roundish shape and fair hair. A woman. Nastja.

'Wsht!' hissed Ellyah. Nastja did not look up. She kept walking, turning the corner and out of Ellyah's sight. Her heart raced. If Nastja was here, there was news. They might be able to move, at last. Where had she gone?

Then she was back. The twisted mess of her light-coloured hair was suddenly visible between Ellyah's feet. Nastja had circled the house to avoid having to stand still.

'Up! Quick!'

Nastja's fingers worked up the wall, inching towards the protruding block that Ellyah used to pull up. Then, they stopped. She was a little too short. Ellyah heard her mutter a colourful swear word under her breath.

She jumped. Kicking out against the lower wall with one foot, she lunged upward, and the leap gave her the extra reach she needed. She clung on grimly, scrambling up the rest of the way. Her face was determined.

Ellyah climbed back up the void and Nastja followed. The attic seemed very dingy after a few moments looking into the light. Luara had dressed, and was sitting beside the candle. Her long, dark hair was tied back, and her pale skin gleamed with a light sheen of sweat.

Nastja was close behind. She had looked calm down in the street, but Ellyah noticed that her fingers twitched and fidgeted, and there was a flush in her cinnamon-coloured cheeks. Her eyes were fixed on the floor.

She took a deep breath, then her words tumbled out in a rush.

'They are after you, Ell. Us. The Mackems. They found the gem dealer, somehow. They have had longer to go around all the city traders, and more people. That must be why they found them so quickly. The dealer gave them my description. And they already think it was you that stole it.'

'Whoa! Whoa!' Ellyah raised both palms. 'Slow down, hen. What happened to the gem dealer?'

'He said he could fence the ruby on,' Nastja continued, more slowly. 'He would either cut it up, or sell it to a single buyer. He didn't want to tell me which, or who he would sell it to. He said he had contacts who could move it over to Buren once it was sold, though.

'I just went to check in, and the Mackems had found him. They got my description from him there, then dragged him away. He'll tell them everything, I'm sure. I'm also sure I didn't lead them to him.'

'How bad is it, though?' Ellyah wondered aloud. 'All they know is that whoever has the jewel was trying to sell it on. They must have known that already.' She tried to tell herself that there was nothing to worry about.

'But now they know that the jewel is definitely still in the city,' argued Nastja. 'They weren't sure of that before. And they know what I look like. So, I can't go out again.' Ellyah ground her teeth. The fact that Nastja's fretting was justified was irritating.

'And,' Nastja went on, with worry in her eyes. What else? 'The Mackems mentioned your name. They suspect it was you already. They are turning the city upside down to find you.'

'My reputation precedes me.' Ellyah grinned, and spread her arms in a mock bow.

'It's not funny, Ell!' Nastja snapped, with heat in her voice. 'It'll be easy for the Mackems now. They know the jewel is in Carhinn. They think you've got it, and they know I'm with you. All they have to do is keep searching, and eventually they will find one of us, and then the game is up. We can't leave, and we can't stay here. We're in a trap.'

Ellyah took a deep breath. She wanted to raise her voice, to rail against Nastja's negativity. She wanted to make her see that this was their chance to escape, and they just needed to think it through.

'We should just give them the jewel back,' said Nastja, in a small voice. Ellyah turned on her. This was too much.

'Give? Give?' she shouted. 'That'd be perfect, wouldn't it? Just give our fortune away. Might as well hand ourselves over to the Mackems right now if we do that, they won't let us get away! I'd rather die trying to escape with it.'

She took a few calming breaths. 'Look,' she continued, in a more reasonable tone. 'They are searching, but it'll take time. There are a lot of hidden spaces in this city. We can prepare a plan and escape before they get to us. If we rush out, they'll catch us, but if we think it through, we'll outwit them. We've got away with worse, haven't we, hen?'

Nastja nodded slowly.

'Carhinn is a big city.' Ellyah sensed she was winning Nastja over. She usually did, in the end. 'Searching every room, in every house, will take years. They could search this house and they wouldn't know this room was here.'

Her mind was already working, thinking of ways to get out beyond the city walls, thinking of ways to hide their identities from the Mackems.

'Disguises might work,' mused Ellyah. She kept a few items of clothing with her that could double as several different outfits. Simple disguises could be very effective. The sort of goons used as gate guards usually lacked the intelligence to look for anything other than an exact match for a description.

Nastja was not finished. 'But, what about the jewel? We might slip past guards, but they are certain to search anything we are carrying. The jewel and the box are too big to hide.'

Nastja was right, again. Any bags, crates or bundles would be rifled through. The jewel could not come through with them, not without risking everything.

Then, Luara piped up.

'I could climb over the walls,' she stated in a matter-of-fact tone.

The wall of Carhinn had been built in modern times; it was made of huge, heavy blocks of square-cut stone. It rose to a height of about twenty feet on all four sides of the city. Above this, a stout timber palisade rose higher still, the lower ends of the thick hardwood logs set firmly in the upper courses of the wall.

The timber palisade had been built so that it overhung the stone walls on the side facing out from the city. Any force assaulting the walls would have to overcome a wooden roof that loomed over their heads. It was designed to be impossible to climb.

Nastja goggled at her, waiting for an explanation.

'Are you serious, hen?' asked Ellyah. 'You've seen how high and steep they are.'

'I can do it,' Luara had said, calmly. 'I've climbed over higher walls. But it will need to be dark. I don't want to climb down the other side to find a bunch of Sentinels or Mackems waiting for me on the other side.'

Ellyah waved that concern away. 'If you say you can do it, you can do it. We'll all move at dusk. Then we'll all meet up on the road to Kereva?' She chose not to ask why Luara had needed to climb over city walls in the past.

'On the road, or in Kereva itself. Once I'm over the wall with the jewel it'll be best to keep moving.'

Ellyah bit her lip.

The thought of the jewel arriving in another city in the hands of another made her feel uneasy. Out of her sight, the riches that the jewel promised could fade away. The opportunity could be lost. Was there a way she could carry the jewel herself?

'Oh!' Luara's blue eyes widened in realisation. 'You don't trust me!' She smiled sweetly. 'You think I'll run off and sell the jewel myself.'

Ellya thought fast. She could not say "it's what I would do", while they were discussing trusting one another. Even though it was the stark truth.

'How do we know you won't?' she asked, eventually.

'The Mackems are after you, aren't they?' said Luara, even as she stood and began preparing to leave. 'They think you have it. So, if I steal it from you then you can go to the Mackems and tell them. You'll be in the clear and you can earn a favour by helping them hunt me down. I'm a stranger down here, I'd have no chance of escaping.' She smiled sweetly again. No one who saw that smile would ever suspect that she could be involved in anything criminal.

'But,' Ellyah replied. 'Then the Mackems would have it.'

She could hear the sulkiness in her own voice, and she did not like it. They did not have any other options. She had no real choice but to trust the older woman, at least for now. At least she had voiced her concerns now. Hopefully Luara would keep trying to win her trust.

'I'll meet you on the road later,' said Luara, with an air of finality, but with a broad smile still spread across her face. 'We can all escape into the night.'

It had been decided. Under the cover of darkness, Luara would take the jewel over the walls. Ellyah and Nastja would leave the hideout at dusk, posing as traders on their way back to the Westra.

Nastja's sulk about the disguise had continued while they made the final preparations.

As she and Ellyah waited for the right moment to leave, they eyeballed each other stubbornly. Ellyah folded her hands slowly across her chest. A chuckle from the corner drew their attention.

'I'd wondered how you two knew each other,' Luara laughed, as she stood. 'Now, I think you must be an old married couple.' Nastja and Ellyah snorted in unison. Luara's face became more serious. 'I should get moving. I can sneak out quickly and hide near the walls until it is dark enough to climb over.'

It was always gloomy up in Ellyah's attic hideout, but her instinct told her it must be near dusk. She nodded. The disguises were ready. They just had to pick the right time to leave.

'We'll give you time to get away, and then we'll go too.'

Luara nodded once and was gone, swiftly and silently.

Ellyah fretted. She did not want to move too early, when it was still light. Dusky gloom would make it harder for any guards to see through their disguises. If they went too late, it would make them look suspicious.

Just a little bit longer, she told herself. She hoped she would time it right. Everything depended on her plan working perfectly.

FOURTEEN

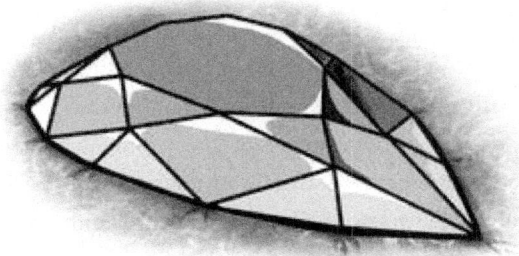

Clayton Moore shuffled through the streets of Carhinn. The crimson glow of his eyes was shrouded by a deep hood.

Hundreds of miles away in Glithoniel, Evane Claes trembled with the effort of maintaining the spell. Every single one of his heavy footsteps was like lifting a sack of rocks. The confines of her cell vanished from her awareness. There was only the churning, draining flow of magic. Nothing else mattered.

She felt herself weakening as each moment passed, but could sense that Moore was closing in.

Skane prowled through the dusky city. He had caught a brief glimpse of the red-eyed figure wearing a deeply hooded cloak earlier in the night, and had wanted to be as far away from it as possible.

'This stinks,' he said, to the tall figure walking beside him. Jhari the enormous, dusky-skinned brawler nodded. Then shrugged. Jhari did what he was told, and questions of wrong or right, natural or unnatural did not seem to concern him.

Flett had told them that the cowled figure would lead them to their marks. The thieves. They had stolen the jewel, and tonight the Mackems would take it back. Flett herself was following closely behind the…thing, while the rest of the gang was spread out through the adjacent streets.

Anyone who tried to bolt would not get far.

Striding through the narrow lanes of Carhinn beneath the velvet cowl of night was not an unusual thing for Skane and Jhari to do. Neither of them had much to fear. The ones they sought had plenty of reasons to be afraid.

Skane clenched and unclenched his fists absent-mindedly. He wondered if he would need to bash any heads this night. He did not care one way or another. It was all part of the job.

The lanes and alleys between the houses at this end of Carhinn were unpaved. His footsteps landed softly, muted by the muddy ground. It had rained earlier in the day. Lights burned behind closed shutters, shining more brightly as the daylight faded away, the candles and sputtering rushlights casting muted shards of orange light over the darkening ground.

A flash of movement caught Skane's eye. A pair of gleaming eyes stared intently in his direction for a moment, appearing in the middle of the street ahead, and then vanished. As Skane stared at the spot where the eyes had been, the dark furry brush of a tail showed in a chink of light. He smiled. He always enjoyed spotting black foxes in the city. They were shy creatures, but could be tamed with the offer of food.

There was a sudden tap on his shoulder. Jhari was motioning down a narrow street to the left.

'Voices,' rumbled the giant, bending almost double to bring his mouth close to Skane's ear. 'Found something.' He strode in the direction of the noise, and Skane hurried to follow.

Cannis Flett and several other Mackems were standing beneath the overhang of a darkened house. Looking across the dimly lit street, Skane could see the unsettling, cowled figure standing against the wall of one of the houses opposite.

No, he was not standing. He was still walking. Walking as if trying to pass directly through the lower wall of the house, face and body flat against the stones, legs moving awkwardly, repetitively. The other Mackems were watching it intently.

Jhari rumbled something.

'What?' Skane turned, cupping a hand to his ear.

'I said, that's not right,' repeated Jhari, patiently.

Skane stepped closer to the other Mackems, noticing a rank, fetid smell that he knew came from across the street. A vague red glow was visible around the edges of the figure's hood and reflecting onto the stones of the house as a sullen, sickly crimson wash.

Then, abruptly, the red light faded and was gone. The hooded figure's jerky movements slowed, and then stopped. Its shoulders sagged and the hooded head lolled. All was still.

'It's in there.' Flett's voice was harsh in the quiet of the evening. 'Spread out to guard any escape. You all know your jobs. Jhari, Skane. The door.'

Jhari crossed the distance to the front door of the house in a handful of his long strides and lowered his shoulder. The door collapsed inwards as the hinges were torn from the frame. It was as though they were made of nothing stronger than stale bread.

Jhari was a sledgehammer in human form.

Without breaking stride, Jhari left the mess behind and vanished into the house. Moments later, Skane could hear vague noises of distress from inside the house. He realised that probably meant that they were quite loud for everyone else. He hurried in, ready for whatever he might find.

The downstairs, as with most Carhinnen houses, was all one low-ceilinged storage area. Chests lined the walls along one side, with a wood store on the other. There were many places that a small, valuable box could be hidden. Yet, Jhari was not there.

A wooden staircase led to the upper floor, carved handrails rising out of Skane's view. He followed the sounds and dashed up the stairs, two at a time. The scene that greeted him was not that of a robber's den.

Lit by the embers of a fire and a single candle lantern, the main upstairs room of the house was unpartitioned, with an ornate iron stove at one end and a wide bed at the other. Shelves around the walls held pots, pans, provisions and an array of ornaments. The walls were hung with thick tapestries and the insides of the closed shutters were decorated with carved, painted patterns.

There was money here, all right. But not dirty money. Not crime.

'Let him go!' A loud shriek pulled Skane's attention towards the bed. A grey-haired woman sat hunched at the head the bed, knees pulled defensively up to her chin. 'Please! We don't know what you want!'

Jhari was standing at the foot of the bed. His head brushed the ceiling beams and his huge fists were bunched at the front of an old man's nightrobe. The man was writhing in that powerful grip, his feet dangling above the floorboards and kicking weakly. He must be terrified.

'Tell,' said Jhari, simply.

Even the nightrobe the man wore was of fine cloth, and his hair was cut level with his jaw in an old-fashioned, respectable style. He was no criminal.

'Please,' groaned the old man. 'My name is Lilir Kepusche. I am a shoemaker. That is all. I have no idea what you want. I have gold…'

'Jhari,' Skane interrupted the man's pleas. 'No. Put him down.' Skane was a simple thinker. The…creature had led them here. So, there must have been a reason. Hiding the theft behind a respectable front was a good idea, but it would work even better if those at the front were unaware.

His eyes scanned the room, and he quickly found what he sought. 'Jhari,' he repeated. 'Come, come.'

At the far end of the room stood a set of shelves. They had been built from floor to ceiling, covering the main beams of the wall. He pointed at the shelves.

'Break this.'

Jhari thrust the old man back onto the bed, where he lay trembling with indignant terror. He strode over, and with an ease that was almost languid he kicked out one massive boot and smashed one of the shelves to kindling. Another kick and the boards behind the shelf cracked and bent back into a void.

'Come on, big lad,' cajoled Skane, grinning. Jhari scowled back and kicked again. Now, a small hole was revealed.

'Keep going,' he said. He had found it. 'I'm going to fetch the Weasel.'

He moved over to the window and shoved the shutters open. The rest of the Mackems were still skulking in the shadows on the opposite side, with the strange figure standing immobile against the wall of the house below.

'Hey,' hissed Skane. 'Send Weez over! We need the Weasel! And bring a lantern.'

Moments later, the light pattering of feet on the stairs was heard as a counterpoint to the rhythmic thuds of Jhari's iron-shod boots. A slender figure appeared at the top of the stairs, glancing quickly left and right as she took in the scene.

The Weasel, whose real name was Wesla Nusel, was a petite, boyish woman. Her reddish hair was trimmed short, like Skane and Jhari's, and her dark eyes were large and wide set. She held a candle lantern in one hand as she approached.

'Get in there, Weez,' instructed Skane, pointing towards the small hole Jhari's boots had made. She nodded without speaking, before ducking and squeezing her narrow shoulders through the tight gap. The Weasel rarely spoke.

There was silence as she moved around in the void behind the furniture. Then, Skane saw her feet disappear swiftly upwards. He listened closely, although he could hear little at the best of times, before feeling as much as hearing her soft footfalls directly above his head. More silence followed.

'Skane?' her high voice called down, hesitantly. 'I think you need to come up and see this.'

Skane motioned to Jhari, who wordlessly kicked at the boards once more, enlarging the hole. It still looked tight.

'Bugger it,' muttered Skane, with feeling. He bent down and squeezed his broad shoulders through the gap, picking up several splinters from the edges of the broken planks as he pushed past.

Then, he was in a dark, claustrophobic space behind the tall furniture. Pushing off either side with hands and feet, he worked his way upwards towards the faint glow of the Weasel's lantern above. She must be standing in the attic space itself.

Skane pulled himself onto the rough boards and looked around. The dim light of the single lantern illuminated the scene. The Weasel stood silently in the middle, able to stand upright easily below the peak of the roof. There were only a few signs left behind, but to Skane's experienced eyes they were enough.

A dribble of candlewax over there. A scatter of breadcrumbs over here. A couple of empty crates stood on the floor, arranged just so, as if used for seating.

Someone had been up here. Probably several people, and for a while. The occupants below would have known nothing about it, if the hideaways had been quiet and careful about their comings and goings. Nice little spot.

He had no doubt that the people who had been here had been cautious, and virtually silent when it mattered. They were professionals. Professionals who had stolen the jewel and had hidden it here.

Professionals who had taken the jewel and left, just in time to avoid being caught in this trap. He sucked a rueful breath through the gaps in his teeth.

Cannis Flett and her mysterious masked master were not going to be happy.

'Where're you two off?' A pair of short-haired figures detached themselves from the shadows of the Westgate, and approached aggressively. Mackems guards.

Disguises in place, Nastja and Ellyah were about to find out whether they were good enough to get them past the gate and out of the city. Nastja's heart had been beating out of her chest as she walked next to Ellyah through the dusky streets, sure that everyone they passed was staring; wondering and, accusing.

Nastja was convinced that the Mackems were already looking for them. She could feel them closing in.

A Royal Sentinel stood motionless at either side of the gate, the sharp points of their ranseurs gleaming ominously in the torchlight. They would not intervene or even move for anything short of murder, though.

Nastja responded, keeping her voice shrill. 'My father is a trader. We are returning to our homes in the Westra.'

'Trading what?' The Mackems' eyes were flinty, but disinterested.

'What is this young man saying?' asked Ellyah in a croaky voice. Nastja resisted the urge to roll her eyes. It was usually much easier if Ellyah stayed quiet.

She had played her part well since climbing carefully down from the hideout, hunching her back over the padding around her middle so it resembled a paunch. Walking with a stiff, shuffling gait she clutched at Nastja's arm as they moved through the streets. She had to admit that even she would have thought Ellya was a frail, elderly old man, at a glance.

'All we have are empty sacks, see?' Nastja opened the drawstring of the leather bag she carried, and showed them the contents; just some rough, hessian sacks. A few items of clothing were hidden beneath. They had betted on the gangsters not being bothered to search properly, once they were sure that the bag was not hiding a box.

They were right. 'Just clear off,' said one, waving them past. Nastja led her "elderly" partner away by the arm.

They walked slowly until they were a good distance from the walls, through the darkened streets of the Westra. A few people moved quietly in the darkness, but the town was quiet.

'We need to find Luara,' hissed Ellyah. Then, revealingly. 'We have to make sure the jewel is safe.'

Nastja remained silent, but dragged on Ellyah's arm. Wordlessly, they hurried off the main street, and away through the mass of shadowy, ramshackle timber houses. Here and there a bonfire burned in a yard, and rushlights sputtered in doorways.

When they were in the deep shadows close to the city wall, Ellyah shook Nastja's hand off her arm.

'Stop dragging me along!' she blustered angrily. 'Where're you taking me?'

Silently, Nastja pointed up, towards what she had noticed from the main street.

A shadow was gliding over the darker shape of the timber palisade high above. Smooth as a spider, it lowered itself down the wall. The logs appeared smoothly cut but there must have been notches and gaps that served as hand and foot holds. As the figure reached the lower part of the rampart, where it overhung the houses of the Westra, it was suddenly silhouetted by the weak, flickering light from below.

It was a person, climbing gracefully downwards. At the lip of the overhang, it suddenly dropped. Nastja's breath caught in her throat. They somehow found another hold, and the fall was held. They swung from their arms, their legs hanging loose in empty space.

Feet still dangling, the figure moved towards the lower walls, vanishing into the deeper shade beneath the overhang. It appeared as though they were swinging from the beams above their head, hand over hand. It was a breathtaking display of poise and athleticism.

Moments later, a shadow flowed down the lower wall like poured liquid. Luara appeared beside them after another few heartbeats, a wide smile on her face.

'That was fun,' she said, breathing easily. 'Shall we go?'

'The jewel?' Ellyah's asked curtly, tone harsh.

'Oh yes.' Luara either did not notice Ellyah's bluntness, or was not concerned. She handed over a small leather sack that had been strapped securely across her back. Ellyah quickly checked that the box was inside, before slinging it across her own body.

A flurry of sudden sounds reached their ears. Raised voices. Running feet. As one, all three heads swivelled towards the noise. It came from the direction of the gate. Something was happening. The quiet of the night was disturbed.

Nastja expected that Mackems' gate guards would now be panicking. She had known they would already be searching the city. Now, they would extend the search out into the Westra. Getting through the gates had needed planning and luck, but now it sounded as if the chase was on.

She glanced at Ellyah. Her eyes were darting, looking for somewhere to hide. That would be no good. The people of the Westra would sell them out to the Mackems in a heartbeat. Their disguises would be no good a second time. They needed a way to get clear of the city, and quickly.

She thought fast, looking around through the gloom of the night. Beyond the nearest cluster of houses was a darker, open area. No bonfires or lights glowed beyond. The dromedary racetrack. With the stables nearby.

'Don't move,' she hissed to Ellyah and Luara, as she darted away.

Nastja swayed with the unfamiliar undulating rhythm of the dromedary's gait. She sat on a stiffened leather pad that served as a saddle, with her legs crossed neatly before her.

The walls of Carhinn receded at their backs, a solid square of hard blackness against the lighter, indigo darkness of the night sky.

She glanced back, her sharp eyes able to make out the rocking, indistinct shapes of Ellyah and Luara as they followed closely behind. She permitted herself a wry smile.

They had escaped. They were leaving Carhinn, and the Mackems, behind.

She could not see if Ellyah was smiling, the darkness too deep, but she hoped that the other woman was pleased. The pair of them had played their part perfectly, and Luara had paid them back handsomely for the trust they had placed in her.

The Mackems had poured from the gate and into the Westra, but the haphazardly arranged streets were a labyrinth even in broad daylight. In the dark, they had no chance of finding anything.

Nastja had stolen three dromedaries, leading them back to the other two women. They had mounted hastily and ridden away. They were free.

Nastja heard hoofbeats growing louder and turned to see Ellyah awkwardly goading her drom into a surge of speed. She came up alongside, body moving up and down with the creature's clumsy trot.

'You were great tonight, Nas,' she said, happily. Nastja glowed inside, heart close to bursting. 'We're in the clear, hen. The Mackems will never be able to track us all the way to Kereva.'

PART THREE

FIFTEEN

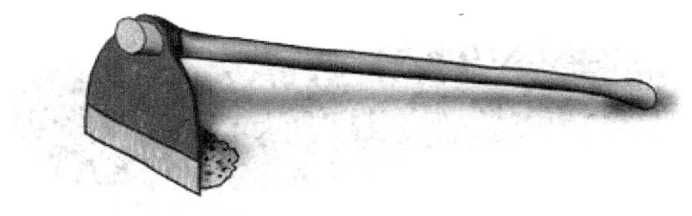

Carilton Tann was a man who saw much.

From his farmhouse in the dusty hills, he saw the sun rise and the moons set, day after day. He had seen many years come and go, seasons turning relentlessly around as he worked this sparse and unrewarding land.

He saw the flight of the birds overhead, observed wild herds of tarpan as they swept down the valley towards the river, and he kept a careful watch for any lions or lynx that might encroach on his land.

So, he spotted the lone figure immediately, as they appeared over the brow of a bare hilltop on the eastern horizon. He watched as the tall person lurched unsteadily down the stony slope. By the time they stumbled and fell, Tann was already moving in that direction.

'Sarm! Caivane!' he yelled, back towards his farmhouse's wide veranda. 'Follow me, and quick! Linil! Fetch a barrow!'

It was evening, and the inhabitants of the farmstead were relaxing after their evening meal. Sunset sucked the warmth from the land, so they made the most of the last gasp of pleasant daylight.

They moved now. The few that Tann had summoned trailed in his wake as he strode out, and the others stood up from their benches to get a better view of what was happening.

It was a mismatched group that leaned on the rail, peering out at the striding, angular figure of Carilton Tann. Men and women from across the Lands of the Great River, and further afield; Tayans, Burenos and Anises, as well as a couple of purple-cheeked half-elves. There was even one who spoke with the accents of Kotev.

Nearly all were displaced from their original homes, for one reason or another. Some were refugees, some had been criminals. All had been exiled or hunted, and had nowhere else to go.

Carilton Tann saw more than just the moods of the landscape and the movement of animals. He saw that everyone deserved a second chance. He thought that everyone should have somewhere safe to go.

When he had come out to the east to manage his mother's smallholding, he put the word out that he was looking for extra hands to help. He paid fair, gave bed and board, and asked no questions about where people had come from, or what trouble was at their backs.

'I've left enough trouble behind me, on my own road,' he said, to those who questioned him. 'I sure as silver don't want to be judged on my past alone. We'll all be judged when we pass through that shining veil, anyway.'

The small farmstead had grown from there, to fill the bowl-shaped valley where it lay. Other houses and storage buildings had sprung up as the seasons rolled by. The few trickling streams that ran through the arid, sandy land had been diverted into channels to water the fields. The community thrived.

Tann's legs burned as he strode up towards where the man, and now he was closer he was sure that it was a man, had fallen.

His legs had collapsed beneath him, and he had rolled bonelessly down the steep slope.

Tann knew he was not getting any younger. His breath came in laboured gasps as he surged up the slope to where the fallen figure lay. Ten years ago he could have jogged up this slope whistling a tune. Twenty years ago, he could have done it armed and armoured. Time was inescapable.

The man had sprawled onto his face, so Tann bent his back and carefully rolled him over.

He was young, surprisingly so. He could not have seen more than twenty winters, and although his cheeks could not have seen a blade for several days, the stubble was thin and wispy. He wore a moustache on his upper lip and his sandy hair was trimmed short at the sides but hung longer at the back, brushing the collar of his pale shirt. His clothes were an unusual style. Tann did not recognise the cut.

'Who's this then?' said Sarm, arriving to stand beside Tann. 'Where in the Five's name has this guy sprung from?'

The Tayan, previously a mercenary fighter, peered down at the prone figure, scrutinising his physique and his garb. Sarm sized up everyone he met, and split them into two groups. Those he could beat in a fight went in one, and those he could not were the other. Very few made it into the second group.

'I really don't know,' replied Tann. He was puzzled. 'Up from Kotev?'

'Don't look Kotevari to me, boss.' Sarm was shaking his head, and Tann had to agree.

The man was wearing snug leather trousers, like those worn by fighters and herders across the wide river lands. The style was unfamiliar, the leather thick and robust. His shirt was cut short too, barely longer than his belt. Was he a serf, or a peasant?

He looked too well fed for that. The breadth of his shoulders and the solid thickness of his arms told of wealth, good food, and a physical life. He was tall, too. Caivane, just arriving beside them, was the tallest man at the farmstead, and Tann guessed that this young man was a few fingers taller still. He had far less bulk around his middle than the portly Caivane, however.

'Oof! That's a climb now, boys!' puffed Caivane, bending with his hands on his tree trunk-like thighs. Rings gleamed across every one of his thick fingers, most of bright tin or yellowish bronze. He had been a small-time swindler in Anish before running afoul of both the authorities and the criminal gangs. He had fled for his life.

'Look at this poor soul.' He stooped over the man lying on the dusty ground. 'Looks like he's been through it, all right.'

Caivane was right. The man's clothes were dirty and torn in places. His skin had a golden hue, but he had dark circles around his eyes, and his lips were dry and cracked. He had dried blood on his hands. Tann knew the signs of war when he saw them.

'We need to get him back down the hill,' he said. 'We'll lift him together. Caivane, you get his legs. Sarm, grab his middle.' Tann himself crouched behind the man's broad shoulders, slipping his hands beneath his armpits.

'Careful now. Lift!'

Between the three of them they lifted the unresisting body, sidling awkwardly down the slope.

'Whoever he is,' groaned Sarm, 'he's a big lad. Sure he's not related to you, Cai?' Caivane chuckled.

Linil waited at the bottom of the slope with a wooden, single-wheeled barrow. Together, they manhandled the unconscious figure into it, and she grasped the handles.

'Another stray dog for your collection, boss?' asked Linil, as she pushed the barrow along a well-worn track between cornfields. Linil had always been cagey about her background, but Tann had gathered that she had travelled to the farm from the region of Kiraband, far to the west.

Tann reckoned that she had come out of the Alrean Empire; Emrys or Timmers, driven into exile by the harsh regime there, or fleeing something. She never told the story and Tann would not ask. She had arrived, exhausted and bedraggled, with her baby girl strapped to her chest. Caurel was already growing into a busy and inquisitive toddler.

'A wanderer,' replied Tann. 'Looks in a bad way. We'll do what we can to help him before we worry too much about where he's from.'

Linil grimaced as she doggedly pushed the heavy barrow along the path. Tann itched to offer to take the handles from her. Yet, he knew she would take offence at the suggestion, the implication that she was not strong enough. She still seemed embarrassed about needing to seek his refuge, when in all other ways she was independent and self-sufficient.

She drove herself hard, whether it be labouring around the farm or gaming against the other hands. Tann had realised that she needed to, needed to feel strong and valuable, and to try to lighten her load would be a false kindness.

As they neared the veranda, more men and women leapt down from their benches to help. Tann could not help but smile, with fatherly pride. Many hands grasped the limbs and clothing of the unconscious man as they lifted him, and carried him into the house.

'Will you come take a look, Ma?' called Tann to his mother, as they passed her seat in the main hall. She was a white-haired woman with piercing blue eyes, and had lived in this same house for fifty years. Elderly, but spry and very determined, she rose from her chair as they carried the man through a door in the back of the hall.

The house had grown gradually over time. Tann's father had laid down the rubble foundations when he was a young man and raised the sturdy wooden beams that framed the house one by one, as he could afford them.

At first it had been little more than a single-roomed hovel with a roof of straw thatch, but first Tann's father and then Tann himself had continued to add more rooms, expanding into the surrounding scrub. The additional space had been useful when Tann had welcomed the first incomers.

At the very back of the house he had added a long, low room and furnished it with several narrow beds. Squeezing though the narrow doorway, they laid the tall man carefully down on one. His feet and ankles dangled off the edge.

Tann noticed a scabbarded blade at the man's waist, and he quickly removed it from his belt. One of his rules was that no-one at the farm was armed. He kept a secure chest in his room where he stored a selection of weapons. This long knife would join the rest, but he took a moment to examine it before he tucked it away. It had an unusual device branded on the leather, like a twelve-pointed star. He had never seen it before.

Moments later, Ma Tann shuffled through the door. She waved the crowd aside as if she were swatting horseflies away, then bent at the bedside.

'Clear out, clear out!' she ordered, irritably. 'Thick as flies around a fresh pat, y'are.'

These were tough people; ex-criminals, soldiers, brawlers and outlaws, and yet they fled at her words like chided children. Sarm left with them. Tann, Caivane and Linil remained in the room.

'Well, he lives,' said Ma Tann after she had gripped his wrists and listened intently at his mouth and chest. 'And he don't seem hurt. Leastways, not hurt in his body. He looks drier than the northern plains, though. Cai, go fetch a jug o'water. He needs to top himself up.'

Caivane strode from the room and she paused, looking up at her son.

'Well, well.' There was amusement in her voice. 'A new mystery for you to solve, my boy.' Carilton was nearly fifty years old but to her, he was always "my boy." 'You draw them to you like you're a beacon burning. I don't know how.'

He smiled. 'Thought you were going to say, "like flies to dung"!'

'Maybe I thought it.'

Caivane returned with a clay jug and cup, passing them to Ma Tann. She poured a little water into the cup and moistened the man's raw lips.

'That's what's needed now,' she said. 'And I sure as silver ain't going to sit up all night doing it. Who'll volunteer?'

'I'll do it, Ma,' said Tann, immediately.

'I'll fetch you a stool,' added Linil.

'Right, so,' said Ma Tann, satisfied. 'Now, just a splash at a time. Slowly catches the badger. Let's not drown the boy afore we've had a chance to introduce ourselves.'

He had sat at the bedside for as long as he could hold his eyes open. Every few moments he carefully wetted the stranger's lips with a drop or two from the cup.

A few other men came into the room as the night drew in, talking in hushed tones before wrapping themselves in their blankets with quiet respect.

'Good night, Master Tann,' they muttered. 'The Five see you, boss.'

He stared down at the young man's face as darkness spread in from the shadowy corners of the room. He tried to imagine the man awake, and upright. He tried to hear the sound of his voice, and the words he might say.

Who are you? He wondered. *And, how did you come to be wandering in those mountains?*

This region, an isolated corner of the Lands of the Great River, was sparsely inhabited. Scratching a living from the thin, sandy soil was difficult. Wandering tribes came this far, occasionally; the Waica and the Meculvy Dutsch, but they never stayed long. Tribes of elves lived in secluded settlements in the northern foothills of the Derufin Mountains, and the fearsome Wild Elves roamed the northern plains.

But, this was no elf.

No one lived east of here. There was nothing but dusty plains, scrubby hills and the fitful wind. Further still, dark, spear-peaked mountains rose on the horizon, uninhabited and impassable. Myths were spoken of a race of giants who lived there, among the snow-tipped peaks, and hurled lightning at each other. Few believed these tall tales, though.

Could he have come up from Kotev? There were rumours of unrest in that southern country, but when was there not? Some said they prepared for war against their neighbours Anish once more. Others said that they would not dare again for many years.

Perhaps they looked north? Kotev was a country of poor land and limited resources. They were always looking across their borders with envious eyes and grasping hands.

This man had none of the look of the Kotevari. He was much too tall, and too fair. Perhaps Kotev had begun to use mercenaries in their armies, or to crew their ships?

He shrugged. He had no idea. As his mother had said, it was a new mystery.

Silence and darkness enveloped the room. Tann kept giving the man tiny sips of water, until he could no longer see the jug.

The first crisp light of dawn brightened the bunk room, and Carilton Tann woke with a start. He immediately looked toward the unconscious figure of the new man, worry gripping him for a moment.

He relaxed. The man's chest continued to rise and fall, deeply and evenly.

The morning light brought no new answers. Tann blinked as the day began, eyes gritty. The aroma of corn grits cooking drifted in from the main hall. His mother was up, and breakfast was on the hearth.

'How's 'ee doin'?' asked Murius, a farm hand with round shoulders and a long, dark beard. Like many Anise, he wore his finger rings on a thong around his neck to avoid them getting damaged by work.

Some days, Murius was up before the dawn to bake bread for everyone. Today, he was only just pulling on his work clothes, so Tann guessed that, as often happened, he had overslept. Tann stood, glancing down at the bed. Some of the greyness around the unconscious man's eyes had faded away overnight. His breathing was even. He seemed at peace.

'Living,' he replied. 'But I'd be happier if he woke up soon.'

'Aye,' said Murius, moving to stand closer. 'If you want to get your head down for an hour, I can keep an eye on him.' He nodded down at the bed. Tann hesitated. He felt responsible for the lad. 'You look right tired,' continued Murius. 'I've been watching you giving him the water. I can do it for a while.'

Eventually, Tann nodded. 'Yes, I think I should rest. My thanks to you, Murius.'

Tann strode to the back of the bunk room and took off his dusty canvas coat, before rolling himself in a blanket on one of the beds. He lifted his head once, and saw Murius settling himself down on the stool. Then, his eyes closed and he was quickly asleep.

The room was brighter. Tann could tell immediately that several hours had passed. His stomach groaned.

Guiltily, he sat up on the bed.

Murias was still at the sleeping man's side, a cup in his hand. Neither of them had moved a muscle. However, his mother was in the room once more. She was sitting on the next low bed, working with a pestle and mortar in her hands.

'I'd say "good morning", my boy,' she said, with a wry smile, 'only it wouldn't be true. Must be past noon by now.'

'I'm sorry—,' Tann began.

'Hush. You needed it. Farm hasn't fallen over or burned down while you slept.' She leaned toward the tall stranger. 'But, I'm glad you're awake now, and I think it's high time this man-child stirred, too.'

Tann rose and slipped his coat back over his shirt of roughly woven flax. He deftly folded the blanket up, leaving it neatly on the end of the bed for the next man before moving over to his mother.

The scent from the small wooden bowl was sharp and pungent. Tann's nose wrinkled.

'Wild mint, *caja*, and camphor,' explained Ma Tann. 'A dab of this should summon him back to the world of the waking.' She tapped at her son's arm. 'My supply of camphor crystal is running low. Hope the merchant trains bring some more this autumn.'

She set the bowl down and stood. Dabbing her fingers into the aromatic green paste, she leaned over the man's face. Tann watched as she carefully smeared a little of the mixture into his sand-coloured moustache.

'Looks like snot,' said Murius, giggling. Ma Tann rolled her eyes.

'He'll be breathing the vapours in now,' she said. 'And these are all herbs of stirring, not settling. Should liven him up better'n a poke in the ribs.'

They watched.

At first, nothing happened. The man slept on, untroubled. Then, his nose twitched. He gave a slight grunt. Tann's heart beat a steady cadence, thumping against his ribcage as he waited.

The man's breathing changed. His chest moved more rapidly as each breath became shallower.

Then, his eyes opened.

They were a slate grey colour, like a mountain lake. They widened and narrowed, as he stared straight up at the ceiling. He blinked.

With a suddenness that caused everyone to take a step back, he swung his long legs off the bed, and stood. In a practised motion that spoke of habit, he too folded the blanket in half, then in half again. Placing it neatly back on the bed, he took a step back.

Then, finally, he looked up. His eyes scanned the room, taking his surroundings in for the first time.

As Tann watched, he saw the man's eyes widen, surprise and alarm flashing across his face.

He moved. First, he raised his hand to his right shoulder, then slapped it to his waist. He grasped nothing but air, but Tann knew he was searching for his weapons.

Now that he was upright, Tann could see even more clearly that this man was a fighter, or a soldier. He had dropped into a fighting crouch, both fists raised. Tann stepped defensively in front of his mother while raising his hands, palms outwards.

He hoped the gesture of peace was clear. The man's height and physical strength were obvious now that he was on his feet. The soiled linen of his short shirt was pulled snug by the breadth of his shoulders and the tensed muscles of his arms.

Please lower your fists, thought Tann. A fight would be painful.

'*Hvar vy eig? Sem vy ther?*'

The man spoke, a rapid rattle of unfamiliar syllables. Tann gaped. It was a language he had never heard before. Where in the world was he from?

The stranger's eyes darted. His fists clenched. His breathing came in shallow, panicky gasps. He took a step backward.

Then, he sagged. As Tann watched, hands still raised, the tall man's head dropped. As if bowed down by the weight of the world, he sat down heavily on the nearest bed. He pressed his hands to his face.

Tann breathed out in a long, low sigh of relief. He had really not wanted to fight against the new arrival, but dealing with those in despair was very familiar.

He silently shooed his mother and Murius from the room, noticing at the same time that the doorway was full of watching faces. He waved them all away. The new man needed to know that he was safe.

Tann sat down on the bed opposite. The bunks were set close to one another, so he had to twist slightly to avoid bumping knees.

Don't touch someone you don't know, he reminded himself.

Long, silent moments passed, with the sandy-haired newcomer staring into the palms of his hands. After what seemed like a very long time, he dragged them away and looked up. His eyes were piercing and filled with a desperate sadness.

What were you running from? What horrors have you seen?

'I don't know as you can understand me.' Tann spoke quietly, gently. 'But my name is Carilton Tann, and this is my place. You're safe here.'

The man stared in what Tann took to be mute incomprehension. Another part of the mystery. Nearly every country in the known world used a little of the Common Speech, even Kotev and as far west as the Alrean Empire. Yet, this man did not understand it at all.

Keep it simple, stupid.

Tann pointed to his own chest with both thumbs.

'Tann' he said. 'Me, Tann.' He turned his hands around and pointed them at the other man. 'You?'

There was a pause. He blinked a few times. Then he raised his own hands, copying Tann's gesture.

'Ee-ane,' he said, slowly and deliberately. '*Eig vy* Ee-ane *Cuh-no.*'

Was that his name? "Ee-ane", or something that sounded that way.

The man, "Ee-ane", was pointing back. 'Tann. *Ther*, Tann.'

'Yea, I'm Tann.' He smiled, in what he hoped was an open and friendly way. 'You are "Ee-ane", right?'

The man gave a weak smile as he nodded. "Ee-ane". Eain. Well, that was a start. He no longer looked like he wanted to hit anyone, although he still looked like he could weep.

'You hungry?' asked Tann, pointing first at his mouth and then at his belly. 'Want food?'

Eain stared for a moment, then touched his own belly. He must be hungry. Understanding seemed to dawn, and he nodded vigorously.

'Come.' Tann stood and beckoned, moving toward the doorway. He glanced back to check that Eain was following. His height really was striking. He was about a hand's width taller than Tann, needing to stoop to pass through the doorway and into the next room.

The main hall was nearly empty. Ma Tann was sitting in her usual chair near the door, and Murius was sat on one of the benches beside the long table. Both fires smouldered; one in the main hearth at the centre and another in the cob-built oven in the corner. Blue-grey smoke drifted up to linger in the thatch above.

Someone had found time to put Murius' dough in the oven, and the savoury scent of fresh cornbread permeated the air.

'Sit, sit.' Tann gestured to a bench and Eain sat, tucking his long legs beneath the table. Tann grabbed a plate and quickly heaped it with what was left of lunch. There were hunks of cornbread, strips of dried goat meat and slippery white chunks of cheese.

'It's not much,' said Tann, passing the plate across the table. 'But it's good enough to fill an empty belly.' Eain glanced around uneasily, but soon enough had picked up a wedge of cornbread and taken a healthy bite.

Murius turned to Eain. 'So, what's your story? Where did you come from? What moons were you born by?'

There was silence. Eain chewed softly and stared back at Murius. His shoulders were tense.

'Uhh…Murius,' said Tann, carefully. 'This fellow won't understand you. I don't think he knows the Common Speech.'

Murius' eyes widened. 'So, how we going to find out his birth moons?'

'He told me his true name already.' Murius opened his mouth to speak, surprise painted across his face, but Tann cut him off. 'And I told him mine.'

'But—' Murius was aghast.

'It's fine, Murius. It's fine. We're friends already, and I guess he's going to be staying a while.'

Murius puffed out his cheeks, but said nothing.

'Can't always stand on tradition.' Ma Tann spoke up from her chair. 'There's a time and place for that stuff.'

'Quite right, Ma. Quite right.' Tann filled his own plate and sat down opposite Eain. He gestured with a hunk of bread. 'This here is Eain. We don't know where he's from or how he got here, but that don't matter. You know we don't concern ourselves with those questions here.'

'Right so, boss.' Murius got up and ambled over to the door. 'I'd best get on to work.'

'See you for dinner, boy,' called Ma Tann.

'Yes, Ma.' Murius slouched into the doorway, but had to duck aside as another figure came through from the other direction.

'Be careful, Bumble,' said Sarm, pushing past Murius and into the room.

'Sorry, Sarm,' muttered Murius, head bowed, as he hurried away. Tann scowled. It was just a nickname, but the way Sarm said it was demeaning and disrespectful. Sarm and Murius both knew that, but the bearded Anise seemed to just accept it.

'Lunch!' Sarm approached the table with a swagger. 'Hard graft this morning, Master Tann. Hard graft. Dug that south channel clear again. Was all choked with flamevine and dirt and shit. Water's running free now. My feelings are happy.'

He seized a plate and sat. 'And look who has joined us in the land of the waking. How are you feeling, fella? You frightened us, my friend.'

'Sarm,' sighed Tann, wearily. 'He doesn't speak our language. You'll have to take it real slow.'

'Doesn't know the Common Speech? So, what does he know? Alrean? Kotevari? They are weird languages but even those folks mostly speak a bit of Common too. He's a bit tall to speak Dwarvish and a bit wide for an elf.' He laughed.

'He speaks a language I've not heard before,' Tann admitted, ruefully. Sarm's eyes widened. They were dark, flecked with gold, and burned in his bronze-skinned face like smouldering coals. He was a broad, belligerent man, and even more averse than most to discussing anything about his past. Tann sensed that darkness lurked there.

'Damn! You sure he ain't just simple? Could have been the heat, the thirst. Dried out his brain, you know?'

Sarm,' said Tann, warningly. Eain was eating stoically, ignoring the conversation or at least oblivious to it.

'I'm joking.' Sarm laughed off Tann's ire. 'But, I'd still like to know where he's come from. He didn't just fall from the sky!' Sarm stood, still chewing, and walked around the table to stand behind Eain.

'Going to be hard to find out if we can't just ask him, isn't it? I guess he doesn't need to talk to work, and with these shoulders he should be a damn good worker, right?'

'We will do what we can to help him fit in,' said Tann, evenly. He was watching Eain, who had started looking uneasy when Sarm had moved behind him.

'Oh, sure,' said Sarm, dismissively. 'And I'll do what I can to get him to help me with my heavy lifting!'

With that, he laid a hand on one of Eain's shoulders, in a way that was intended to be friendly and familiar.

Tann saw the danger, but could not react quickly enough.

Eain's legs straightened as he raised his left hand to where Sarm's lay on his shoulder. At the same time, he lifted his right arm. His hand pointed to the ceiling and his lower arm was level with his shoulder. Sarm opened his mouth, expression quizzical.

Eain spun. He pivoted on the balls of his feet, and his right elbow clamped down over Sarm's arm. As Eain turned and his weight was pressed down, Sarm was pushed helplessly down and around. His head bounced off the aged boards of the table with a resounding thud. It had taken a few heartbeats.

The whole bench tipped over backwards as Eain stepped away. Sarm slithered down onto the floor beside it, hands clutching his face. Tann glanced down at the table to see if Sarm's head had left a dent.

'*Eicha snert!*' shouted Eain, in his own language. '*Eicha snert ehg!*'

He backed across the room, eyes wild. Tann stood and raised his hand, trying to think of something to say. A moment later, Eain had turned and he was gone through the doorway.

'Goatshit,' swore Tann, softly. 'That's torn it. Sarm? You still with us?'

Sarm groaned. 'He smashed my skull. I can't see straight!'

'Ma, can you see to him?' Tann was striding to the door. 'I'm sure he'll live.'

He had to catch the new man before he got too far. There was nothing in several days' ride, in any direction. If he fled, he would a find nothing but a hard death out in the barren, dusty hills.

He did not to have to search for long.

The tall, lean figure of Eain was plain to see, stood at the edge of the garden that spread around the house. The fields of crops were further south, filling the bowl-shaped valley, and the brown and white splashed shapes of goats could be seen roaming the nearby hillsides.

The garden was well watered thanks to channels that had been cut from the higher ground, and it stood as out as a pool of verdant lushness amidst the harsh surroundings. Here, flowers bloomed in sprays of purple, red and white. Bees hummed. Sprawling herb shrubs filled the spaces, a mix of flavourous plants and those with medicinal qualities.

It was the green heart of the small community that Carilton Tann had built.

Eain was leaning heavily against one of the tall, carved gateposts. He shook his head as he stared out at the bleak landscape beyond. A rough track ran indistinctly from the gateway and out into the far distance, but apart from that there was nothing.

Tann approached slowly.

'Eain.' He said the name carefully. Eain glanced up and Tann raised both hands, palms outwards. He felt as though he was approaching a wild animal. The man was scared, trapped, and ready to lash out. 'No harm will come to you here, Eain. No harm.'

Eain stared for a moment. Clearly, he could not understand the words, but Tann hoped that his tone would communicate his intentions.

'*Eig eicha thann hathae voi geidh. Eicha thann hvar eig get faer...*'

He sounded uncertain. His tone was questioning. He was full of doubt.

Tann gestured back toward the house. 'My home. Understand? My home can be your home. For as long as you need. Can you understand that word? "Home"?'

Eain blinked. Tann thought that at last something had got through, and some understanding had been reached. Then Eain spoke again.

'*Eigh haf eicha heimma.*'

Tann could not understand the words, but this time the meaning was clear. Eain's voice was filled with bitter sadness.

'I have no home.'

SIXTEEN

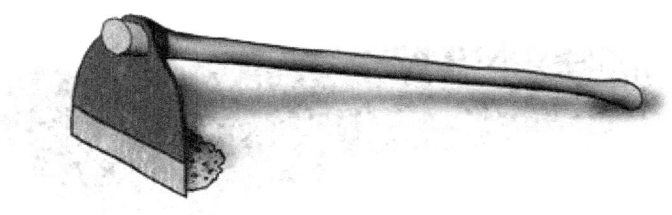

'He's been shouting in his sleep.'

Murius was talking about the new man, Eain. Several weeks had passed since his arrival, but he remained the most common topic of conversation around the farm.

'He thrashes around and wails,' continued Murius. '"No, no," he says. Or, "nai, nai", which is probably the same thing, right?'

It was lunchtime, and various of the farm's inhabitants were filtering in and out of the main hall for a bite, before going back to work. A couple of children ran past the veranda, their merry laughter bubbling into the room. Tann chewed a mouthful of bread slowly, listening to the conversation.

'Look hard in his eyes,' said Linil, without looking up. 'There's a story there. A sad one. Maybe if his speech improves, he will tell it to us.'

She sighed as her daughter Caurel picked up a handful of bread and rubbed it all over her own cheeks, completely missing her mouth. She giggled.

Caurel had been a babe in arms when Linil had arrived at the farm. She had already grown into an energetic and inquisitive toddler. Tann reckoned her and her mother had been at the farm for six seasons.

Would the child grow up here? When might Linil decide to move on? Questions that Tann could not answer. He mentally waved them away.

'He's ended up in the right place,' Ma Tann spoke from her chair in the corner. 'We don't need to know his history, and we don't need to guess. It ain't anyone's business but his own.'

Tann nodded. Sarm shook his head.

'Until he hurts someone else,' he muttered from where he was standing, leaning on the wall. His thick black hair had gown longer still, drawn to one side and tied by his right shoulder in the Tayan style. 'We know he's violent. If he's gone in the head too…it's like living with a wild dog.'

'We've all had to live with you for long enough,' said Linil, blandly, pushing a strip of goat jerky into Caurel's gummy grin. There was laughter.

The bruise on Sarm's head was fading but the man was still smarting from the humiliation. He fancied himself as the tough guy of the farm, and yet Eain had put him on the ground seemingly by accident.

To Tann, Eain's instinctive, decisive reaction spoke of rigorous training. Military training. His action had been fast, precise and without conscious thought. As far as Tann could see, Sarm was fortunate that Eain had not broken his arm.

To Sarm, it had been an affront. His pride was hurt. It was threat to him. He spoke against the new man at every opportunity, knowing full well that Eain could not understand the insults, and could not respond. At least, not yet.

Because Eain was learning.

From the first day, when Tann had led him around the farmlands as an introduction, Eain had tried to copy the words for things as Tann had pointed them out.

'Fence. Field. House. Goat.'

Tann had said each word and, haltingly, Eain had repeated it back. It was a start. Some words were surprisingly similar. The sounds Eain made for "sky", "tree" and "house" were all very familiar. He seemed happier when he was able to communicate, even just a little.

He was still a long way away from being able to tell his story, even if he wished to.

They had walked through the southern fields, where corn and beans grew in patchy rows. Some plants grew tall and green, while others were yellowing and withered. A healthy crop of tabac and *kanab* for smoking grew well here; they were his main export crop. He had little interest in smoking himself but there was a good market for it across the plains and all the way to Kiraband.

'It's tough living out here,' said Tann as they walked, 'but we make it work. Everyone pitches in.' He knew that Eain could not understand much, but he felt that silence would seem unfriendly.

The sun was warm on their backs as they followed the straight path between the fields. The track climbed more steeply as they walked further from the house. Eain's face gleamed with sweat. Water gurgled quietly in neatly cut channels to either side of the path.

Tann fanned his face with his wide-brimmed hat, then put it back on his head. The crops petered out and scrubby bushes and grasses dotted the sandy slopes ahead. Goats wandered freely, grazing stoically on the tough vegetation.

'Damned things will eat a whole field of crops, if they can get in. Checking and repairing fences is a daily job. Maybe that's something you can help with? Soon enough.'

Eain looked at the goats with calm interest, nodding.

A few more brisk paces and the ground flattened out. Before them lay a bleak plateau. The gritty soil gave way to flattish shelves of ochre rock which was marked in places with dark or green streaks, showing where water sometimes flowed. Knife-edged peaks of crumbling stone rose in the distance, and a small, still lake spread before them.

Trickling, ephemeral streams ran from this lake, fading away into the dry landscape. Digging channels to capture this intermittent water flow had been arduous labour for Tann when he had returned to take over the farm.

A spring rose from the cracked rocks near the farm, bubbling out at the base of the lower slopes. That had been enough when it was just his parents here, but now they needed a lot more water. The lake overspill, when channelled, now provided a source of irrigation through even the driest summer months.

He turned and looked north. Eain stood beside him.

'This is all we have,' he said quietly. 'Maybe, all we need. All I need.'

The land fell away before their feet in a gentle slope. The farmhouse was visible as a dark, blocky shape amid the greenery of the fields and garden. Other, smaller buildings were dotted nearby; the newer houses of some of the other inhabitants. They built their own homes and spread out as their numbers grew. Now, it was like a small village. Beyond the farmstead all was drab, dry and colourless.

Hillsides extended in long, sloping ridges to his left and right, forming a natural bowl between their embracing arms. More dusty hills rolled away eastward, and the menacing bulk of the eastern mountains rose darkly on the distant skyline.

To the left, the hills dwindled in height, until they merged with the formless, featureless plans of the eastern extent of the Lands of the Great River.

This far east, the river was no more than a fan of twisting streams that ran down from the mountain ranges to the north, south and east. The waters broadened as they ran westwards, merging with other streams and flowing relentlessly towards Kiraband. On either bank a strip of green reached out, adding life and colour to a small swathe of the plains.

All of that was a long way out of sight, even from this elevation. Tann's sharp eyes scanned the vista before him. He loved this view, and hated it. Loved it, because it reminded him of all that he had worked for; to establish this sanctuary, this community, deep in this remote but magnificent landscape. Hated it, because; where else could he go now? What else could he do?

It was a constant reminder that he was trapped, in a cage of his own making. But, his decision had been made. He could never go back to what he had been before.

Silently, he led Eain back down the track towards the house. Before they were halfway there, something made him pause. He shielded his eyes against the sun and gazed out across the plain.

After a few heartbeats, he was certain. A plume of dust showed where a horse and rider were travelling along the track to the farm. They were approaching fast.

He glanced at Eain. The tall man raised an arm, pointing toward the trail. So, he had spotted it too.

They hurried down the path, through the fields towards the farmhouse. Tann liked to think that he was fit and hale for his age, but having Eain loping easily along behind him made him feel older. He was winded and sucking the air deep by the time they reached the gate. Eain was barely breathing.

The rider approached. They were small, and as they grew nearer Tann could see that she was a woman. A woman who had travelled a long way across the forbidding plains, alone.

She reined in, a few paces away from where they stood. Dismounting easily, she led her lathered horse towards where Tann and Eain stood in the gateway. She was a short and slight, and dressed in travel-worn rider's leathers with a broad strip of cloth across her brow as a headscarf. Reddish hair, tied in two rows of complex plaits, showed above the scarf.

'You are Carilton Tann?' she asked, her voice strangely toneless. She had no accent that Tann could place. She stepped closer, waiting for an answer.

Her eyes were intense, and dark, and Tann would have described her face as pretty. There was something slightly unsettling about the sharpness of her gaze though, and Tann could not help noticing that her attention was directed towards Eain.

'That's me, and this is my place,' Tann replied, throwing open the gate. 'May I ask what moons you were born under?'

She paused. She blinked. 'My moons? Of course. I was born with Kalua a waning crescent and Jura full, and my name is Anndra co Jorto. I have ridden from Ben Gedrin to find this place.'

'And you must have ridden well indeed,' said Tann. 'There are many hard leagues between here and Ben Gedrin. We have stables out back the farmhouse. Bring your horse on through, and then come for a drink at the house.'

She bowed her head graciously, and followed Tann. He noticed the way that she and Eain locked eyes as she walked past. Tann smiled a small, knowing smile.

'I do not think Eain Connow is wild, or violent,' said Anndra. Tann had not actually noticed that she was in the room until he heard her voice. 'He has a gentle soul, but he has seen much. Suffered much. He will tell you himself, when he can.'

Several weeks had passed and both Eain and Anndra had been accepted by the inhabitants of the farmstead. It was like they had always been around.

Tann caught his mother's eye, and they both smiled. Sarm rolled his eyes. None had missed the way the new woman seemed to gravitate to where the tall stranger was at any time.

'That's a sweet thing to say, dear,' said Ma Tann, and there was laughter in her words.

At that moment, the doorway was shadowed and then filled by a massive figure. Caivane. Over six feet in height and seemingly just as wide, the former Anise swindler was a huge man. His hair was white-blond and his skin was ruddy, cheeks full and puffy beneath his small, twinkling eyes.

Eain followed him in, stooping to avoid hitting his head on the lintel. Where Caivane was round and bulging, Eain was spare and lean. A good few inches taller than even Caivane, Eain towered over everyone else.

Caivane had taken Eain under his wing over the last couple of weeks, relishing the challenge of teaching the foreigner the Common Speech. He was learning surprisingly quickly.

'Lynx got one of the kids, boss,' he said, helping himself to a hearty lunch.

'Another?' asked Tann, exasperated. The wild lands surrounding the farm were full of predators, and a young goat was an easy meal. 'Did you find it?'

'No, no.' Caivane's jowls wobbled as he shook his head. 'But there was blood on the ground, and paw prints nearby. Eain saw drag marks, too.'

Eain's head snapped up when he heard his own name. 'I help...goats,' he said, haltingly.

'*With* goats,' corrected Caivane.

'I help with goats,' repeated Eain, proudly.

'Eain helped,' said Murius. 'Well done, Eain!' The tall newcomer grinned broadly in response.

'Yes, well done Eain,' said Anndra, quietly. Tann was not sure whether anyone else was intended to hear that.

'I eat food,' said Eain slowly, moving toward the table. Tann smiled now. The joy of seeing someone who arrived with no hope beginning to recover never faded.

'Now, boys,' said Caivane, leaning forward. Inevitably, this was a prelude to one of his tall tales.

'I did some work for a fellow out near Annida, a good while back. Each night I took home a barrow full of hay for my horse. Each night he waved me through. Little perk of the job, you know?'

He paused, smiling widely as he looked around to check that all were listening.

'By the end of that season I had stolen thirty barrows from him!' He slapped the table, roaring with laughter. Tann laughed too. He had heard the story many times, but seeing these people he had brought together so happy made his mirth feel fresh, and new.

These were the good times.

'Hey, hey! Whoa! Easy now, boy!'

Caivane rarely raised his voice, so hearing him shout from across the farmstead in sharp, worried tones instantly drew Tann's attention.

Two days previously, a timber merchant had visited the farmstead and dropped off a load of man-sized logs.

'Cyle!' Tann had greeted him warmly. 'What news?'

Their fathers had known one another, and when Darigho Tann had struck out eastward to find a quiet place to farm, Cyle's father, Hrvha, had offered to load a wagon with timber for firewood and building and drive it over, now and again. The sons had honoured their fathers' arrangement.

'Nowt good,' said Cyle, in grumpy tones. He hopped down from the seat of his wagon to fall in beside Tann as they walked toward the house. 'War in Tayo, as usual. Rumours about Kotev gathering spears. Steady stream of dwarves, armed to the teeth, crossing the Riverlands.'

'On their pilgrimage?'

'Aye, looking for that Hidden City or some other children's tale.' Tann chuckled. The dwarf tribes took the story of a lost dwarf city, filled with ancient riches, very seriously. Everyone else laughed it off. There was nothing hidden on those wide plains apart from grit, rocks, and a bit of sand.

They went up the step and onto the veranda. Linil and a couple of others went past in the opposite direction, carrying bags of dried tobacco leaf as payment for the wood.

'Wild Elves been seen too, Carilton,' continued Cyle. 'Only in the north as yet, but it's still bad news for travelling traders.'

'You going to be safe riding back?'

'Aye,' Cyle spat. 'Don't worry about me. I travel fast and stay south. Let's all hope they don't start moving further south.'

Since Cyle's delivery, teams of labourers had been working on chopping the large logs into smaller chunks for the woodpile. Caivane and Eain had gone at the logs with a long saw at first, and today they would have been splitting the cut rounds with long-handled axes.

Tann had been working on a new boundary hedge, carefully cutting partway through the stalks of the thorny shrubs he had planted, before weaving them together. They would grow into a dense lattice of branches. The goats might munch the outer leaves and shoots, but even they would not be able to get through the thorny tangle that the hedge would become.

The shouts continued. Tann dropped his heavy work knife, and hurried toward the sound.

When he arrived breathlessly at the scene, Caivane was holding his axe before him defensively. Eain was backing away, with his own raised threateningly behind his shoulder. His eyes were wild. He radiated fear, and confusion.

'He took a great swing.' Caivane spoke quickly, eyes fixed on Eain's face. 'And his axe stuck in the log. Something just…changed in him. By the time he had pulled it free it was like he didn't know where he was.'

They watched Eain, who made no move to approach. His gaze flicked between the two men desperately.

'I thought he was going to brain me with that axe, boss,' finished Caivane.

'Eain.' Tann took a step forward, hands raised. 'Drop the axe, son. We are your friends. Please.'

Eain stared back. There was incomprehension in his eyes. His gaze flicked over Tann's face as if seeing it for the first time. Or, as if seeing something different to what was really there.

He dropped the axe. '*Nan aftir. Nan aftir! Eig hafa sorch.*' He backed away. '*Eig hafa sorch.*' He turned and fled, heading towards the western hillside.

Tann caught Caivane's eye. He had no answers to the questions they asked.

The next morning was worse.

'Master Tann, I think you need to come see this.' Murius scratched his beard worriedly as he appeared in the doorway of the bunkroom. He was still wearing the grubby underclothes he slept in.

When Tann entered the room, all the other beds were empty; their occupants long risen and gone to begin the labour of the day. Except one.

Eain's bed.

'He don't seem to want to get up,' said Murius. 'I'm not sure he can.'

Tann stepped closer. The tall foreigner was curled up on one side. His blanket had been kicked off and was puddled on the floor. His long legs were bent tightly, and his knees were drawn up to his chest. He shuddered and twitched. He did not appear to be sleeping.

'*Nan, nan,*' he muttered. '*Han bloaith. Han bloaith. Ba vy minn kehna.*' His hands were curled into claws, his fingers tense and gripping.

Tann chewed his lip. He had seen people this way before. It was so many years ago that he had almost forgotten, but there were some things that would never fade from his memory.

The terrible thrill of battle. The clash of weapons. The screams and wails of the hurt and dying. That had been his life, once.

He still had the occasional nightmare, but he had mostly shut the horrors of the past away. For some, they remained too vivid, too powerful. They relived them in their waking moments, and became shaking, haunted shadows.

Was that what was behind this young man's troubles? Is that the fate that awaited him? Tann's heart ached to think of it.

'Let me see him, please.'

Soft footfalls sounded behind Tann, and he turned to see Anndra entering the room. She looked tiny, almost childlike in a loose work smock. Her auburn hair hung loose to her shoulders.

'This is the men's bunk room—' Tann began, hesitantly.

'I know,' she replied. Her intense, dark eyes were fixed on Eain. 'But I can help him. Let me try, please.'

Tann paused. Then, he shrugged. Since her arrival, everyone seemed to have accepted Anndra's presence. He had not overheard anyone discussing her story, or questioning how she came to be there. It had certainly not crossed his own mind. Which, now he thought about it, seemed strange itself.

It probably did not matter, and there was certainly no harm in letting her try to help the lad. He stood aside.

'Of course,' he said. 'It must be worth trying. I'll close the door behind me.'

'Thank you, Carilton Tann,' she said.

As he left, she was already sitting down on the nearest bunk. She leaned forward and began to speak in a low voice. He could not hear the words. He closed the door.

They emerged an hour or so later. Many eyes studied them as Anndra led Eain into the main hall. Word had spread, and even though Tann had suggested they all went back to work, many had found a reason to remain sitting at the long table. Tann supposed that life at the farm was usually pretty quiet.

Eain sat, and Tann's mother pushed a steaming cup of tea before him. The herbal scent of camomile wafted around the room.

'Thanks you,' said Eain, slowly. He smiled weakly, but his face was pale, his eyes darkly lined. 'I...better now.' He glanced at Anndra as he spoke.

Tann wondered what the new woman had done or said in there, but it really was not his business. Perhaps it was nothing. Perhaps she had just kept him company until his fit subsided.

Eain sipped his tea. It soon became clear that he was not about to hit anyone or fall into another fit, so the gathered crowd gradually stood and went back to work.

Tann also had things to do, but felt he should watch the lad a while longer. In truth, he wanted to figure the puzzle out. He wanted to understand.

'Tann?' It was Eain. He had stood while Tann had been lost in his own thoughts. 'I can use…?' He paused while he thought of the word. He mimed cutting. 'For make hedge.'

'My knife?' guessed Tann.

'Yes!' Eain grinned gratefully. 'Knife. I make hedge more.'

They had worked together on the thorny hedges previously, and Eain had seemed to enjoy it. Tann unclipped the long, sheathed knife from his belt and handed it over. He made sure not to hesitate when he passed Eain the blade. There must be trust.

'Careful,' he said. 'Very sharp.'

'Yes,' said Eain, nodding. 'I careful.' He headed for the door and Tann noted, without surprise, that Anndra stood to follow.

'I'll come too,' she said, in her slightly toneless and unaccented voice. She hurried after him and they both went out through the front door.

Tann blew out a sigh and stood. There was more going on here than he understood. He walked through the door and leaned on the rail. Perhaps, he thought, as he watched the tall, rangy man and the small, slight woman walking away, side by side, it was actually very simple. Some people found a connection with another very quickly and unexpectedly.

'Look now, maybe that's what he needs.'

Caivane leaned on the rail beside Tann, his meaty hands gripping the beached wood. The supporting timbers groaned beneath his weight. 'We all need a bit of that sometimes, right?'

He turned to Tann with a suggestive grin, which died on his face when he remembered who he was talking to.

'Sorry, old friend,' he muttered, embarrassed. 'It must still be hard for you. Even now.'

'Forget it,' said Tann. 'I wish them well.'

Tann had been married, once. It was so long ago that sometimes it seemed like the life of someone else. A story he had been told and had half remembered.

Yet, Elsia Tann had been very real. At a time when he was alone she had been a blessing from the Five. She had arrived in his life like cool water on a raw burn.

And, just as quickly, she had been taken away forever.

Tann had been a soldier and then a general, fighting a war on foreign soil. His army had pushed the battle lines further into the Swarthland of Tayo, leaving their supply camps further and further behind.

A ruthless mercenary leader named Wolt Wose had led his band behind the lines to attack and destroy the camps.

Elsia Tann had been in one of those camps.

Wose's savage mercenaries had swept the camp's flimsy defences away. They killed everyone in the camp, but raped the women first.

In moments, Tann's life had been burned away.

He could not remember how he felt when the news had come to him and for that he was grateful. He remembered desiring death. He remembered trying to ride off immediately in pursuit of Wose, and he knew that he had been physically restrained.

He had found a jug of wine instead. Then another. Until all he could remember was the pain, and the rage. It seethed within him, and he hated himself for what he had done. The army had no more use for him and eventually he rode away, alone, and left his old life behind.

The next few years were a blur, but one day the news came to him that Wose had led his mercenaries away from the wars of Tayo and Buren, and into a life of banditry in the Lands of the Great River.

This had sobered Tann up like a bucket of cold water dousing his face. This was his chance for revenge. He spent months painstakingly tracking Wose down, before recruiting a band of trusted warriors to help him. Of course, he did not tell them his true reasons.

They defeated Wose's band of outlaws as they tried to storm a village near Kiraband. Tann himself had taken on Wose in single combat, and had emerged victorious. And he had felt…nothing. No valediction, no glory, no satisfaction of justice served. He did not even feel guilt at the death that his crusade had caused. He just felt empty.

So, he had thrown down his sword and shield, and walked away from that life without a backward glance. The hardship of life on this farm had soon engulfed him, distracting him from his memories. Like leaves on the breeze, they had drifted away.

He knew though, that there were still raw wounds deep inside. Caivane knew it too, and moved silently away, leaving Tann alone with his thoughts.

SEVENTEEN

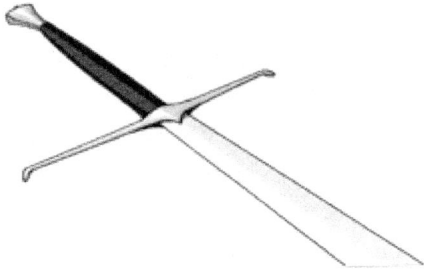

Eain's legs burned. He sucked at the air, and it seared a trail down to his empty lungs. Sweat streamed from his face, mixing with the freezing rain. His hands clawed at the mud, an inch from his nose.

It smelled of pine resin and damp. It smelled of pain. It smelled of failure.

A pair of immaculately clean boots appeared at the edge of his field of vision. There was not a speck of mud on them. Their cleanliness mocked him.

A hard, hook-nosed face was lowered next to his own.

'Problems, Connow?'

The unsympathetic, questioning tone somehow managed to imply that any and all problems rested with Eain, and that the owner of the voice had none. The boots turned and walked away, the heels receding rhythmically from his view.

Eain felt shame wash over him, colder than the rain. Shame, anger and burning hatred for those arrogant boots and their arrogant owner. The surge of emotions sent fire to his muscles. He pressed up with his arms and pushed forward with his legs.

It hurt. It hurt like his skin had been shredded and then washed in vinegar. It was good. In a handful of paces he was running again. After ten more he overtook the Claihedehme. His footsteps splattered on the muddy ground as he accelerated.

'Run, Eain!' jeered the Claihedehmore. 'Run faster, you lazy swine! Run, Eain!'

Now, his feet were slipping on a gravelly slope.

'Eain! Eain?' called a different voice. Jeering, questioning or encouraging; he could not tell. He looked around, puzzled. There was no forest, no mud and no other runners, just a sandy-coloured slope that rose before his face.

The shouting figure approached.

'Eain? Are you well?'

It was Carilton Tann. Of course, it was. There was concern in his pale eyes.

'Sort your life out, Eain Connow!' he barked. Except that Tann had gone again, replaced by Arall Rathvedd, his face contorted into a rictus of indignant fury. 'Pump your legs and run, you idle shite, or I'll be pumping my boot up your arse!'

Eain knew why Rathvedd was so angry. He had disobeyed an order. He had been told to lead them to Vekwicc. He had been told to keep them safe.

But he had led them into danger. And now they were all dead.

Their faces flashed before his eyes; Kater, Foinn and Edich. Poor, trusting Edich. He had put his faith in the wrong person and had died a pointless death.

Edich's brother Arin would ask what had happened, and Eain would have to admit that it was all his fault. He had watched Edich die, and he himself had escaped. He had run away. Like a coward. A worthless coward.

His knees buckled and he fell again. He expected his hands to sink into sucking mud or to grasp springy heather but instead his palms were prickled by sharp, gritty soil.

All Banahgar would hate him for what he had done, of course. That is why Rathvedd kept shouting at him.

'Eain? Eain?' Tann's voice was closer. He did not sound angry, but he must be. 'Linil, no! Don't touch him. Just leave him be. I think he's going through something. Help? No, I don't think we can right now. Not yet.'

Eain rolled onto his back. The sun was searingly bright, high in the pale sky. He closed his eyes, then opened them again. The sun remained where it had been. His fingers, curled and tense, raked into the soil and felt dry, bare earth. This was not Banahgar. He had left that country far behind.

Yet, the guilt would not leave him alone.

'Tann,' he said, keeping his voice steady. 'I am fine.' He was not. 'I slip on slope.' Another lie. He sat up. Tann lowered himself down to sit next to Eain. Linil waited nearby, arms crossed.

'We go work?' He looked to Tann, checking that his words made sense, and trying to read the other man's reaction to his fall.

'I reckon we sit down here for a moment or two, yet,' replied Tann, calmly. 'Ain't no hurry.'

Eain was grateful that Tann did not shame him further. He had already gathered that Carilton Tann was a man who was sensitive to the feelings and moods of those around him. He reminded Eain of the very best of his Claihed teachers, the ones who told hard truths gently, and pulled you up rather than knocked you down.

He was also grateful that Tann continued to speak slowly, using simple words. His understanding of the new tongue, that everyone here spoke to one another, was growing. Many of them talked too quickly for him to understand fully, however. He felt like a child and knew that was how they saw him too; one who knew little and had much to learn.

He pointed up at the sky. 'Cloud. Is cloud?'

'Correct, my friend,' confirmed Tann. 'That's a cloud. Don't see too many of those this time of year.'

Eain watched the wispy, insubstantial white shape as it was driven across the sky by a persistent westerly wind. Away in the distance, more clouds gathered as they approached the bulk of the eastern mountains.

In this land they called them the Wolfteeth, but he knew them as the Beinuirm Skele. The mountains that marked Banahgar's western border. The mountains on the edge of the world.

Except, that they were not. The world continued, the sharp, rocky peaks giving way to arid rolling hillsides and then onwards to this place. And there was no going back.

Even as he thought of his home country a tightness gripped his chest, a claw around his heart. He had betrayed everything that was important, and the perpetual presence of those dark ridges on the eastern horizon was a constant, inescapable reminder.

He dropped his head. His eyes saw nothing but the dun soil between his legs as he waited for the churning in his body to subside. Though several weeks had passed since his arrival, things were getting more difficult, not easier.

He had fallen easily into the rhythm of farm life once he had recovered from his lonely journey. Ma Tann inspected him daily and made sure he kept on drinking plenty of water. His body healed.

He rose early, laboured all day, and ate well. Some nights he slept without nightmares. Many more, he knew, he cried out in his sleep or woke screaming. Questions circled endlessly like the dark soaring birds that glided tirelessly over this dry land.

How had he been the only one to survive?

Had he been wrong or right to investigate the village?

Should he try to return? Would he ever be forgiven?

Would it have been better if he had been killed along with the others?

No answers, only questions. He could find no peace from their nagging.

As the Kotevari ranks had closed in, his eyes had gone dark. His sight was dimmed as if a heavy cloud had passed over the noonday sun, and despair gripped him. Panic, horror and needling guilt.

When he had raised his head again, he was surprised that he still lived.

The Kotevari spearmen had backed away, although their weapons remained levelled at his chest. The cavalry had formed a wider circle behind, hemming him in against the looming quarry wall. There was no escape.

Two mounted figures pushed through the ranks of knights, their eyes fixed on him. One was the richly dressed man with shining, damp-looking hair. His sword was still sheathed, and he glared down from his horse with an imperious expression.

The other was the noblewoman, her hair an unnatural red. It was as vivid in colour as the brush of a fox or the fur of a squirrel. She drew a short, thin-bladed sword from her waist, and pointed it in his direction.

'*Meer-eh at-eh!*' she cried, in a commanding tone. Eain could not tell what her order meant, but the army immediately took a forward step.

An entire army against one man. He felt a sudden fury. What cowards they were! He would not let soldiers so weak take him. In a moment, he had summoned his resolve and was ready to act.

He planted the tip of his greatsword in the stony ground. It found purchase after sliding a few inches into the surface. Leaning the long sword back toward the quarry wall, he shoved the thumb-thick, forged quillons on one side of the hilt into a deep crack. Pushing hard, he felt it jam.

He would have one chance at this. One slip, and he would be captured or dead in moments.

With one hand on the rounded pommel, and the other on the hilt, he jumped. Teeth clenched, arms tense, whole body pushing upwards, he got his foot up onto the hilt.

Quickly, before the sword slipped away, he stood. He prayed fervently to the Brothers as his fingers inched up the blank quarry wall.

Please! He thought. *Let there be something.*

Then, his fingertips curled over a square-cut edge. He gripped with all his strength, and pulled hard. He found small, flaky edges which he used for his toes, walking his feet up closer to his hands.

He lunged upward again. This time, he was high enough to face an unpleasant fall to the ground as well as the enemy below, but once again his hand found a good hold.

Above, a wider crack opened up, leading toward the top of the wall. The width of a fist, Eain immediately knew that it was his best chance of escape. A route to freedom.

Banahgar was dotted with disused quarries as well as natural crags and escarpments of dark, rough rock. Climbing them, racing up them, challenging each other to feats of increasing daring and strength were common pastimes for Claihed soldiers in training.

Eain was more than a competent climber, and he knew just how to climb this sort of crack. Hand in, clench a fist with a thumb tucked into the palm, then pull up higher once your hand was securely jammed. Feet followed, turned sideways to ram the toe of each boot into the same crack.

He raced to the top of the sheer wall like a squirrel up a tree.

Shouts of fury and anguish rang out from below as he reached the top and pulled over onto level ground. Looking back down, he saw the cavalry scattering and riding furiously away, looking for ways to skirt around the edges of the quarry and give chase.

There would be no easy escape.

He exhaled and got to his feet. Even at that point, he had not despaired. Even with all the blood and the death, he still moved with purpose. The need to warn the rest of the Claihed had driven him on.

Yet, he had failed at that, too.

'Are you ready, big man?' asked Tann, moving to stand closer. Stooping, Eain gripped the handles of the barrow and continued pushing it up the hill. A short time later his back was bent and sweat dripped freely from his brow as he plunged his shovel into the hard ground.

Maintaining the irrigation to the farm needed constant labour. In this dry land, channelling what little water ran across the ground to flow down to the fields below would ensure that there was enough food for everyone, for this season and beyond.

Tann had hopefully cast around for volunteers to help recut the existing channels and to dig new ones, and had been visibly surprised when Eain had quickly raised his hand. The other, more experienced farmhands had been clearly reluctant.

Eain knew that the labour would be a distraction. A distraction from the incessant questions, and the harrowing memories that would not leave him be.

They had walked up the slope behind the farm, Eain pushing a barrow laden with digging tools. They struck out for the rocky shelves of the high plateau, where water constantly trickled down the slabs from the lake beyond.

With a pit dug in the right place it could be collected. With a carefully placed trench it could be channelled to run toward the edge of the plateau. Tann had created a network of these small trenches, which fed a wider ditch that began at the crest of the slope. As the months passed they silted up, and had to be laboriously dug again, or irrigation would be lost.

Eain bent over, scraping the wide blade of his mattock along the narrow channel. He pushed the damp soil down the slope and watched as the cloudy water trickled along behind. It was satisfying.

The sun climbed, the air grew warmer, and sweat ran off him as he worked. Ma Tann had adjusted the largest spare work smock she could find to fit him. What little breeze there was tugged at the loose fabric, but cooled his skin beneath.

He silenced his thoughts with focus on the work in hand, barely aware of the passing of time.

'Eain.' Tann's voice intruded abruptly into his dreamlike state, an unknown time later. 'Time to go.'

He glanced up. The sun was at its zenith, pounding down with a dry heat that felt like a physical presence. They had made a habit of resting and eating during the warmest part of the day; the few hours that followed noon.

'Yes,' said Eain, simply.

He loaded his tools, the mattock and shovel, back onto the barrow and followed Tann and Linil down the slope. There was a burn of fatigue in his shoulders. He enjoyed the familiar sensation. It was a good pain.

The thin, stretched-wool clouds were still flying high across the pale sky. Eain followed their path with his eyes, squinting against the bright noon light. The wind cast the wispy clouds against the dark bulk of the eastern mountains, where they thickened and turned the sky from pale blue to stern grey.

He had been told that those mountains were impassable for his whole life. That they were edged with blade-like rocks, their flanks sheer as a sword. The tales were known by all.

Except...he had crossed them.

Desperate and alone, and almost delirious with guilt and grief, he had happened on a pass through those mountains. And he had left Banahgar.

The same feelings welled up once more with the memory and he staggered, almost falling. He caught his balance and kept walking, not wanting the others to worry, or to question him. He screwed his eyes shut tightly as the painful memories overwhelmed him.

He ran. He ran with increasing desperation as the pursuit went on.

His joy at reaching the lip of the quarry had been short lived. Dense woodland grew here, thin birches that clustered tightly together. Ferns and briar spread between the slender trunks, carpeting the shady forest floor with green.

He could hear the shouted commands of the Kotevari nobles from the quarry floor. The rustling and crashing sounds of vegetation being crushed and broken came from everywhere else. They were coming for him, and they were approaching from every direction.

He had no choice but to run. The leaves and brambles of the undergrowth slowed his progress, tearing at his clothes and creating a racket as he forced his way through. He left a trail of broken branches and crushed plants in his wake that a blind man could have followed.

Onward was the only option. He struck out in a westerly direction, following a low, indistinct ridge that must be south of the village. He wanted to head north, but whenever he tried to turn in that direction his path was blocked by thick, thorny undergrowth that overhung steep, rocky escarpments.

The chase was not far behind.

The army of Kotev must be to the south. He could not escape that way, not without risking being caught almost immediately. Evading capture was his only aim, for now. Keep running, move faster than the pursuers could, then find a way to get back to Vekwicc or Osturbrost. Or maybe Sudvirke, where he could be closer to the action.

His blood cooled the longer he ran, though, and the thrill of his escape was replaced by memories of the horror that had preceded it.

As he ran, he saw Edich slain once more, the spearhead gleaming coldly as it burst bloodily from his chest. The image of Kater falling flashed before his eyes again and again, haunting him, dogging his steps. They were all gone. They would go no further within the Claihed, because they would never again draw breath.

Because of him. His decisions. He had led them into that trap where the only escape was death. He had led them away from the marching route that would have taken them to the safety of Vekwicc. All that blood and loss of life was his fault.

The landscape funnelled him on, ever westward. A high, rocky scarp rose steeply on his right, to the north. The light was beginning to fade as the afternoon wore on, but even so, if he broke from the cover of the woods and attempted to gain the ridge, he would be visible from miles around.

He was alone, and tired. His legs burned, his stomach was empty and he was already carefully eking out what little remained in his waterskin. His pursuers were many, and although he could not see them he had to assume that they would keep up the chase.

He slowed, walking a few steps as a brief rest. A sharp noise came from somewhere behind. A branch breaking? He broke into a laboured run once more.

As his breath came in gasps he tried to imagine reaching the safety of one of the fortresses. He would be able to stop running. But, what would he say? What could he say? That he had led a host of young soldiers to their death? That there was an unknown enemy army on the doorstep, and he had probably led them to the gates?

Shame engulfed him as he thought of it. Had anyone ever failed the Claihed so utterly? An answer came to him, unwanted and unwelcome. A name.

Cerle Connow.

Tears of frustration and despair sprung into his eyes, and he staggered. Pushing himself upright off the trunk of a sturdy oak, he managed to continue running. His knees sent stabs of pain up his legs, but he ignored them.

If he returned like this, he knew that the inevitable comparison to his traitorous, cowardly grandfather would be made for ever more. He would never be free of his shadow.

What else could he do? Go back to Keldfirth, and tell his parents that they needed to hide a deserter?

Keep running, said a quiet, sly voice in his mind. *Keep running and you will never have to face these questions. Your grandfather did it, you can do it too.*

Eain's lip curled as he suppressed a sob. He felt as though he was backed into the box quarry once more, with nowhere to go. Maybe it would have been better if he had died there, too.

There would be no welcome for him now, anywhere in Banahgar. Only judgement and condemnation.

The ground was rising steadily. A long, wooded valley had channelled him directly west. He had stopped thinking about his route, or his destination. He had only enough energy to continue straight ahead.

It was dusky amid the trees, with shards of cold, grey light stabbing down here and there illuminating patches of the forest floor. He saw a growing brightness ahead. As he approached, he realised what it was. He had climbed so high that he was at the treeline.

Bare, grassy slopes rose before him as he paused between the last, stunted trunks. The surrounding hills were high, steeply sided and crowned with rugged outcrops. Ahead, though, a low pass led onward and beyond.

He decided that he needed to risk breaking from the cover of the trees. He was sure that he could still hear the occasional raised voice or breaking twig, but now they were dim and indistinct. Distant.

He took a quick sip of water and ran toward the pass. The grass was soft and soothing beneath his bruised feet. The air around him cooled with the gain in height, and as the evening drew in. He was deep in the western ranges of the Dall. He was totally alone.

Despite the forlorn sense of isolation, he felt that this was where he belonged. He could do no harm, here.

He had fought though, had he not? He had tried. And yet, now that he remembered the battle, he felt only disgust at the spilling of blood and the waste of life. He felt shame at his part in it.

He had been brought up on stories of the Brothers and their ferocious skill in combat, their glorious bravery. He had felt no glory as his sword cleaved flesh and bone. It made him feel sick to his stomach, even to recall the sensation.

He was no true warrior. No soldier. He was a feeble, soft-hearted coward.

'You'll never be hard enough. You'll never be strong enough.'

Morgan Blane had said those words to him, glaring down on him as Eain recovered from attempting an impossible sword technique. Eain had been gasping with exertion and frustration. Blane had been impassive. 'You will hesitate in the moments when you need to act without mercy. You will fail.'

Blane had been right.

His breath came in anguished gasps of exertion as he reached the pass. A long, narrow ridge stretched away to his left and an imposing, rocky hill rose to his right. But, that was not what caught his attention.

Spread before him, filling his entire field of vision from right to left, north to south, was the Beinuirm Skele.

The sun was just about to set behind one of the highest peaks and so the whole range was cast as a dark, forbidding silhouette. A black, jagged mass, the tips of the summits seemed to stretch up to scrape the very clouds.

He was drawn. In these peaks, he could escape. The Kotevari would not find him, and neither would the Claihed with their questions, their condemnation.

He would seek out a dark cave, and while he hid there he might also escape the burning guilt and shame that he felt like a lit torch against his skin. Maybe the blood and the screams in his memory would subside, and he would find peace.

Peace in life or death, at that moment he did not care which.

Yet, he had survived, and had found himself in this place, Tann's place. He pushed the uncomfortable memories away and concentrated on the rough path before him. The heat was rising, and lunch was calling. His stomach growled.

His past was a different room now, and he had to shut the door and lock it behind him. Memories could be forgotten. Pain could be ignored.

'It's only pain boys! Won't hurt when it's gone!' The voice of Rathvedd came back to him once more. It had been his catchphrase when his charges were labouring over a tough training session.

Eain shivered. He stopped and closed his eyes, steadying himself.

'Are you well, Eain?'

Eain turned, and for a moment he saw Rathvedd again, reaching out from the past. He flinched. Tann stepped back as he saw Eain's alarm. Of course, it was just Tann.

'Yes,' Eain replied, letting out a deep breath. He patted his stomach. 'Hungry.'

Tann nodded, and they made their way back down to the house.

Ma Tann described lunch as a "mess of beans". A heavy cauldron simmered on the hearth, full of thick, lumpy soup. Various vegetables from the garden were chopped and stirred in with the beans, along with an array of herbs that Eain could not name.

The workers queued up to ladle a spoonful into clay bowls, before finding somewhere to sit and eat. By the time Eain had arrived many had already eaten and gone. Murius was just shuffling off to the bunk room for a rest, but Caivane, Linil and Sarm were sitting on the benches at the long table.

'Hail, hail!' exclaimed Caivane, welcoming them warmly with outstretched arms. 'Good morning, Master Tann?'

Tann was filling his own bowl. 'Sure,' he replied as he sat down. 'Eain and Linil put in some hard work up there.'

Eain knew that they were both speaking loudly and slowly to help him understand. Caivane had limitless patience in teaching him new words and helping him with the language. His comprehension was growing but he still had much to learn.

Sarm cut in with a question, his speech rapid, and Eain could not follow. He picked out the word for "irrigation" in Sarm's quick patter of words.

He lowered his head to his food and ceased paying attention. The beans were full of flavour and very filling. He ate with enthusiasm.

His bowl was empty when he heard someone say his name. He raised his head to see Sarm looking straight at him. Talking about him. Eain concentrated, trying to understand the words.

'Maybe we should try to find out where he came from,' he was saying. 'We should all know the truth.' There was a belligerent tone to his voice. Ever since their first confrontation, the man from Tayo had been openly hostile toward Eain.

It had not taken the form of physical aggression. They had got a good measure of each other during that first tangle, and Eain was pretty sure that Sarm had sensed then that he was outmatched. Eain was a hand's width taller and much broader. Sarm was no fool. He did not need to throw fists when he could throw words more easily. Eain had got the idea that Sarm had been quietly spreading his dislike, his mistrust.

Now, he was voicing it openly.

Tann's hand was raised warningly. Caivane leaned forward, anger creasing his broad face.

'Your mouth does too much hard work, boy,' he hissed. 'You know we don't ask those questions here!'

Tann turned to Sarm, his words growled low and fast, in an undertone that Eain could not understand. Sarm shook his head, chuckling.

'We know something of everyone else, right?' Now Sarm spoke more slowly, words he intended Eain to hear and comprehend. 'We know that Tann was a soldier in Buren.

Caivane was a' – the big man shot him a warning glare, 'a *trader* in Anish. Linil, we at least know she's from the Alrean Empire. And you all know everything about me. But him? Still secrets and mystery.'

'He does not yet have the words in the Common Speech.' Eain turned in surprise. Anndra had appeared and was standing behind him, protectively.

The slender woman from Kiraband had been a comforting presence these last weeks. They just seemed to keep bumping into one another around the farmstead. Eain could not have said what they had talked about, but he felt like he had learned a lot of the language from her so far.

She had certainly told him a lot about Kiraband, the bustling frontier region between the wild expanse of the Lands of the Great River and the civilisation of the southern countries. There could be opportunities there. Away from the shadow of the Beinuirm Skele. The shadow of his past.

Sarm scoffed. 'He knows enough. Enough to tell us something, if he wanted to.' He leaned closer to Eain. 'Tell us, big man. Tell us where you came from. Tell us what you did.'

Eain opened his mouth. He thought of Banahgar. He thought of Edich, Kater, Foinn and the others. The memory of the screams of the dying and the smell of fresh blood overwhelmed him once more. He could not bring himself to speak.

'See?' Sarm leaned back, triumphant. 'He could say, but doesn't want to. I think he's done something bad. Something he's ashamed of.'

'Sarm, stop this!' Tann's voice had a warning tone.

'The truth should out, Master Tann,' said Sarm. 'What if there are hunters looking for him? We can all see that he was a soldier. What if he's a deserter? A traitor?'

They were unfamiliar words, but Eain knew what Sarm must mean. The rest of the room faded away into insignificance as his eyes locked onto Sarm's face. That angular, dark-skinned face framed by the long hair pulled rakishly to one side. That face, with its slight, knowing smile.

Sarm said one more word. 'Coward.'

Eain stood. He stepped up onto the bench, then across the table as he launched himself at Sarm. Something wordless and primal drove him. He was suddenly possessed with an animal fury.

He heard Anndra cry, 'No, Eain!', but it was too late. His weight knocked Sarm backward off the bench. The pair crashed onto the floor, Sarm's back thumping hard onto the rough timber planks.

He was not smiling now.

Eain raised himself, sitting astride the smaller man. He lifted a fist. He heard the word "coward" echoing around his mind. He threw a punch.

Pain shot through his knuckles as Sarm's head snapped back. Fury still coursed through Eain's body. He could not suppress the desire to lash out. The need to hurt.

He threw another punch. It was painful. The skin over Sarm's cheekbone split and blood welled. Eain hit him once more. Sarm groaned. More blood spread across his face. That smiling face.

Then, strong hands were gripping him. He tried to twist away, to lash out at them, but they had grasped his wrists. They held him firmly.

He felt himself being lifted, dragged and guided to the door. Then, he was thrust out onto the veranda. He turned to see Tann and Caivane staring at him as they stood before the doorway.

Their eyes were wide with shock and condemnation. Silently they judged him, and they shamed him.

He looked down. Blood was smeared across his knuckles. So red. Red blood, blue sky. Once more, all that he had brought was pain.

He collapsed to his knees. He had to go.

EIGHTEEN

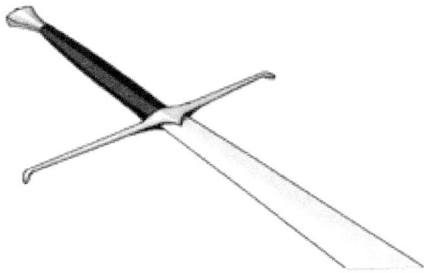

The coming of the wagon trains spoke of the change of the seasons. Like the turning of a wheel, the year circled around and the evenings began to draw in.

Eain had a feeling that the arrival of the wagons would bring change for him too, although he had yet to put his finger on exactly why.

The last few weeks had been hard work. All hands had been needed, spending most of daylight hours away from the farmhouse. Time was spent harvesting the ripe crops in the fields, or roaming the surrounding landscape to forage and hunt.

Stores were gathered, prepared and divided. Where they had surplus it was sealed in barrels or boxes for trading. Meat was cured and salted. Grain was siloed beneath the dry ground. With the labour of all, they made ready for winter.

'Just stay away from him,' Anndra had said, coming back to Eain where he sat on an ochre-coloured rock.

Tears had welled in his eyes after the fight with Sarm. As he stood on the veranda before the disapproving stares of Tann and Caivane, his hands had begun to shake. Like so many others, they had put their trust in him and he had let them down.

He fled. He turned, and strode away up the path, climbing the steep slopes once more to try to find some space, some air.

He found a flattish rock and sat. There was the slightest breeze up here and it was cooling, reviving. He tried to be calm. His heart fluttered and his fingers still trembled.

He stared out westwards. Featureless dun plains stretched away to vanish into the hazy distance. He was suddenly struck by the alienness of his new surroundings. He was so accustomed to dark mountains and green hills that he still expected to see them when he rose each morning.

These colourless, scrubby hills and wide, flat expanses barely seemed real. He felt very small in this new world.

The horizon to the east was more familiar. Too familiar. He could not manage to look in their direction without feeling that same stab of guilt and shame. It was almost too much to bear. Maybe he needed to be somewhere he could not see those dark mountains?

When he turned his head away from the distant peaks, Anndra was approaching. She had managed to walk within a handful of paces without Eain noticing. It was puzzling how she managed it.

'You must not blame yourself,' she said, sitting down beside him. He moved along slightly, to make room on the rock for her slim frame. She sat close, but did not touch him at all.

'How can I not?' he replied. 'My temper caused it. My fists drew his blood.'

'He sought it, whether he knew it or not. He sees you in pain, sees you suffering, and deliberately provokes you.'

'I didn't need to hit him,' muttered Eain, bitterly. His mouth twisted into a frown. Once more, he felt close to tears.

'And that you did causes you more pain. You care, because you are a better man than you know. Do not despair of yourself, Eain Connow.'

He could think of nothing to say in reply. He did not understand why she was so kind to him. Why she cared. Fleetingly, he wondered why he found it so much easier to talk to her than to anyone else. With Anndra, it felt like they spoke the same language.

'What will you do?' she asked, after a long silence.

Eain sighed. 'I suppose I should go back down soon.' He put his hands on his knees.

'I mean in the future. Do you think it is a good idea to stay here?'

Eain felt uncomfortable. He felt bad enough about his own thoughts of flight. Her words made it seem as though they were clear for her to see. He did not answer.

'If there is pain in your past that endures in your present, you must look to the future.' He shook his head. What was she trying to say?

'If you cannot go back, nor remain where you are,' she explained, patiently, 'then your course must be onward.'

She reached out and laid her tiny, delicate hand on his arm. It felt light as a butterfly, cool as fresh snow. 'Onward,' she repeated.

Together, their eyes turned westward. The rough wagon track was suddenly a vivid line across the arid plain. Where would it lead him, were he to follow it? Was it good enough that it would take him away from this place?

He stood, and Anndra walked next to him in silence as they made their way back down to the farmhouse.

The wagons began rolling in a few weeks later. The temperature had already begun to drop across the Lands of the Great River. Those traders that came from the north wore fur hats and jackets with fleecy collars.

The occupants of the farm worked in long-sleeved smocks as they unloaded supplies from the wagons and lifted their own barrels and crates on in their place.

'Oh, ho!' exclaimed Caivane, shading his eyes and gazing out up the track. 'What's this now, boys? Who's a-coming?'

Before a trailing cloud of dust came a flat-bedded wagon, drawn by a single shaggy ox. Two short, stocky figures rode on the seat of the cart. A group gathered to watch their approach.

The wagon drew up beside the farmhouse, and Eain was surprised to see that it was not just the distance that had made the figures riding it appear small. They were both less than five feet in height, the top of their heads not reaching Eain's chest. They looked similar to each other, with fair hair, ruddy skin and pale eyes.

'Dwarves, lad!' whispered Caivane as they moved toward the wagon. 'Watch what you say.' Eain shrugged. He just would not say anything.

The pair of dwarves were a man and a woman. Both wore loose shirts with baggy sleeves, and both were clad in pleated skirts that hung down to their knees. Eain had never seen anything like them. He had heard of the wild dwarven tribes that attacked Banahgar's north, but they were described as feral, and savage. This pair were nothing like that.

'Hail, hail! Greetings to the master of the house!' barked the male dwarf, standing to attention beside his wagon. 'We come with goods from our steading. May we trouble your hospitality while you consider our offer?'

Tann had already appeared from the house, and after hurrying over he lowered his head toward the dwarf. 'Hail, my friend from afar. Greetings returned to you. My house is yours while I consider your offer.'

To Eain, this had the feeling of a formal, traditional greeting. They were both speaking clearly and loudly, so he had little difficulty understanding.

'I was born with Kalua waxing fat and Jura young,' continued Tann, 'and my name is Carilton Tann. This I share freely and without obligation.'

'My moons were Kalua full and Jura waning half,' replied the dwarf, then more warmly; 'My name is Wochenjera Chitsiru, and you have already met my wife, Okondeka Chitsiru.'

'Of course, of course!' Tann strode forward to clasp the dwarves' hands in firm handshakes, one after another. 'It is good to see you once more, my friend Jera.'

'And it is very good to finally arrive, Master Tann. Our journey here has been long, and over-warm!'

'In that case, let's not linger out here! Come within, and we will pour a cool drink. Deka, please follow me. I trust you are well?'

'The Five remain generous, Master Tann,' replied Okondeka as she headed for the house.

'Caivane?' said Tann, an aside as he passed. 'You know what to do.'

'Come on, Eain-boy,' he said. 'Let's get this stuff shifted.'

Together they unloaded a couple of barrels from the wagon, along with a roll of cloth wrapped in canvas and a few heavy jute sacks.

'Oats,' replied Caivane, in reply to Eain's question. 'Master Tann likes the way the dwarves dry and roll oats. And that's a bolt of spun wool. Useful.'

'What about the barrels?' asked Eain.

'Dwarven mead,' replied Caivane, with a broad grin. 'The good stuff. Hopefully, we'll get a little taste later tonight.'

It was supper time when all the supplies had either been loaded onto other wagons and driven away or stored around the farmhouse. Only the dwarf wagon remained. It appeared as though Wochenjera and Okondeka Chitsiru were staying the night.

They ate roast goat, and roots mashed generously with butter. Nearly all the farm hands had gathered in the hall, so some had to eat standing up. It felt like a feast.

Then, after eating and drinking, Okondeka leaned back in her chair and began to sing. With her feet on the table, she sang in a breathy, sonorous tone.

Eain's stomach lurched. It reminded him instantly of the breath-singing of the Banahgarian Sjonacaidh. The bards and musicians of his own country. He was transported. The words that the dwarf intoned in her rich, melodious voice meant nothing, but to Eain they spoke of a depth of history in the same vein as the Banahgarian sagas.

The simple melody painted a picture of sadness and loss. The feeling of grief was clear, even in an alien language. Eain struggled to hold back tears.

There was silence when the song was over. A few of the audience nodded knowingly.

'What is that song about?' Eain blurted out the question before he could stop himself. Caivane had told him to stay quiet, but he just had to know.

Wochenjera fixed him with a flinty glare. 'You know the story of the King Set in Stone, do you not?'

'Eain is from…a far land,' Tann interjected, apologetically.

'I'm sorry,' muttered Eain.

'It's a fine tale though, boys,' said Caivane.

'It be. Some say it is more than a tale.' Wochenjera's voice was enigmatic.

'Will you tell it?' asked Caivane. 'Please? For Eain.'

Okondeka smiled slightly. 'Perhaps if my cup were filled with mead once more, my voice could find the strength to tell that tale.'

Tann grinned, jumping up to fetch the jug. He poured a generous measure of the dark, bittersweet spirit into the clay cup before her.

'An honourable man,' she said, inclining her head graciously. She took a deep draught and settled herself more comfortably in her seat.

'So,' she began, her voice rising in volume dramatically. 'The tale begins many years and many miles from this place.

'King Wadyera ruled over the great kingdom of Dziko Zatsoparo from his city and palace of Mzinda Bisani. He was sundered from his queen, Wanzeru. She was wilful and proud and disapproved of his ambition. She left Mzinda Bisani with her own warriors and journeyed north. She did not return.

'One day, a wandering merchant, a human, arrived at the palace gates. She was a stranger in the city. She came from none knew where and her wares were rare and mysterious. She was neither young, nor old.

'They were granted an audience with the king, and spoke to him thus:

'"*Wise King Wadyera, I would win your favour and make a trading alliance with the glorious city of Mzinda Bisani. As a token of my good faith, I would gift you one of these four sacred items.*"

'She opened the ornate, elegant case that she carried, and within were four ancient heirlooms that flowed with secret power. King Wadyera's eyes widened as he beheld them.

'First there was a metal bowl, carved with angular patterns and mystic symbols. Next, was a pair of curved daggers, crafted from black glass, with jewelled hilts and wickedly sharp points. Third, was a necklace of cunningly linked plates, which shimmered and gleamed as it moved. Last of all was a wooden flute, thick as a man's arm. It made a haunting, breathy tone when carefully blown.

'*"Choose your favourite of these treasures, o-king!"* cried the merchant. "*And I will give it freely to show my respect for your power and wisdom."*

'Yet Wadyera was proud, and captivated by the beauty and the mystery of the artefacts. He desired them all, and could not abide the thought of any of the rulers of neighbouring kingdoms possessing them.

'So, he took the case away from the merchant and sent them hence. He felt it was his right, as the king of Dziko Zatsopano. It was befitting to his authority. The merchant walked away from Mzinda Bisani without a word, but there was a knowing smile on her face.

'For a time after this, all was well. Possession of the four items brought King Wadyera great fame and many travelled to Mzinda Bisani to see them. The glory of the kingdom of Dziko Zatsopano increased. Until, that is, the next night when the moons were full. The milky light of cartwheel moons shone down from an indigo sky alive with twinkling stars, while Wadyera slumbered uneasily in his grand bed, alone.

'Something disturbed his dreams. Some foreboding of coming danger, of hidden threat. And then, the whole mighty palace shook, rocked from its very foundations. Rumbling crashes filled the night air, followed soon after by screams of pain and terror. He woke.

'Wadyera dashed to his balcony and looked down. A hole gaped in the lower walls of his beautiful palace, and from the lowest basements four shapes emerged. They were creatures, beasts of mystical horror. The King realised immediately that they had come from the four magical artefacts. They had been brought to him as a trap by the devious merchant.

'The first, and greatest was the huge *torenko*. The metal bowl had become its colossal, domed shell. Beneath this armour carapace, the creature crawled on four legs as thick as mighty forest trees, and its scaly head bore a mouth filled with teeth like the points of spears.

'Smaller, but faster and more deadly was the *mphaka-langando* – the powerful and agile bear-cat. Two great fangs curled from its ravening jaw, alike to the curved obsidian daggers. It sank those long teeth into any it could catch, and it caught many that night.

'Scaled and shining like the linked necklace, a two-headed snake slithered along the streets of Mzinda Bisani. They named it *njoka-ziwiri*, and it had fangs to bite as well as a great, twisting body that could squeeze the life from a dwarf with ease.

'Last to emerge into the lamplight of the terrified city was the sinuous *nyamai-yait*, the armoured weasel. It was a long, lithe creature with astonishing speed. Armour plates ran all along its back, overlapping and impossible to pierce. The armour resembled the wood of the flute, from which the *nyamai-yait* had transformed.

'They were huge. They were ferocious. They rampaged through the city through that long night, killing and destroying without pause or mercy. Many died, or fled the gates, before the king could raise his mighty army. They formed ranks, shoulders set together, and drove the four creatures from the ruined city.

'But, that was just the beginning of the troubles of King Wadyera and Dziko Zatsopano. For the monsters ranged widely across the kingdom, wrecking homes, destroying fields and farms, and everywhere killing, killing, killing. Within weeks, the kingdom was decimated beyond repair. King Wadyera was desperate.

"*'What can I do?*" he wailed to his generals. "*We cannot defeat these creatures and we cannot endure their rampage. I would take aid from any quarter. I would pay any price to be rid of them.*"

'The very next day, the merchant appeared once more. They stood proudly at the ruined gates of Mzinda Bisani and Wadyera knew that he had no choice but to treat with them. He went down to her.

"'*You are ready to make better decisions?*" she asked of the King.

"*Yes,*" he sighed.

"'*You are ready to act with honour?*"

"'*Yes. Yes!*"

"'*You are ready to be humble in light of your greed?*"

"'*Please, just help. I will do anything,*" pleaded Wadyera.

"'*Very well. The bargain is struck. The price will be paid.*"

'And then she cast off her cloak, and revealed her true form. The King gaped, for before him stood one of the Others, as if conjured from myth and legend. Her bones were delicate and her skin was translucent. She had very wide eyes that seemed to see all. There was an unknowable power about her.'

Eain frowned. He did not understand this word, "Others". He gingerly raised his hand, and immediately felt all eyes on him.

'What is it?' he asked, trying to put the words in the right order. 'Who are these "Others"?'

'A fairy story,' responded Sarm, with a quick grin.

'You must have heard of the Others?' asked Wochenjera in his deep, gruff voice. 'The hidden kin? The shining folk?' Eain shook his head.

'Story goes,' said Tann. 'Long, long ago, before the elves came here from across the sea, and before the dwarves emerged from the roots of the northern mountains. Before any of the new races, there was a people who lived all across these lands. They could work magic and speak with the animals. They built much with their powers, and it was thanks to them that the lands were made safe, first for the dwarves and elves, and then much later for humans.'

'But the dwarves were first,' cut in Wochenjera.

'Quite so, Jera.' Tann smiled at the dwarf. 'The Others slowly dwindled as time went by, and lost most of their power during the Diminishing.'

'Which is another children's tale,' added Sarm with a snort.

'Some say so,' conceded Tann. 'Some others say it really happened and it's why we don't see any magic these days. Some also say that the Others still linger in quiet places and wild woods, and that they touch our affairs with subtlety when the need is great. Who knows the truth?'

Sarm rolled his eyes. Eain blinked. He had never heard any of this before. The stories he knew from childhood were all histories of Banahgar. Of course, they were true. Yet, there was disagreement in these lands about whether their own tales were true or not. It was confusing, but he wanted to hear how the tale ended. He wondered if the greedy King would be punished, and if he would learn a lesson.

'Deka, please.' Tann turned to the dwarf woman. 'Please, finish your fine tale.'

'Thank you, Master Tann,' she said, graciously. 'I think I will. When King Wadyera saw one of the Others before him, he knew that he had fallen into a trap. And also, he realised that he had entered into a bargain for which he did not know the terms. But, it was too late!

'For, at that moment, the Other gathered her hidden power. The very air rippled and swirled. Ribbons of coruscating blue energy shot away from her body in four different directions. The throne room was lit by that eerie light as the moment stretched out, and then suddenly, it stopped.

'"*It is done,*" she said. "*I have placed the beasts under control once more. A temple has risen to each, spread at each corner of this wide desert.*

The keys are hidden so that none who do not have the proper knowledge can ever free them again. Your lands are safe."

'"*But, my lands are ravaged,*" said Wadyera, voice full of bitter despair and regret.

'"*Restoration of your lands was not part of the bargain."*

'"*Dealing with the Others is a quick way to find your hoard emptied,*" quoted Wadyera sadly.

'She smiled. "*And now,*" she said. "*I will take payment."*

'She raised her slender arms and the power flowed, but this time the waves glowed orange. King Wadyera staggered back, and sat heavily on his ornate throne. As the spell intensified, the very air vibrated, and the whole palace shook.

'Wadyera tried to raise his hands to shield his eyes, but could not move. He tried to turn his head away but found it locked in place. He felt stiff, as though frozen. He knew only terror.

'When it was over, Wadyera was turned to stone. Locked into his throne. His whole mighty army, thousands strong, along with everyone else that remained in Mzinda Bisani were now no more than statues. The Other shrugged their cloak back onto their narrow shoulders and left that place, never looking back.

'Behind her, she left only silence. A whole city, eternally frozen in place like carved rock. As the years passed, the desert was blown over that place and buried the walls, the homes, the once-were-dwarves. Mzinda Bisani vanished beneath the plains and the hidden city became a myth itself.

'Dwarves still speak of it with regret, and hope. It is a symbol to the dwarves of the danger of greed. It is a reminder of the price to be paid when we meddle with mystical forces. It is a dream for some, that one day it may be found, and be restored to its glory as the centre of a new and independent dwarf kingdom.'

Her tale was finished. She bowed her head as the audience hammered on the table and the walls with the heels of their hands, showing their approval.

Eain joined in. He had understood nearly all the story and had been captivated. He could not stop thinking about the idea of a magical race with enigmatic morality and supernatural powers. He had never heard anything like it.

He looked to Anndra, a broad smile on his face, but she looked perturbed and uneasy. With a small frown, she stood and left the room.

NINETEEN

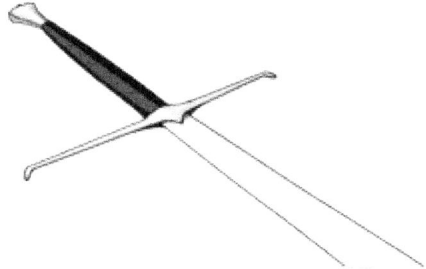

Wochenjera and Okondeka rolled away in their wagon the following morning.

Anndra's face was blank as she and Eain looked on, the dust cloud raised by the wheels hanging like low cloud in the still morning air. She still seemed pensive and tense. Her fingertips were pressed tightly together at her waist.

Eain wondered where the dwarves were headed. What would they see on their journey across this bleak land? How would it feel for those dark eastern mountains to recede into the distance, and for there to be new ground on every horizon?

'They would not take you where you wanted to go,' said Anndra. Once again, it felt as though she could see his thoughts.

'I like it here,' said Eain, truthfully.

Anndra smiled. 'I know. But can you find peace? What if Sarm, or another, angers you again? How would you feel if you hurt someone more seriously?'

Eain was silent. Anndra spoke only truth. He was surrounded with things that transported him back to Banahgar, reminded him of what he had done. Reminded him of the pain he had caused.

He dreamed most nights. Stern, silent faces appeared before his sleeping eyes; Arall Rathvedd, Morgan Blane, Helden Haradsson and so many others. They looked down upon him and he was a child again beneath their stares, clumsy and ashamed.

He woke from those dreams anxious and whimpering. Yet, they were not the worst. He saw dead faces. They lay on the green grass. Edich, Kater and Foinn, blood soaked and pale. He knew they were gone forever. But, sometimes their dead eyes opened and their white fingers reached for him, clutching at him.

'Join us,' they said, their voices hollow. 'Join us in the lands of the dead.'

He woke screaming from those dreams and the guilt was a blade between his ribs.

'Where could I go?' he asked. To wander out onto the plains alone was to die.

'When the time is right, you will know.'

Eain paused. 'Would you come too?' His voice was quiet, uncertain. Anndra looked up at him, craning her neck to meet his eyes with hers, which were wide and shadowed. She shook her head slightly, and Eain felt his face fall. What had he expected, really?

Why would she travel hundreds of miles across the plains to reach this place, only to leave again so soon?

To be with you, said a silly voice in his mind.

He shook his head, willing the thoughts away. She was fighting her own battle and did not need his burden too. Leaving Banahgar had destined him to be alone.

Light faded. Shadows lengthened. There was a gusty, insistent wind that tugged at Eain's face and hair. The box quarry and the pursuit were behind him and he strode onwards, ignoring his growing fatigue.

He could not see another living thing. He was totally alone in the vastness of the mountains, and felt very small. He felt like he did not belong here. He felt like an intruder.

Peaks reared up before him, dark and forbidding. The softer slopes of the Dall were behind but there was only war, death and shame there. He had to keep moving forward.

He stumbled on in the gathering gloom, and noticed the vaguest of paths beneath his feet. A narrow track wound through the short heather, exposing flattish rocks beneath. He looked ahead and thought he could discern the route, curving around the steepening slopes to vanish over a crest between two frowning crags.

He put his head down and pumped his legs, his gait somewhere between a run and a walk. Thought was not necessary.

Hurrying as the light fell further, he pushed himself past a straight sided boulder with the flat of his palm. His brows furrowed as he glanced down. Beside his hand, and about the size of his spread palm, was a carved symbol.

It was a circle, crossed with lines that divided it into twelve segments. It somewhat resembled the crown of Banahgar, the symbol of the Claihed, but without the points of the crown or the emblazoned sword. Just a circle.

Eain moved on.

The path climbed steeply. Eain sweated despite the growing chill of the evening. He should stop for the night. Travelling through the mountains in darkness was dangerous, but somehow, he felt compelled to keep moving.

A short, rocky step led upward. He put his hand on the rock and noticed another circular symbol, clearly carved into the grey stone. He climbed past it and stepped up onto a rocky plateau.

Before him was a long, steep-sided vale. Towering, sheer crags loomed on either side, tall and unclimbable. Nestled between, still and glassy, was a mountain lake. It stretched away from Eain's feet, shining like a sword's blade. Numb and fatigued as he was, Eain was moved by the grandeur of the sight.

To his left, flat-topped stones poked their heads above the water in the outflowing stream. They were spaced a pace apart, as if deliberately placed as stepping stones, and Eain followed their path unhesitatingly.

On the far side he found another circular symbol, noticing it without surprise. An indistinct trail seemed to follow the banks of the lake and deeper into the valley. The presence of this path, and the symbols that lined it, seemed like a sign. It was enough encouragement for Eain to follow them, and to feel as though in some way his steps were guided.

Soon, he was at the head of the lake. Narrow waterfalls traced undulating white paths down the crag that rose before him. They tumbled into a swift stream at the base, that pooled and fell over smaller steps in noisy surges on its way to feed the lake. He turned away from the waters and began to climb.

A narrow gully ran up the back of the valley, bounded and overhung by rocky shelves. Loose scree slithered and scraped beneath the soles of his boots as he struggled upward. As he climbed higher he passed the occasional circular symbol, carved into the angular walls.

His hands shook as he reached up, pushing with his legs as he pulled with his arms. He was almost at the limit of his endurance, but it did not matter. Reaching the top was his only aim.

A bigger, wider symbol carved deeply into the rock greeted him at the top of the gully. The intersecting lines were deeply incised, but the grooves had been worn to roundness by time and weather.

He left it behind without a backward glance as he staggered on into the darkness. Not long afterwards, his knees buckled, and he collapsed. He was spent. He rolled down into the lee of an overhanging boulder and slept until dawn.

He shivered to recall the dismal cold of that lonely dawn. His conviction of the previous night had evaporated like morning mist, leaving just doubt and guilt, along with fatigue that was bone deep.

Yet, he had known that he could not go back, so he had struggled to his feet and staggered onwards, the rising sun at his back.

He did not remember the rest of his journey clearly, but knew that a couple of days later he had arrived in this valley. Without that fortune, he would have died in the wastes and his bones would have been buried by the sandy, shifting soil.

Footsteps approached. He turned to see the lean frame of Carilton Tann. The man's self-possession and natural authority reminded him of the soldiers of the Claihedehmore. He had nothing but respect for Tann and tried to brush away the negative feelings that his presence invoked.

'How are you feeling?' he asked, stopping beside Eain.

'I'm…fine.'

Tann nodded knowingly. 'Sure. You liked the story that Deka told?'

'Yes, good story,' replied Eain eagerly. A question occurred to him. 'Is it…is it a true story?'

Tann sucked his teeth. 'Tough question. I can't rightly give you a straight answer. What I can tell you is that even the dwarves themselves can't agree about it. Half say it's a tall tale, a fable to warn against greed. The other half say that it's real history, and that the Hidden City is still out there somewhere, buried beneath the northern desert.'

Tann shrugged, unconcerned.

'But.' Eain was still bursting with questions. 'The Others? And the magic?'

'Yea, it's a fantastical tale. Maybe a bit of history woven with a healthy ladle of myth. But the dwarves really think they will find the city one day and rebuild it. A new northern kingdom where they will live in peace and wealth. Well, half of them, anyway. The southern tribes who are still believers make a pilgrimage to the Great River and beyond, searching and digging. Maybe they'll find a buried city one day. More likely they won't. Doesn't stop them trying.'

'I would like to see it.'

'Then you need to travel a good way west, and a decent step north, too!'

Tann chuckled. His laughter died as he realised that he had touched on one of Eain's worries. Stay, or go.

'Look,' he said, turning to face Eain and looking up to meet his eyes. 'We both know it's hard for you to stay here. I've been around enough soldiers and fought enough battles to understand what you are going through.'

Eain opened his mouth to speak, but Tann cut him off. 'No need to say anything. Your truth is your own. The past is gone.'

'Master Tann,' said Eain uncertainly, after a moment's thought. 'I don't know what to do.'

Tann leaned in closer, lowering his voice. 'I knew a man. Like you. Good soldier, good man, and a brave, brave fighter. But, he had just seen too much. Too much blood, too much pain. He couldn't face holding a blade anymore, not as a soldier, as a warrior.'

Eain was listening. This man, Tann, seemed to see right through him, as if he knew everything that went on in his mind.

'He started working as a guard,' continued Tann. 'On the wagon routes. He couldn't bear fighting and war, but he could use his skills to protect others. It still scared him, but he found the courage to be a shield when he couldn't be a sword.

'He was the bravest man I ever knew.'

Eain blinked. He knew what Tann was trying to say. He saw the wisdom, and the slender branch of hope that he was extending.

'And did he find peace? Your friend?'

Tann turned away, and when he spoke again, his voice was thick.

'Yea. He found peace.'

Eain watched the trail incessantly from that point on. He felt as though there was a rope around his body, tugging at him, drawing him westward.

The next day, he had asked Tann about the lands to the west.

'Kiraband,' he replied, definitively. 'That's where I'd head. It's a frontier region between the plains to the north and east, the Alrean Empire to the west and Re'Emsser to the south. The capital is Ben Gedrin. It's a rough, low place but if you want to find work, that's where you need to go.'

He explained how many of the traders rode a circular route to align with the seasons; north from Ben Gedrin in the spring and summer to escape the heat, then along the southern plains beside the Great River's south bank through autumn. They would winter in Kiraband and start again the following spring.

'They pass through Annida, but that's little more than a staging post of a town. Goods come up from Anish over the Rujrweh pass and onto Kiraband from there.'

Eain thanked Tann for his advice, and went back to work.

He was climbing onto the veranda for a break, a couple of hours later, when Ma Tann emerged from the doorway. She was clutching a bundle of skins.

'I made this for you,' she said, holding something up.

It was a jacket, made of goatskin. The leather was smooth and soft, the colour of the farm's sandy soil. When Eain put it on, the lining was furry and comfortable, with thick bands of white fur at the collar and cuffs.

'Thank you,' he said, admiring the coat. 'Very much.'

'Don't mention it, boy. I just figured you had nothing to wear in the cold, and we had nothing as would fit you.'

'Ready for a journey,' said a voice from beyond the veranda. Eain looked around, and straight into Anndra's wide, dark eyes. Her expression was unreadable and her gaze was intense. He had no idea what she was thinking.

He glanced down at his hands. Why did he feel sad at the thought of leaving her behind? When he looked up again, she had gone. And the next day, another wagon train arrived.

From his vantage point in one of the higher fields, Eain watched it approach. It wound across the plains like a snake emerging from a mysterious cloud as the wheels raised dust.

The evening sky was painted with clouds like salmon scales, pale patches against the fading rosy pink. There was barely a breath of wind but the patterned sky spoke of change. It might be a blowy night.

He slung his shovel over his shoulder and ran easily down the path. Across the fields, he could see others doing the same. The new arrival was a significant event.

As the wagons appeared from the swirling dust, the lead wagon driver stood up on his seat. His arms were outstretched and his long, curling hair blew out behind him.

As they drew up beside the farmhouse, he leapt athletically from the wagon and landed like a cat. His wagon rolled to a halt, the horse standing placidly between the shafts as the dust settled.

He impressed Eain immediately. He was a tall man, overtopping Carilton Tann by the width of a couple of fingers, and was lean as a snake. His travelling leathers clung to his spare frame like a second skin. Even travel worn and covered with the dust of the trail as he was, he had a regal presence.

Tann rushed forward, crying a greeting. 'Hail! Hail traveller! The moons have been kind to guide you here, and the Five bless us with your arrival.'

'Hail to you, Carilton Tann,' responded the newcomer, striding forward and extending his hand. He and Tann shook hands vigorously, wrist to wrist like warriors. 'It has been a long road, my friend.'

Two further wagons drew up behind the first. Each was drawn by sturdy draft horses and the drivers were dressed like their leader.

'Now then, boys' exclaimed Caivane as he shuffled up to greet the newcomers. 'Tressin Oke, as I breathe! We thought you'd run into trouble when you didn't show up last year.'

'Aye, aye,' said Tressin Oke, hands on hips. 'Trouble, there was. The Wild Elves were restless, so I stayed in Kiraband. The dwarves are making pilgrimages this year, so trade is good and the roads are safer.'

He spread his arms wide, raising his voice as if in proclamation. 'But now, we are here! We bring the finest produce of these lands and beyond, from west, north and south, to trade with the honourable Carilton Tann and his noble household. Let wine be poured and songs be sung this night!'

He laughed, and Tann laughed with him. Oke wrapped his skinny arm around Tann's shoulders, and they headed for the house together. Before they got there, Oke turned and his eyes caught Eain's. They were dark and sharp, twinkling like smouldering embers. He fixed Eain with a curious gaze, his stare travelling quickly up and down as he took in Eain's height and stature.

Then, he was gone. He stepped confidently into the house, and the crowd followed.

The evening was raucous. Oke had arrived with several barrels of Bureno wine, apparently to trade with Tann. But, he insisted that they were rolled into the farmhouse and opened immediately.

Soon, everyone had a full cup while a couple of young goats roasted on spits above the hearth.

Eain had never tasted wine before. It was dark in colour and had a flavour that was somewhere between bitter and sweet. He was not sure that he liked it, but he found himself wanting more. Before long, the room was swimming slightly.

After pouring the wine, Oke had introduced his wagoners to the room.

'Mayla,' he said, gesturing to a short, broad woman with her hair in tight braids. 'Not my wife.' Mayla rolled her eyes.

'Whose is she?' ask Sarm, to laughter from the room.

'I'm mine,' retorted Mayla.

'Reela, and Haf.' Oke seized a couple, arms around their shoulders, and presented them. Haf had much of the look of Oke about him. He was tall and slim, with long dark hair. His was pulled back and tied behind his head, and his long, pointed nose scanned the room.

Reela had a hand around Haf's arm. She was slightly shorter than her partner, with pale hair and luminous blue eyes. She edged slightly behind Haf, self-consciously.

Oke introduced the rest of his team, a mix of men and women who were all stained from travel and tanned from a life working outdoors.

'And last—' announced Oke, with a flourish. 'Our shining star, our songbird.' He reached out and pulled a scruffy young man out into the centre of the room. He had been skulking quietly near the wall. 'The one and only Mahr Mehlan!'

Mahr Mehlan was short and somewhat stout, with closely cropped fair hair and a faint sprinkling of stubble on his soft chin. He looked awkward and uncomfortable being the centre of attention.

'Where is it?' asked Oke, exasperated. 'Where's your *zito*? Come on, boy! I brought you all this way, play. Play!'

Mayla passed an object to Mehlan, and he gripped it in a familiar way.

Eain had never seen anything like it before. It was made entirely from wood, seemingly carved from a single block. The back was rounded and Mehlan pressed this close to his body. The front was finely sanded and oiled to show off the rippling grain of the wood. A strip of darker wood had been set at one end and four narrow strings ran across this from pegs at the top to the other end of the body.

As Mehlan held it, he passed his thumb through a hole bored through the neck and set his fingers to the strings. In his other hand he produced a wooden rod which had been whittled into a rounded point. He paused for a moment, the point of the rod over five deep, wide holes bored into the body. His posture had changed completely. At once, he was confident, his body upright and his head raised.

He closed his eyes and brushed the tip of the rod across the strings. Eain was astonished by the sound.

Clear, woody tones rang out from the instrument. The sound was bright and joyful. He moved the fingers of his left hand expertly, and plucked the strings again, and this time the chord was mournful.

Eain only knew Banahgarian music; the metallic pounding of anvil and drum, and the low moan of the pipes. He had never heard anything like the music that Mehlan was making with his *zitol*.

Mehlan shifted smoothly from chord to chord, and the soft ringing tones painted musical pictures of vivid landscapes and moods in Eain's mind.

'Play something we can dance to, boy!' bellowed Oke, voice now thick with wine. 'Someone beat out a measure for him.'

Caivane raised his meaty fists, bringing them down onto the table in a steady rhythm. Others copied. Mehlan began playing again.

This time, the wooden rod moved up and down rapidly, and his fingers danced across the strings as the *zitol* rang with an intricate, repeating melody. Alongside the steady thump of Caivane's drumming hands, the effect was hypnotic.

Men and women stamped their feet in time and Eain felt his own foot tapping. Then, Mayla launched herself into the centre of the room, the table pushed to one side, and began a complex dance. Her feet kicked and stomped, and she whirled and swayed to the beat.

Haf and Reela followed, clutching each other and soon the room was a mass of swirling, shifting bodies. Laughter filled the air in counterpoint to Mehlan's spiralling tune.

After a while, a hand clutched Eain's arm. He spun. It was Tann.

He leaned in close and spoke loudly to be heard over the noise. 'I want to speak with Oke, before he is too deep in his cups.' Eain nodded. 'I'll get his attention.'

They glanced across the room. Oke was in the middle of the dancers, waving his arms above his head in total disregard for the rhythm of the music.

'Tressin!' called Tann. 'Tress!' He beckoned vigorously as the lead wagoner looked up, then danced over to them.

'I've missed your fine hospitality, Tann!' he enthused.

'It's not like this here every night, you loon!' retorted Tann. Oke cackled at his words. 'We need to speak seriously about something.'

'Now?'

'It's better now than later.'

Oke tilted his head in acknowledgement. Tann led the way, and the three men strode out into the quiet cool of the night.

'Guess this is going to be about man-mountain here?' said Oke. He leered up at Eain unsteadily, although his eyes were sharp.

'He wants to move on,' said Tann. 'Wants to go west, maybe find some guarding work around Ben Gedrin.'

'Aye. Plenty of strongarm work around on caravans going through Kiraband. Always is.'

'Will you take him? He can earn his keep on the way, guarding and shifting stuff for you. Then you can drop him off when you make it through to Ben Gedrin.'

'I wasn't looking for anyone,' admitted Oke, ruefully. He turned to face Eain. 'Why would you want to leave, big man? It's a pretty nice place. This guy—' he indicated Tann. 'Ain't the worst boss.'

Eain thought hard. Oke had a strong accent, but the drink slowed his speech and actually made him easier to understand. What could he say? He could not admit the problems he was suffering. It would make him sound crazy.

'I like to travel,' he began, haltingly. 'See the plains and the cities. I have not seen this before.' Both men were listening and nodding, Oke with interest and Tann in encouragement. 'I am not from here,' Eain continued, more boldly. 'I am from…somewhere else.' He tailed off.

Oke chewed his lip for a moment.

'I'll take you on,' he said, suddenly and decisively. 'I'll take you on as a handler and as a guard. No pay. Meals and passage only for payment. Agree?'

He stuck out his hand. Eain grasped it.

'Agree.'

'Wonderful. Let's seal it with a drink. Come on, Tann, let's open another barrel!'

He danced off and back into the room, Tann at his heels.

Before Eain could follow, he noticed a figure stood at the far end of the veranda. A small, slight person with dark eyes that gleamed in a shaft of light from the doorway. Anndra.

She waited. Something about the way she stood, a stiffness in her bearing, showed unease and hesitance. Slowly, Eain approached her along the veranda, his steps marking a quiet rhythm on the wooden boards.

'I heard,' she said, voice just loud enough to be heard over the sounds of music and laughter inside the house. 'I heard, and I think it's what you need.'

'I hope it is,' said Eain. 'I want to stay here. But, I cannot.'

He knew it was the truth. The warm arms of kindness that most here had thrown around him could not hold back his past. He needed to move on.

'I know. I see it.' Anndra's eyes were sad.

'I will miss you.'

'You will not. Life is a road and you must keep moving along it.'

'I will miss you,' Eain repeated.

Anndra took a step closer. 'I will give you two things to remember me by.' She reached into a pocket and produced a small wooden object. 'First.' She placed it in Eain's hand.

He lifted it up into the light. It was an exquisitely carved likeness of an eagle. Its wings were spread as if soaring on the wind, and the sculptor had picked out every detail of the feathers that clothed them.

'Maneg,' murmured Eain, thinking of the Banahgarian goddess of wisdom.

'The Skyfather,' said Anndra, 'sees all travellers and knows all paths. He will guide and protect you.'

She moved slightly closer. 'And second.' She raised her head, standing up on her toes to gain extra height. Her lips brushed his. Eain inhaled deeply at the sensation, the soft warmth of her mouth pressing momentarily against his. Then, she was stepping away.

'Anndra—' He was surprised and confused, but also suddenly felt calm, and more certain about his onward path. He knew he was making the right decision.

'No more words,' she said. 'No more goodbyes. We will meet again in this life, Eain Connow.'

She turned and walked away, and was soon swallowed by the night. Mehr Mehlan played a slow, sad tune on his *zitol*, and as the melody echoed out through the darkness Eain slumped heavily against the rail, thoughts whirling.

Eain's mouth was dry. He squinted against the bright light of the morning as a dull pain throbbed behind his temples.

He was riding on the tailgate of a half-laden wagon, and his stomach lurched and groaned every time the wheels hit a bump. He could not sit like that any longer.

Jumping down, he suppressed a queasy groan as he landed, and began walking. Moving off to the side of the track, his long strides let him keep pace with the slow-moving wagon train easily.

'Leaving so soon, my friend?' Tressin Oke called down from his high seat on the lead wagon. He was grinning broadly.

Eain shook his head. 'Need to walk a little.'

'It's a long, long way to Ben Gedrin on foot!' laughed Oke. 'Hope you have good boots.'

'Yes, yes. Strong boots.' Eain made a face as his stomach lurched and his breakfast rose.

Oke waved a clay bottle. 'I got medicine if you are sick!'

Eain's face fell and he blew out his cheeks in disgust. Oke laughed again and took a deep swing of wine.

Oke had roused them all in the watery light just before dawn. He looked bright eyed and laughed at their groggy expressions.

'Up and out!' he cried. 'The long road beckons!'

Eain had dressed in his newer clothes, but pulled on his Banahgarian leather trousers. They would be comfortable for travelling. Lastly, he had picked up the new goatskin coat made by Ma Tann and shrugged gratefully into its soft warmth.

As he stepped out onto the veranda, he was glad of the thick layers. There was a new, fresh bite in the air. A brisk wind swept over the farmstead beneath an achingly clear sky. Autumn was on the way.

Eain had done what he could to help prepare the wagons, but for the most part he had just felt like a hindrance. The rest of Oke's people worked with the efficiency of repeated practice. He looked around constantly for Anndra, but she was nowhere to be seen.

'Eain!'

He turned to see Tann striding toward him from the house.

'I think you should take this.' Eain looked down, and his stomach gave a lurch.

Tann was holding out his own sheathed seax. The symbol of the Claihed stood out in a dark, vivid brand on the brown leather of the scabbard. He shied away. Yet, it was his, and he was to be travelling as a guard.

'Yes,' he said, taking it and hooking it onto his belt. 'Thank you. For all.'

'Don't mention it. It was a wise fate that brought you here. I hope the same fate favours the rest of your journey.'

Eain reached out and they shook hands, gripping each other's wrists like the warriors both had been.

'I will remember.' Eain's voice was thick with sudden emotion.

'Sure. Call in if you ever come back this way.' Tann smiled, but then Oke was calling out the order to leave. Eain hurried to find a seat on one of the wagons, and before he knew it the farm and the gathered, waving inhabitants were juddering backward into the distance.

He had endured the swaying and bouncing of the wagon on the uneven trail for as long as he could, his stomach and head protesting, before jumping down to walk instead.

Oke's bottle made a clatter as he tucked it beneath the seat. Eain walked on, eyes on the distant horizon. No other soul or living creature could be seen across the wide, barren lands crossed by the road.

What lay ahead? What sights would he see? Would he find the peace that Tann had promised?

Only time would tell.

TWENTY

A breath of wind stirred the branches above, and the roof of leaves fluttered and swayed. The colours were muted in the grey light of another cold dawn, the green, yellow and gold of the canopy washed out and indistinct.

Callan Fraevar blinked in the growing brightness of the morning, forcing himself to alert wakefulness. The last few weeks had passed in a rapid haze, and it was often difficult to remember where he was each time he awoke.

He cast aside his blanket and sat up. There was a dull ache in the muscles of his arms and legs, and his stomach clenched and growled with hunger. Yet, he felt more alive than ever.

Yesterday, he thought. *What happened yesterday?*

It came back to him in a rush of images. Yesterday's dawn, the Claihedehmore tapping him on the shoulder to tell him he was needed. Daylight hours spent skulking through the forests waiting for dusk. Then, as darkness fell, launching the attack and springing their trap.

His hands clenched with the sudden desire to hold his greatsword again. To swing it in battle, to feel it biting flesh. He craved seeing the enemy cast down by his blade, seeing them turning to flee and knowing the glory of victory.

These last few weeks had been a gift for Callan, and today would be a special day.

Of course, there had been fear, too. And pain, and a measure of horror. Many of his fellow Claihedehlar had already been sent to the great hall of the ancestors, their lifeblood draining into the dark soil of Banahgar.

Most had not gone easily. It was not like the sagas, where men gave valiant speeches before fading away with heroic dignity.

Death in battle was brutal. Young men clutched at gaping wounds that vomited blood, while others tried to hold their guts in and screamed in childish terror.

Callan had seen all this, and had shrugged it off. In his heart he knew that those that had died so far were the weak. Weak in body, short of skill, or simply lacking strength of will.

The strong prevailed. The strong lived to fight on and would be the ones to win this war for Banahgar.

Like me, he thought, and smiled wolfishly.

And today, his strength would be formally recognised.

'Get a move on, children!' A gruff voice cut through Callan's thoughts. Raidth Scaepar, a harsh Claihedehmore and a savage fighter prowled through the clearing, barking his commands. 'I'm sure your dreams are full of beautiful maidens, but if you think you can lie around 'til lunchtime then you are very sadly mistaken! Up!'

Callan was already moving, standing and quickly rolling his blanket into a tight roll. He stowed it on his back and then slung the baldric of his greatsword around his shoulders. The solid weight of the weapon was a comfort. With it in place he felt complete.

'Grandmaster will be in camp today,' continued Scaepar. 'If he finds dirt on your boots there will be consequences. If he sees a blunt sword there will be consequences. How can you greet the Grandmaster with dirty boots and blunt swords? Sort your lives out, now!'

Callan knew full well that "consequences" was just another word for "pain". He set to work making sure his kit was all in order. It was helpful to have the distraction. It would be hours yet before the Grandmaster, Helden Haradsson, arrived, and Callan hated waiting. It was boring.

The camp was tucked away in a deep wooded dell in the northern Dall. The men went about their preparations with soft footsteps and quiet voices. Smiles and laughter were scarce.

The road was about an hour's march to the east, and Kotevari forces could be moving along it now. If they got a sniff that there was a Claihed camp so near, then they would be able to stride into the words and encircle them. They would be trapped, and wiped out.

However, Callan was confident that the enemy had no idea where they were. The Claihed had taught them to fear that northern road, and they would only travel along it with slow caution. They also knew that to blunder into the surrounding woods was to invite a quick death.

The Claihedehmore were like ghosts in this uneven, forested landscape. Ambushes could be set, sprung, and the position evacuated in heartbeats. They could strike Kotevari forces when they were on the move, or encamped, and fade away without a trace.

It was only this that prevented the north of Banahgar being overrun.

Until the Kotevari controlled the northern road, they could not advance further into Banahgar. The Claihed could not let that happen. They all knew they had to fight for every yard of Kotevari progress.

Another of the Claihedehmore came over to where Callan sat on a fallen branch, waiting. Friian Fiesbladd was tall and open-faced, with hair that was prematurely white. He took on daily life with a calm pragmatism that he retained even in the heat of battle.

'How are you feeling?' he asked, sitting down.

'Fine,' replied Callan, honestly.

'Not nervous?'

'No.'

What was there to be nervous about? If he could face the maelstrom of a night ambush, he could cope with what would happen in the forthcoming ceremony. The worst part would be speaking before the Grandmaster, and that was nothing compared to a spear heading for his ribs.

'It's a momentous day for you,' added Fiesbladd. Callan nodded. 'You have done the country proud, you know. We were up against it, and losing, before you and the other Claihedehlar joined us.'

Callan shifted uncomfortably at the sincere praise.

The fleet that had sailed up Osturfjord and landed above Sudvirke had been assailed immediately. The Claihedehmore had set traps around the landing sites, and attacked the Kotevari as they tried to set up their camps. Boats were burned, tents were slashed in the night and supplies were either stolen or just thrown in the river.

The enemy were beset on all sides, and unable to make any progress.

Until, that is, until the second Kotevari army had begun to move through the Dall. A small group of Hniffare had taken warning to Vekwicc, fortunately, so the Claihed were not taken completely by surprise. Nevertheless, now they were forced to fight on two fronts; one to the south, one in the west.

Their front lines creaked. They were at risk of being caught between the hammer and the anvil.

The Masters had no choice but to deploy the Claihedehlar. Sverlaeggare were called up as reserves and the Claihedehlar, like

Callan, were sent to join the Claihedehmore in the west or in the south.

Callan recalled his first battles, the upper and lower ranks of the Claihed fighting side by side. Attacking in the half-dark of dawn or dusk, chaos reigned. Many fell in those raids.

When they drew back into the woods after each raid and counted heads, naming the lost and the dead had become a grim routine.

Yet, their lines held. They fought desperately and used the terrain, which they all knew so well, to their advantage. They halted the advance and bought the occupants of the plains of Ostur and the northern Dall time to escape to the highlands of the north.

But, we cannot hold them forever, thought Callan. *Soon, we will all fall.*

He was staring into the distance when Fiesbladd stood and clapped a hand firmly to his shoulder.

'I will stamp for you, soldier,' he said. 'I just might do it quietly.' He eyed the trees as if armed men might appear at any moment, as he moved quietly away.

The hours passed. The soldiers checked their kit and checked it again. Callan dozed, the bright sun filtering through the trees above and casting shifting patterns against his eyelids.

A murmur began, and spread around the glade like a breath of wind through leaves. Callan's eyes snapped open. Men were rising hastily and brushing themselves down. The same few words were on all lips.

'He is here.'

Helden Haradsson entered the clearing with quiet authority. His face was flushed as if he had been running but his breathing was even. To Callan, he was an unimpressive sight, despite his reputation. He spoke with wisdom befitting his years, of course, and his skills in battle were spoken of in hushed tones. Yet,

Callan found his eyes sliding away from the man. He projected no threat.

The man who followed on the Grandmaster's heels was the opposite. The more Callan had learned about the way of the sword and the deadly dance of battle, the clearer it had become; Morgan Blane, the River in Flood, was a wolf among hounds.

He was a battle-hardened predator and every angular line of his lithe, muscular body projected alertness. Even as he strolled casually into the glade he resembled a crouching animal, ready to pounce. Ready to kill.

Callan noted with a thrill that a second blade was scabbarded across Blane's back, at the opposite angle to Blane's own famous greatsword. Callan's sword.

'Men of Banahgar,' began the Grandmaster. His voice was soft, like the sigh of the wind, but all other talk silenced as he spoke. 'Your stand here has already been worthy of the sagas. Without your bravery, your skill, and your cunning, we would now have enemy armies to our north and to our south.

'The whole Claihed knows of your valour. We sing of those who have already gone to the ancestors' long hall. We will honour the sacrifice they made. We will never give up.'

Blane leaned forward to whisper in the Grandmaster's ear. Haradsson nodded as the Master leaned back, sinewy arms folded across his broad chest.

'But, we have other business this day,' said Haradsson. 'Claihedehmore, you know what must be done.'

There was a sudden bustle of decisive movement. The slight sounds of crackling leaves and snapping twigs filled the air as men moved in all directions, while Callan remained still. Moments later, he stood alone at the far end of an avenue. The other men formed each side, facing inwards, and he could see the tall, lean figure of Morgan Blane stood at the far end.

In the ensuing hush, the footfalls of the Grandmaster seemed loud. He strode out from one side to stand facing Callan, looking down the avenue.

'Men of the Claihed,' he began, in his usual quiet but forceful tone. 'Who is this that approaches? Who is he that darkens our door?'

The words were addressed in Callan's direction. In the fortress, in peacetime, they would be bellowed, and this ritual performed before the whole of the Claihedehmore. In war, many compromises had to be made. The heart of the ritual, known as *Verthan* or "The Becoming", would remain the same.

Fiesbladd stood. 'This man is known to me. He is called Callan Fraevar. He comes with a challenge.'

'And will you accept his challenge?' asked the Grandmaster.

'Nay, I will not draw blade against this man. I will let him enter.'

'Do any others know this man?'

'Aye, this man is known to me,' said another of the Claihedehmore as he rose. 'He is called Callan Fraevar. He has passed through danger to be here.'

'And will you ask him to tell of this danger?'

Callan took another step forward as the Grandmaster asked the question.

'Nay, his presence proves that he has overcome the danger. He needs not speak of it.'

'Is there one more who would speak for this man?'

This was the third and final question put to the assembled men. Who would answer? Would any?

'This man is known to me,' came the answer, growled in a low voice. Callan realised with a thrill that the speaker was Morgan Blane. 'He is called Callan Fraevar, and he seeks an invitation.'

'And will you invite him in?' The Grandmaster's voice increased in intensity as the ritual reached its conclusion.

'Nay,' replied Blane. 'It is not my place to invite any into this house.'

'Why not?'

'This is the house of Kell, and Kell is not at home.'

The Grandmaster faced Callan once more. 'I will take the responsibility to speak in Kell's stead, while we await his return.'

Kell had formed the Claihed before vanishing from Banahgar, many years ago. The same ritual had been repeated times beyond counting since then.

'Come, Callan Fraevar,' said the Grandmaster, with an air of finality. 'Come in now, if you would join us. Or turn away and do not return to this place.'

Callan cleared his throat. He felt uncomfortable speaking before so many, but he had to play his part in the ritual. He summoned his courage. Everyone was looking at him.

'I come,' he said, face colouring as he strode forward along the avenue of faces. 'And I accept your invitation with humility, and gratitude. I will enter this house and join my brothers as we wait for Kell to return.'

At the end of the avenue, he stopped. The Grandmaster stood before him. His open, blocky face was blank and unreadable. Glancing down, Callan took in the long, metallic gleam of the sword lying near his knees.

His sword!

This ritual usually took place in the fortress of Vekwicc, high in the northern mountains within the region of Naen-Giata. The great hall could fit the entire Claihedehmore and torches would flicker on the walls beside great tapestries depicting scenes from the Claihed's history.

The Grandmaster would stand beside an ancient stone podium which was draped in fine red cloth; the *pallar*. Here, the *pallar* was a stack of logs and the cloth was a folded blanket, but the item it held had the same significance.

Callan fought the urge to reach down and grasp the tightly bound hilt, and to hold the sword aloft. He craved to feel the perfect weight and balance of the weapon. He tucked his thumbs in his belt. It was not quite time.

'We welcome this man,' stated the Grandmaster. 'We will not fight him. We acknowledge the challenges he has faced. He may remain in this house, the house of the Claihed, until he is dead, or until Kell returns.'

There was a pause. Callan felt the unfamiliar flutter of nerves in his belly, like the twitching of a flock of tiny birds.

'But,' all was suddenly still and silent, as the Grandmaster continued, 'is he our brother?'

The question lingered in the air. Then, Morgan Blane stamped his foot. In the great hall at Vekwicc the stamp would ring out like the boom of a great drum. Here, it was a muted crackle. The effect was no less exciting for Callan.

Blane stamped again and this time more feet moved in unison. Again, and again, until every man in the clearing was beating the soles of their boots against the forest floor in a steady, hypnotic rhythm.

The Grandmaster was smiling down. It was time.

Callan stooped and reverently wrapped his hands around the hilt of that magnificent sword. It was long and heavy, even compared with other Banahgarian greatswords. It had been made to suit his own strength and height.

He held it steady with the point down, then in a single sweeping motion he kicked the blade, outwards and upwards. The point swung up and he slashed it through the air in a smooth figure of eight.

Holding it upright, with the hilt by his chest, he paused. The ricasso, the blunt section at the base of the blade, was before his face.

He had had no idea about his Sword-Name. Other lads had talked about it constantly and some seemed to have decided what it would be by the time they became Sverlaeggare. Callan had not given it a moment's thought. It had not seemed to matter.

Then, when he had been called up to fight alongside the Claihedehmore, a phrase had begun to repeat in his mind. Before and after battles he spoke it, silently and secretly, repeating the words to himself. It was like mantra.

It became him. Or he became it? In those dark, desperate skirmishes, when he burst from the trees to hunt and to kill before melting away like a shadow, he began to truly know himself.

When he was told that his deeds had marked him out for promotion, had earned him the right to become one of the Claihedehmore, he had known his Sword-Name immediately.

And now it was time to speak it aloud.

He brought the hilt of his new sword to the left side of his chest. There was a soft thump as every man watching copied the salute.

Callan raised his voice as he spoke the words.

'This is Dusk Wolf.'

'I am Claihedehmore!

'I am Banahgar!

'I am alive!'

PART FOUR

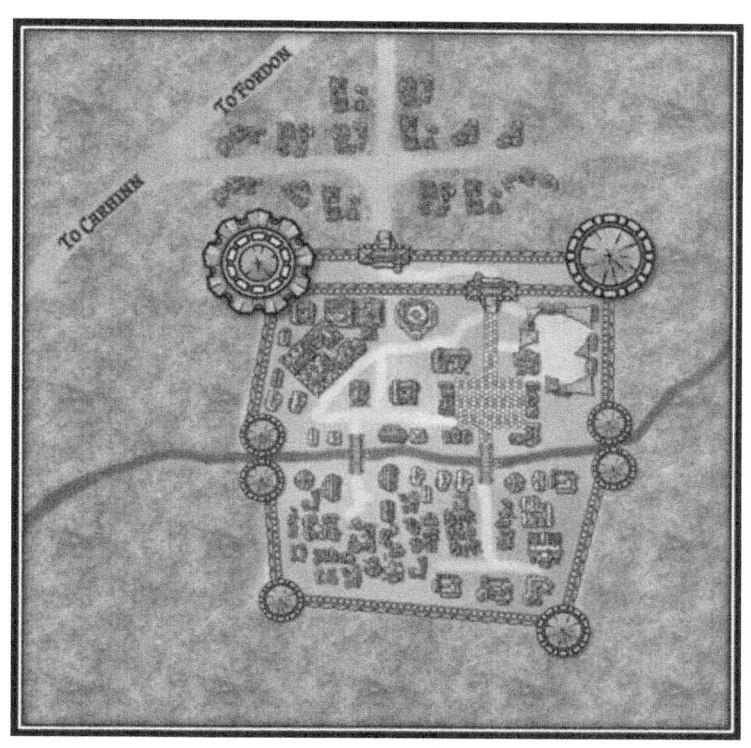

KEREVA

TWENTY ONE

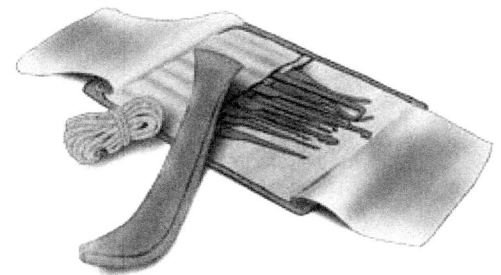

Scaffolding wrapped around the city walls. Long wooden poles, lashed together with coarse rope, rose toward the sky like reeds along a riverbank.

Rickety ramps led up to walkways that ran along near the uneven tops of the walls. Like an army massing to defend the city from invasion, scores of labourers swarmed along the ramshackle structure. Instead of spears and swords, they carried stones, tools and buckets of mortar.

They sang as they worked. A lone voice rang out into the still morning air, confident and clear. It sang a well-known local song and after a few lines a host of voices joined in chorus.

> *Ne'er kill a bird, my lad.*
> *Ne'er harm a wing.*
> *Let the flocks fly free, my lad,*
> *E'er thou wouldst be king*
> *'Twas easy to forget, that day*
> *And he unwound his sling.*
> *They cried 'put that stone away,*
> *E'er thou wouldst be king'*

The last echoes of the melody faded away, and for a time there was just the steady sounds of labouring workers mingling with the normal noises of the surrounding city.

Dawn had not long broken but the city was alive with sound and movement. The chatter of the labourers and the barking shouts of the foremen formed an indistinct grumble over the sharp, percussive sound of tools on hard stone.

Ellyah stepped back from the open window, breathing in the familiar air of her own city. Kereva. She felt like she was truly home. She felt like this is where her luck would change. Her face broke into a broad smile.

'Let the flocks fly free, my lad,' she sang. 'E'er thou wouldst be king!'

She tailed off as she moved back over to the hearth, where she stirred a warming pot of barley porridge.

'The crows are in fine voice this morning,' said Nastja from where she sat on the floor beside the door.

'Piss off,' retorted Ellyah without looking up. A snort of laughter came from the bed where Luara lay, still wrapped head to toe in her blankets.

They were holed up in a single tiny room at the back end of a larger storage building. The room itself was little more than a cupboard, but had been fitted with a hard, narrow bed and a small hearth. The window opened out into the shadow of Kereva's east wall, with the seemingly permanent scaffolding almost overhanging the building.

This had been their home and hideout for the days that had passed since their hurried journey here from Carhinn.

They had ridden the dromedaries through the darkness along the great diagonal highway that ran from Carhinn to the northeast of Anish.

As she rode, jerking awkwardly with the unfamiliar rocking motion, Ellyah tilted her head constantly. Listening for the sound of galloping hoofbeats approaching them from behind.

A fast horse, ridden hard, could catch them as they trotted along. If the Mackems had enough mounts, they could make a good chase this night. Ellyah did not like to admit it but they, and the jewel, remained in danger.

The dromedaries were capable of a short burst of speed, but how long could they gallop, if a pursuit overtook them? Could it be long enough to escape? Or would they be caught?

Ellyah fretted the hours of darkness away, but as they got further away from the city she began to relax. A chase would have been on them by now. They had done it. They had escaped Carhinn with the jewel. For now, they seemed safe.

Just before dawn, as the sky was tinted with the vaguest silvery glow, they dismounted. An orchard grew beside the road here and they led the dromedaries between the ghostly trunks and ducked under branches heavy with fruit.

Out of sight of the road, even as the first golden fingers of dawn probed through the trees, they let the dromedaries loose. As the beasts wandered away, they wrapped themselves in blankets and took it in turns to sleep.

When the sun had risen higher, crowning the pear trees with vivid wreaths of light, they found the road again and set off on foot. As they began their day's march they munched on fresh pears, gathered from around their resting place.

'I don't really like pears,' said Nastja sadly. Ellyah could not think of a civil retort, so held her tongue.

All through that morning there were no signs of pursuit. They passed a few lone riders as well as laden carts drawn by oxen or ponies, heading toward Carhinn. They walked without speaking much, but the more miles passed beneath their feet the more that the silence was filled with a comforting sense of relief.

Soon, the orchards gave way to fields of wheat and barley, ripe, golden and ready for the scythe. The air was damp and the countryside seemed to steam as the sun cleared the horizon, beaming down across the upright ranks of stalks like a proud general admiring a parade.

After three more days walking, the land began to rise around them, the road climbing and descending shallow rolling slopes while lumpy green hills bunched up ahead. In the distance, the first sharp black peaks of the Singing Mountains could be glimpsed, although the taller bulk of the mighty Derufin lay further north and out of sight.

They kept a steady pace each day, strolling easily along the hard-packed earth of the road. At night they found outhouses and barns to sleep in, creeping in under the cover of darkness and leaving again before dawn.

Evening was drawing in on the fifth day when they crested a small rise and looked down into the sheltered vale where the city of Kereva lay. It was an older city than Carhinn, with walls that varied in height and age, indicated by the colour of the stone. It was built on a roughly square footprint, with study round towers at three of the four corners, and a larger tower that was the lord's palace to the northwest. Rebuilding work was constantly underway, repairing and adapting the layout to meet the latest fashions.

Ellyah increased her pace to ensure that they reached the gates before dusk.

Once through the gates, Nastja led the way along the inside of the city walls. The square, tall houses of the nobility that occupied the city's northwest corner were pale, but by the time they crossed the river, the water was inky black in the low light. Nastja led the way with purpose.

They had discussed where they could stay as they walked, trying to reach a decision.

'I want to stay at the Claypit,' stated Ellyah.

'Where every single person in there will know your face,' countered Nastja. 'We should find somewhere we can stay out of sight while we decide what to do with the jewel.'

Ellyah had pouted. 'I like the Claypit.'

The Claypit was one of the oldest taverns in Kereva. It was a low, raucous place but was always alive with music and talk. It served the best ale and cider in the city, too.

It was also a pit of gossip, and if Ellyah or Nastja showed their faces there then their presence would be common knowledge across the city by midnight, along with a dozen theories about their business.

In the end, Ellyah had been forced to admit that Nastja was right, and that lying low for a while was prudent. She had felt her face twisting into a scowl of annoyance, and forced herself to smile pleasantly instead.

Maybe, she told herself, when she had sold the jewel and was rich, she would buy the Claypit herself. She could live there in comfort. A queen in her palace.

The porridge bubbled and she stirred it vigorously a few times. She lifted the pan away from the embers and divided the lumpy meal between three mismatched bowls.

'Breakfast is ready, my hens,' she called out, in a singsong voice. She passed a bowl to Nastja, and Luara emerged, wild-haired, from beneath her blankets to grab another.

They ate in silence. Ellyah had thrown a handful of chopped prunes into hers, for a sweet bite, and she found the creamy porridge delicious and filling.

Nastja was picking at hers half-heartedly.

'Something wrong?' asked Ellyah.

'It's just a bit runny.'

'Porridge is nice like this. Goes down easy.'

'No.' Nastja looked away. 'This is how you like it. It's not how we like it.'

Ellyah stared at Nastja, then looked toward Luara. The older woman shrugged noncommittally. Nastja just could not help finding fault.

'Fine,' said Ellyah, trying not to sound grumpy. 'You can make our breakfast tomorrow.'

'If you want me to,' said Nastja, emotionlessly. Then: 'Did I say something wrong?'

Ellyah summoned her patience. 'No,' she said, after a moment. 'It's nothing.'

Luara was smirking.

'I think we should start making contacts today,' said Ellyah, as she gathered the bowls. 'What do you think?'

'There are four dealers in Kereva who might be able to fence the ruby,' replied Nastja. 'And I can think of five other…general traders who might be interested.

By "general traders", she meant smugglers. Legitimate-seeming merchants who used their lawful trading as a front to hide their more profitable sideline in moving goods illegally.

'They won't all give us a fair cut though,' Nastja went on. 'Two or three—' she paused, as if adding up in her head. 'Yes, three, will try to rip us off. And we will need to be careful, Ell. If word gets around that we are here, trying to shift a valuable gem…' she tailed off into a meaningful look.

'Simple disguises?' said Ellyah, as a suggestion.

'Yes,' replied Nastja.

Ellyah strolled through the marketplace alone. She wore a short, dun-coloured smock with simple hose. Her long dark hair was tied up tightly and tucked up underneath the rough wind of thick linen that served as a commoner's cap.

No one spared her more than a disinterested glance.

This time, her rings were her own. She had put them back on with some relief after they had escaped Carhinn. Like any Anise, she felt uncomfortable without them, felt uneasy hiding her true history. It was sometimes essential in her line of work, though.

Her first ten were a mix of the dull greys of pewter and iron. Her early years had been simple, but secure. The other twelve rings were a ragtag mix of lead and iron, with a couple of bright brass rings representing her best years. As she looked around the marketplace, rings flashed on most fingers, a record of each person's class and fortunes.

Her face was set in an expression of slightly blank concentration, and she feigned an interest in the wares of the stalls she passed. Inside, she was bubbling with delight. She had grown up in this city and knew every cobbled street and muddy lane. She was home.

The familiar sounds of daytime Kereva washed over her as she strolled lightly through the streets. Small livestock in pens and cages bleated or clucked, the percussive ring of the smith's hammer was loud over even the roar of the furnace, and everywhere was the noise of people.

People chattering. People bartering. People laughing, arguing or simply exchanging greetings.

The flow of communication was endless, like the rain teeming down into a still lake and creating ripples that spread, collided and grew. She ached to hear every word, to listen to the stories behind each conversation. There would be so much she could learn, so much she could use.

'You're trying to rob me, cock! And in broad daylight, too!' exclaimed a trader, hands firmly grasping the fleeces he was selling. 'If I sell them for that, then I may as well just lie down in the gutter and starve. Is that what you want?'

'...and you know my Uncle Trojne?' a common woman was saying to another, leaning in close as though sharing a secret. 'Well, his wife don't know but he's been seen with one of the barmaids of the Claypits after dark. The one with a touch of *helfishness* about her face? I know! The scandal!'

'Come closer.' A dark clad man beckoned to a teenage girl in a dirty smock. 'You get that boss of yours to let slip when he's shifting his next load of spice, and there's be good money in it for you. You do a favour for me, I do a favour for you, see?' He smiled, a yellow-toothed leer.

Ellyah caught all these snatches of conversation, and more besides, as she moved gradually through the city. The last one made her prick up her ears, and she was hard-pressed not to stop and listen in to the rest. It could have been worth much.

The trade in some spices had got so fierce that the criminal gangs had taken notice. Supply from Kotev had fallen off and prices had never been higher. There was a lot of money to be made trading legally or illegally, and the gangs wanted to control that trade. Simple theft had also never been more profitable.

No, she reminded herself. *Not here, not now.*

Last time she had left Kereva it had been under the cover of darkness with all the brawlers of a rival gang at her heels. They had overreacted to her...seizing an opportunity. Seizing something they regarded as belonging to them. She had barely escaped with her life.

It would be better if she was not recognised this time. Besides, that sort of news was not what she was supposed to be listening for. She was trying to find a way to sell that jewel. Could any of her old contacts help? Were they still in Kereva? Were they even still alive?

All questions that she hoped to answer over the next few days, but she had to be careful.

She was forced to be frustratingly tentative that day. She dared do no more than pause outside the doors of a couple of different gem dealers, staring quickly inside to see if she could spot any familiar faces.

If she was going to make contact later, she had to be sure. She had to be discreet. It was vital that she gathered all possible knowledge before acting. Her future depended on it.

Heavy clouds scudded overhead, driven by a steady southwesterly wind. They massed over the Singing Mountains, filling the sky as though it were a thick woollen blanket. The light faded as the afternoon wore on. Rain was on the way.

She hurried back toward the south-east of the city. The nearest tower loomed large in her vision, rising above the walls to keep a watch over the surrounding land. Like the walls, the tower was draped in a robe of scaffolding. The whole city was constantly being rebuilt or renovated in keeping with the needs of the times.

It was a common joke that every stone of the upper towers served an apprenticeship in the lower walls, before graduating to a higher location.

Fat, heavy spots of rain broke across Ellyah's face as she dashed toward the dark doorway of the storage shed. She checked left and right to make sure she was not observed, before ducking through the door.

A gloomy corridor led through the building. The northern end comprised one large barn-like room, but the southern half was divided into smaller areas by high timber partitions. The whole building was little used, and Ellyah felt the fleeting touch of cobwebs against her face as she followed the corridor south.

At the end, she was faced with a sturdy door of aged wooden planks. To the touch, it felt securely locked, but Ellyah pulled a slim metal rod from her tool roll and inserted it into the lock. She pulled it upward with practised confidence. There was a solid click, and the door swung inwards.

Beyond, was an office. It was clearly owned by someone who had little time or inclination for proper record keeping. Linen scrolls, rolled and tied or just screwed in a ball, lay all over the table and littered the shelves that ran around the walls. More tellingly, empty wine flasks dotted the floor.

The disorder made Ellyah shudder. She moved through the mess swiftly and through another, narrower door.

From the outside it appeared little more than a cupboard, but behind was a room of similar size to the office. Ellyah had not said so but thought Nastja had done well to think of this place and to lead them here. They were unlikely to be found, either accidentally or by their pursuers.

'Afternoon,' said Luara, looking up with a quick smile. 'I went to the market.'

Several small sacks stood near the hearth and a selection of fresh fruits and vegetables were stacked neatly nearby. Luara did not know the city, and had no useful contacts, but it seemed she had nevertheless made herself useful.

As Ellyah sat heavily on the bed, Luara added several handfuls of rice to a pan of water over the fire. Reaching into smaller sacks, she added some small, wrinkled dried fruits and a pinch of vivid yellow curcumin. A savoury scent filled the air, borne on the rising steam.

'I thought you would be hungry,' she said, daintily stirring the contents of the pan with a long-handled spoon.

'Hungry?' Ellyah thought for a moment. 'Yes, I suppose I am. Haven't eaten since dawn.'

'Well, there we are then,' replied Luara, satisfied. 'There'll be plenty to eat, soon. Nice to be home?'

'Yea,' replied Ellyah, quickly. 'But I didn't find much out. I can't ask too many questions, it would be suspicious. But if I do nothing but watch I'll never learn anything. It's frustrating.'

'We have a bit of time, yet. You just need to be patient.'

Ellyah swung her head around to look at Luara. The older woman was wearing an expression of bland innocence, eyes wide, lips in a half smile. Was she being subtly provocative? Ellyah did not know her well enough to be sure. She chose not to argue the point.

As she stood to change her clothes, she noticed for the first time that there was a lumpy bundle of blankets lying beneath the narrow window. As she looked closer she saw that the bundle had some messy fair hair. It was Nastja.

'How long has she been back?' asked Ellyah, incredulously. She pulled the rough smock off over her head and reached for her own shirt. It was somewhat stained from the long, rapid journey and she wrinkled her nose at the smell.

'She came in one chime after you went out.'

'What? She was supposed to be looking for contacts to help fence on the jewel!'

Luara shrugged. 'Said she was tired because she'd been awake all night. And the city was too busy. Too loud.' She lifted the steaming spoon to her lips and took a tentative taste. 'Nearly ready,' she said. 'Nastja curled up in the blankets straight away, and she's not moved since.'

Ellyah fumed. This was typical of Nastja. On her good days she could solve insurmountable problems, and act quickly with an intuitive sense of the best course of action. On a bad day, it was like being around a toddling child having a sulking tantrum.

'Am I supposed to do all this by myself?' Ellyah asked of the world in general, despairingly.

'She didn't look good when she came back,' said Luara, speaking slowly as though choosing her words with care. 'She looked...frantic. Scared. I think we should let her sleep it off, maybe she'll feel better in the morning.'

'Maybe you're right.'

'Come and eat.'

Ellyah sat, lowering herself to the floor to sit cross legged near the hearth. The warmth was comforting and welcome. Outside the window, the splattering roar of the pouring rain was loud.

'Make sure to save some food for Nastja,' said Ellyah, as she filled her own bowl. 'Although she'll complain. She'll say you should have put some piment in, or more pepper. She always knows best.'

The two women shared a smile as they spooned warm, fragrant rice into their mouths. It was filling, warming food.

'You grew up here?' asked Luara between mouthfuls. Ellyah nodded.

'I lived in the slums near the south of the river,' she replied. 'Not sure the house is still there. I've not been to check.'

'And your parents? Are they still here?'

There was a long, pregnant pause. Ellyah considered what to say. She decided on the truth.

'My parents are dead,' she said, simply. 'They were murdered.'

'I'm so sorry.'

Ellyah waved a hand. 'It happened so long ago I can barely remember it. I mean, I can't remember what it was like before.'

'How old were you?'

'About six.'

Luara nodded. 'So what happened to you?'

'Someone found me. Took me in. Raised me.'

Suddenly, Ellyah did not want to talk about her early life anymore. 'What about you? Did you have parents?'

Luara chewed for a moment, thinking. 'One of my parents was around when I was growing up. The other one was not. I still haven't decided which of them was the better influence.' She smiled weakly.

'We're still here, hen,' said Ellyah, softly.

'Aye, we are. For now.'

Luara paused. Her eyes flicked to the corner of the room. A nondescript leather bag was tucked away there, and inside was the jewel. So much rested on that jewel.

'Do you have a plan for how you're going to find a buyer for it?' she asked. 'Really?'

'No. But I'll find a way.'

'We're still in danger as long as we have it.' Luara's eyes had hardened. 'If we can't sell it, we should give it up and disappear. They will stop chasing us if we don't have it.'

Then what? Ellyah wanted to retort angrily. *We starve to death in some other hideout? Or try to take normal jobs? What would we be, barmaids?*

She chewed her lip instead. With enough money she could truly escape. Away from the cities, away from criminals, and away from all the painful memories.

'I won't give it up,' she said. 'We'll sell it somewhere. Even if we have to keep walking for another three months. They'll get bored of chasing us eventually.'

The rain continued to drum on the roof, and the wet sounds from outside told of the muddy street being churned into a swamp. The gusting wind caused the timbers of the building to creak and groan, like badly greased cart axles.

Ellyah blew out a breath, and turned to stack the bowls by the hearth. The fire had died but the embers still glowed, filling the room with a comforting warmth.

'Guess I'll turn in,' she said.

'Me too,' said Luara, standing and moving over to the bed.

'Oh. Are we sharing?'

'Warmer,' replied Luara as she wriggled onto the hard, narrow bed and made room beside her.

Ellyah shrugged and sat down, before swivelling around to lie next to the older woman. They were both long in the habit of sleeping fully clothed, including their boots. Both had learned from bitter experience that it was sometimes necessary to make a swift escape, even in the middle of the night.

The bed was not wide, and Luara lay on her side to leave room for Ellyah to lie down on her back. In the dimming light of the glowing hearth, Luara's eyes were wide and gleamed with deep fire.

'I'm not sure I'll be able to sleep straight away,' Ellyah murmured. 'My mind is racing.'

'You'll drift off,' replied Luara softly. 'I'll look after you.'

As she spoke, she reached out and gently smoothed the hair on Ellyah's brow. Ellyah sighed as Luara's hand stroked across her head. Shutting her eyes, she relaxed as Luara's fingertips ran through her hair, then trailed across her cheek and down to her jawline. She could hear the other woman's steady breathing.

Luara wriggled closer. Ellyah was suddenly very aware of the sensation of Luara's body pressing firmly against her own. She was slender, but strong and muscular. Her proximity was warm, reassuring and yet somehow also very alien.

Ellyah was not sure how she felt, but kept her eyes closed. She did feel more relaxed now though, beginning to drift off to sleep.

Her eyes snapped open. What was that noise?

She thought she had heard a soft click, only just audible over the noise of the rain. What was it? Something moving outside the building? Something being blown over by the fitful wind? Or, had the sound come from inside the building?

Another sound. It was a footstep, she was sure. In the next instant, she had jumped out of bed.

She moved silently across to the door and checked that the wooden latch was in place before pausing to listen. She could feel Luara moving behind her, and was equally aware of the subtle sounds outside. Aware of the threat.

Nothing happened. All was still.

Ellyah barely dared to breathe as she crouched before the door. Maybe, she had imagined the sounds. Maybe.

With a tearing crash, the door was ripped from the frame and flung into the room. Ellyah had no chance to move before it hit her full in the face.

She was flung backwards, and the last thing she felt was the back of her head colliding jarringly with the end of the bed.

There was a stab of pain that shot through her skull, then everything faded to black.

TWENTY TWO

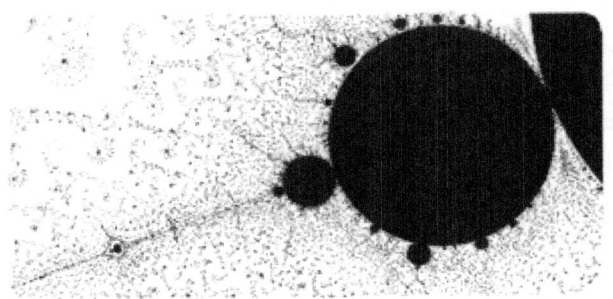

He was drunk. He had thrown down his reaping hook in the middle of the afternoon and stormed off in the direction of the nearest village.

Now, it was dusk. The door swung inwards and shook violently, even as he stepped unsteadily into the house. Nastja usually made herself scarce on these occasions, but this time she was not quick enough.

'Food,' he grunted, toward her mother; his wife.

Wordlessly, she set a wooden plate with a small loaf and some soft white cheese before him.

'Want meat!' he snarled, rounding on his wife. He was only a slight man, with slender shoulders and a wiry build, but when he was deep in drink he could still be frightening. Like a wild animal.

'We haven't got any meat,' sighed her mother, wearily.

'Insolent bitch!'

Her father stood. His fist swung. Her mother did not move to block the blow, or even try to avoid it. She knew that it would just make the next punch harder.

The noise when his fist hit the side of her head was flat and dull. Her mother toppled sideways. The sound when her head bounced off the shelf beside the hearth was sharp and woody.

The sound of her body hitting the ground was soft, and horribly final.

Nastja had looked down, knowing already what she would see. Her mother lay on the ground with her eyes wide open, and did not move again. Nastja had run through the open door and had not looked back.

She still heard those terrible noises in her dreams. The dull slap, the sharp crack, and the soft thud.

That harsh sound of a skull bouncing off hard, unyielding wood echoed through her being.

Her eyes opened. This time, it had not been in her dreams.

Looking up from her position on the floor she saw that the whole door had been ripped from its hinges. It lay across the floor, and a huge, dark figure was stepping over it. The way he had to stoop to fit beneath the lintel suggested a towering height.

That woody crack…it had been so familiar.

Then, she noticed Ellyah sprawled on the floor at the foot of the bed, and her skin tingled with a chill of horror. Glistening blood made a damp, shining mess in the hair on the back of Ellyah's head.

Nastja stood, shrugging off her blankets. This time, Nastja knew she must stay and help.

As she moved toward the intruder, he turned away. He dropped into a defensive crouch which dropped his head a few inches lower than the ceiling beams. He was a truly enormous man, or perhaps a half-elf.

He swung a fist, then twisted his body as though avoiding a blow. Of course, Luara. She was putting up a fight. Her adversary was just so big that he blocked her from view.

Nastja scanned the room. They needed to escape. She needed to help Ellyah. They must take the jewel with them. She planned her actions quickly.

Luara was backing away. Her fists were raised, and she was moving constantly. Her opponent was not just tall, he was broad and had thick, powerful arms. She could not let him land a blow.

She was watching him like a hunting hawk, ready to duck or dodge any time one of those great fists swung in her direction.

She danced close, risking a hit while she jabbed toward his ribs. She was keeping his attention, that was the main thing.

As Nastja stepped silently onto the bed, Luara spun, bent low, and came up again holding the wooden spoon she had used to eat her dinner. For a moment, her opponent was puzzled and as he hesitated she jabbed at him with it.

He grunted in pain, slapping a hand to his thick neck. Nastja edged closer, creeping across the bed. He still had not noticed her.

Luara lashed out with the spoon again, catching the dark-skinned giant with a rap across the knuckles. He growled, snatching his hand away.

It was time.

'Hey,' said Nastja, loudly and clearly.

He turned.

As his head came around to face hers she thrust out a hand. He was caught completely by surprise by the blow and did not have time to even raise his arms.

The heel of Nastja's hand caught him beneath the chin as she twisted her whole body from the waist. She was not especially strong, but need gave her extra power, and she had timed the blow perfectly.

His head snapped back. His mouth lolled open even as his long legs buckled. He fell backward into the doorway. It seemed to take a long time, like watching a building collapse.

'Help me,' she barked toward Luara as she jumped down from the bed. 'There'll be more of them on the way.'

Working together, they pushed the giant's legs out beyond the doorway, noticing movement in the next room as they did so.

'The door!'

They lifted the door and propped it horizontally across the doorway. Nastja held it in place while Luara dragged the bed across the floor to reinforce the barricade.

'That won't keep them out for long!' panted Luara. 'We need to work fast!'

Nastja was darting around the room, collecting essentials. 'The window.'

Luara nodded. She did not need detailed instructions, which was fortunate. As they dragged Ellyah's limp form across the room, a furious face appeared in the partially blocked doorway.

'They are going out the window!' they shouted, their words spoken thickly and indistinctly.

Nastja went through first, climbing over the sill and jumping down to stand in the muddy street. Inside the room, Luara bent down and wrapped her hands around Ellyah's body. With a grunt of effort, she lifted Ellyah up and pushed her across the sill. Nastja took her weight and eased her out to slither softly onto the wet ground.

Fat drops of rain poured from the darkness and ran down Ellyah's face, slack and emotionless.

'Now what?' Luara leaned in close to make herself heard over the weather's cacophony.

'There,' said Nastja, pointing.

A wagon stood in the lee of the wall. It was lit by the paltry glow of a single shrouded candle lantern, seemingly hung from the rail. Squinting through the darkness she could see two sturdy ponies hitched to the shafts. Strangely, a tall crate stood upright on the bed of the wagon.

Between them they half dragged, half carried Ellyah over to the wagon. Even as they set her down on the boards, the slapping sound of running feet on mud reached their ears.

A group of men had appeared around the corner.

They could only be Mackems.

Luara dropped lightly from the wagon. As they had hurried from the room she had made sure to wrap her sword belt around her waist. Now, she drew her matching pair of shortswords and held them low.

'Now,' she said, stepping forward. 'It's my turn.'

They spread out, beginning to surround her, but before they had taken two steps she danced sideways and one of her slender blades scythed out. The cloaked gangster holding a cowled lantern clutched at his throat as blood poured over his fingers. It looked black and shone wetly in the dim light.

He dropped the lantern to the sodden ground and it went out. Aside from the small circle of yellow light in which Nastja sat, the rest of the scene was cloaked in darkness, black as pitch.

Grunts and cries of pain broke the stillness of the night. Nastja could see nothing, and she wondered if Luara was being overwhelmed, beaten by the clubs and pierced by the daggers of the Mackems.

When a hand grasped the rail of the wagon, she jumped and reached for her small belt knife.

'Drive! Go! Now'

It was Luara, climbing into the back. Nastja flicked the reins and the wagon was dragged into motion. Slowly. Too slowly.

Running feet sounded through the gloom, and another hand grasped the rail. A man's hand. Luara slashed down precisely with those swift blades, and the hand was gone in a spray of blood.

Nastja turned her head for a moment, to see Luara moving to the back of the wagon. She hung off the crate, which was lashed to the wagon bed with thin cords, and peered into the darkness.

Urging the pair of ponies to greater speed, Nastja was glad that she knew the city well. She was planning to head straight for the closest bridge, before turning onto the wider streets that led to the north gate.

They could not stay in the city, and could not return south. North was the only way they could go, if they could escape that way without being caught.

A sudden shriek from Luara made her turn again. She had jumped back from the crate, which was rocking from side to side. A shuffling, rhythmic thumping was coming from within.

'Well, I don't like that!' exclaimed Luara. She quickly cut through the cords with her swords, before giving the crate itself a solid kick. It teetered on the back of the wagon for a moment, then toppled backward to land in the mud. There was a solid crunch as the timbers broke apart with the force of the impact.

Through the gaps where the planks had shifted, a sullen red glow shone fiercely. It was bright enough to wash the nearby walls with crimson.

'Keep going!' said Luara, fear filling her voice. Nastja turned back to the road, clicking her tongue at the ponies.

What had caused that strange light that shone from within the crate?

They turned right around a sharp corner, and continued down a narrow street. The stony faces of the buildings flashed by on either side, illuminated momentarily by the wan light of the cowled lantern.

'Ellyah?' Nastja raised her voice to be heard over the hiss of the rain and the rattle of the wagon. She kept recalling that awful noise, and the damp spread of blood across the back of Ellyah's head.

There was no response for a moment, as Luara stooped across Ellyah's prone form, trying to hold herself steady as the wagon lurched along the bumpy street.

'She's breathing,' Luara called out. 'But she's not waking up. There's a lot of blood around the back of her head…but I think it's stopped bleeding now.'

Nastja thought quickly. They had to leave Kereva. They needed to head north. They needed a healer for Ellyah. She knew where to go. Fordon.

Before her, the narrow street opened out into a dark, open space. The city square. Flickering orange glows from the open windows of several inns cast the area with a ghostly half-light. The edges and corners of the square were shrouded in deeper darkness.

She hauled on the reins and the cart turned sharply left. The wheels slithered onto cobbles and the whole wagon began to judder and shake with a staccato rhythm.

'Don't slow down,' growled Luara.

Half-turning, she saw Luara crouched in the rear of the cart, Ellyah lying still between her legs. She scanned the darkness as the wagon seat bounced beneath her. What had Luara seen?

A hand grabbed the rail with a sudden slap. The wagon rocked as another pair of hands appeared at the other side. Faces followed as the attackers began to climb up. The desperate, growling faces of Mackems gangsters.

Luara lunged out with her swords. There was a cry and thud as someone fell away to hit the ground, left behind as the cart rattled on.

At the same time, the second attacker swung their leg over the rail and stood. They threw their hands towards Luara. Nastja watched with half an eye, gripping the reins tightly, opening her mouth to cry out.

But Luara had already seen the danger. She leaned toward the rail and kicked out backwards. It looked almost casual. Her boot caught the attacker across the body, and they staggered. As her foot came down she shifted her weight backward, still facing away from her attacker and stabbed out behind her with one of her swords.

The sharp point sunk deeply into the gangster's side, and as they slapped a hand to the wound, Luara twisted and struck them powerfully in the chest with the flat of her left hand.

They toppled backward over the side of the wagon, to be swallowed by the night.

The cart had only jolted on for a few more racing heartbeats when it was rocked once more. This time, though, Luara barely had time to turn before a new attacker had scrambled up onto the back.

Nastja glanced around to get a look at them. In the low, upward glow of the shrouded lantern they had a menacing, spectral appearance.

It was a man, tall and extremely broad around the shoulders. His ears jutted out and his head rose like a dome though his thin, rain slicked hair. Thick, strong fingers flexed as he faced Luara.

'Just the jewel,' he shouted over the chatter of the cart and the hiss of the rain. 'Just want the jewel, that's all. Give us it.'

'No,' said Luara.

The Mackem rolled his neck, legs spread to balance himself against the rock and sway of the surging wagon. He drew a short, heavy bladed knife and an iron-capped cudgel, before taking a step forward.

Nastja was forced to concentrate on steering the wagon as the gateway through the inner way loomed ahead. The guards to either side could only watch the wagon surge past, their surprised expressions lit by flickering torchlight.

She sawed at the reins and the cart turned to the left, rattling onwards through the narrow space between the inner and outer walls. It was an ink-dark canyon illuminated only by the glow of the torches in the shelter of the gateway and the swaying candle lantern on the wagon.

Weapons clashed behind Nastja's head, and she turned. Luara and the burly Mackem were still facing each other, both too preoccupied with keeping their footing on the swaying wagon bed to attack wholeheartedly.

Luara thrust with one sword and slashed with the other, but her opponent responded quickly and beat the strikes away.

Then, the yawning mouth of the gateway in the thick outer wall opened to her right, and Nastja concentrated on steering through and out of the city. The dark tunnel of the gateway receded quickly and the cart jolted out into the countryside.

The road twisted and turned through the outer township; a ramshackle sprawl of roughly built houses that huddled in the lee of the city wall. Even in the dark, it reminded Nastja of Carhinn's Eastra and Westra.

The rattle and clash of weapons colliding broke the stillness of the night. Nastja did not dare to turn her head, but could feel the combatants moving around wordlessly behind her. She could sense them both striving for an advantage.

A grunt of effort. A metallic, slithering sound. Then, a dull thud and a groan of pain.

Now, Nastja could not restrain the urge to turn around.

The man was moving toward her. He lifted a foot to step over the prone figures of Ellyah and Luara. His cudgel was held loosely in one of his meaty hands, but it carried no less of a threat. He was ready to use the weapon.

'Just you and me now,' he yelled. 'Stop the cart and give us the jewel. I'll let you all go.'

Despite his muddy, indistinct pronunciation, Nastja thought from the look on his face that he was telling the truth. He had the air of a man at work, and his job was to get his hands on the jewel. Nothing more.

The cart juddered on, soft earth beneath the wheels.

Nastja made her decision.

She leaned on the reins, sending the cart across the road and over the edge. The road was raised above a steep sided ditch on either side. As the wheels on one side of the wagon slewed off the hard-packed dirt and into the ditch, the whole thing tipped sideways.

The Mackem man lost his balance, lurching across and sprawling over the rail. Nastja hung on desperately, trying to prevent the whole wagon or either of the ponies being lost into the depths of the ditch.

She glanced back, and saw one of Luara's legs rising. She kicked out at the man as he clung onto the rail. Once. Twice. Three times.

The third kick tipped his balance, and he swung over the rail. His feet waved despairingly in the air before he vanished into the night.

Nastja heaved on the reins once more, and the ponies trotted gratefully back up onto level ground. She could hear a rhythmical roaring sound. She realised it was her own ragged breathing.

Luara climbed over to join her on the driver's seat. She was gingerly dabbing a growing bump on the side of her temple. Blood oozed.

'Ouch,' she said.

Nastja said nothing. That really had been far too close to complete disaster. They had been lucky to escape. How did the Mackems keep tracking them down?

'How do they keep finding us?' said Luara, like an echo of Nastja's thoughts.

The night rushed by, the surroundings invisible beyond the small circle of guttering lamplight. The rain still fell in hissing sheets, pattering on the damp wood of the wagon.

I don't know, thought Nastja, although she could not bring herself to say the words.

'I don't believe it's chance,' she began, thinking as she spoke. 'And I don't believe any of those thugs have the skills to be tracking us. Not that easily. We barely made a ripple in Kereva, the word could not have spread that we were there at all, let alone exactly where we were. It doesn't make sense.'

'It feels like they will keep finding us, wherever we go.'

'Yea. But how?'

Nastja suddenly remembered the red glow that had shone out in the dark street. Shining out from inside that tall crate.

The same red glow as from the ruby.

'The jewel,' she said. 'They must be able to follow the jewel itself, somehow.'

How?

'I don't understand how that can be.' Luara glanced back where it was stored, in a leather bag tucked behind the seat. 'But it would explain a lot.'

'Do you believe in magic?' asked Nastja, abruptly.

Luara's stare was incredulous, eyes wide and shining in the low light. 'Do you believe in faeries?' she asked.

'Yes, I think so,' replied Nastja, before realising that Luara's voice had been laced with sarcasm. She continued. 'People say there used to be magic in the world. We shouldn't rule it out. No other explanation really makes sense.'

'You're saying they are tracking us by magic?'

Nastja shrugged in response.

'We should get rid of it!' Luara suddenly sounded shrill.

'No,' replied Nastja, quickly. Her thoughts went immediately to Ellyah. She was determined not to give up on this. This was her big, final job. Her dream. Nastja had to be a part of it, and to help make it a success. 'If the Mackems want it this badly then it must be very valuable, very important, or very dangerous. Probably all three. Someone will pay well for it.'

'The Mackems?' Luara was smiling. 'Sell it back to them?'

'Trying something like that would be the best way I can think of to get our throats slit. No, we can't do that. But, if we can sell it on to someone who thinks they can, and isn't scared of the Mackems…'

'I've got an idea,' said Luara with a decisive tone.

'Go on.'

'My lovely hometown,' she said, 'is run by criminals. The governor has no control and it's also where all the trade of the Riverlands goes or comes from. I'm certain we could sell anything there.'

'Ben Gedrin?' asked Nastja.

'Yes, Ben Gedrin. It'll be dangerous but if there's anywhere in the world we can shift it, it's there. It also gives us a chance to leave the Mackems behind by crossing the Derufin Mountains.'

'It's still "us" then?' said Nastja. 'I wouldn't blame you if you decided you'd had enough after tonight. I'm sure you could vanish.'

Luara looked thoughtful. 'I know there are a couple from the fight at the hideout who won't remember my face, because they won't remember anything ever again.' Her sweet smile belied the savagery of her actions. 'But I'm fairly sure the big guy who got on the wagon will remember me.'

'I'm sorry you ended up involved,' said Nastja. 'I never understood why you were. Just for the money?'

The cart rattled on as Luara gazed out into the night. She was silent for so long that Nastja wondered if she had caused offence.

'I don't have anywhere else to go,' she said, eventually, and her voice was uncharacteristically quiet and sad. 'And I don't know how to do anything else. All the people I knew and trusted are…gone. I was alone until I met Ellyah and when she talked about her dreams it made me feel like life might be…fun, again. I'd rather be in danger with some people I like and trust than be safe and alone.'

She looked very emotional. Her brow was furrowed with fine lines and her eyes were wide and shining. It was like she was close to tears. Nastja knew she should say something friendly and encouraging.

'We are happy to have you with us. You're a very useful person.'

'That's nice of you to say,' said Luara, her usual smile returning. 'So, the plan is to go to Ben Gedrin?'

Nastja nodded in agreement. 'Yes. First, we stop in Fordon, but quickly, to take Ell to see a healer. I know one who I hope still lives there. Then we make for the Rujrweh Pass toward Annida, and head for Kiraband once we're over the mountains.'

'Then back to Ben Gedrin,' shrugged Luara.

'To Ben Gedrin,' repeated Nastja.

TWENTY THREE

'What do you want? Go away.'

The figure in the doorway looked exactly as Nastja remembered. He had wild, unwashed hair that hung to his shoulders and was dressed in a short, dirty robe that appeared to be made from sacks.

Pale eyes burned intensely from a face that looked too young. At this moment, they gleamed with anger.

They had arrived in Fordon. Nastja and Luara had taken turns driving the wagon through the night, only slowing to a walk once they were well clear of Kereva. They had been determined to keep moving.

By mid-morning, the town of Fordon rose before them.

The town rose on a hill at the north of a wide vale. This was bounded by the Kereva Hills to the south, the King's Dyke to the east and the bulk of the Singing Mountains rising to the north. All the towns in the area were fortified although local treaties had brokered a fragile peace between Anish and Kotev.

The whole eastern extent of the vale was studded with lakes; sapphires strung on the necklace of the Tohruvy River. They ran in a chain from Kereva northward to the very feet of the Singing Mountains, and Fordon lay beside the greatest, and most northerly of these; Lake Mjafte.

Fordon was built atop a low hill, a solitary sentinel of the higher mountains beyond. The walls encircled the very summit of the hill, and the town huddled on the flat space within.

At the far side of the hill, a grand keep rose. This had been home for generations of a local noble family, and the keep of Fordon was said to be impossible to take. Few armies had tried. The rear of the hill was too steep to climb and the entrance at the front was reached by a winding causeway, cut into the hillside.

To approach the town, travellers or attackers alike were forced to slowly climb this snaking path and sheer, grey stone walls loomed above, bounding a huge gateway.

The gates were wide open and Nastja drove the wagon through them surrounded by a steady flow of other traffic. A constant stream flowed in and out of the town. Wagons, piled high with goods bought or to be sold rumbled on side-by-side with lone traders pushing barrows, as well as simple travellers, mounted or on foot.

Nastja was unsurprised to see groups of dwarves among the crowds. Fordon lay near the trade route they often used between their mountain home and the Rujrweh Pass, the only way north through the Derufin Mountains. She saw only common dwarves in pleated skirts and baggy shirts; their knights and nobles were rarely seen outside of the Severed City.

As she turned the wagon off the cobbled main street and onto a muddy lane, a dwarf woman on the corner clasped her hands before her waist and raised her voice in a clear, simple song.

She sang in Dwarvish, so Nastja could not understand all the words, but the melody was sad and melancholic.

She tugged on the reins and the weary ponies came to a grateful halt before an untidy shack. It looked out of place beside the tall, neat stone buildings that lined the street. A groan from the wagon bed told her that Ellyah was at least awake.

'Where are we?' she asked, voice groggy. Again.

She had woken a few times during the night, confused and alarmed. They had explained the head injury she had suffered and their subsequent escape from Kereva.

'But, I'm fine,' she had said, before suddenly leaning over the rail and vomiting noisily. 'My head hurts a bit,' she admitted, before slumping down and falling asleep once more.

'Where am I? What's going on?' was a repeated refrain whenever Ellyah stirred. In the end, Luara got in the back of the wagon to keep a close eye on her, and to make sure she did not do anything too stupid. Nastja was very keen to get a healer to look at her.

She hopped down from the wagon and tapped her knuckles on one of the doorposts of the shack. The door itself was a stained length of oiled cloth, frayed at the edges and muddy where it brushed the ground.

'Clear off,' said the healer with a gesture, after he had emerged from behind the flimsy door.

'We need a healer,' said Nastja, standing her ground. 'And you are one. I remember.'

'Remember?' he asked, suspiciously.

'Yes, we have met before. I have had healing from you before.'

'Well, I don't remember. A lot of people come knocking on my door. *People.*' He invested that word with heavy scorn.

'Our friend has an injury,' said Luara, from her seat on the wagon. 'Will you at least look at her?'

'What sort of injury?'

'She hit her head,' replied Nastja. 'Hard.' She was trying to remain patient.

'That was careless. How did she manage that?'

'It's a long story,' growled Nastja through gritted teeth, 'that doesn't matter. Can we bring her in? Please?'

'Oho!' hooted the healer. 'That's how it starts. Some excuse to come into Mateck's home, and then the interrogation starts. The accusations!' His face was twisted in fury.

'Mateck the healer,' said Luara, slipping down from the wagon and walking closer. 'We don't know what you're talking about, but we aren't going to accuse you of anything. We just want to help our friend be well again.' She gazed up at him with wide eyes. 'Will you help us?'

His eyes flicked between the two women. His anger subsided visibly as the moments passed.

'Fine,' he snapped eventually. 'Bring her in. But don't touch anything!'

Together, Nastja and Luara managed to lift Ellyah from the wagon and get her standing upright. She was the tallest of the three, but was slender. Luara was probably heavier and almost strong enough to carry Ellyah on her own. As they dragged her across to the shack, her arms around their shoulders, she woke.

'Where am I?' she asked, once more. She sounded muddled and confused. 'Just put me back to bed, hen. It was a busy day.'

Nastja looked across to Luara, who caught her eye and giggled.

Inside the small, round shack was chaos. There was no furniture. The bed appeared to be a dirty woollen blanket, folded onto a floor of rushes over bare earth. Open wooden crates lay in a haphazard distribution around the walls. These were brimming with powders of various colours, herbs both fresh and dried, and here there were what looked like fragments of rock.

They carefully sat Ellyah down on a clear patch of floor, and leaned her gently against the wall. It was made of birch rods tied together with twine, and shifted unsteadily. Her eyes snapped open.

'I'm in a witch's house,' she said, after a moment. 'Nas, why am I in a witch's house?'

'A witch?' asked Luara, surprised.

'A witch!' growled the healer, Mateck, raising his hands and curling his fingers like claws.

'The witches are the best healers,' said Nastja, blandly. 'They have a lot of knowledge that has been forgotten. They study. They learn. They don't rely on superstition and old tradition.'

'I see at least one of you has a little sense,' said Mateck. 'Or a sweet tongue.'

Luara snorted. 'She is sensible,' she admitted. 'Is your knowledge of healing the reason they let you keep your house here?'

'What are you trying to say?' He turned to Luara in mock outrage. 'Are you suggesting that I do not seem of the same class as my neighbours? Is that what you're saying?'

Luara gave him a level look. 'Yes.'

He shrugged. 'You're right. They only put up with me because of the services I offer. Or, rather, the nobleman and traders who would have me run from the town are forced to put up with me because their wives would kill them if they touched me.'

He sat down on his ratty blanket, crossing his legs beneath himself.

Luara was still unconvinced. 'Services?'

'Oh yes,' he replied, eyes rolling. 'There's much that I can put right with the correct herb or brew or—' he paused, knowingly. 'Ointment. I can go into more detail if you'd like?'

'No. It's fine.'

'Yes, thought you'd say that. Anyway, the good, rich people of Fordon come a-flocking and all I demand in return is that they listen to what I have to say. That, and a handful of copper, of course. Man cannot live on righteous truth alone. I know, I've tried.'

Nastja was getting impatient. They were here for Ellyah, after all. But Luara was still curious.

'So, what exactly is it,' she asked, gazing intently at the scruffy man, 'that you feel the need to tell your visitors?'

'Not much,' he answered. 'Just that everything you have been told, your whole life, about the gods and the veil and the glorious judgement after death is a hollow lie. It's all a sham designed to keep the rich, rich and the poor in the dirt.'

'Are you serious?' She turned to the others. 'Is he serious?'

'There's no more proof that there is anything beyond this mortal realm than there is that lightning-giants roam the northern mountains. It's nothing more than a cradle tale, and it makes children from honest folk.'

Luara scowled. 'And what would you have them believe?'

'Nothing!' he cried, raising his voice excitedly. 'Believe nothing! Deny faith! See, hear, speak and listen. Find joy, meaning and satisfaction in the here and now! We are given a short span of years in this world, and we must use them well. Use them better.

'The world is beautiful, mysterious and full of enough wonder without wanting to tell one another foolish children's tales and live as though they were true. What matters is who you are, what good you can do, and how many lives you can touch for the better. Think on this, act on this, and suddenly you will be free. Free of fate and in control of your own life.

'I promise you this. That is all I have to say.'

Luara sat down, eyes wide and more questions on her lips. Nastja cut her off.

'Will you look at Ellyah now?' She paused, then put a note of pleading into her voice. 'Please?'

'Impatience.' Mateck wagged a chiding finger in Nastja's direction, but stood and moved over to where Ellyah sat. 'Lean forward,' he ordered briskly, and began probing the back of Ellyah's head with his fingertips. She took sharp intakes of breath as he touched the area around the injury, but otherwise stayed quiet.

'She's taken a mighty blow to the back of her skull,' he said, rising and moving to the other side of the hut. 'But it's not broken. Brain all still within.' He laughed at his own joke.

'Why am I in a witch's house?' asked Ellyah.

'Not now, Ell.'

'When did this happen?' asked Mateck, returning with a wooden bowl of water and a small cloth.

'Last night. Late,' replied Nastja.

'And has she slept since?'

'Yea, we couldn't keep her awake through the night.'

'She woke up, so I guess she will continue to do so. Lucky girl.'

He bathed the back of Ellyah's head with plenty of water, then began cleaning away the blood that was dried and matted in her hair with gentle dabs of the cloth. Ellyah grimaced, and hissed in pain. Once all the blood was washed out of her long, dark hair he reached into one of the scattered boxes and drew out a small, lidded jar. A sweet smell filled the room as he removed the lid.

'Honey,' said Nastja, knowingly.

'Of course.'

Mateck parted Ellyah's hair and dabbed it all over the gash. Nastja watched with interest. He set the jar down and produced a long strip of surprisingly white cloth. With this he bound the wound, wrapping it several times from the back of her head and around her temples.

Ellyah turned to Nastja when it was done. 'Do I look beautiful?' she asked, grinning.

Nastja did not reply, but she noticed Luara's smirk.

'If it were me,' he said. 'I'd avoid moving too much. Get plenty of rest.'

Nastja and Luara glanced at one another. Their journey so far had been far from restful.

'We don't have anywhere to go,' said Nastja.

'So?' Mateck was wiping his hands on a dirty cloth. He looked between Nastja and Luara, eyes darting, before throwing his hands up with an exasperated noise. 'Fine, she can stay here while she recovers. Two days, though, that's all. And you'll have to pay!'

'There's a wagon and two ponies outside,' said Nastja. 'You can have them.'

'What's wrong with them?' he asked, suspiciously.

'Nothing. We just don't want them anymore.'

Mateck shrugged in acceptance. He waved his hands dismissively towards a curtained off area at the rear of the hut. Drawing back the curtain, Nastja found a small heap of blankets. It would have to do.

Four days later, Mateck peeled back Ellyah's bandage and examined the wound on the back of her head. His lip curled in a disinterested sneer.

'It's fine,' he said. 'No pus, no visible bone. No leaking brains. Boring, really.'

The days had been long, with Nastja and Luara taking it in turns to sneak out into Fordon, hooded and cloaked, to fetch food while Ellyah mostly slept. The smell of the hut pervaded everything.

Mateck had mostly ignored them, apart from when other customers knocked on the door and he insisted that they hide silently behind the curtain.

'You'll probably have a headache for a while,' he said. 'Wine will help.'

'Wine?' asked Luara incredulously.

'Yea. Wine helps with most things, I find. In the correct quantities.'

Tying the bandage back in place, he helped Ellyah to her feet. Making shooing motions with his hands, he ushered the three women toward the sack cloth door.

'Go away,' he said. 'I'm really busy. And I'm tired.'

Outside, Ellyah was squinting in the bright daylight, the bandage bright on her brow. More rain had blown through during the night but the day was fine. The clouds were high and a patchy blue sky showed between their writhing white shapes.

'Right,' said Ellyah, clapping her hands eagerly together. 'You heard the man. Let's find an inn.'

The Crossways Inn sprawled. It sat on the intersection between the two busiest roads in Fordon, although some said that the Crossways had been there first and the roads had just been built to lead to the inn.

The high wall of the town's inner defences rose at the end of the main street. Where the street passed through the wall, a sturdy gateway led through to a wide courtyard with the keep, solid and timeless, looming beyond.

Tall, elegant buildings lined the streets. They were built from stone, cut square and fitted together with the fine tolerances of master craftsmanship. It was a far cry from the haphazard layout of Kereva and its jumbled mix of buildings. Fordon had been built with planning, and with wealth.

The inn itself was built from the same pale, well-dressed stone as the surrounding shops and civic buildings. It had many windows, which were filled with panels of horn scraped thin enough to let a cheery orange glow to shine through.

Ellyah led the way through one of the many doors and into the warm, welcoming interior. She seemed to have recovered a little already, although she had asked why they were in Fordon at least twice on the walk from the witch's shack near the town walls.

'A drink, and some food,' hissed Nastja as they crossed the common room to the bar. 'And then we leave. We can't linger.'

'Yes, yes,' said Ellyah dismissively. 'Wine, please! And something to eat. What do you have?'

The barmaid was olive skinned and slender, and when she spoke the accent of northern Anish was thick on her tongue.

'We got mash and stew today,' she said. 'And we got Bureno or local wine, my hens.'

'Local wine is fine.'

Ellyah slipped a copper ring from beneath her sleeve and handed it over, and the barmaid set a clay flask on the bar along with three wooden cups.

'Sit anywhere you like,' she said with a smile, 'and I'll bring you some food over.'

The inn's interior was like a grand hall in a lord's mansion. The horn windows meant that the wide room was lit with a cheery, yellowish light. Nastja was used to taverns that were shadow-haunted and gloomy, even in the middle of the day. This room was bright and welcoming, even though the walls were made of thick stone.

Embroidered wall hangings depicted mythical and historic scenes; Hawat and Jutat facing one another, holding the Twin Swords; Tureank the Hunter pining for his lover Conferan; and the stern, noble faces of the Many Kings sat around the table signing the unification of Anish.

'I could get used to this,' murmured Ellyah as they sat at a broad, polished table. 'When I've sold the jewel I might use my share to buy this place.'

'Hush,' said Nastja. 'Keep your voice down.'

So, the knock to the head had not helped to change Ellyah's mind about that. Not that Nastja was surprised. Ellyah changing her mind, or even admitting to a mistake, was not a common occurrence.

Ellyah poured dark, rich wine into the three cups before pushing them across the polished surface of the table. She raised hers.

'Let's drink to still being alive!' she said, with a broad smile.

Nastja did not feel like cheering. 'A drink, and some food,' she hissed, 'then we go. We can't risk being caught again.'

Luara nodded. Ellyah shrugged an agreement.

Nastja sat back in the sturdy, high-backed chair and cast her eyes around the room. Even if the other two were relaxed, she had to keep watch.

A pair of traders stood by the bar, deep in conversation. Both wore the mid length robes of a moderately prosperous merchant. Nastja noted that the closest merchant's robe and cap were embroidered, while the other's was plain. Their rings were bright and polished.

The woman with the embroidered clothes was making directed, assertive gestures while the other clasped his hands across his stomach. He shook his head in denial, but his manner was meek and resigned.

It was clear to Nastja that the trader woman was about to get the favourable end of whatever business they were concluding, and while the other was unhappy about it, they knew that the outcome was all but decided.

Further across the room, beside one of the many hearths, a group of three older men sat around a table. Their robes were long and cut from fine cloth, in rich shades of blue or green. Gold thread shone. These men wore many rings, for the many years of their lives and plenty of them were bronze or copper or even silver.

One was older than the others, his well-trimmed hair shot through with silver strands. He spoke with fervour, hands working in the air to conjure up dreams and possibilities. Before him was a small stack of wood-bound books. His wrists gleamed with the sheen of silver money rings.

The two younger men handed over some of their own, before standing to leave, each clutching a copy of the book. More of these Charterists, spreading the written word of the gods. There was clearly money to be made there.

As the two men hurried past the table, the barmaid approached bearing plates. Thick orange mash, probably a mix of turnip and swede, was topped by a stew of minced meat and beans.

Nastja was pleasantly surprised by the food. The mash was heavy with butter and seasoned with salt and some other spices she could not identify. The meat was probably mutton or goat, but well-cooked and drenched in a flavourful sauce with pepper and mint.

The three ate hungrily and the wine flask was soon drained.

The afternoon was wearing on, however, and the inn was starting to fill up. Labourers rubbed shoulders with rich merchants and well-dressed nobles as they clamoured for the attention of the serving staff.

Nastja scanned the crowd constantly, worrying that the Mackems could burst in at any moment.

As she was trying to watch the whole inn, a delicate flourish of musical notes shimmered through the smoky air. At the fair end of the room, a golden-haired young woman plucked at a harp. A bard, about to entertain the crowd.

'We can't stay,' hissed Nastja, in Ellyah's direction. She had turned in the direction of the singer, a broad smile across her face.

'But, the music…' pleaded Ellyah.

'Steyfan was a noble son and Helien just a serf…' sang the bard.

'The Mackems,' stated Nastja, simply. Ellyah frowned. 'She's just going to sing the ballad of Steyfan and Helien. I'll tell you it on the way.' She stood.

'Fine.'

Ellyah and Luara stood and followed Nastja, squeezing carefully through the thickening crowd.

Had they taken the time to look at the jewel in that moment, they would have seen that its usual fiery glow was dimmed. The jewel sat in its plain, wooden box; dull and inert. As they passed the threshold of the Crossways, the fires in its heart burst into life once more.

TWENTY FOUR

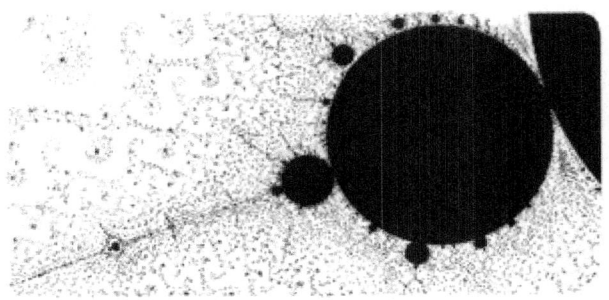

'Young earl-in-waiting Steyfan Jukeev was reckless and irresponsible. His father had died when the young noble was barely five, leaving him an orphan.'

The three women had hurried from the Crossways, at Nastja's urging, all suddenly paranoid that the Mackems were about to burst from every doorway they passed.

In response to Nastja's worry, Ellyah had declared that she had a plan, and moved to lead the way. The taller woman set the pace with her long strides as they passed through the wide gateway in Fordon's outer wall and swiftly down the winding causeway.

At the foot of the hill, they ignored the wide track that continued north and east from the direction of Kereva, and instead followed a smaller path around the foot of Fordon hill westward. As they contoured around the hill, which rose steeply to their right as flatter farmland stretched away to their left, Nastja kept her promise and told them the tale.

'Too young to come into his own,' Nastja continued as the path began to climb toward the rugged mountains. 'Steyfan was left in the care of the household nursemaid, while Duke Vashil of Ostier appointed the Seneschal Tsvethan as trustee of the estate. When young Steyfan came of age, Tsvethan would hand down the keys to the keep at Fordon, and with it the wealth of the estate.

'The nursemaid, Irinla, brought the young earl up alongside her own children, Damek and Helien. They never forgot that Steyfan would one day inherit the earldom, but in all other ways Irinla treated him as though he was her own child.

'As they grew toward adulthood, tensions began to grow. Steyfan felt that Damek would use his status for his own benefit. Damek thought that Steyfan behaved as if he was already the earl. His manner had become haughty and superior. The pair argued frequently, Irinla and Helien wrung their hands with worry.

'Meanwhile Seneschal Tsvethan ran the earldom as though it was his own birthright. He made good decisions and the wealth of the influence of the estate grew, but he was not minded to share it. As Steyfan grew closer to his age of majority and inheritance, Tsvethan drew up a plan.

'Steyfan and Damek often went hunting in the woods and rides abutting the Singing Mountains. Not far from where we are now,' added Nastja, gesturing across the grassy land before them, to where patchy woodland darkened the rising slopes. 'One spring day, they were riding together, following the trail of a boar.

"'*We have lost the spore of the beast,*" said Steyfan. "*Brother, check back and see if it turned off our path further back.*"

"'*You mistake me for a servant as usual, brother,*" replied Damek, with bitterness. "*Check the backtrail yourself.*"

"'*It was your job to follow the trail, brother,*" said Steyfan. "*So, you should be the one to find it again.*"

'They argued. Damek accused Steyfan of being proud and superior. Steyfan shouted back that Damek was envious and greedy for wealth and power that was not his by right. Damek shouted that he wished Steyfan was gone from his life.

'Steyfan rode away alone, in a cold fury. He urged his horse up a steep trail to be far from where Damek stood. That was when the killers found Damek.

'Tsvethan had hired a band of outlaws to find the young earl-to-be and do away with him, while making it seem like a simple robbery. They found Damek instead.

'Sometime later, Steyfan rode back down through the woods. Half his mind was to apologise to Damek and be reconciled. The other half was to continue the argument, and to prove that he was in the right.

'That is when he found Damek's body. His guilt and remorse were profound when he beheld the bloody mess that was the remains of his foster brother. But, worse was to come.

'For word had already returned to Tsvethan that his hired bandits had killed the wrong man. And he quickly saw the opportunity that this presented. He spread the tale that it was Steyfan himself that had done the murder, in an argument that had got out of control. All in Fordon had seen the two of them exchanging hard words in the past, and so the story was widely believed. Steyfan's name was cursed as a murderer.

'Tsvethan barred the gates and made Helien a hostage in the keep against any attempt that Steyfan made to return. He had no choice but to go into exile, renouncing his claim on the earldom as a consequence of the crime. He took a new name and joined the king's army as a common soldier.'

Nastja trailed off into silence. The path had climbed steeply as she talked, and they found themselves high on a hillside. The plains and fields that surrounded the lone hill of Fordon spread out into the distance behind them. Groves of stunted, twisted oaks stood to either side of the path, the first tinge of autumnal yellow showing at the tips of their lobed leaves.

'Well?' Luara's voice carried a hint of annoyance. 'Then what happened? Surely that's not the end of the story?'

Dusk was near. The day had been clear but a band of cloud had gathered above the peaks of Damowedd, some distance away to the west. The sun dipped behind these like a lantern screened by a gauzy curtain, and the sky was shaded more deeply with orange and pink as each moment passed.

'We should make a camp,' said Ellyah. 'But a little bit further up so that we can see in all directions. The Mackems have always surprised us when we've stopped before. We can find a spot up here where they won't be able to come near without us seeing them.'

'That makes sense,' agreed Nastja. 'As long as we can see all the way down the trail and back to the Kereva road. It seems like we are taking the long way round, though.'

'It gives us a chance of giving them the slip,' said Ellyah, leading the way further up the trail. 'I know another road that leads where we are going.'

At the crest of the hill, the ground flattened out. Undulating grassy hillocks led away across a plateau until in the dusky distance the dark mass of the Derufin Mountains began to rise. They chose a small, bowl-shaped depression backed by slopes of springy heather. One of them could sit as lookout at the entrance and keep watch down their backtrail, and Ellyah checked that there was also a good view to the north.

'We might be here for a few days,' she warned. 'Make yourselves comfortable.'

Nastja eyed Ellyah suspiciously as she laid her blanket down at the back of the bowl.

'What are you looking for?' she asked.

'There's a road to the north that crosses the plateau,' replied Ellyah. 'I wanted to see if I could make it out.'

Nastja seemed unconvinced. 'It's just another road. It'll only take us to where we could have got to quicker by the main road.'

'It'll help,' replied Ellyah. 'Trust me.'

'I want to hear the rest of the story!' Luara was sitting against the slope, blanket wrapped tightly around her body. Her eyes were pale in the dimming light.

Nastja sat down in the entrance of the bowl, lifting the collar of her coat to keep out the chill of the evening. One by one, the stars began to appear, glimmering and vanishing as wispy clouds moved across the broad sky.

She began to talk.

'Several years passed. Steyfan, under his new name, had begun to earn himself a reputation as a brave soldier and a conscientious leader. He now saw his past behaviour in a new light, you see? He saw how his previous arrogance and entitlement had led to Damek's death and the imprisonment of Helien.

'He wore his guilt heavily, and the weight of it made him a better man. A man who, without his famous name and without his destined inheritance, had to prove himself anew. And prove himself he did. Time after time, he threw himself headlong into the chaos of battle. He put himself where the fighting was most ferocious, thinking only of victory and the safety of those he led.

'Now a great captain, he received a call for aid from an allied manor that was under siege. He rode there with all haste and fell on the enemy like a thunderstorm. They were swept away, the siege was lifted, and the manor was retaken as a bastion for the king in the civil war.

'But! There was more. More than Steyfan could have ever guessed. For when the hostages were released from their captivity in the manor house there was one he knew better than any other. One he knew like his own kin and one he now realised, he desired with all his heart. Helien.

'He gaped as she came to him, standing amid the ruin of battle. He could not understand how she came to be there.

"*My Steyfan,*" she said, flinging her arms around him. "*I have searched long for you, but it is you who have found me.*" And Steyfan's troops learned his true name, and realised at last who he really was.

"'*Seneschal Tsvethan kept me a prisoner as surety against your return,*" Helien explained. "*He knew your heart. He knew you would not risk him hurting me.*"

'He grasped her fair hand. "*Tis true,*" he said. "*But, how did you escape?*"

"'*Tsvethan employed a grim-looking woman as a jailer. Little did he know, but the woman was an old friend of my mother, Irinla. She hated him, although she could not gainsay him directly, and had pity for my plight.*

"'*Together, we made a plan for my escape. The jailer feigned a fainting fit, but handed me the keys to the locked door that restrained me. Before anyone else in the house noticed, I made for the stables and escaped on a swift horse. I thought I would be safe here, but…alas!*

"'*But now you are here, Steyfan. And all is well!*"

"'*Yes, now I am here.*" There was fire in young Steyfan's eyes. "*And the usurper Tsvethan has a hold over me no longer.*" And all that stood nearby were amazed at the change that had come over him. He was lordly, and full of wrath. Vengeance was in his eyes.

'He spoke, loud enough for all his army to hear. "*I claim my rightful name and title at last. For I am Earl Steyfan Jukeev of Fordon. I was wrongfully accused of murder. I was wrongfully dispossessed of my lands and inheritance. I ride to claim them back. Who will follow me?*"

'The roar of acceptance was deafening. The army rode like a gale, blown on the wind of justice. Yet none of the swiftest riders could keep pace with Steyfan on that journey. He arrived at Fordon ahead of the vanguard. He was the very tip of the spear.

'Tsvethan's army watched his approach, but fled before his wrath. He was driven by just fury, and none could stand before him. Soon, he faced Tsvethan in the great hall of the mighty keep. The Seneschal would not fight. He pleaded, he begged. He twisted and turned, and lied, but Steyfan was merciless and demanded satisfaction. He bade Tsvethan to pick up a sword. He called the Seneschal a coward and a traitor. Tsvethan's unwilling fingers curled around the jewelled hilt of his ancient blade.

'They fought. Tsvethan was a skilled duellist but Steyfan's strength had grown in his exile. The keep rang with the sound of clashing steel, but Steyfan quickly gained the upper hand. With a guttural roar, he ran his opponent through, and the duel was over.'

'Did they get married afterwards? Was there a grand wedding?' Luara could not restrain herself from interrupting.

'Of course they did,' replied Ellyah. Her voice was thick and muzzy as if close to sleep.

'Steyfan and Helien were married that very day,' said Nastja, irritated to be interrupted. 'Earl Steyfan governed the earldom wisely and fairly from that day on, and his descendants live in the castle to this day.'

'Lovely story, thanks hen.' A rustling came from Ellyah's direction as she rolled herself deeper into her blankets. The steady breathing from the other direction suggested that Luara was already asleep.

Nastja stayed awake for a while longer. As the wind whispered through the heather, she stared down into the darkness of the plains. Nothing moved. Not a flicker of a torch or the glow of a cowled lantern lit even a square yard of the ground. All was still.

She was not happy with the mystery Ellyah had created about their onward journey. If Ellyah chose not to talk about something, it usually meant that she knew Nastja would not approve, or would point out flaws in her plan. Nastja worried.

Her eyelids grew heavy as she gazed into the darkness, and before an hour had passed she was sleeping too.

TWENTY FIVE

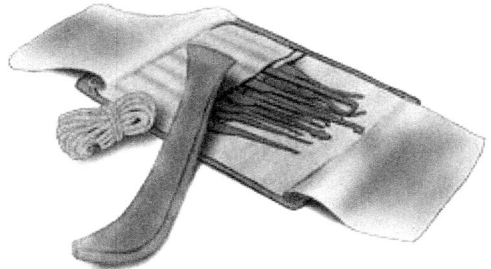

Ellyah woke suddenly. Her surroundings were unfamiliar. How had she got here?

The dawn was grey and overcast, shapeless clouds clinging to the slopes, and shrouding the sky. There was a chill in the air and an autumnal dampness. Dew had sprinkled her blanket with a multitude of shining beads.

The season for sleeping outside was nearly finished for the year. In a few more weeks there could be frost dusting the ground with its powdery white crystals. Money would need to be found for inns or guest rooms, were they still travelling.

Money. Travel. The pieces began to fall into place, memory returning.

The jewel, of course. They were still trying to sell the ruby. Once they did, money would be no issue. She would sleep on a feather mattress in a warm room, every night.

She sat up, and was greeted by a stab of dull pain from the back of her head. The room in Kereva, and the door tearing from its hinges and throwing her back. It was there in her mind, but almost as though it were a dream.

She knew what had happened, but her memories since that event were patchy and fragmented.

She would recover. She had to. And, she had to make sure that Nastja did not find out that she was still in pain, and still struggling to remember things. She would only worry.

'Good morning hens!' she said, brightly. 'Still no sign of anyone chasing us.'

Nastja groaned in response, pulling her blanket further over her face. Luara signed heavily but unrolled herself and stood. She shook and wriggled her hands and feet, trying to get warm.

Ellyah turned to rummage in her pack for something to eat, and Luara began stretching. She bent double and twisted from her hips, swivelling her body from side to side. Ellyah eyed her as she took a bite from some hard-baked flatbread. Luara was far too energetic.

She knew that they would soon ask her why they had come this way, and what they had been waiting for these past days. She knew that there was a good reason, that it was part of her plan. She just could not remember exactly what that plan was. She hoped it would come back to her soon.

'So,' she began, keeping her voice casual. 'Tell me more about where we decided to head to?'

'Ben Gedrin, in Kiraband.' Nastja's voice was muffled by her blanket. If she noticed that Ellyah seemed unsure of the destination, she gave no sign. 'We can't sell the jewel in Anish. The Mackems will keep finding us. But like Luara said, you can move anything through Ben Gedrin.'

Luara nodded. 'The gangs in Ben Gedrin won't be scared of the Mackems.'

Ellyah nodded too, in sage agreement. She remembered now. They had talked about this more than once over the days they had spent in this grassy hollow.

The plan did make sense. She had heard about the chaotic lawlessness of Kiraband, where the underworld held the reins of power. Ben Gedrin itself lay on the bank of the broad Lake

Gedrin, the confluence of the Great River and the Alrean river, and many roads intersected before the city. Ben Gedrin was a hub for trading every type of goods imaginable. Ellyah could only think of one problem.

The Rujrweh Pass.

It was their route to Kiraband; a rough, rocky road that wound up the sides of a steep valley cutting into the heart of the Derufin Mountains. Ellyah knew that trade streamed back and forth across this high pass. A village stood at the foot of the pass, Kalojne. The Mackems would be waiting there, ready to cut them off and take the jewel.

Fortunately, Ellyah had a plan. All it needed was perfect timing, and a little bit of luck. So, they had been waiting.

The weather had been grim, with low, grumpy clouds hanging low over the undulating grassy ground of the plateau. The dark, frowning faces of the distant Derufin loomed over the northern extent of these bleak, boggy highlands.

Ellyah put her hands on her hips and sucked in a few deep breaths. She had hurried to the top of this hillock; a slightly higher undulation in the shapeless mass of green and brown, for a better vantage point. The climb had not been easy. She was damp on the outside from the weather, and clammy from sweat inside her clothes. It was unpleasant.

She gazed out into the distance. From this height, she could just about make out the road.

A pale, unlikely ribbon ran across the plateau. Ellyah had never seen it before, but she knew that while the eastern end of this trail led to the Rujrweh Pass, the western end began at an ancient and mysterious city.

A city that was two cities. A city that was built both underground and on the plain. The Severed City. The city of the dwarves.

It lay on the border between Anish and Buren, tucked away in the mountainous duchy of Damowedd. It had been built in the distant past into the high cliff of The Schism, and in later years had been extended away from the cliff, across the dividing river and into the north of Buren. It had a dwarf name, but Ellyah only knew it as The Severed City.

The dwarves had built the road to provide an easy route to northern Anish and the Lands of the Great River, without needing to pass through Buren. They maintained it, and guarded it, and few others used it.

So, when Ellyah saw the shapes of many figures in the far distance, moving along the road, she knew she had found exactly what she had been waiting for. She grinned. Turning, she galloped back down the hill to fetch the others.

'Dwarves?' asked Nastja, surprised, when Ellyah told her what she had seen, and what she had planned.

'I hoped I had got the timing right,' she replied, smiling broadly. 'It's a way we can sneak past the Mackems when we get to Kalojne.' She busied herself rolling up her blanket and packing her things away in her pack.

'With dwarves?' asked Nastja, puzzled.

'Yea, we'll just tag along with them. The Mackems won't dare touch us then. If we're careful, they might not even spot us in the crowd.'

'Interesting idea,' murmured Luara, but Nastja was more forthright.

'You can't just "tag along" with a dwarven column! They hardly ever speak to outsiders. We'll be lucky if they don't attack us.'

'We have some silver.'

'That would make it worse!' groaned Nastja. 'You can't just pay off dwarves. Offering money to dwarves we've not met before is about the most offensive thing you can do. It's implying that they do not have enough wealth of their own. We can't do that.'

'I'd like to hear your better idea,' said Ellyah, angrily. Nastja looked thoughtful.

'Well,' she said, after a moment. 'We are here now. But you must let me do all the talking.'

'Why? Aren't I charming enough?'

'Please, Ell. I've had some dealings with the dwarves before. Your plan might work, but you need to trust me.'

Ellyah nodded and they strode forward. They needed to be careful of their footing on the damp, tussocky grass, but before long they stood on one of the road's banked verges. Nastja frowned, preoccupied, as they sat down to wait.

The column approached swiftly, and soon the waiting women were able to pick out the different dwarves that comprised the party.

At the head of the group were several mounted knights, short legs spread wide over the barrel-like bodies of their sturdy ponies. They wore grey plates of thick, heavy armour over their shoulders and chests. Grim, dull iron helmets covered their heads and the upper halves of their faces. Narrow slots in each faceguard provided the barest glimpse of pale, piercing eyes. They were an imposing sight, their short height not lessening the aggressive threat they projected.

More knights rode at regular intervals down the length of the snaking column. Between them, keeping pace on foot, were a host of common dwarves. Men, women and children were all dressed in pale, coarse shirts of thick linen, and skirts of pleated wool. They strode along the road with energy and determination. None lagged behind.

All the men and most of the women wore large sacks, belted around their bodies, as if setting out on a great journey. They walked lightly though, as if the weight was no burden.

The first knights were within an easy bowshot when Nastja stood. In an instant, their swords were drawn. They heeled their mounts forward, hefting their heavy, single-edged blades.

'*Kunama bwino! Kunama bwino!*' cried Nastja. '*Migodi yanu ikhale yakuya ndipo miyala yanu ikhale yolemera.*'

Ellyah goggled at her friend. 'You speak Dwarvish?'

Nastja looked back curiously. 'You don't?'

The dwarf knights paused, puzzled. In their hesitation, another figure rode forward to the front of the column. He too wore a pleated skirt, but was bare-chested even in the chill of the morning. Chains around his neck were strung with many yellowing teeth, and there was a short cape of grey fur across his back.

He roared with laughter as he approached. 'Oh, ho ho!! Here's a puzzle indeed! A strange outsider woman who springs up from the turf, speaking Dwarvish!' He laughed again. His accent was earthy, but he spoke the Common Speech clearly. '*Kunama bwino pobwezera. Nkhandwe isalume.* What brings you to this place?'

Nastja inclined her head slightly at his greeting. 'My name is Nastja Mjette, and these are my companions Ellyah Jerim and Luara Orsini. We are making a long journey.'

The lead dwarf laughed again. The knights behind him remained poised and alert. His hair and beard were both a reddish-brown, long and braided. His face was round and jolly, but there was a sharp intelligence in his pale eyes.

'We're all on a journey,' he replied, sagely. 'Moving through space or time. What matters most is the destination, yes?' He paused, then asked. 'Where're yer headed?'

'We must make for the Rujrweh Pass,' said Nastja. 'And then onwards through the Riverlands.'

'We travel int' same direction, also toward the Pass of Anish.' He gestured down the line of the column. 'What an extraordinary coincidence.'

'Where are you going after you cross the pass?' asked Luara. Both Nastja and Ellyah glared at her. Ellyah knew that dwarves could be touchy, and Nastja clearly had something in mind to win them over. Fortunately, the bare-chested dwarf remained cheerful.

'We're making the pilgrimage, of course!' Nastja nodded, but Luara stared back blankly. He went on. 'You've 'eard of Mzinda Bisani? The Hidden City? We journey to find it, wherever it lies in the northern plains.'

'You mean, you're going to *try* to find it,' said Luara. Ellyah bit her lip.

He smiled benignly. 'My faith is strong. I know the city is there somewhere, and I know that we shall find it, when time is right. And, I believe the time is close. Do yer not feel it? There's change int' air. Peoples are moving, finding new ways, making new wars. Things that were lost are being found once more, for good or for ill.'

Ellyah was suddenly uncomfortable, reminded of what she carried hidden in the bottom of her pack. She shifted uneasily, thinking about that ancient, mysterious jewel that glowed with unearthly, mystical fire.

'Yes, I'm a priest of Wölfin and I 'ave faith,' he went on. 'Wölfin will guide our steps and the Hidden City will be found. A new dwarven realm will be born. Our troubles will be over.'

'And now,' he said, more briskly. 'We must gan our way. The morning marches on and will not tire.' He lifted his reins, and the knights gathered behind him copied the action.

'Let us join your pilgrimage,' blurted Nastja. 'For a short way. Please.'

The dwarf paused, one eyebrow raised.

'The road is dangerous for three women alone,' Nastja explained. 'We would be grateful for your protection. And we can pay.'

'Pay?' The dwarf was taken aback. He frowned. 'What do you have that would possibly be useful to us.'

'Stories. I know many and will tell them as we walk. I will pay for us to join you with tales.'

The dwarf priest paused, eyebrow raised. Then, he laughed heartily once more.

'Very well!' he exclaimed. 'A bargain is struck! This one will be our bard, and will entertain us as we journey onwards. Yer'd better tell the tales with skill, the knights get impatient when they're not entertained. Let us ride!'

True to her word, as they travelled during the days that followed, Nastja told tales.

She told the story of Steyfan and Helein once more, but this time she rendered it as a grand, romantic epic. The characters gave lengthy speeches and Nastja was able to embroider the basic story with drama and sentiment.

She told the tale of Hawat and Jutat and the forging of the Twin Swords, heavy with the weight of ancient history, and then the tragedy of Tureank the Hunter. She even told the silly story of the fairytale people known as the Coyvid, who somehow stole the Twin Swords and used them to create their own mischief.

The journey passed quickly and easily, with Nastja's clear voice ringing out over the walkers and riders. With everyone preoccupied by the stories, any tension that might have arisen between the dwarves and the humans was averted.

At Nastja's suggestion, they camped slightly apart from the dwarves. She had a large square of oiled cloth in her bag, and it was the work of moments to string this between two spaced birches. It was not much of a tent, but kept off the worst of the misting rain.

'How much further?' asked Ellyah. She had not thought much beyond finding a dwarf convoy to travel with. The journey across this bleak landscape was already becoming a dull trudge.

Talk had been sparse throughout that first day. The dwarven families seemed shy and reluctant to even meet their eyes, and the knights were solemn and inscrutable beneath their heavy helms. Even Nastja had spoken little, apart from telling her stories.

'Two more days,' she said eventually, 'until we reach Kalojne, at the foot of the Pass of Anish. There is a campground there. People usually overnight at the bottom of the valley, so they can get all the way across in a day. Whole groups have frozen to death by getting caught at the top, and even in summer it's dangerous in the dark.'

'Right, so.' Ellyah thought for a moment. 'We can use the dwarves to hide from the Mackems at the pass.'

'I don't think they are tools just to "use",' retorted Nastja. 'Were you planning just to hide behind them?'

'You would have to bend over a lot,' put in Luara, grinning. 'You're much too tall for a dwarf.' Ellyah glared at her, then flashed a tight smile.

At that moment, they were interrupted by a deep, booming voice, ringing in the evening air.

'Evening's greetings, human ladies!' It was Khandwe, the dwarf priest. 'May I approach?'

'*Indeh*! Yes, of course,' called Nastja.

Khandwe appeared in the triangular mouth of the tent, still bare chested. His skin, slick with rain, glistened in the light of the dwarves' smoky campfires.

Even Nastja would tower over his squat form, and Ellyah guessed he must be several inches short of five feet in height.

His hands were large and strong, and they gripped a staff topped with a bare wolf's skull. He sank easily into a seated position, laying the staff across his knees.

'You fare well?' he asked. 'The pace was comfortable for you this day?'

'It was fine,' replied Nastja quickly. 'We appreciate you allowing us to join you.'

In truth, Ellyah's legs ached. The dwarf knights rode at a relentless walk, and allowed few breaks. The common dwarves seemed to keep up with little effort, despite their short legs. Ellyah had not even heard any of the children griping. She felt like griping. It was especially annoying to see Nastja being treated like a celebrity after this whole idea had been hers.

Khandwe waved Nastja's comment away. 'You've paid for yer passage. You entertain us and make each mile shorter.' His face became serious. 'I must ask yer something. Yer've a need for safety, and to travel quickly? What is it that yer fleeing from?'

Before they could answer, he went on. 'I'm a priest of Wölfin, and my preoccupation is the safety of my pack.' He indicated the other dwarves with the point of his elbow. 'Spiritually or otherwise. I am also no fool. Three human women, trying to cross the high *vidda*, and travelling so light? This in't usual. A tale follows at yer heels.

'So, I must know, does it put my pack in danger? We would prefer to be prepared for what may come.'

There was an uncomfortable moment. Nastja opened her mouth, and Ellyah knew that she was about to tell him everything.

'We were robbed,' said Ellyah, before Nastja could speak. 'By a criminal gang in Carhinn. The Mackems. They stole something valuable from us. A family heirloom.' She glanced around. Nastja and Luara's faces were mercifully blank.

'We stole it back,' she continued. 'And that caused quite a stir. Gang politics, you know? They chased us to Kereva, and so we thought it was best to leave the main road at Fordon. We hoped we could lose them by passing through the Singing Mountains.'

'We were fortunate to meet your pilgrims,' added Nastja. 'To show us the way through to the pass. If we can cross over into the Lands of the Great River, they will give up the chase.'

It was a convincing tale. Ellyah had always found it best to mix in a good amount of truth into any lie. What she had said was nearly all true, anyway. She had just added the first robbery, which is absolutely the sort of thing that the Mackems would not hesitate to do. She felt no shame about the lie, but she was glad Nastja had helped rather than hindered the telling.

'A tale of adventure and daring!' boomed Khandwe, with a grin. 'These Mackems won't find yer 'ere. May I ask, what's the nature of this treasure?'

'I'd rather not say,' said Ellyah, warily. She peered out into the darkness suspiciously to make her point.

The dwarf priest stood. 'Very well. You and yer treasure will be safe while you are with us. This 'un,' he pointed at Nastja, 'has impressed us with her Dwarvish and her tales. We trust her and you can trust us.'

'My thanks to you, Khandwe-wulf,' said Nastja, using the priest's formal title and bowing her head. Ellyah rolled her eyes.

'Rest well,' he replied, standing and moving away. 'We will travel far tomorrow, and the road will be harder than today.'

When he had vanished into the night, Nastja rounded on Ellyah.

'You didn't need to lie to him!'

Ellyah was unfazed. 'Yes, I did.'

'He's a priest! And he has been kind to us.'

'That doesn't matter.' Ellyah leaned closer. 'If I'd told him the truth, and he figured out just how keen the Mackems are to find us and the jewel, he might well decide he'd be best leaving us by the side of the road, and saving him and his people some bother. Maybe with our throats cut. And the jewel taken.'

'He said we could trust him,' said Nastja, in a small voice.

'It doesn't matter. He doesn't need to know the truth. It won't help him or us.'

'I still don't think we need to lie. I think you're wrong,' said Nastja. Ellyah felt her face harden.

'I don't care what you think,' she spat, before she could think to restrain her anger.

Nastja stared, face blank. Then she stood and left the tent without another word. Luara sat silently, clearly uncomfortable.

'Nas,' called Ellyah, softening her voice. 'This is the best way.' There was no reply. Nastja had wandered off into the damp darkness.

The following morning, the mood was tense. Nastja had returned, deep in the night while Ellyah had been fast asleep.

She had slipped silently beneath the spread canvas that formed the makeshift tent, and roller herself in her blanket. The subtle movement must have disturbed Ellyah though, and she woke even as Nastja's breathing was deepening.

As Ellyah stirred, trying to make herself comfortable on the damp, lump ground, the argument with Nastja came back to her mind. Was Nastja really so trusting? She was usually no fool. This small lie kept them all safer.

It was stating, so bluntly, that Ellyah was wrong that had really made her lose her temper. Ellyah never minded admitting she had made a mistake, but in this instance she was certain she was not. Being cautious, and creative with the truth, was the right thing to do. Nastja would see that, she was sure. She would come around.

Fretting over this kept her awake a while longer, even though it was long into the night, and as she lay in the darkness she became aware of an unusual sound. It took her some time to be sure, but gradually she was able to pick out the low rumble of voices singing.

One voice rose, picking out a low, quavering line of song, and then others joined in repetition. It was at once eerie and mournful.

Wriggling around so that she could peer out from under the tent, she could make out the silhouettes of some of the dwarves. They were sitting around fires that burned low, singing softly in a murmuring language that must be Dwarvish. Midnight must have passed some time before.

Perhaps dwarves did not sleep? Ellyah had not spent enough time with them to know.

She certainly needed to, and wriggled back into a comfortable position before shutting her eyes. The background noise of quiet song gradually lulled her back to sleep.

'Are you hungry, hen?' Ellyah asked Nastja as she stirred the following morning. 'I've got flatbread, dried fruit, some jerky...?'

'No,' replied Nastja, simply, before rising and packing away her blankets, heavy with dew. Ellyah chewed her lip. Clearly, Nastja had not forgiven or forgotten overnight.

The camp was struck with precision and efficiency in the cold, grey light of a cloudy dawn. Ellyah and Luara found themselves hurrying to catch up as the column moved out, winding eastward on the pale, gritty road.

Nastja had been ready for some time, and Ellyah could make out her shock of fair hair toward the front of the line as she walked beside Khandwe's pony.

'For what it's worth,' said Luara as they hurried along, side by side. 'I think you were right not to tell the priest the whole truth. It wouldn't help anyone.'

Ellyah was pleased. 'Exactly! They don't need to know. And, thank you,' she added. 'Nice to know I'm not going mad.'

Luara shrugged. 'I didn't tell you to make you happy. I just think it's the right thing to do if we want to look after ourselves. Nastja must realise that too, however hard she finds it to lie.'

There were big lies and little lies. Lies that you told in order to get something done, and lies that were entirely selfish. People told lies every day to spare others' feelings, in ways that were essential for relationships to be maintained. Yet, Nastja saw them all the same; an evil that people used to deceive one another.

Ellyah thought it best to leave Nastja alone for a while, so for the remainder of the day she stayed toward the back of the column with Luara. The common dwarves bustled along the rocky track alongside the two women, but paid them little attention.

As Khandwe had promised, the road today was harder. The high plateau gave way to folded, broken ground as the indistinct ridges of the Singing Mountains merged with the foothills of the Derufin.

The cloud was higher, the air clearer, but the summits of the peaks that rose menacingly to their left were still hooded with shifting grey.

The road rose and fell as they travelled east, the dwarves marching up and down the steep hills at the same relentless pace. The knights glared out across the surrounding hills, eyes shadowed beneath the iron cowls of their helmets. Their hands hovered close to the hilts of their short, broad-bladed swords as if constantly expecting attack.

None came, and the column continued on at the same speed until the cold tones of dusk began to dim the sky. Ellyah sat gratefully in a patch of twiggy heather, footsore and exhausted. Her legs ached.

Luara was rummaging in her pack, and produced some small, tied sacks a moment later as Ellyah lay back. She still looked fresh.

'I want a hot meal,' she said. 'I'll see if some kind person will share their cook fire with me.' She strolled off.

The dwarves had split quickly into groups at the end of the day's march. Small fires burst into life across the heath, although Ellyah was not sure where they were finding the fuel. Maybe they burned heather? Or rocks?

Luara approached one of the groups. The knights had removed their helmets, but heavy plates of armour still gleamed on their shoulders and backs. She flashed them her most winning smile, and was utterly ignored. They did not even acknowledge her presence.

Eventually, she found a family that let her share their fire and their food. She beckoned Ellyah over to join them. They ate well that night, although the food was flavoured with unusual spices and their company spent the meal conversing quietly with one another in rapid Dwarvish.

As the light fell, Ellyah could see Nastja in earnest conversation with Khandwe. She was grateful to wrap herself in her blankets and shut herself away from it.

She was curious, though, about what she had witnessed the previous night and made herself stay awake as the night deepened. She watched as the fires burned low and the dwarves laid themselves down, wrapped in their coarse blankets. So, they did sleep.

However, in the later hours of the night, Ellyah stirred once more to hear the gentle mumble of quiet song. A single voice, then an echo of many, as if in reply. Once more, when she looked up she could see squat figures outlined by the soft glow of the campfires. Once more, she went back to sleep, puzzled.

The mountain village of Kalojne bustled. It was an hour after dawn, and already people were moving in the direction of the tollhouse.

Ellyah felt like her eyes had been rubbed with sand and her feet beaten with a bat. The journey to this point from Fordon had been hard. Relentless walking at a pace that was just too swift to be comfortable, sleeping on the ground each night. She craved a soft bed beneath a solid roof.

Her head wound had healed well during the journey, although her memory of the events leading up to their meeting with the dwarves were still patchy.

They had come far, to the very doorstep of the Riverlands. It would not be much longer until they could pass through Kiraband to the city of Ben Gedrin, where they would sell the jewel. Then, they could escape. They would take the gold and disappear. She would start a new life where none knew her past. She took a deep breath, almost able to taste that future.

A bump near her waist reminded her of the present. A rounded shoulder jostled her as the crowd moved along together. The dwarves had struck camp as the dawn broke and were filing towards the mouth of the pass.

To her right, a steep and winding road led back down to the vale of Fordon, and then on southward to Kereva. A small village had grown where the same road crossed a small patch of flat land before heading up to the pass.

Traders did good business selling provisions to travellers, or quick meals of pies and stuffed vegetables. Others repaired leather items; riding harness, boots or clothing. Trappers and hunters sold furs and heavy woollen blankets. Travelling over this high pass was demanding, and there were always those trying to make a living by selling to those in need.

To Ellyah's left, the tollhouse sat astride the onward path like a guard. Originally built as a fortification against attacks from the northern lands, now it existed just to extract a measure of silver from those who would use the pass. Royal Sentinels kept watch on either side and on the wall above, like gilded statues.

The dwarves filed slowly forward, the knights now dismounted and leading their stout, bad-tempered ponies. Ellyah found herself pressed on one side by the cold, angular armour of a knight and the bare, clammy skin of Khandwe the priest on the other. Nastja was just ahead, standing tall in contrast to the dwarves on either side.

She had still not spoken to Ellyah, keeping her vow of silence through the entirety of yesterday. Ellyah did not know what to do, but did not feel that she was in the wrong. Nastja would just have to come around to the fact that Ellyah was right. She could wait.

As the crowd filed forward slowly, Ellyah gazed out to the south where the road passed between the simple wooden houses of Kalojne. Then, she froze. There, waiting beside the road was a wagon with a pair of ponies hitched to the traces. A wagon surrounded by a small group of rough-looking men and women. A wagon bearing a tall, upright crate that stood behind the driver.

The Mackems.

'Nas! Nas!' she hissed, urgently. Nastja turned and Ellyah pointed frantically, away to the south. Nastja's eyes widened as she too gazed back down the road.

What could they do? Even if they passed through the tollhouse ahead of the Mackems, they would be on the same, narrow trail and only a few hundred paces ahead at best. They might even be in view as they climbed. They would be caught.

Ellyah ducked, trying not to stand out. Nastja turned, leaning down to face Khandwe.

'It is the thieves,' she whispered. 'The thieves are in the village. They will be right behind us over the pass. We'll never be able to escape.'

Khandwe frowned, thinking. Then he raised his voice to be heard by all in the group.

'We do not tolerate thieves. None should take whatever they want. We will stand against this.' Then he added more quietly, with a wry grin. 'Yer've won me over, Nastja. Yer part of my pack now, wherever you go.

'As it turns out, now is the time for the rest of my pack to pray to Wölfin. We must gather our strength and fortitude anew before the next stage of the pilgrimage.'

He stopped walking and raised his hands toward the sky.

'*Ankhondo a nkhandwe!*' he bellowed, in Dwarvish. '*Phukusi liyenera kupemphera. Tetezani paketi! Tetezani paketi!*'

The dwarves moved instantly, swarming around like ants from a stirred nest. Khandwe turned to Ellyah and Nastja.

'The knights will protect the pack. They'll not be moved. You should go, now.'

As he spoke, the dwarven knights stepped away from their ponies and spread out into a line across the road, shoulder to shoulder. They moved in perfect, practised unison. One of the knights barked out an order, and they all drew their heavy, single-edged swords and hefted their square shields.

Behind this barrier of steel, iron and muscle, the rest of the dwarves dropped to their knees. They bowed their heads as

Khandwe stood before them. An angry crowd was already massing before the dwarf knights, but there was no way through.

'Go!' repeated the dwarf priest. 'May Wölfin hunt with you. May you find fortune.'

Nastja hesitated for a moment.

'He's giving us a way to escape,' said Luara.

'Come on, Nas!' urged Ellyah.

She blinked. 'Yes. Let's go.'

She turned away, and the three of them hurried toward the tollhouse. If the dwarves could block the trail for an hour or more, they could get far enough ahead to escape.

In a hurried daze, they rushed through the wide gateway. As Ellyah crossed the gatekeeper's palm with a few scraps of silver, she could hear raised voices and angry exclamations over the monotonous drone of Khandwe's sermon.

She did not look back. Through the gateway, the Rujrweh Pass opened before her. A long, winding and well-worn track cut into the hillside and rose steadily, turning this way and that, to pass through a steep notch high above. Steep and craggy mountains rose in all directions, their sides broken and unclimbable and their peaks shrouded in low cloud.

Beyond, were the Lands of the Great River, and that is where Ellyah was determined to find her fortune. Beyond this pass and within the walls of Ben Gedrin, she would find her destiny.

TWENTY SIX

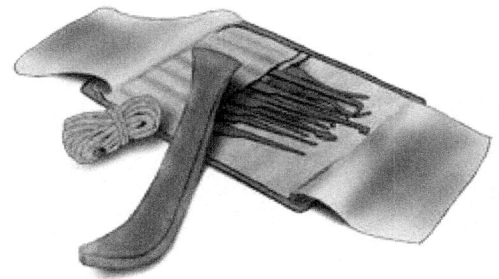

The journey from the northern end of the Rujrweh Pass had felt slow. The road from Anish flattened out onto the plains of the Lands of the Great River, with one path continuing northward toward Annida, and another veering to the left; the westbound road to Kiraband and Ben Gedrin.

To Ellyah's eyes, the landscape before them was harsh, and alien. Sand-coloured plains stretched away into the distance, the monotony only broken by the occasional frond of yellow grass, waving in the slight breeze.

The hills behind them were bare and stony, and rose to forbidding dark ridges of bare black rock, that loomed oppressively over the land below.

Nastja was talking to her again, which was helpful. They seemed to have left the argument behind as they crossed the pass from Anish into the Riverlands. Nastja seemed to have acknowledged that Ellyah had been right all along; they were wise to hide the truth from the dwarves. That she would openly admit that was too much to hope for. It was enough that the dispute was put aside, and that Ellyah had been right.

The rapport that Nastja had established between herself and the dwarves, particularly the priest Khandwe, had also proved useful in the end. Nastja knew that, so Ellyah was sure that it did not need to be said. In any case, the atmosphere as they began the next stage of their journey had been cheerful. They were almost there.

They had left the road and picked their way along the fringes of the foothills. The terrain was rough. The way was pathless, winding over rounded hills and down into narrow vales, and crossed loose and blocky ground. There was a fair amount of muttering about this, but the decision had been made.

'We know that the Mackems are behind us,' Ellyah had stated at first, and repeated regularly. 'Maybe they will go on to Annida first, and maybe they won't. But either way, they will be on our trail sooner or later. If we are on the road they will find us, and we will have nowhere to hide.'

'But,' argued Nastja. 'They have found us so easily so far, wherever we were. It might not make a difference whether we're on the road or not. And if we're on the road we can move faster, and maybe stay ahead of them.'

She glanced over at Luara and she and Nastja shared a look. Was there something they were not telling her?

'They're driving a wagon, aren't they?' she asked, looking from one to the other until they nodded in agreement. 'They won't follow us off road, then.'

'I can find you a path to Ben Gedrin that avoids the road,' said Luara, forestalling any further argument.

It was a slower route, but they did not see another soul. Nastja scrambled to the summits of low hills every now and again to check their back trail. Nothing moved. No-one followed.

On the fifth day after crossing the Rujrweh Pass they came upon a trickling stream in a deep cut, square-sided gorge about the same depth as a man's height. Luara was suddenly agitated, but seemed excited.

'Ooh. Oh dear! This is interesting.'

'Is it?' said Nastja.

'We can cross easily,' said Ellyah. 'Just need to drop down carefully and scramble up the other side.'

'No. Yes.' Luara seemed distracted, biting her lip and looking north, her eyes following the path of the gorge.

'I mean,' she said, gathering herself. 'I know where we can cross. And if we're careful, it might give us a quicker way to get to Ben Gedrin.'

'If you're sure,' said Ellyah.

They had followed her without argument, the afternoon light shifting from pale orange to dusky pink as they strode along the eastern bank of the gully. Luara would not answer any questions about where they were headed, and seemed unusually cagey.

As the sun set the vague, glowing lights of a village shimmered ahead.

'Sure this is a good idea?' asked Ellyah in a quiet hiss. She had strode forward to walk beside Luara.

'Trust me,' replied the older woman, confidently. 'But keep quiet.'

She led them quickly and carefully across a simple bridge made from aged logs lashed together. Ellyah realised with a start that they were on the road.

'Follow,' whispered Luara, then slipped away to skirt the nearest buildings. Ellyah and Nastja hurried to remain close, two more shadows in the night.

A little further on, Luara darted into an open-sided structure. The scents of warm animals and hay told Ellyah immediately that they were in a stable.

'Transport,' whispered Luara from the darkness of one of the stalls. 'We're safe if we can stay ahead of the Mackems, right?'

'Stealing?' asked Nastja.

'Borrowing,' replied Luara, a slight laugh in her words. 'Someone here owes me. A few people, actually. We'll bring them back later.'

Ellyah's eyes were adjusting to the gloom and she could now see that the stalls were clean and well-tended.

'We could spend the night here,' she suggested. 'We could still be on our way by dawn.'

'Na, don't want to risk getting caught here.' Luara appeared from the shadows leading three saddled horses. 'If we have to ask for permission they might say no. And the Mackems might catch up while we're napping.'

Neither Ellyah or Nastja were minded to argue, and they mounted up and rode out through the silent village. Luara hung back slightly, and as Ellyah turned to watch she noticed that the older woman was staring intently at a particular house. She shook her head as if trying to avoid a troublesome fly, and kicked her mount into a faster trot.

'Something wrong?' asked Ellyah, as Luara caught up. She hesitated, an uncertain expression on her face.

Then she smiled. 'Just the past, as usual.'

Ellyah did not ask any more questions, and the three women rode away into the night.

Five days later, the walls of Ben Gedrin rose before them.

The candle burned low. Evane Claes sat cross-legged on the floor, and any that opened the door would have seen her practising her nightly meditations on the Veil.

Apparently practising, for in reality the wonders of the Veil were far from her mind. In truth, she merely waited. Waited for the allotted hour, in impatience and with worry. The summons this night was unusual, and she fretted over what it might mean.

As she sat on the floor, eyes closed tightly, her skin crawled and throbbed with pain. It burned. It froze. It itched. She felt as though it must be red and blistered, marked and marred by scars and welts.

After the jewel had escaped her clutches in Carhinn, then Kereva, and lastly across the Rujrweh Pass she had been punished, and punished mercilessly.

Desya, in his wisdom and righteous fury had flayed her skin with lashes of power and scorched her being with great gouts of magical flame. She had endured the torture silently, knowing it was deserved, and knowing she paid a fair price for her failure. But, she still hoped she would be given another chance.

Part of her wondered if this summons was to be punished once more, but when that happened she was usually dragged abruptly from her slumber. This felt different. It felt like a beginning, not an end.

So, she waited, full of uncertain anticipation.

The candle guttered. It was deep in the night. Nothing stirred, all the other priests must be asleep by now. It was time.

She unfolded her legs and stood. Locking the door, she retrieved her mask from beneath the bed before turning and sitting down. Forcing aside her worries, she set the mask to her face and concentrated. Whatever pain and suffering awaited, she would meet it with conviction. Her mission was all that mattered.

It was not difficult to summon fervent belief in Desya this time. The pain that crawled over her skin was an unforgettable reminder.

She felt the familiar surge of power; that primal force that came directly from the demon. It flowed easily but did not fill her whole being as it once had. Like a few quick bites when the stomach was empty, her fatigue made it difficult to draw the amount of power she had in the past.

The chase for the ruby had been demanding. She had been forced to draw more and more power to communicate with the Mackems, and to animate Clayton Moore-that-was, without time to fully recover. Her resilience was being drained.

Nevertheless, it would be enough. She could rest easily when the jewel was recovered.

Even with the limitations, the sensation of the magic filling her body caused her to shudder, and her lips to part slightly. A small sigh escaped as she wove the spell. The arch appeared, lighting her cell with a ghostly purple glow as it grew. With practised ease, she drew it to herself, and was within it, and then passed through.

She found herself looking at a familiar room. The storeroom of the merchant's shop in Carhinn. Now that the merchant herself was…gone, the shop was disused. It served as an occasional meeting room and store, but mostly it was left empty.

The room was not empty now. A single ladder-backed chair had been set near the centre of the room, and a broad-shouldered figure was sitting in it.

They had a deep, dark hood pulled low over their face, but Claes could tell from their outline and attitude that it was Cannis "Butcher" Flett. She was ill at ease, hands clasped and shoulders tense. For a woman of her fortitude, these were signs of real worry. Worry about the significance of the summons.

She would not have forgotten the fate that had befallen her former leader, Brin Gallit.

She glanced up as Claes' face appeared in the room, peering up from beneath the hood. She caught a glimpse of the mask and lowered her face again, deferentially.

'I serve,' she said, simply. Claes was pleased. Flett had a fearsome reputation and a strong stomach when it came to violence, but had fallen into line. The Mackems leader balanced the force of will to see orders carried out with the right amount of subservience and eagerness to please.

The ruby had escaped with the thieves while she led the Mackems, that was true. But, Claes acknowledged in her own mind that Flett was not to blame. The thieves had repeatedly outwitted even her brightest thugs. She had not expected it.

Of course, if it would spare Claes further punishment, Flett could still be blamed yet.

Claes bade herself to remain silent. To speak might betray a hint of her nervousness to Flett and that would appear weak. Better to hold her tongue, and let the gang leader worry.

Moments passed. Impatience forced idle, pointless words to Claes' lips, but she clamped her teeth together.

Then, something *happened*.

A small swirl of purple light grew in the opposite corner of the room, expanding to form a familiar portal. Claes' eyes widened as she watched something happening that she had believed only she could do.

How could this be?

A dark shape appeared in the centre of the room. It moved through the portal, like a head thrust through a circular window. Beneath her own mask, Claes gaped.

It was another masked face, and it could have been the twin of her own.

Before she had time to speak, to question this astonishing appearance, another purple shimmer caught her eye. Then another.

Soon, the room contained five purple window portals, and five matching silver and black striped masks. From behind the eye holes they stared balefully at one another.

Though Claes was horrified, and enraged that there were others when she believed that she was special and unique, she held her tongue. She could think of nothing to say that would not sound petulant or reveal her ignorance. She would not give them the satisfaction.

There would be an explanation. It had to be. She had been summoned, after all. Moments later, it came.

You have gathered at my bidding.

Desya's voice thundered in her ears. She noted that some of the other mask wearers seemed to flinch, and Cannis Flett's head jerked visibly backward. The demon went on.

The time has come for you to know of each other.
I require you to combine your powers.

There was a moment of quiet. Each masked face moved subtly, looking toward one another as if trying to gain insight or find clues. Had each thought they were only one? Or had the others been in league for some time? Questions that were impossible to answer, yet.

In times gone those that followed me were great in number and powerful. They built temples and honoured me with worship. This will be restored.

The jewel is the first step. Locate it. Bring it to me. The thieves have gone north. Use your forces and servants to find them. The one who does this will be well rewarded.

Claes thought hard. She must be the one who recovered the jewel. She must be. How could she gain an advantage?

Work together, or apart. I care not. But know this- to fail is to suffer.

Abruptly, his presence was gone and the five strangers in identical masks were left in silence. Who would be the first to speak? Who would take charge?

Claes bit her lip beneath her mask. She stood on a knife edge. She had to make the right decision in this moment, and in the days to come.

Her whole future depended on it.

PART FIVE

TWENTY SEVEN

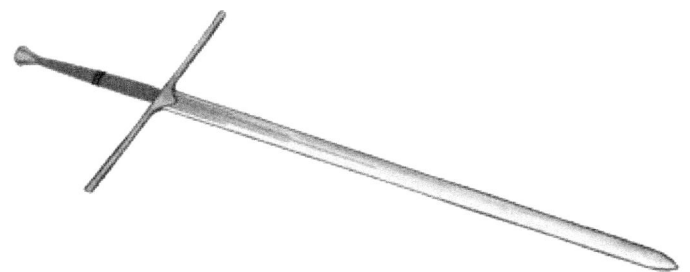

He had seen the sun rise this day, the rosy fingers of dawn grasping the horizon, and now he stood in the insipid grey light of dusk. He had not moved a single step. He had eaten nothing, and drunk only a few gulps of water.

His lonely, unmoving vigil was not unusual. Not for a member of his order.

Grey eyes, like a still pool reflecting cloudy skies, stared out impassively from beneath a gilded helm. The helmet was heavy, like the ornate plates he bore on his shoulders, chest and back but he carried the weight stoically.

His oaths bound him to his watch, and strengthened his will. This was what he had promised to do; to stand, to watch, to endure. To complain would be dishonourable. Even to begrudge his duty in thought was an offence against the order.

His eyes flickered as he blinked rapidly. Aside from methodically tensing and relaxing each muscle in turn, this was the extent of his movement. The fading light picked out the spear points and dull grey helmets of the enemy lining the walls of the fortification opposite. He studied their movements for a while, without interest.

They would not attack. Not now. And, if they did tomorrow or the next day, then they would face a thicket of spear points.

This was the other part of this man's sworn duty; to fight, to defend, and to protect.

For he was one of the Royal Sentinels of Anish, and had served them with his strength, endurance and his patience for many long years.

He had long thought that this was how he was destined to see out his days; standing vigil on a wall like this, practising and training, or simply waiting to be called to action.

But, something was changing,

He sighed, no more than an elongated breath. He was getting old and starting to feel it. He served his watches, trained hard and was mostly able to keep up with his younger colleagues, some less than half his age. Despite his robust physicality, of late he was starting to feel the strain. His feet would be sore tomorrow, and his back would ache.

How long could he continue?

There was the faintest scrape of leather on stone, and he turned his head a fraction. The gleam of polished bronze told him that another Sentinel had joined him, even as the sun was setting. As he had known they would.

'Dusk has fallen. Your vigil is ended. You must let another continue the watch.' It was the deep, melodious voice of a female elf.

'Is there another with the strength to stand until the dawn?' he replied, giving the formal response.

'One has come,' she said. 'Her oaths will hold her while she stands.'

'May your watch be peaceful.'

'May your rest be long.'

Deftly, he leaned his polearm so the blade lightly touched hers. The metallic sound was soft and faded quickly in the evening air. As his replacement stepped forward, he turned on his heel and strode away.

The matching armour made all Sentinels look alike, but he recognised Cusevadu. She was a young elf, barely fifty years old, and had only become a Sentinel in the last year. She was a demon when training and her endurance was growing, although she still had much to learn about patience. She would be a fine addition to the Royal Sentinels, if she could master her scorn for authority.

Tatayga she had called him, directly to his face. It meant "grandfather" and was an unflattering comment on his age. There were many elves in the Sentinels who were far older but they did not have the same creased skin and grey hair. He acknowledged that to them, he must appear so ancient as to seem close to death.

He had punished Cusevadu for her impertinence, but without anger. And she had accepted the pain without complaint. He remembered the event with a slight smile as he moved to the steps that led down off the wall.

He had been known by many names over his long career. They called him *Apaicitudu*; "The Stranger". They called him *Videsi*; "The Foreigner"; and they called him *Maunanga*; "The Silent One". He spoke with many, but remained silent about his past.

Flickering torches lit his downward path. The steps were tall and blocky, and led to the soft ground behind the wall. The cloak of night was spread about him now, the first stars appearing in the inky heavens above.

Despite the gloom, the path behind the wall was well lit by spitting rushlights and the occasional brazier. Other glimmering lights shone high above his head, seemingly floating in space; it was a tall watchtower, not a constellation of orange stars.

The path turned away from the wall and led down into the Sentinels' camp. Movement in the gloom showed where other Sentinels who had just been relieved of their watch were heading to their homes. Gilded armour glinted like hot embers as it reflected the flames.

Referring to the village of timber-built houses as a camp did not adequately describe the nature of the settlement. Royal Sentinels had camped here in times long past, pitching rough tents behind the walls. Gradually, the tents had been replaced with small wooden houses once the permanency of their watch was realised.

The perimeter of the village was bounded with timber screens, and only the Royal Sentinels were allowed within. The screens were decorated with historical scenes, painted images from the Sentinels' past.

It was too dark to make out the detail now, but he remembered clearly the first time he had seen the set of daubed images that depicted the Sentinels' formation.

He had gaped. He had moved closer to study the detail, and the annotation. Then, he had staggered slightly and sat down heavily. Because suddenly, many pieces had fallen into place, with one fact rising unavoidably from the rest.

The founder of the Royal Sentinels was a man named Kell. Kell, son of Leowrac, last King of Banahgar. Kell, who had vanished into a voluntary exile and taken the legendary Riversword with him.

The Sentinel reached the door of his home and removed his helmet. He tucked it under his arm and brushed his shoulder length grey hair back behind his ears before reaching for the door handle.

Discovering the truth about Kell's exile, or at least part of it, had shaken this man to his core. It had also been a thrilling moment. For he was Banahgarian himself.

His name was Cerle Connow, and he was also an exile.

He opened the door and stepped into the house. It was a simple dwelling, with a single room and slanting walls formed by the low, pitched roof. It was dimly lit, the fire in the hearth burning low, and the sparse furnishings cast the corners with deep shadows.

He was quietly and carefully placing his armour on pegs protruding from one of the walls, when a groan from the bed caused him to turn. He shrugged out of his leather arming jacket and moved swiftly over to sit on the edge.

The occupant of the bed stirred, looking up at him. She had a head of long, tangled brown hair which was streaked liberally with grey. They shone like strands of silver in the glow of the embers. Pale eyes, heavy with sleep, regarded him steadily.

'War,' said Indaella Connow. 'I dreamed of war again tonight, Cerle.'

He reached out and stroked her hair. Her dreams were vivid and seemed real to her, and she often needed to be soothed and comforted after she woke.

'Tell me what you dreamed, my love,' he asked, gently. 'Tell me of the war.' Cerle had learned to take the scenes that appeared in his wife's dreams very seriously. Her visions were what had led them to leave Banahgar and begin a fruitless search for Kell and the Riversword. They were the reason he had sworn his oaths as a Royal Sentinel; to discover what had become of Kell.

'War, in Banahgar,' she began slowly, gathering her thoughts. 'But not the final war…man against man. Both sides dressed in red. Red blood on white snow.'

It sounded like any dream, but Cerle nodded his head in resignation. The tale rang true with the rumours he had heard today. He had not wanted to believe it, but he had seen the Kotevari troops moving with his own eyes. The stories of the Teliyade had persuaded him, and Indaella's dream was all the confirmation he needed.

Kotev had invaded Banahgar once more.

'We should return. To Banahgar,' he clarified, when she looked up sharply at him. 'We have talked about it many times. I cannot deny my duty to my country any longer.'

'Our quest—' said Indaella.

'Has failed. We always knew it would be difficult to follow Kell's trail, and many years have passed now. We still know nothing of what happened to the Riversword. Maybe it is not our fate to return it to Banahgar after all.'

Indaella shook her head. 'I was so sure we would find it. That we needed to find it.' Her eyes shone sadly in the dim light. 'What of your oaths to the Sentinels?'

'My watch is complete,' he replied. 'I have done more than my share. My country must come first and it is calling. I cannot spend my last days on foreign soil, knowing my brothers are fighting.'

Maybe, if I return there can be redemption, he thought.

He could only imagine the stories that would have been told about him during his years of absence. Perhaps, if he returned to join the defence, he could silence some of those accusing voices.

'You have plenty of days to live yet, my love,' said Indaella with a warm smile. 'When will we leave?'

'Tomorrow.' Cerle was decisive. 'There is no time to waste if the Claihed are already embattled. And, we must cross the Beinuirm Skele before the first snowfall.

'I will buy a horse with a cart in the morning. We will head north and cross the Rujrweh Pass. It is not a difficult journey.'

As he spoke, he glanced across to where his Royal Sentinel armour hung on the wall. It had been part of his identity these last few years. The thought that he had worn the heavy plates for the last time was a strange one.

Then, he shifted his gaze to the opposite corner of the room. His greatsword stood there, leaning in the corner. Stands With

Kings, was his Sword-Name. The blade had gone unused for a while, but it remained sharp, still ready. Slinging the long weapon across his back once more would feel like he was already returned to his old life in Banahgar.

His years to date had taught him that there was no shame in humility. He could admit that he had not achieved what he had set out to do. He had not located the Riversword, or even found a trace of where it had gone.

Yet, he had tried. Indaella's visions had suggested that a great calamity would befall Banahgar unless that legendary, ancient weapon was returned to the country. Cerle had tried. Maybe there were paths of fate that Indaella could not see. He was just a man, and he had devoted a large part of his life to this search. He was comfortable in admitting that he could do no more.

As he lay down and sought sleep, he was nevertheless haunted by sadness over his failure as well as faint hope for his own redemption. As he drifted off, he was haunted by questions to which he could find no answers.

TWENTY EIGHT

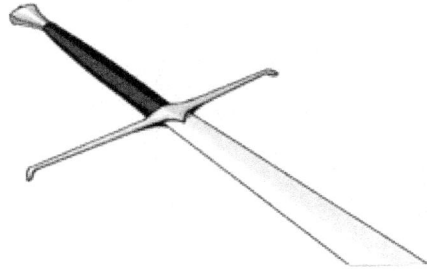

Pale blue, wispy white and flat, dull beige. The sky, the clouds and the ground that stretched away unbroken to every horizon.

For many days, Eain's world had been reduced to these few basic colours. They streamed past his vision and stretched away relentlessly in every direction. The wagon train rolled across the plains, steadily leaving Tann's farm further behind.

The plaintive sound of Mehr Mehlan's *zitol* rang out as the wagons rumbled along, mingled with the tremulous wail of Tressin Oke singing at the top of his voice.

> *I'll follow the road to Kiraband!*
> *I'll chase the setting sun.*
> *Oh, I'll follow the road to Kiraband,*
> *That's where I'll have my fun!*

Eain strolled along beside the lead wagon, long strides covering the ground as quickly as the laden caravan could move.

'What a racket,' said a voice at Eain's shoulder. He turned his head to see Reela striding along to catch him up. She had to hurry to match his pace.

'I like the song,' replied Eain. 'It is an old song?'

'No!' scoffed Reela. 'He just makes them up as he sings. Thinks he's a bard. I promise, a few more weeks with us and you'll be keen for him to shut up too.'

Reela gave him a grin. The breeze whipped a few stray strands of her ash-blonde hair across her face. Eain turned back to watch where he was going. He much preferred to walk, while the rest of the company rode on the wagons whenever they could. Reela often jumped down to talk to him, although she could not match his pace for long.

Her company was easy and she had welcomed him to the group. She chattered about where they were going, and what they might see. Some days, though, it seemed that she did not have a good word to say about anyone else who rode with the caravan.

'Mayla won't stop bossing me around,' she complained. 'She's not my mother.'

Or, about Mehlan. 'He's a lazy freeloader. Never lifts a finger. Look how soft his hands are.'

She even talked of Oke himself with scorn. 'He's a moon-eyed dreamer, Eain. You can't get him to be serious about anything.'

She even moaned about her partner, Haf, saying he could be boring and tight-lipped. Eain felt uncomfortable at overhearing such things, and kept his own lips pressed shut. Haf himself had never spoken to Eain, and Eain was certain he had caught the man glaring at him on occasions, hostility in his eyes.

As the days wore on, Eain fell easily into the steady rhythm of the caravan; walk all day, taking few rests; stop as they sky began to turn dusky; eat a simple meal, mainly beans or corn grits, and then roll himself in blankets and furs to soften the hard, rocky ground and try to get some sleep.

Eain found that he slept well, either beneath one of the wagons or out in the open with the stars like jewels decorating the vast sky. The first few mornings saw him wake with stiff, aching legs but that soon eased as he became used to the miles of walking required.

As they put more distance between them and the farm, and as the distant eastern mountains faded lower on the horizon, Eain found himself feeling more at ease. He could not forget his guilt and shame, but the tearing sensation within him faded. His night terrors became less frequent.

Oke sang most of the time, either made up nonsense songs, or what he called the *songlines*. These were meandering rhymes that described the curves of the road and the sweep of the hills beside it. Oke said he could find his way by the *songlines* better than any map.

Eain mostly walked in silence, alone with his thoughts, so he was grateful for Reela's occasional company. The whole caravan was serenaded with barely a pause by Mehlan's *zitol*, and Oke gave him regular orders to keep playing.

Eain stole a glance at the pudgy musician, sitting on the second wagon. Reela was doing no more than stating a fact when she said that he never did any work. The rest of the team had to pitch in at every isolated farm they passed, loading and unloading boxes, barrels and sacks. But not Mehlan. Oke actually forbade it. Eain supposed it did not matter.

'Hey! Big guy!' called Oke. 'Come up here, I ain't getting down to walk.'

Dutifully, Eain jogged over and climbed up next to Tressin Oke. Long-limbed and slender, he sat on the seat of his wagon as though it were a throne.

'I know you all want to know why I carry him as a passenger?' Eain did not respond. He got the impression that Oke was going to tell him anyway. Oke nodded knowingly.

'I was in Annida,' he began. 'Real good place to pick stuff up or move it on, but not good for much else. No life. Anyway, I'd bought a wagonload of dwarf slate, to take through Kiraband and sell in Ben Gedrin. Good market for it. They'd have less fires if they roofed the whole city in slate.

'One of the handlers working in the yard was—' He gestured over his shoulder with a thumb. 'That boy. I saw right away that he was struggling. Couldn't lift more than two at a time. Sweat was running off him. He was a mess.

'So, I said to him, "you don't look a natural at this, boy". And he answered, "no, sir. I'm a player". Well, that answer got me curious, so we got to talking. He told me that he had studied the *zitol* since he was a little kid, and had hoped to travel the world earning his way with his music. Only, his master had got himself some bad debts and to settle them had to sell everything, including all the instruments, and send the boy out to labour for his keep.'

He paused, scanning the horizon.

'Maybe I'm soft, or dumb, or something worse but I couldn't bear the thought of that poor, weak boy labouring away with those dreams dying inside him. So, I found the *zitol* with a trader, bought it back, and put it in his hands. He didn't want to play at first. Shy, you know? But I bade him to play, and passed him some copper, and he played. And, well—you've heard him? It was like the Veil itself was singing to me.'

'It is a beautiful sound,' added Eain in agreement. Oke inclined his head in acknowledgement.

'We made a deal. He rides with us, and keeps us entertained. And when we hit civilisation he earns his keep by playing. With me with him to make sure he's treated fair, of course. He earns a nice handful of copper, I can tell you. We share it and by the time we get to Ben Gedrin he'll be set up to carry on south into Re'Emsser and find his own fortune.'

'Is a nice thing to do,' said Eain.

'I thank you for saying so,' replied Oke. 'Just seemed like the right thing to do. And I like the sound! It cheers us all up.'

They sat back then, the soft melody washing over them as the landscape rolled by slowly. To their right, the plains rolled away like a tight, brown blanket. The odd scrubby bush broke the monotony, but little else. On the right, dull hills drew nearer. They were little more than hummocks covered with sandy soil, rising from the plains to the south of the road and forming low peaks and shallow valleys. They at least gave something slightly different to look at.

Eain stayed with Oke for a while, resting his legs as Oke chatted idly about the weather, their destination, and anything else that crossed his mind. Eain got the impression that Oke was bursting to ask about his past, but he did not. Perhaps Tann had instructed him not to.

A high-pitched bird call sounded from the scrubby hills to the left of the wagon track. Oke's head snapped around in the direction of the sound.

'Mehr! Quiet!' he called out, eyes scanning the hills. Another call came, a rising, whistling call that ended as a shrill squeal.

'What bird is that?' asked Eain. It was a call of no bird he had ever heard before.

'It's not a bird,' replied Oke without looking round. 'It's a person. People. The Meculvy Dutsch are near.'

'The what?' Eain was used to having to ask for explanations of tricky words or phrases, and Oke had used a couple of unusual words that he had never heard before.

'The Meculvy Dutsch,' repeated Oke. 'The Walking Birds. They are an old tribe of hunters that live all along these hills.' He was peering into the dull brown peaks and valleys, dotted with dry, twisted trees, with avid intent.

'They move like ghosts,' Oke went on. 'Never see 'em out here. Hear them, sure. Those whistles are how they talk to each other. One of them would have been a question, the other an answer. Probably talking about us!'

Oke continued to glance this way and that as they continued along the road. After a couple of hundred paces more, he shouted out triumphantly.

'Aha!' he hauled on the reins and with an uncomfortable lurch and shake, the wagon turned off the road, veering to the left.

Before them, a flat-bottomed valley ran back into the hills, away from the road. Shallow, stony slopes climbed away on either side and a trickle of water, barely enough to wet the pebbles, ran along a shallow gully in the middle.

Further away and hidden from the road, a small stand of wizened trees grew like a collection of sweeping brooms planted in the ground. They had dark green, serrated leaves and rough, hoary trunks.

'I thought so!' Oke punched Eain familiarly on the arm to make his point. 'I bet this is where the Meculvy Dutsch were hunting. Or maybe they were just whistling to tell us about it, in their own weird way.' He shrugged. 'Either way, this is a perfect place to spend the night. We can have a proper campfire for once!'

He turned, raising his voice. 'Resting here tonight, my good people! Let's chop some wood and get a fire going! Mehr? Play!'

They drove the wagons as far up the gully as possible before the ground became too rough, then unhitched the horses. The wagoners set about their tasks with workmanlike haste.

Mayla was unconvinced. 'Are we safe here, Tressin? There's no way out.'

'It's fine. It's perfect.' Oke tried to placate her. 'You heard the Walking Birds whistling? If they are nearby then it's safe. They wouldn't be hunting otherwise.'

'It feels like a good place,' agreed Reela. 'Wood to burn, water…I'm happy to be here.'

'Exactly, my girl,' said Oke, nodding. 'Exactly. The lions will have scarpered too, with the Whistlers around. They love a bit of roast lion!'

'Can we just get the fire going?' mumbled Haf. 'I'm hungry.'

Mayla continued to grumble, but before long a few trees had been felled and roughly chopped. They were quickly built into a bonfire, and as the dry wood burned it gave off a pungent, resinous scent. Eain found it comforting.

Haf was on cooking duty, and mixed some dried beans, barley and a bag of dried mushrooms with water from the brook. Standing the big, heavy pot at the edge of the fire, he poked at it half-heartedly with a stirring stick while Reela moved between the trees, searching for fresh herbs.

As the stew cooked, furs were laid on the ground and blankets were unrolled. Eain pitched in to help as the evening drew in. Mehr Mehlan accompanied all the activity with gently strummed chords on his zitol.

When the food was ready, they clustered around to fill their bowls. Eain took his food away, looking around for a spot to sit. The only place he could find was next to Haf.

For a few moments, they ate in slightly uncomfortable silence. The stew was watery but flavourful, and Eain was very hungry. The fire had burned lower and Haf's face was lit by the shifting flames, the angles of his high cheekbones casting the top of his face into moody shadows.

'You like fighting?'

Eain was momentarily taken aback by Haf's question, and wondered if he might have misunderstood. Haf must have noticed his confusion, and went on.

'In Ben Gedrin,' he explained, 'they stage bouts between the best fist-fighters around. They've got elves, dwarves and humans on their lists. Half-elves too. It's great getting to see a man or an elf give one of those purple-skinned mongrels a beating!'

'Haf, stop!' Reela had sat down on Eain's other side, and leaned across to chide Haf. 'You're boring him with that kind of talk.' She laid a hand on his arm, unseen by anyone else in the low light.

'No, it is interesting,' replied Eain. He did not want Haf to be upset, or to get in the middle of an argument between the pair. 'I didn't understand what you said about elves. And half-elves?'

'Never seen an elf?' Eain shook his head, and Haf explained. 'Well, they aren't the most sociable of folk but you see them now and then. They are mostly tall, taller than you, he- or she-elves. Skin like polished blackwood or coal.

'A lot of them are ferocious fighters. Strong and quick, quicker than most men. Built for it, see?'

Reela giggled. 'The elves all have to fight with their shirts off, too!'

'Why?' Eain was puzzled.

'To show that they aren't, you know, scarred.' Haf drew a couple of lines across his chest with the tip of his finger. 'To show that they aren't one of the Wild Ones.'

Eain nodded. He understood now. Tann and the occupants of the farm had told tales of the Wild Elves of the plains, savage tribes who cut their own skin deeply to leave livid scars across their chests. They were universally feared and hated across the Riverlands.

'And half-elves?' Eain had met a couple of half-elves at the farm. They were quiet and went about their work stoically and shyly. Apart from their purple-tinted cheeks and upswept ears, they seemed like anyone else.

'Yea, mongrels.' Haf spat on the ground. 'Think they are special. Better than us. Never met a poor half-elf, always got their hands in our pockets.'

Reela leaned forward again. 'Maybe, Eain could become a prize fighter,' she said, changing the subject. She wrapped both of her hands around his upper arm. 'Look how strong he is! And so tall!'

Eain was glad that the darkness covered his face, as he felt it colouring, heating. He could sense Haf's displeasure without needing to look in his direction.

The conflicting feelings of anxiety when he considered fighting for money, and the simultaneous enjoyment and embarrassment caused by Reela's touch was too much to bear. Abruptly, he stood.

'I must make water,' he said, forgetting the proper words in his flustered state. 'Then I sleep. Good night and good rest to you.'

He was tired. He had been walking from dawn until dusk for many days, and sleeping on hard ground each night. His eyes felt hollow and gritty, and his legs and feet throbbed.

Yet, as he lay down that night, wrapped snugly in furs and blankets, his mind whirled with questions. Sleep was elusive.

Tressin Oke seemed worried. His smile had not faltered and his constant patter of talk had barely slowed, but Eain could read tension in the set of his shoulders.

What had happened here?

They had left the hollow vale an hour or so after dawn. It was an overcast and cool morning, and something about the low cloud seemed to weigh heavily on his spirit. The conversations of the previous night, and Reela's touch, still lingered unsettlingly in his mind, too.

'We will be turning off soon!' Oke called as the wagons lurched back onto the road. 'Old friend of mine lives a couple of hours further. Hope we can trade some of Tann's tabac for some leather. If we're lucky, he'll have some beef, too. Let's keep rolling!'

Oke's friend's farmstead was a good two miles north of the road, at the end of a rough, winding track. As they approached, a small stand of evergreen trees screened the house from view. Oke was singing tunelessly as he drove his wagon through a small gap between the dark branches.

His whole posture had changed the moment that he had set eyes on the house. He tried not to show it, but it seemed straight away as though something was wrong.

The house was built from wide, stripped logs, with a single low storey and a wide, slanting roof which was thatched with reeds. It lay beside a placid, shallow lake that was fed by a trickling stream that ran through the trees from the south.

Beside and to the rear of the house, rows of thorny bushes formed wide enclosures for livestock. But, they were completely empty. Not a living creature could be seen. Between the house and the surrounding land, nothing moved. Even the house itself looked…dead.

Oke jumped down from his wagon and hesitantly approached the house.

'Eain!' hissed Reela, urgently. 'Go with him! Guard him!'

Ean felt guilty as he started forward, hurrying to catch the wagon leader. As Reela had pointed out, this was his job.

'Padan!' shouted Oke as he raised his hand to the door of the house. 'You there? It's Tressin Oke.' He put his hand to the wooden latch and started to push it open.

'Wait.' Eain reached out and placed a hand on Oke's shoulder. He gathered his courage. This is why he was here. 'Me first.'

He stepped ahead of Oke, squared his shoulders and opened the door.

The house had a single room, partitioned into separate areas with woven screens. No rushlights burned, and the fire was black and cold. Tiny shafts of light stabbed into the interior through tiny chinks between the logs. It was just enough to see by, as Eain edged inside.

'Hello?' Oke's voice was hesitant as he followed on Eain's shoulder. There was no reply.

Eain shook his head. 'Nobody is here,' he said. The place was empty.

Oke looked around the interior once more, then strode back out into the light. He walked around the house and out into the enclosure, head swinging side to side as he looked for some clue. Reela had come over from the wagon, and she and Eain followed Oke as he prowled, this way and that.

'Look,' he said, pointing at the ground near the lake. The hoofprints of many oxen were visible there, the imprints clear in the dark mud. 'Ox stood here recently. Since the last rain. But they're nowhere near here now. I don't understand.'

'They have gone,' said Eain. Oke shook his head in denial and confusion, but whatever other explanation crossed his mind, he chose not to share it.

They left that eerily still place behind soon after, gratefully turning their wagons around and rolling away.

Eain was deeply disconcerted. Not just by Oke's worry and disconcertion, and not just by the atmosphere of fear that had hung over the place. There was something else.

As Oke had stomped out of the house, and Reela had come to stand in the doorway, he had noticed a mark. It was a dark streak marring the dry rushes that were spread over the floor. He had missed it on his way into the house, but noticed it now as the morning daylight filled the doorway.

His eyes had lifted to meet Reela's, and the understanding was instant. They had both seen the dark stain, but neither wanted to be the one to speak out.

He had spent the time until the wagon train had rolled away from the farmhouse dwelling on it, and trying to avoid meeting Reela's eye. Should he tell anyone? What should he say?

Something made him hold his tongue though. It may have been the desire to save the others from further fear. It may have been the hope that Reela would speak up instead. For, the more he thought about it, the more certain he was.

What he had seen on the floor of the house was a streak of dried blood.

The being who called herself Anndra co Jorto let her horse slow to a halt. The creature was exhausted. She could feel its confused fear through its trembling flanks.

She had been riding for weeks, urging her mount to keep going, eking out its strength and endurance. It was essential that she returned to this place, and quickly. Going any slower could have cost her life.

As she rode, she had thought deeply about Eain.

Her kind had been watching the world for years, waiting for someone like him, and as soon as they had sensed him taking the first steps of his journey they had sprung into action. Anndra had been sent to meet him, to assess his strength, to do what was in her power to help him. Had she done enough? Only time would tell.

She could not see the future so there was no way to be certain. Lack of surety was difficult for her to process. She was unused to dealing with those mortal areas of grey uncertainty that lay between "right" and "wrong". The usual ways of examining the possibilities of the future had been obscured by a source of chaotic, dark magic. It was not yet understood, and had given the elders great concern.

Anndra, as she called herself, had done exactly as the elders had instructed. She had calmed the child, soothed his raw pain, and helped him communicate with those around him. That mortals could not express themselves with pure thought was an inconvenience.

Most importantly, she had set him on his path.

He could not have stayed where he was. His mind was too fragile, his scars too fresh. Besides, there was a task that they required him to perform. He had to begin, before it was too late.

She knew that she had done what was needed, and that deceiving him had been necessary, and crucial. It was logical. And yet, she felt pain. She had invested some of her emotional capacity in him, in order to help him. A connection had been made. She had touched him, and passed her ancient protection to him and in that moment she had seen into his heart.

She grieved anew to think of it. She had seen it all, his fears, and his shame, and the great care he had for all around him. He would have to fight many battles on his journey ahead, and she flinched to think of his gentle soul being put through more violence, more suffering.

But, she reminded herself, this was all necessary. One man's hardship was nothing set against the fate of the world.

She took a step forward, feeling soft grass between her toes for the first time in half a season. As if brushing past an invisible curtain, she knew she had passed back into one of the ancient and hidden strongholds of The Others. Her people.

There was no visible transition, but she herself *changed*. The human clothes were gone, as were the crude physical features she had worn as a disguise.

She had made the reservoir of power she carried within her last for as long as possible during her task, but until this very moment she had been very close to depletion, and collapse. With every step she took, closer to the twisted green mass of the wild wood before her, she felt herself being replenished like cool, fresh rain pouring into a wide-necked ewer.

She was home. And, now she must tell her family of all she had done, and all that she knew of the man, Eain Connow.

TWENTY NINE

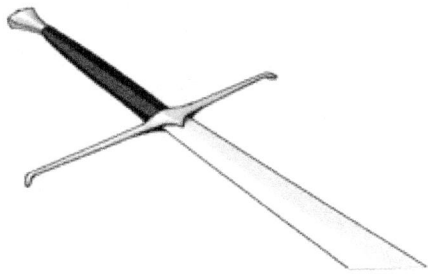

Dark clouds gathered as the wagon train rumbled on.

The road wound around low hills and scrubby slopes, still heading westward. The same featureless plains stretched away to the north, although here and there the ochre ground was punctuated with the iron-grey shimmer of small lakes.

When Eain turned his head to look left, the southern skyline had become dominated by dark, jagged mountains.

'The start of the Derufin,' Oke had said when Eain asked. 'Highest mountains in the world. Only way through is the Rujrweh Pass, up ahead and away to the south. We'll be following the ridge most of the way to Kiraband.'

The slopes rose steeply and with sheer, angular flanks. The peaks were sharp tipped, reaching for the sky like grasping claws. Around the summits, obscuring the very highest, thick clouds piled high as if driven by a wind from the south.

The darkening sky matched Eain's mood; sombre and fretful. The deserted farmhouse with the troubling smear of dried blood had unsettled him. He had caught Reela's eyes once or twice and could see that she worried too.

The whole group seemed disturbed by the experience, which was why, Eain told himself, he had not added to their worries by mentioning the bloodstain. Part of him still felt like he should, but he did not want to be the one who made things even worse.

He pulled the collar of his coat up higher, and walked on.

It felt as though it could rain at any moment. Mayla glanced often at the sky as the wagon train ground along the road. Silence lingered uncomfortably. Eain glanced up at Oke as he walked beside the lead wagon. The leader's eyes were fixed sullenly on the onward road. He was not singing today.

Maybe, he should quietly tell Oke what he had noticed. The streak of blood might mean something to him. He might know what could drive off a family and their herd of cattle without leaving a trace. He might, but it would not be anything good.

It had only been one small patch, too. It could have been from freshly slaughtered meat, or a minor injury. Why scare everyone, just for that?

Raised voices cause him to turn. A couple of wagons back, Reela and Haf seemed to be arguing. He could not hear the words but Reela's brow was furrowed in obvious anger, while Haf was staring impassively straight ahead.

Eain dragged his eyes away, not wanting to pry. He noticed that Oke had not turned, but was gently shaking his head. There was no surprise on his face. Then, Haf raised his voice in annoyance, his words carrying clearly through the cool air.

'You can't stop looking at him!'

'I'll look at who I damn well want!' retorted Reela, equally loudly.

There was a thud of feet landing hard on dirt as she jumped down from the wagon. Eain glanced around to see her striding forward, moving to walk along on the other side of Oke's wagon. Every line of her tense body showed frustration and anger.

Their journey continued for the rest of the day, with little talk. The thickening clouds hung above their heads like an oppressive, physical force.

By the time Oke had given the command to make camp for the night, a gusty wind was blowing a drizzling rain over the caravan in sporadic showers. Oke led them off the road and northward, the wagons jarring and jouncing over the rough ground. A piece of flat ground next to a small stream provided a good campground, and they drew the wagons close together and stretched sheets of canvas between them as a shelter.

The rain came and went throughout the evening, and they were able to get a small fire lit during one of the dry spells. It was enough to heat a pot of thin stew.

Reela and Haf were sitting on opposite sides of the hasty camp, refusing to look at one another. The atmosphere was tense and uncomfortable, and Eain was relieved when Oke stretched and yawned. That was the wordless signal that he thought it was time they slept.

As he curled up in his blankets and furs once more, Eain could not help wondering whether he had caused the argument. Reela had been very familiar, and Haf could not have avoiding noticing.

He had not encouraged Reela though. She had been the one who had initiated a conversation, each time. This was not something for which he should blame himself.

As he drifted off to sleep, though, he felt the unease of an awkward guilt.

Eain woke with a cold breeze lifting his blankets. They must have slipped down as he fidgeted restlessly in the night, and where his skin was exposed it pebbled in the cool air.

His eyes felt gritty and his body was clammy with cooling perspiration. The urge to wash came over him, and he recalled the small lakes he had seen the previous day. Bit by bit, he rolled himself out of his blankets as silently as possible, then crawled out from beneath the wagon and into the morning light.

The thick clouds had cleared during the night, and the sky above his head was clear and almost colourless. Dawn was about to break, a bright glow rising in the east. There was an invigorating freshness in the air.

His boots were somewhere beneath the wagon, with his coat, so rather than risk disturbing anyone else this early he walked away from the camp barefoot. The gravelly soil prickled the soles of his feet, but it was no worse than uncomfortable.

He strolled easily as the morning sky brightened at his back. A patch of dark green foliage in the lee of a low hill suggested the presence of water, and when he pushed through the low shrubs he found a small, still pool.

There was not a breath of wind to cause a ripple, and the surface was glassy. He doffed his shirt, throwing it over one of the nearby bushes. He swore in Banahgarian as it flew further than intended, falling out of sight into the tangled roots. No matter, he would find it again afterwards.

He sank to his knees on the bank of the pool. For a moment, his reflection stared back at him from the surface, grey-eyed and unshaven, before he dipped his hands into the cold water. His image broke into shifting, blurry pieces as the surface was disturbed. Cupping his hands, he lifted them to his face.

As he washed, his mind worked. He did not know what to do about Reela and Haf. It felt like his presence alone was driving a wedge between them. It made him feel awkward and uncomfortable.

He did not know why Reela behaved like she did. If she had promised to Haf then she should surely want him to be happy? It often felt as though she deliberately tried to upset him. It was strange. Eain wracked his brain for anything he could have done to encourage her, but there was nothing. So why did he still feel guilty?

He filled his hands with clear water once more, before pouring it down his face and body. He felt like some of the dirt and sweat of his long journey was washing away as the water ran down him to drip onto the dry ground. He cast another handful over his head, as if it could rinse away his worries about Reela and Haf.

A splash of water could have washed away that blood from the farmhouse floor. He still doubted himself about that issue. Was he right to keep what he had seen to himself? Or, should he tell Oke? Perhaps, Reela should tell him. Should he talk about it with Reela? He did not want that to trigger further arguments between Reela and Haf, though.

If it was significant, the wagon leader should know.

He paused. Water dripped through his hair and ran in chilly rivulets down his chest and back. He made his decision. He would tell Oke. Perhaps it would turn out to mean nothing.

Then, he heard the first screams.

His head snapped around. A high-pitched shriek of fear split the air. More raised voices echoed off the hillsides, muted and indistinct with distance, but nevertheless sharp with urgency.

He stood and pushed his way back through the low shrubs, heedless of the twiggy branches prickling his bare skin. Emerging on the other side, he broke into a run. His discarded shirt was forgotten as he dashed back towards the campsite, small stones digging painfully into the soles of his feet.

As he rounded the last shallow-sided hill, he found a scene of horror and chaos.

The wagons had been drawn into a line with the horses hitched between the traces, ready to leave. But, before they had a chance to go anywhere, they were attacked.

He could see some of the wagoners atop their vehicles, trying desperately to fend off the attackers with hand tools and wooden staves. He heard Reela's voice, crying out Haf's name in pleading terror.

The attackers were…Eain had but moments to study them as he closed in on the battle, and struggled to understand what he was seeing.

They milled around the wagons astride horses of their own. They were all tall, and bare-chested, men and women alike. They were armed with stabbing spears and the odd axe, and they thrust them mercilessly at Eain's companions.

As he watched, open-mouthed in fear and confusion, he saw a pair ride down Mayla as she attempted to flee. A spear sank deeply into her back, between her shoulder blades, and she fell with a wordless grunt.

Eain's mouth went dry.

The two spotted him, one pointing in his direction. They wheeled their horses around, eyes fixed on him. Eain slapped his hand to his waist, searching for his seax. It was not there.

He had left it with his coat.

One of the attackers threw a spear, and he ducked. It missed him by inches. The other lashed down with her axe as her horse thundered past, but Eain dodged and grabbed her wrist. Dropping his weight and holding tight, he dragged the axewoman off her horse.

She tumbled to the ground, but quickly jumped to her feet. Eain could now see that she was an elf. On foot, she matched him for height but was slender and long-limbed. Her scalp was shaven and her whole head was covered with incised scars, reaching down over her face in an intricate pattern.

As she moved to attack him, he noticed that her torso was likewise laced with scars. What manner of people would disfigure themselves so? Were these the Wild Elves?

Then, she was on him and he had no more time to wonder.

She swung her axe savagely, and he swayed back. In the moment she was off-balance, he lunged forward. His right arm came up and he drove his elbow into her throat. As she gagged, staggering, he twisted to palm the backswing of her axe away. In the same motion he seized her wrist and pulled it toward his rising knee.

There was a solid crack of impact and she dropped to her knees. Her teeth were clenched in pain, but she made no sound.

He sensed the next attack before he saw it, and spun on his heel. He crossed his forearms and lifted them, catching the shaft of a thrusting spear and ducking beneath. Clenching his fists, he drove a flurry of rapid punches to the elf's exposed ribs. The feeling of snapping bone beneath his fists was sickening, and he felt a gust as all the air left his opponent's lungs.

The elf doubled over, and Eain drove his knee and up into his face. The elf's nose smashed flat, the bones cracking against Eain's kneecap, but he had no time to dwell on it. There were many more, and wagoners were falling everywhere he looked.

His breath came in gasps and his hands were shaking. The urge to run was powerful. He wanted to flee, to leave the fighting behind. But, the urge to defend the others was stronger.

As he dashed toward the wagons, two struggling figures wove across his path. One was Haf, wrestling uselessly with a towering, russet-skinned elf. Eain increased his pace, but was too late. The elf reached around Haf's body from behind and drew a jagged-bladed knife across his throat.

'No!' Eain's voice sounded shrill in his own ears. Haf's lifeblood poured from his throat, spreading across his pale shirt like a crimson fan. Before Haf's body hit the ground, Eain charged at his killer. He barrelled into the slighter elf, and they tumbled to the ground together.

Eain saw the elf raising the bloody knife, and reached out quickly to pin that wrist to the ground. The elf struggled but Eain was heavier, and his strength was amplified by desperation. He swung his left arm, smashing his elbow into the elf's scarred temple. The elf reeled back as the bony point split the skin near his eye. Dark blood welled.

Before he could react, Eain lashed out with his elbow again, this time to the elf's throat. He gagged and croaked, struggling to breath. Without thinking about it, Eain grabbed the dropped knife and plunged it into the elf's neck.

Leaving him bleeding out on the rocky ground, he rose.

'Eain! Help!'

Eain turned toward the sound to see Tressin Oke fighting desperately. He was standing, long legs spread wide, on the bed of one of the wagons. He had a scythe in his hands and was whirling it around, holding the elves at bay. Reela was beside him, fending attackers from the other side away with sweeps of a shovel.

If he could reach Oke and Reela, and stand beside them, maybe they could drive the elf raiders away together. Maybe he could protect at least two people. Maybe.

He took a step forward, but another elf warrior leapt into his path, axe swinging. Eain swayed aside without conscious thought and lashed out with a fist. As the elf reeled back Eain pressed forward, striking again and again with hands, elbows and knees. He left the elf in a heap, bloody and unconscious.

Oke's wagon was only a few strides away, and the leader still stood. Reela clung close to his back, shovel outstretched in desperate defence. The scythe Oke wielded spun in blurring arcs, sweeping toward any that tried to climb up toward him. As Eain closed in, Oke caught his eyes for a moment. They were wide with terror.

Then, they widened further. The scythe fell from his fingers. His hands dropped to his belly, curling around the haft of a thrown spear. At the same time, strong hands grasped the end of the shovel and dragged it from Reela's fingers. Heartbeats later, a she-elf had leapt up beside them both. Oke was defenceless as she dragged her knife across his throat.

Reela lunged away, trying to jump from the wagon, trying to escape anywhere. But the elf woman was too quick. A hand snaked out and took a handful of Reela's long, fair hair. She shrieked with pain as the she-elf tugged her viciously backward and thrust the knife into her back. Reela's mouth gaped but no sound emerged.

Eain watched in helpless horror as Reela was stabbed again and again, and dropped to the wagon bed, her clothes dark with blood.

Eain staggered sideways, a low moan escaping his lips. It was all but over.

He came to a halt, and something inside him chilled, and hardened. He clenched his fists. He would not go down easily. Maybe some of the wagoners had run away. He would try to buy them time.

Last night's campfire circle was beneath his feet, and he set a wide stance above the blackened ash. More elves were approaching. He lifted his head and regarded them dispassionately. Let them come.

They attacked.

He was in the *claidah*. His instructor, Rathvedd or another hard faced Claihedehmore, calling out the moves. Their harsh, barking voice reverberated off the stone walls.

'Palm strike! Forearm block! Elbow strike! Grab! Twist! Kick!'

The hard points of his body struck flesh as he moved around the campfire circle, but he barely registered the impacts. His mind was elsewhere.

'Do it better, Connow!' The voice from his past was ruthless and unrelenting. 'Concentrate! Do it again! Again!'

Again.

It had happened again. Once more, others died while he lived. Once more, he was to blame. Once more, he had failed. A sob escaped his lips.

It took him a few moments to realise that the fighting had stopped. He stood, bloodied fists raised before his chest, but none attacked.

Elves lay sprawled about his feet. Some were groaning, others were still and silent. Ten paces away, more scarred elves waited in a ragged line. Every eye was on him.

Their dark skin gleamed in the morning light. Their complexions ranged in colour from tanned leather to coal black. He- and she-elf alike were similarly covered in scars, livid lines that seemed to radiate outward from their chest. The heart was at the centre.

This would be the end. They would attack him together and he would be overwhelmed. Their axe blades and spearpoints would pierce his flesh. He hoped it would be quick.

Then, one stepped forward. He was taller than Eain, unnaturally narrow about the waist and with long, slender limbs. His scars made a spider's web across the dusky skin of his chest and face.

Deliberately, he returned his curved axe to his belt while glaring directly into Eain's eyes. Without looking away or seeming to blink, he lifted his right hand and drew a finger slowly across his chest. The gesture seemed to follow the line of one of the scars that was cut over his heart. Then, he made that hand into a fist and raised it beside his head.

Eain blinked. He had no idea what was happening. Without a sound, the other elves copied their leader's gesture; they drew a finger across their heart-scars and then raised their fists.

Eain watched dumbly, still waiting for death.

As one, the elves dropped their hands and turned to leave. Eain stared uncomprehendingly. As he watched, rooted to the spot, they silently gathered the dead and piled it onto one of the wagons.

Eain saw the bodies of Oke and Haf dumped unceremoniously on top of one another, along with the sad, deflated shape of Mehr Mehlan. He would never find fame as a musician. The sight of Reela's flowing golden hair on top of the pile was a knife in his gut. Gone forever.

The elves rode away without a backward glance, drawing the wagons behind them. Eain watched them dwindle, and slumped to his knees, unable to grasp what had just happened.

Why had they spared him? What did the finger and fist gesture mean? What should he do now?

Part of him wanted to pursue the elves, to confront them, and to make them fight again. Part of him did not believe that all the others could truly be dead. He should try to rescue them.

He climbed to his feet. The rocky ground dug into his bare soles as he stepped forward. He had not taken more than a few steps before images swam before his eyes; Haf, Reela and Oke bleeding out through their ruined throats, Mehlan's broken body, Mayla's screams.

They were dead.

He fell to his knees again, and did not move for a long time.

The sun was higher when he found the strength to raise his head again. It was warm where it touched his bare skin, although the rising wind had a chilly bite.

Streaky clouds surged across the sky, like dead leaves blown across the rippled surface of a clear lake. Eain rose to his feet, his body heavy with weariness. He felt numb. He felt as though this must be a dream; a nightmare. How could this have happened?

He could not comprehend it. Worse, he could not find a way to feel anything, any way to care. He just felt empty.

Feet. His feet hurt and felt cold. He wandered slowly through the discarded piles of possessions, things that the elves had clearly not thought worth taking. His boots were still there, and he put them on.

His hands also felt sore. He raised them, noticing with mild curiosity that they were covered in blood, the knuckles split and raw. Wash. Water. His hands shook as he set off.

He found his way back to the small lake and washed his hands clean. The water dripped back into the lake, stained with pink. He also wiped off the blood that had splattered up his arms from his elbows, and across his chest.

He had been shirtless. Why? Shirt. He remembered throwing his shirt. Pushing through the bushes he found it and put it on. Now what?

His mind drifted as his body moved around the campground, collecting things he would need to survive. A waterskin, a leather sack holding a few rounds of hard-baked bread and a little dried meat.

Last, he found his goatskin coat and put it on. It provided a soft, comforting warmth against the growing chill. His body felt shivery now. His teeth chattered.

He buckled his seax on once more and began walking. He reached the road and paused. Should he head back toward the farm, or onward west? The answer was clear.

Onward.

All he could think was that he needed to leave what had just happened behind. Get far away. He could not find the strength to let himself feel anything. He did not have the strength to care. It was too much.

He turned, the westward road stretching out ahead. He began to walk. He knew he had to keep moving. He was still in danger.

THIRTY

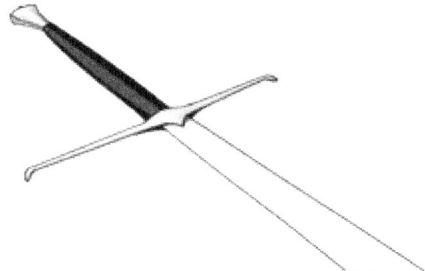

The days passed in a relentless trudge. Endless ochre slopes marched away to Eain's left, while the inhospitable and featureless expanse of the plains stretched out of sight to his right.

He saw no one but felt unfriendly eyes watching him constantly.

The westward road hugged the foothills of the soaring southern mountains. The daytimes were mostly dry but cool, and their saw-toothed summits were a stark black silhouette against a crystalline blue sky.

Day by day, nothing seemed to change.

In a way, he revelled in the solitude. He was able to stretch his legs, and cover the ground quickly. The more distance he put behind him, the less real the fate of the wagon train seemed. There were none around to judge, to speak to him of what he had done, what he had seen.

At night, though, he was haunted by dreams of pain and blood. Pain that he had caused, blood that he had spilled.

At least while was alone, he could not cause anyone else to be hurt.

The road remained empty. Eain feared to venture north of the track in case the Wild Elves returned. Where possible, he walked to the south to be less conspicuous, but the roughness of the slopes often forced him back down to the hard-packed trail.

He had no way of finding food. He ate sparingly from the small stock he had taken from the ruin of the wagoners' camp, knowing he could not replenish it. He could not afford the time to stop and hunt, and knew nothing of the game in this strange land. Likewise, he had not the knowledge of the plants he saw to tell which could sustain him, and which might kill him.

So, he marched on with a stomach that growled and clenched, and with legs that felt weaker with each passing day.

He was sustained by his determination to reach Kiraband, and the city of Ben Gedrin. That is where he had decided to go, and he held onto that as his goal. Every weary step took him closer.

He remembered the others talking about Annida as a town that was somewhere on the way. If they had described the journey time to reach it, he had not been listening. He had no idea how long he would need to eke his limited supply of food out for.

He wished he had paid closer attention.

Evening was falling on the fourth or fifth day since the elves' attack. He was struggling to remember. He was finding it difficult to think about anything beyond putting one foot in front of the other. Annida. Kiraband. Ben Gedrin. He had to keep going.

The westering sun was in his eyes, a hazy reddish glare, as he stumbled off the road to look for somewhere to spend the night. His food was all gone and he was down to the last few drops at the bottom of his waterskin.

He should be afraid, but he was not. All he felt was apathy. He would keep moving while he still had strength to stand, but if he fell then at least he would find peace.

A shallow gully opened unexpectedly before him, the hollow gurgle of a narrow stream loud in the surrounding silence. He stooped to wet his dry lips, then glanced upstream. Stony banks rose on either side, and between them lay a sheer wall of rock, about the height of a man. The stream trickled down this small cliff; a feeble waterfall that covered the rocks in a glistening sheet.

Above, Eain could see the matt green fronds of a stunted tree. A sign of more water. He edged along the slope and clambered up the rocky edge of the falls. The stone was cool and sharp beneath his hands. Beyond was a narrow pool, where water that ran off the higher hills collected, before dripping over the edge to gurgle down the gully and out onto the plains.

The steepness of the hills relented before the edge of the water, leaving a flat space to one side. This would be an ideal place to spend the night, sheltered by the hillsides above and next to this clean, fresh water.

He cast himself down at the water's edge and drank deeply. He felt the cool, crisp water wetting his moustache and chilling his stubbled cheeks as he gulped great mouthfuls down into his belly. It was not food, but for the moment at least, he was sated.

His stomach felt tight as a drum as he rolled onto his back to rest. Small stones pressed sharply against the back of his head as he gazed vacantly up into the clear, fading sky.

His hopes were also fading.

He lay there for some time, as the light leached away. Night would soon fall, and like every other night, he would face the darkness on his own.

A sudden sound roused him from his stupor. A whistle. It started low then increased in pitch to a high note, before stopping. The echoes died away quickly and silence returned like it had never been broken.

Eain sat up. Once more, he knew that it was not a bird call. The Meculvy Dutsch. Should he be wary? Were they dangerous? He recalled Oke saying that the Walking Birds only hunted where it was safe.

He did not have the energy to worry.

The shadows were deep in the narrow valley as he pulled his blankets from his pack and wrapped himself in their comforting folds. He thrust a hand into the pocket of his goatskin coat, and his fingers wrapped around an angular wooden object. Anndra's carved wooden eagle.

He closed his eyes tightly as emotions threatened to overwhelm him. He suddenly wished for her, her calm presence and gentle wisdom. He gripped the eagle tightly and prayed. He prayed to Maneg for wisdom, and he prayed to Kell and the Twelve Brothers for the fortitude he would need to survive. He wished Anndra was there beside him, in his arms.

As his eyelids closed, he thought he heard another faint whistle, but it could not hold back the dark embrace of sleep.

The morning air was a frosty caress across his face. His eyes felt heavy as he forced them open, and was surprised by the brightness. He had slept much longer into the morning than usual.

His empty stomach shuddered, and he grimaced as hunger pains rose like the clutch of invisible claws. He despaired anew. How could he get through this day with no food?

Maybe he would reach Annida today. Maybe Maneg, the eagle-headed god, or the Brothers would answer his fervent prayers of the night before. Maybe Anndra…he dismissed that thought. He was alone.

He sat up slowly, gathering his fragile strength. Gathering his courage. His blankets slithered down to pool in his lap, and he began to rise. Then stopped.

Beside where he had been sleeping, on the narrow shore of the pool, was a sack tied with a leather cord. It was not his. He had never seen it before.

He stood, looking around warily. The hillsides remained bare and empty. Nothing moved apart from some gauzy clouds drifting high overhead. Cautiously, he reached for the sack and untied the cord with quivering fingers. A mouth-watering, savoury scent filled his nostrils as he opened it, and he could not restrain himself from thrusting his hands eagerly inside.

It was full of food.

There was a stack of unusually square flatbreads, wrapped in linen. They were freshly baked and when Eain took a large bite it had a rich, herby flavour. Aside from the bread there were strips of jerky, some fruits he did not recognise but had a sharp, tangy scent and two small clay pots. One contained a reddish paste which was oily and had a pungent flavour, and the other was filled with yellow honey.

He did not understand. This food had clearly been left for him to find when he woke. Someone had placed it here while he slept. Could it be a trap? Was it poisoned?

Eain dismissed this. If an invisible watcher had wanted him dead, they could have easily ended him last night while he was asleep and defenceless.

He ate, hungrily but carefully. It would be a waste of food to gulp it down too quickly and make himself sick. He also still had no idea how long the rest of his journey would take. He would have to make it last. But now, he had the strength to continue.

He packed the food away in his pack with his blankets, filled his waterskin and made his way back down to the road.

Could he dare to assume that someone out there wanted to help him? The prospect lifted his spirits as he struck out westward, his long strides eating up the miles.

The next few days passed uneventfully. With a full belly, Eain strode along his path with renewed vigour. He felt as though he was leaving his past behind, step by step.

The soft flatbreads gradually went stale and hard, but retained their flavour. He had eaten the last of them that morning, and then the strange paste around noon. All he had left was the pot of honey, which he intended to save for as long as he could.

The landscape remained unchanging. Bare plains to his right, hills rising to jagged mountains to his left. The road stretched away unremittingly before him, vanishing into the hazy distance.

He squinted against the bright sunshine, looking around constantly for any signs of settlement or civilisation. The road was empty of other travellers. There was nothing.

His mind played tricks.

That morning he had been convinced that he heard the grinding rumble of wagon wheels on the gritty surface of the road. He knew immediately that it must be Oke, catching him up at last.

The attack by the elves, and the battle, and all the blood … that must have been a dream. A horrible dream. It could not have really happened.

He stopped, waiting beside the road for the wagons to roll past. There was silence. The wind twitched the longer hair at the back of his neck as it blew in petulant gusts.

Then, reality came crashing back down. They were all gone. Dead. He had seen them die; Oke, Reela, Haf and the others. They would never come this way again.

His knees buckled and he collapsed to the ground. Great, heaving sobs wracked his body as grief overwhelmed him. He craved someone to be there with him, Anndra, Tann, his own mother…He was so alone.

His hand went to his pocket, his fingers wrapping around the hard wooden shape of the eagle once more. He gripped it until it hurt, the sharply carved beak and wings digging into the skin of his palm. His despair passed.

He was stronger alone. He did not need to care about anyone else. His journey was all that mattered now. Annida. Kiraband. Ben Gedrin.

He continued.

A shallow cave was his resting place that night. He sat with his back against the angular rocks of the cave wall, watching the sun set in a blaze of angry red light. Setting over his destination.

The honey was almost unbearably sweet as he licked it from his dirty fingers. The pot was almost empty. He had intended to save some but the sweetness on his tongue was irresistibly soothing.

He faced a day tomorrow with an empty stomach, once again.

Clutching the carved eagle, he fell slowly into a worried, fitful sleep.

There was another sack of food waiting for him when he woke. It had been placed in the mouth of the cave, not two paces from where he slept.

He scanned the dry dirt around the cave entrance, but could see no signs of a boot or a bare foot. Whoever was providing these gifts could move silently and with great stealth. Eain was intrigued.

Aside from what Oke had shared, Eain knew nothing about the Meculvy Dutsch. Well, he knew they spoke in whistles and moved through the hills like ghosts. But, what type of being were they? Men, or elves? Or something different?

If they were willing to share food, then they cannot have seen him as an enemy. Perhaps, if he could speak with them they could provide guidance. It would be useful just to know how much further it was to Annida. It sparked a vague hope in him. Maybe, he was not completely alone.

He packed up and strode away from the cave. Thinking that he might have his supplies replenished again, he ate less sparingly over the following days. There was bread, dried meat and shrivelled dried fruit, sweet and chewy. He dug into his sack every few hours, and made good progress.

The scenery began to change. The plains to the north were slightly greener, dotted with slender trees that bore dangling fronds that swayed in the gentle breeze. The high mountains to Eain's left seemed more distant. The summits were still sharply outlined, but they were remote, marching away to the southeast.

The rolling foothills still rose closer to hand, the road picking a winding path at their scrubby feet.

It was sunset once more when he wandered off the road, weary and footsore, finding himself in a grove of small trees. Their trunks were gnarled and rough, and so dark the wood appeared almost black. He had decided to try to make contact with the Meculvy Dutsch.

He ate his fill before curling up in his blankets. With a concentrated effort, he allowed himself to rest without sleeping. The trees sighed in the breeze, and Eain listened intently for any other sounds.

What felt like a couple of hours had passed, and Eain had heard nothing. He felt the persuasive hand of sleep trying to drag him down the land of slumber, and fought against it. He pressed his nails into his palms, concentrating on the sharp sensation.

Then, he heard it.

The subtle scrape of a leather sole on rocky ground. The unmistakable sound of stealthy movement. He opened his eyes, but kept them narrowed to slits. He was ready.

There was the soft scuffle of a sack being laid beside him, and he sat up abruptly.

He caught the briefest glance of a tall, grey-clad figure. They were hooded and masked, and they wore robes that brushed the ground. Eain caught their dark eyes for a moment, before they turned and were gone into the night.

He jumped up and tried to follow.

'Wait!' he called, desperately. 'I am a friend!'

It was no use. They had vanished as if they had never been there. As though they were no more than a spirit, or a half-remembered dream. Eain cursed.

A couple of low, elongated whistles floated through the night as Eain sullenly rolled himself in his blankets once more.

The next day, the road left the hills and struck out across the plains.

Eain staggered. He tried to focus on the path ahead but the low sun burned into his eyes, forcing him to look down. His mouth was dry, his lips cracked.

He had run out of food two days ago. He had drunk the last tepid drops from his waterskin this morning. He had nothing left, and his strength was failing.

Several days had passed since he had struck out from the grove where he had set his ambush for the Meculvy Dutsch. That food parcel was the last he had received, although he did not know if that was down to his attempt at making contact, or because the road had broken away from the foothills.

When his food had started to run low this time, he had considered turning back toward the hills. But, something inside warned against it. He knew he must keep moving forward. Annida. Kiraband. Ben Gedrin.

He clutched his wooden eagle tightly, and trudged on.

The plains to either side were almost featureless. Thin, scrubby grass swayed in the nagging breeze. Far to the north, at the extent of his vision, Eain could almost imagine that the ground began to slope away.

The southern mountains had receded into hazy distance; now just a spreading, bulky shadow on the distant horizon. There was not a drop of water to be seen. Even a small rain shower would have been welcome, but the sky remained stubbornly clear and blue.

The road ahead continued without a curve or bend. When he glanced behind, he was greeted with an identical view. He felt as though his weary steps were getting him nowhere. He walked and walked and nothing changed.

He did not know it, but he was travelling the stretch of road known as the Dry Leagues. No watercourses ran anywhere near the road for a hundred-and-fifty mile stretch between Annida and the hills to the east.

None lived here, and only well provisioned travellers would attempt the journey.

His legs felt as though they were filled with water. His head was heavy. Perhaps, he thought, if he rested for a time, it would give him the strength to go on. As soon as the thought crossed his mind, his knees buckled and he collapsed at the side of the road.

Exhaustion and thirst swept over him like a heavy blanket. His eyes closed, and the blue sky above faded to grey, then black.

As he lost consciousness, he wondered idly if this was how death would take him. It was strangely peaceful.

The ground beneath him swayed. His whole body rocked from side to side as the very world seemed to jolt and judder.

He carefully opened his eyes. His senses were confused. He struggled to link his memory and his present sensations. Where was he?

'He wakes! He wakes!'

A voice from near his head was shrill in his ears. He looked up to find a young boy staring down at him. His hair was fair and his eyes were blue, and his skin was fair but sun darkened. Eain noticed that he wore a band of plaited reeds around his brow.

'Where am I?' asked Eain. The boy looked away bashfully, and did not reply.

Eain sat up higher, looking around. He was in the back of a large wagon of an unusual design. The perimeter of the wagon bed seemed to be formed from narrow wooden boxes, with hinged lids. He had been laying on a blanket woven with geometric patterns but that itself was laid on panelling of shining, well-oiled wood which had been planed and sanded smooth.

'He must not speak with you,' put in another voice. A woman had turned from where she sat, next to the driver. 'As you are a stranger to us, and not one of the Waica.'

She too was fair-haired but hers was tied in tight braids that ran from her hairline and back to the nape of her neck. They were tied over the band she wore across her brow, formed of what seemed to be copper rods, bent and twisted over and around each other to create a complex pattern.

'But,' she continued. 'I am happy to see you awake. We found you sleeping beside the road in the middle of the Dry Leagues. Not safe! We could not leave you there.'

She smiled. After spending so long alone, the sight of a human smile sent a radiant warmth to Eain's soul. He also appreciated his good fortune in being found at all in that hostile, arid expanse.

The woman was clearly the boy's mother, they had the same pale, round eyes. He was sitting in the opposite corner of the wagon bed, staring intently. Eain had to assume that the fair-haired man driving the wagon was the boy's father.

He had not turned around once yet, but Eain noticed that he wore a band of what seemed to be intricately woven hazel twigs.

Eain looked beyond the driver. The plains still stretched away to either side, but up ahead Eain thought that he could make out blocky shapes that could have been houses.

'Where are we going?' he asked.

The woman frowned. 'It is too early for those questions. You are still a stranger to us. We must know you first.' Her stare became more penetrating. 'What moons were you born under?'

Eain now knew to expect this question at a meeting, and he had learned how to answer.

'My birth moons were Kalua full and Jura old.'

She nodded. 'What have you made?'

'What?' He was taken aback by the question.

'What have you made, in your life?' she repeated. 'What have you created?'

His mouth opened but he did not know what to say. What had he made? The truth was that he had made nothing. He was a soldier. Had been a soldier. What had he ever created?

Apart from pain and death, said a cruel voice deep inside him.

'I made a fence,' he stammered, thinking quickly. 'At my friend's farm. I bent the branches of a hedge to make the fence. It was to keep goats inside.'

The woman nodded slowly. 'A worthy creation,' she said, 'if simple. What land were you born in?'

Eain was again surprised at the question, and the word was out of his lips before he could think to lie.

'Banahgar,' he said. 'I was born in the land of Banahgar.'

She blinked. 'I have never heard this. Is this place to the north of the Great River, or to the south?'

'Neither,' replied Eain. He felt he owed her the truth. 'To the east. Over the Wolfteeth Mountains.' He used the name for the mountains he recalled Carilton Tann had used. No-one this side would know what he meant if he said the Beinuirm Skele.

'There is no land there.' Her voice was cold. 'None ever came from there. You are lying, or I will name you outlander. One who comes from elsewhere.'

'Yes,' Eain admitted. 'I am an outlander.'

'Stop.' Her voice was harsh as he addressed her husband. Now, she turned back to Eain. 'Get off my wagon, outlander.'

'What? Why?'

'Now. You have received our aid, but you are an outlander and we cannot know you. Cannot trust you.'

Bewildered, Eain climbed off the back of the wagon. The boy wriggled across the wagon bed to keep as much distance as possible between Eain and himself. Once Eain had climbed down, the woman moved to the back and started lifting the lids of boxes. She pulled out some linen-wrapped packages and threw them down. They were parcels of food.

'The Waica do not leave strangers to starve,' she said sternly, looking down from her high position on the wagon. 'But we do not carry outlanders. It is twenty miles back to Annida that way.' She pointed in the direction from which they had come. 'Or, thirty miles onward to the next village. It is called Feorhryc. Choose your path, stranger.'

Then, she sat once more and the wagon rolled steadily away, the train of other wagons following behind raising dust into the air.

Eain was left alone once more, surrounded by a shifting cloud.

Where should he go now?

THIRTY ONE

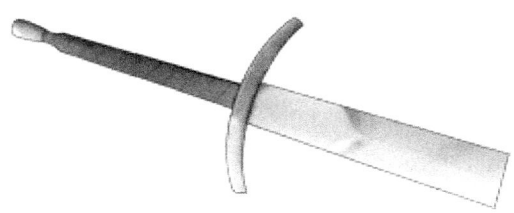

Holt Cookson rose with the dawn. He always did, these days.

He slept lightly and as soon as the first grey link of the sunrise found its way through the chinks in his shutters, his eyes were open.

The room was cool as he dressed without urgency. He had various things to do, but could take all day over them. The village of Feorhryc was sleepy, and in normal circumstances life ran at a slow pace.

Holt pulled on thick woollen trousers and a long coat. Autumn was truly here, and the temperature seemed to drop daily. It felt like it got colder every year, but then he wondered if he was just starting to feel his age.

A bite of yesterday's bread washed down with a gulp of chilly water was enough for breakfast, before he seized his staff and opened the door. Stepping down onto the main street, he sucked in a breath as a cold breeze knifed through him.

'Holt!' a voice hailed him, and he turned to see Bryllin, a younger man with round cheeks and mousy hair, pushing a wheeled barrow along the street.

'Be you well, Bryllin,' called Holt in greeting.

Bryllin bobbed his head. 'Aye, Holt, all well. I'm out to get some roots dug. I'll put them in the main barn, right?'

'Right, Bryllin.'

Holt sighed inwardly. The lad did not need to ask him that. He knew where to store roots, just as well as Holt did. But, the youngsters had been raised with the tale of the time that bandits had overrun the village, and the heroic and dramatic battle that had seen them off.

Holt had been right in the middle of it, of course. With what had happened, he really had no choice but to become the village elder. Anyone else who took the title would only have asked him for advice anyway.

Fion would have done a better job. Fion was a stronger character than him, more able to bend people to her will, better at making difficult decisions. Fion had gone, though. She had ridden off to start a new life in Ben Gedrin, and in many ways Holt envied her. Feorhryc was full of ghosts.

'One more thing, Master Holt,' added Bryllin. 'I checked the stables, too. All the horses are still there this morning.'

'That's good Bryllin, well done.'

Three horses had been stolen from the village a few nights previously. Holt had been puzzled, and still was. Why steal just three, and not empty the whole stable? It was good news that the thieves had not been back again, though.

Bryllin trotted off toward the fields, and Holt walked away in the opposite direction.

Feorhryc was built to either side of the main road that ran between Ben Gedrin and Annida. The inn had been here first, a stopping point for weary travellers, but then the nearby stream had been diverted from its deep cut gorge into irrigation channels, turning arid plains into fields. Now, it was a small but stable settlement.

Holt had reached the inn, and old, stone-built structure when something gave him pause. He lifted a hand to shade his eyes against the watery sun, and peered out along the eastward road.

Something was moving there. Someone. A lone traveller, approaching the bridge that spanned the stream. That seemed unusual.

It was Holt's job to keep the peace here, so he needed to find out who this was, and what had brought them to Feorhryc at dawn, on foot. He put his chilly hands in the deep, woolly pockets of his coat and strode toward the bridge, his staff tucked beneath his arm.

Holt paused just before the wooden span of the bridge and regarded the approaching figure. It was a man, a young man. He was dressed in snug leathers, like a rider, although there was no horse in sight. Not the horse thief, at least.

He walked with an unsteady gait, swaying from side to side. Holt hoped he was not drunk. He hated managing drunkards.

'What's your business, friend?' he called out, as the man stepped onto the other end of the bridge.

'No business,' replied the man, and his voice was croaky with fatigue and thick with an accent that Holt could not identify. 'Just travel. To Kiraband. Ben Gedrin.'

Holt gripped his staff more tightly, as he noticed the long fighting knife scabbarded at the man's hip.

'You're on the right road to Ben Gedrin, friend. But maybe you should take a break.'

Holt stepped back warily as the man came closer. He was tall, with hair the colour of straw. His eyes were fixed on the road. Holt had been around enough violent men to get a sense of when there was a threat, and he was not alarmed by this man, despite his size.

'I don't want to be trouble,' he said, making as if to walk a wide arc around where Holt stood. As he tried to take a longer stride, he staggered slightly. Holt sucked his teeth. This man was not going to go much further, and if he tried to carry on he would end up dead beside the road.

It would be more trouble to have to worry about his fate. Holt made a snap decision.

'Take a moment before going on,' he said, moving to follow the young man. 'I'll fill your waterskin and find you a bite to eat. I can open up the inn for a quick rest.'

The man paused, thinking. His eyes were shadowed and grey, his skin parched and dry. After an age, he spoke again.

'Yes,' he croaked. 'Please.'

The sky was brightening, a cool breeze riffling through Holt's hair as he led the stranger toward the inn. He kept a pace or two of space between them, watching the traveller carefully out of the corner of his eye.

Trusting without reason was foolish.

As Holt reached the door of the inn and put his hand to the handle, the fair-haired man staggered slightly. Holt raised his arms, either to catch him or ward off his falling body, but the man moved past to slump against the wall of the inn. Looking again at the man's size, Holt was not sure he could have caught him. He was a hand taller and broad in the shoulder.

'Tired,' sighed the man as he leaned on the inn's ancient stones.

'You can rest up here,' replied Holt, opening the door.

The inn was the biggest building in the village. Most of the interior comprised a single room, a broad hall the full width of the building. Tables and benches were arrayed around two hearths, one at either end. Both were grey and lifeless at this early hour.

The landlord, Alwyn Oleman, served ale from a table at the far end, and beyond that was a narrow door which led through to the rooms where he lived with his wife and family.

'Sit yourself somewhere,' said Holt over his shoulder as he strode toward that door. Ducking quietly through, he found himself in the Oleman's living room. The family were still sleeping, so he moved carefully as he gathered a heel of bread and a jug of water.

Carrying them back into the main hall, he found the bedraggled young man sitting motionless on one of the benches. His eyes stared blankly forward at nothing.

What have you been through? Thought Holt.

'Eat. Drink.'

Holt set the jug and the bread on the table and stepped back. His eyes flicked to the wall behind, where a long, broad sword was hung.

It was a trophy. A memento. Holt shuddered. They called it the Wose Blade, and it was a symbol of the battle that had been fought to free the village from the clutches of the bandit Wolt Wose.

Holt found it difficult to look at the sword without feelings of regret, guilt and grief. Wose and his bandits had murdered his wife Mali, and Fion's husband Bruk. It seemed so long ago that Holt often struggled to recall Mali's face, but the loss lived inside him and he grieved for it every day.

Fion had managed to recruit a band of mercenary warriors to aid them in their fight against Wose. At the height of the battle, the leader of the mercenaries had duelled with Wose, and had eventually slain the man, leaving him bleeding out on Feorhryc's main street.

Except, that was not exactly what had happened.

The mercenary had defeated Wolt in single combat, but he had not killed him. In a cold, vengeful fury he had begun to torture Wose. It was a long-awaited revenge for another murder; Wose had raped and killed the mercenary leader's wife.

Holt had not been able to bear it, and had seized the first weapon he could lay his hands on. It was the brutal, heavy sword belonging to Wose's dwarf lieutenant, Sturi, and Holt had used it to run Wose through.

This had become the Wose Blade. This is what the other villagers had wanted to keep as a reminder of victory. This was one other thing that made it impossible for Holt to forget how he had dealt death that day. How he had taken a life to save the soul of the mercenary leader, Carilton Tann.

The man was wearily chewing the bread, in between taking deep, grateful swigs of water. It looked as though he had not eaten or drunk for some time.

'There's more, if you want,' said Holt, looking down at the young man with concern.

'Just tired,' he replied, before lowering himself to lie sideways on the bench. Moments later, Holt could hear the even sounds of snoring. He was asleep.

He must need it, thought Holt, strolling toward the door. *Maybe he will tell me his story when he wakes again.*

It was high noon when Holt returned to the inn. He had a fresh loaf tucked under his arm and a couple of dried figs in the pocket of his coat. The loaf had been thrust upon him by the village baker's wife.

'We appreciate everything you do for us, Master Cookson,' she had said. It had been impossible to refuse. He felt embarrassed by the praise. He did so little to help them. They needed no help. And he certainly did not deserve the title "Master". He held no land.

As always, he had shrugged and thanked her, and moved along. He felt like he was working up a debt that he could never pay off.

Ducking back into the inn, he found Alwyn Oleman quietly moving around the room, sweeping the floor.

'Holt,' he murmured, nodding his head in greeting. Then, he laid a finger across his lips and gestured toward the back of the room. Holt glanced over and saw the stranger lying on the bench. He was still fast asleep.

Well, thought Holt. *He did say he was tired.*

He sat down at the table, opposite where the sleeping man lay, and tore the loaf open. It was nut brown, speckled with seeds and still steamed slightly. A perk of the job, he supposed.

Before he had taken more than a few bites, the door slammed open and the skinny figure of Alwyn's son, Caill, burst through.

'Da! A wagon has just pulled up and I don't like the look of the folk getting out!' he cried. Then, he noticed Holt. 'Master Holt,' he said, in a calmer tone. 'I think you should come outside and see this too.'

Holt got to his feet, but he had not taken more than a couple of steps when the doorway darkened. A solidly built man ducked through, followed by several others.

They were dressed in smocks and hose, with sturdy boots. Holt took a step back as they spread out into the room, looking them up and down. They were a mix of men and women, and all clearly southerners, with olive skin and dark hair. Their fingers were thick with many slim rings, forged from different metals.

The size of the last man to enter the room caused Holt to stare. He was a giant, his head close to the ceiling beams and with skin that was the colour of charcoal. Holt worried for a moment that he was one of the Wild Ones, but he was not scarred. His very presence was intimidating though, and he seemed to loom over the whole room.

The first man to enter spoke.

'Be you well, be you well all,' he said, cheerfully. His voice was thick and nasal, as if someone was pinching his nose as he spoke. 'We hope today finds you healthy and hale. And helpful.'

'We don't want any trouble,' replied Holt, warily. 'We can open up the bar though, if you're thirsty. Alwyn?' He motioned toward the barrels and the innkeeper began to move in that direction.

'Stand still,' rumbled the giant, and Alwyn froze.

'We just want to talk,' said the leader. 'Ask.'

He stepped a little closer to Holt and smiled. He was not an especially tall man, but the thickness of his neck and the breadth of his shoulders told of great physical strength. A sturdy club hung at his belt.

'If you're bandits—' began Holt, but was cut off.

'We're on the trail of some thieves,' he said, folding his arms. 'Women. They have taken something that belongs to us, and were heading this way.'

'Have you seen them?' put in the huge half-elf in his low rumble.

'No.' Holt did not hesitate before answering. There was something about these people that rang a warning bell in his mind. They were smiling, but it made him think of the way a hunting cat bared its teeth. There was no warmth there, only hunger.

Bandits still ranged up and down the great road, preying on the unwary. People around here had become used to travelling with care, or in large groups. Holt had heard that dwarf pilgrimages had been coming over the mountains again, and it would take a brave or foolish bandit to try attacking a caravan guarded by a force of fully armoured dwarf knights. Travel would be safer while they were abroad.

There had been rumours, though, of Wild Elf attacks near the road. Even bandits spoke of the Wild Elves in fearful tones.

This group did not look like bandits, though. They looked like outlander travellers and had clearly come from far away.

'So sure?' the leader was asking with a sneer. 'You look like a friendly man. Can imagine you believing a sob story coming from a pretty face.'

'They ain't been here,' replied Holt, folding his own arms. 'And that's all there is to it.'

'You won't mind if we have a little look around then? Check a few barns, stables, outhouses? Make sure nothing has slipped your memory. Be easy to hide three women here.'

At the mention of stables, Holt thought of something. Three thieves, three horses stolen. Had the three women these thugs were chasing passed through Feorhryc just a few nights ago?

'Three?' asked Holt, before he could think to restrain his tongue. The leader glared in his direction even more intently.

'That's right,' he said. 'Three. Ringing a bell now? Got 'em hidden here? Know where they went, maybe?'

'I already told you they ain't here, and I ain't seen them.' Holt felt his anger growing, and took a step forward. 'I don't care for being called a liar, and I don't care for your tone. I think you have overstayed your welcome. Time for you to leave.'

'Spoken like a man hiding something.' The leader half turned. 'Jhari, grab the boy.'

As the looming figure of Jhari reached out for Caill, there was a soft, metallic sound from behind Holt. All motion in the room seemed to stop. A single word was spoken into the ensuing silence.

'No.'

Holt turned. The stranger was awake, and on his feet. His pale eyes burned with intensity. The broad, gleaming length of the Wose Blade was in his hands.

It was a long sword, and the pommel would reach up to Holt's chest, were the point on the ground. It was much too long to swing in a confined space such as the hall of the inn. The stranger clearly knew this and was holding it half-sword, one hand on the end of the long grip and the other on the ricasso, just below the hilt.

It was a stance that spoke of familiarity and practice with weapons. It was a stance from which he could be deadly.

'No,' he repeated. 'Enough. He said leave, so leave.' He took a step forward.

There were a handful of intruders standing behind their leader. Holt counted five or six, but they were clearly taken aback by being confronted by a single man. A man who looked ready and capable of spilling blood.

The leader scowled, brow furrowed in thought.

'Come on,' he said, eventually. 'We'll catch the thieves in Ben Gedrin anyway. Let's go.'

He turned, and they followed him back out into the street.

'Thank you,' muttered Holt to the stranger, who was still holding the all-too-familiar sword. The man did not react at all. Holt turned away and headed for the door.

By the time he stepped out onto the street, the southerners were already rolling away. The sky was clear but a biting wind swirled around Holt and the innkeeper as they watched the wagon dwindle into the distance.

A tall crate was standing on the back of the wagon, lashed in place with ropes. It stood upright like a single finger raised in warning, and Holt stared at it as the wagon left the village. The whole encounter had left him with a sour, uneasy feeling.

'I did not like them.'

The tall stranger stood beside him. His accent was unusual, the words sounding angular and blocky. His pale eyes were hard as he glared out at the westward road. He still held the sword loosely in one hand.

'Nope,' agreed Holt. 'Me neither. I had a feeling they wanted to flex their muscles and would have hurt someone just to show they could. Until you stood up, anyway. Thank you for that.'

'Why would they need eight fighters to hunt three women?' wondered the stranger, ignoring the praise. 'I think they were not saying truth.'

'You're right. A gang of horse rustlers could have emptied the stables. But they only took three. That makes me think it was more likely some people who were desperate to put some distance between themselves and whoever was chasing them.'

From what he had just seen, that made good sense to Holt. That gang were fighters and thugs, that had been clear. He could think of many reasons why a person would be anxious to be far away from them.

'But they are still chasing. The women are still in danger,' said the stranger. Holt looked him up and down. The vague, fatigued look in his eyes when he had arrived in the village had gone, replaced with a determination. 'I will follow them.'

'If you think that's the right thing to do.'

He nodded. 'Protecting people is the right thing to do. What I should do.' He glanced down at the great sword, eyes widening as if noticing it for the first time.

'That looks right in your hand,' said Holt. He already felt relief at the prospect of it leaving the village. 'I reckon we can find you a baldric for it. If you think that'd be useful?'

The stranger was silent for a time, alternating glances westward and down at the weapon.

'Yes,' he said, after a while. 'I think that is right.'

'I'm Holt Cookson,' he said, introducing himself. He felt they were already past the sharing of birth moons. 'Feorhryc is grateful to you. What's your name?'

The young man looked at Holt, fixing him with a grey-eyed stare.

'I am called Eain Connow.'

THIRTY TWO

A bitter wind whipped around the long, lean figure of Skyle Burns. The sky was as grey as if roofed with slate, and the familiar surroundings of the dale of Vekwicc looked flat and lifeless.

Vetundaeghur was a week away yet, but winter was coming. The first snows would fall soon, blanketing all Banahgar with white. They could not come soon enough.

The lake stretched out behind him, silver as a sword blade. Gusts of wind drove small, white-tipped waves across the surface to lap insistently at the stones of the shoreline. Burns turned his back on the water and strode into the village.

Squat, blocky stone houses with slate roofs stood to either side of the main street. They clustered around the rushing, chattering stream that flowed toward the lake, but were also dotted over the steeply sloping sides of the valley. Above the houses, tussocky grass gave way to broken, rocky slopes and then bare, jagged rock. The sheer ridges above the valley were high and forbidding, and rarely climbed.

Burns smiled to think of his own time in Vekwicc, and the attempts he had made to climb all the neighbouring peaks as a young man. The fire, and the foolishness of youth.

He turned his eyes away from the lofty peaks and looked toward the fortress, which sat at the head of the valley. Today, his business was not with hills and mountains, but with a man who needed to be reminded of his sworn duty.

The gates of the fortress were open and he breezed past the two wardens with a simple nod. They knew who he was. They were a pair of smooth-cheeked Sverlaeggare with wispy moustaches. Every spare man of the Claihedehmore and Claihedehlar had been sent south to fight.

Fighting a war that they were steadily losing, thought Burns, ruefully.

They needed something drastic to turn the tide.

The courtyard beyond the walls was filled with young men and boys, performing sword drills, sparring with one another, or lifting weights. They were all very aware that if the Kotevari continued to push their lines northward, they would all be needed to fight. These soldiers all looked so young.

Heads turned and many eyes followed his path as he strode across the Claidah. His age, and the unusual hilt of his unique greatsword marked him out, even to those who did not know his face.

'Continue,' he said to a group of Sverlaeggare who had paused their practice to watch him pass. They turned, startled, and returned guiltily to their drills.

He stopped beside the sour-faced Claihedehmore overseeing the morning's training session. He was a northerner with reddish hair and a thin, braided beard. His arms were thick with muscle and were crossed sullenly across his broad chest.

'Master.' The Claihedehmore saluted, right fist to left shoulder. Burns returned the salute, casually.

'I need to see the Bear,' he said. 'Is he in the fortress?'

'Aye, master,' replied the Claihedehmore. 'You've come at the right time – early. The honourable Master is not at his best in the afternoons these days.'

Burns blinked, but not in surprise. He knew of the Bear's tendencies, and where he went to seek solace when afraid or under stress. The bottom of a barrel.

'Thank you, soldier.' Burns moved toward the door that opened to the interior of the fortress. 'I'm certain I'll be able to find him.'

The Master in charge of the fortress had his quarters in rooms that opened directly off the great hall. The smell of baking bread filled the room and Burns' stomach growled. As he crossed the hall, he noticed that the door to the Master's quarters was closed. He strode over to it and stopped outside.

'Is the Master of Vekwicc fort in his quarters?' he asked, raising his voice to be heard clearly through the thick timbers.

'Begone,' came the grunted reply. 'I'm busy.'

Now, Burns struck his fist against the door. A hollow boom echoed through the hall.

'It is Skyle Burns,' he called. 'Say now if you are naked, else I am coming in.' An irritated growl was the only response. Burns put his hand to the handle, and let himself in.

The room was deep inside the fortress and windowless, and it stank. A poorly tended fire spluttered and smoked in a dirty hearth, and the air was hazy. The source of the worst of the smell was sitting in a chair facing the guttering flames.

'Master Munrae,' said Burns, stepping carefully into the room to avoid the empty clay flasks that littered the floor. 'I had heard that you have found a way to ease the stresses of war. I see the rumours were not exaggerated.'

'Always so clever, Burns,' spat Munrae. His words slurred and spittle shone in his bushy moustache and beard. Maichen Munrae was a huge man, with towering height and massive breadth of shoulder. His dark hair grew out in a wild, tangled mass giving him an untamed, feral appearance, even when he was sober.

Right now, he was drunk. Burns could smell *vochvior*, a strong Banahgarian spirit, in every breath and there was an open flask propped between his massive thighs. His thick fingers were curled around the neck.

Munrae lifted it and took another deep swig. 'The Grandmaster sent you?' His voice was thick with drink, his tone aggressive.

'I was just passing by, and thought I would visit my old friend,' replied Burns, calmly. Then, as he preferred not to tell lies, he added. 'But yes, he did. He asked me to bring a message.'

'Well then, hand it over and piss off.' Munrae extended a meaty hand, and Burns smiled grimly.

'It is not a written message,' he said. 'It is a suggestion for the Master of Vekwicc to consider.'

'You always speak in riddles, Burns. Just spit it out and leave me in peace.'

Burns steeled himself for what he was sure was to come, and began.

'The war goes badly. Kotevari forces advance up the Sudvirke road toward Osturbrost, and up the Dall road toward Naen-Giata. Toward you. Banahgarian blood and the valour of the Claihedehmore have slowed their march, but nevertheless, still they come.'

'And the Grandmaster thinks I am such a fool that I know this not?' Munrae clutched his flask protectively.

'He thinks you know this very well. Too well.' Burns took a deep breath. 'And he thinks you fear what may happen next.'

Drunk as he was, Munrae was on his feet in a heartbeat. A moment later he was looming over Burns, fists clenched.

'Fear! Fear?' he bellowed as he stepped closer to Burns, teeth bared. Burns remained calm, staring up at the bigger man impassively, but it was an effort. "The Bear" in full fury was a fearsome sight.

Maichen Munrae was the biggest of all the Masters, and one of the most physically imposing men in the entire Claihed. Often known by his Sword-Name, "The Bear's Claws", or simply, "The Bear", Munrae was strong enough to wield two greatswords at the same time. One in each hand.

Burns could see them, standing in the corner of the room. They were slightly shorter than a typical greatsword but broad, heavy-bladed and flared at the tip. In battle, Munrae swung them with brutal power and balletic grace, and only a fool would underestimate his skill and mastery.

Yet, as adept as he was in battle, his weakness was in waiting for it to arrive. He worried. Given the responsibility of leading Vekwicc, he had to watch over the youngsters while the soldiers he knew all marched away to fight. And die.

This assignment had not been kind to him. It had taken all his willpower not to rush away to the front lines, and every day he dwelled on the fate of those that were there, and the eventual fate of those who were not. The Grandmaster had not foreseen the war when he had assigned the responsibility.

'How dare he speak of fear?' Munrae's eyes were wild.

'He speaks as one who knows you,' replied Burns calmly. 'And respects your courage in battle, and your prowess. As do I.' He bowed his head slightly, raising his fist in salute.

'Yet you come here and insult me!' Munrae raged.

Burns saw the blow coming from the slight tension in the big man's huge shoulders. It was clumsy and slow, almost as if it were intended to miss. He swayed aside, steering Munrae's huge fist to one side with open hands. Grasping his wrist and hand, a deft twist was all that was needed to control the strike.

He thrust Munrae backward, bending his wrist uncomfortably, and the big man was unable to resist. He staggered back to slump down into the chair once more. Burns said nothing, and Munrae looked up sheepishly. Munrae could not beat him, and they both knew it. Burns would not shame him by mentioning this again, though.

'What's all this about?' he said, after an awkward pause.

Burns spread his arms. 'We need more troops. We cannot train them fast enough. The Grandmaster sent me to ask if you would consent to allow him to use all the forces under your command.'

'But he has authority over all the troops here.' Munrae was puzzled.

'Not all of them.'

'Yes, all of them. The Sverlaeggare and the Hniffare…they answer to him, ultimately. If he orders them to march, they must march.'

'Yes, and he does. But it is not those troops that I mean.'

Munrae was silent for a moment, brow furrowed. Through the fog of drink it took a few moments for realisation to hit. Then, his eyes widened.

'You can't mean…' he muttered.

'Yes,' replied Burns, locking eyes with the bigger man. 'The Skjilde.'

'But…' Munrae's eyes darted around as his brow furrowed. He took some time to get his thoughts in order. 'It is not the way!'

'But why not?' Burns stepped forward. 'They are fit, they are well trained and well disciplined. They are children of Banahgar like us, and they have the same right to fight and die our the country as we do.'

'Women have never fought in our wars!'

'Yet, they will fight in this war, sooner or later. Later, if we leave them behind and are overrun. Then, they will face the spears and swords of Kotev alone. We shall be gone to the great halls of our ancestors. They are garrisoned here, now, and under your command. They cannot march without you giving the order.'

Munrae looked distraught. Burns knew that the truth of his words was evident, and yet Munrae was fighting a battle against the power of tradition and precedent. The Grandmaster had given him authority to order The Bear to release the Skjilde to fight, but in this fragile state such a challenge to his authority might be the end of him.

'I...I am not sure I can do it,' stammered the great Bear.

'The Grandmaster thought you might say that. And so—' Burns moved swiftly to the door and opened it. 'He sent another to offer his considerable wisdom.'

For a moment there was silence. Then, Munrae's eyes widened. From the great hall came the rhythmic clack of metal striking the ancient flagstones. The sharp, regular sound grew louder, and then a figure entered the room, leaning on a staff of smooth oak.

Like Burns, he wore a long Banahgarian greatcoat, the aged leather marked and stained by travel. The hilt of a unique greatsword rose over his right shoulder and he swept the staff from side to side, as if feeling the ground. Munrae dropped to his knees before the newcomer.

'Master!' he cried. 'My Master!'

'Rise, Maichen,' said the new arrival, reaching out to grasp Munrae's shoulder.

'Master Farguson thought you might pay more attention to advice, if he were the one to bring it to you.'

Graigor Farguson felt his way across the room and sat. It was a wonder of the Brothers that he had been able to make such a journey to get here alone. But, Farguson was far from normal, even by the standards of the Claihed. He was blind.

After losing his sight to a Stobyvar spear he had been forced to retire. There was great sadness in the Claihed at the loss of such an experienced warrior and knowledgeable teacher, but none realised that he had not given up. He went away and trained himself to wield a greatsword without sight, before returning and demanded to be retested.

He had passed, to the shock of most and retaken his Masterhood, although with a new Sword-Name; The Eyes of the Sword.

'I would always heed your words, my Master,' murmured the Bear, lowering his head in contrition. As a Claihedehlar, Munrae had witnessed the strike that had taken his Master's eyes, and had fought like winter's fury to protect the injured man. He had won his own Sword-Name that day.

'I know you strive always to do what is right,' began Farguson. 'And to be seen to do what is right. You fear that others will judge you. You fear that they will think ill of you.'

Unseen by Farguson, Munrae nodded sadly.

'You are a leader now, my friend. You must lead. You must make decisions on behalf of those who follow you. It is not important that those you lead like you. It is vital that they trust you, and trust you to make difficult decisions. That, is leadership. That is courage.'

'It just does not feel right,' mumbled Munrae. His eyes were red and watery. He added, more loudly. 'It is not how things are done!'

'And what is it that feels wrong to you?'

'To send the Skjilde to war!'

'Yet, what does your wisdom tell you is the correct decision?'

There was a pause. Munrae bunched his great hands into fists.

'I must send the Skjilde to war. I must allow them to fight alongside us, for their country.'

'Yes,' said Farguson, smiling. 'And no. You will not be sending them anywhere. You will march with them as their commander. These are the Grandmaster's orders.'

Munrae scowled, then his face brightened into a grin. He laughed. 'That bastard always knows!'

Burns cleared his throat. 'You can lead no-one looking like this.' He gestured at Munrae, and the chaotic mess that lay strewn around their feet. 'May I suggest that you go to the lake and bathe, while I remove...temptation.' He strode over to the shelf, where there was a row of full flasks, all containing more *vochvior*.

Gathering them in his arms, he turned to see Munrae standing near the door. The huge man's demeanour was suddenly nervous.

'I cannot walk past the men as I am,' he muttered. 'It will shame me.'

'Do you think that they do not know what you do in here, alone?' Farguson's tone now had a hard edge. 'You must know that they already whisper of how fear has gripped you. Go past them now, and go with pride.'

'They will see me as a failure!' Munrae blustered. 'As I am! There is no pride.'

'They will see a man with humility,' said Farguson, gently. 'They will see a man who admits to his fear and attempts to conquer it. They will see you as you are.'

'They will love you anew, brother,' added Burns. 'Go and wash and I'll get some steaks cooked.'

'No such luck!' grunted Munrae, ruefully. 'Supplies aren't getting through. All we've got is brawn.'

Burns smiled. 'I have brought you a special delivery from Osturbrost, my friend. When you are clean we can eat well, and plan our next move.'

Munrae grinned, a toothy, bear's snarl. 'Yes! The Kotevari will never beat the likes of us!' Then he was gone, marching through the great hall like a powerful predator on the hunt.

'Thank you for coming, my old friend,' said Burns to Farguson. 'I am not convinced I could have persuaded him alone.'

'For Banahgar,' replied the blind Master, simply.

'Aye, for Banahgar.'

With the Skjilde to bolster their numbers, their lines would be able to hold until the ice and snow of winter would make any further advance impossible for the invaders. Spring's thaw would bring a new assault. All the Masters knew that. But they would work out how to ford that stream when they stood on the bank.

The war was far from over.

PART SIX

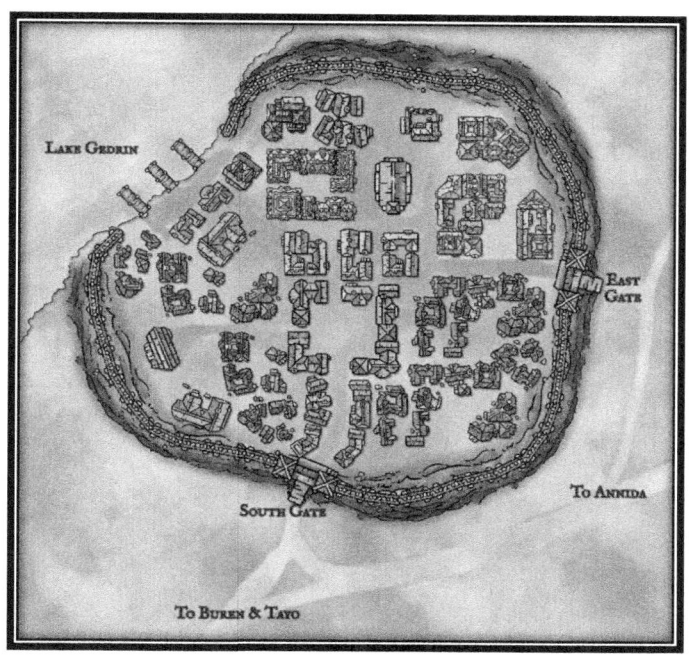

Ben Gedrin

THIRTY THREE

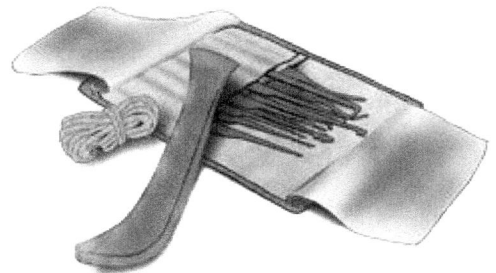

Ellyah stopped dead. She stepped to the side, then darted forward again through a small and closing gap. People were all around her, seemingly moving in every direction, heedless of what was before them.

Ben Gedrin was a city that hummed with activity. After so long in the wilderness, the bustle of a city, and such a lively one, was almost overwhelming.

The buildings were all made from roughly cut timber, stained a dark brown. They overhung the muddy street and loose planks sagged near their heads. Many looked like they could collapse at any moment.

The people alongside them and those passing in the opposite direction moved purposefully and shirts and trousers were as common as robes and smocks. Travellers came here from many different places. Most bore a bulging pack or stacked basket; goods bought or to be sold.

Everywhere Ellyah looked deals were being struck, people were bartering loudly and with exuberance, and copper or silver money rings were changing hands.

This was a city where a smart operator could make a quick and easy profit.

Then she looked down. Huddled against the lower walls, in the worst of the dirt, were more people. These were not purposeful. These had no money rings, and their clothes were little better than stained rags. They held their hands out in supplication but were ignored.

Ellyah saw men and women, faces gaunt and grubby, their hands trembling with the cold or with fear and despair. And she saw children. Small bundles of quivering rags, some clinging fearfully to slumped parents but many more on their own.

She looked away.

She glanced back to check on Nastja and spotted her slightly behind, blank-faced and moving stiffly. Ellyah reached out and pulled her gently forward by the arm. They hurried to catch up to Luara's hooded figure.

'When I was a child, I always wondered why the city was fortified,' Luara had mused, as they had tethered their horses beneath a lean-to stable outside the city walls. The thick hardwood logs that comprised the defences rose high above their heads. 'It's not like anyone is going to attack it!'

They had slipped the stable hand a few scraps of copper, and headed for the earth causeway that led to the main gate.

'Why not?' asked Nastja as they passed beneath the gateway and began to jostle their way along the crowded streets. Ellyah noticed that Luara had pulled her hood up as they approached the city and had remained cowled since. She wondered if she should copy.

'Well, first,' began Laura, speaking back over her shoulder. 'It's worth so much for trade. Nearly every nation in Re-Emsser and the Alrean Empire buy from, or sell to Kiraband and the rest of the Riverlands. It all passes through here. And second,' Luara turned off the main street and they hurried to remain at her heels. 'The minute an army was seen approaching, the gangs would join forces and fill the walls to defend the city. It'd be a bloodbath. Not worth it.'

They had turned into a dingier part of the city. Timber houses with shingle roofs loomed over the dirty street. Luara moved confidently. She seemed to know exactly where she was going.

'So, why the walls?' asked Ellyah. If it would never be attacked, why ring the place with such a sturdy fortification?

'Control,' replied Nastja, speaking over Luara's reply. 'With the walls so high, only way in or out is by the docks, or through the gates. If you have a strong hand and a long reach, you can control everything. Supply, demand, taxation…'

'And that's what the governor and the militia do?' asked Ellyah.

Luara replied with a short laugh. 'Try, maybe.'

'The gangs,' said Nastja definitely, and Luara nodded. She had stopped before a dark door in a looming, dirty building of aged and stained timber. It had a forbidding appearance, but the enticing scent of roasting pork wafted out from within.

'I'll say more later,' she said, setting her hand to the door handle. For now…quiet, and careful.'

She opened the door.

They walked into a dimly lit and smoky tavern. Most of the downstairs was a single wide room, but a serving hatch to one side served as a bar. The rear wall was pierced by a of pair of wide double doors, currently flung open onto a paved area.

The source of the smell was evident as a pig's carcass was turned on a spit over a smouldering fire.

They moved across the floor, weaving between rough tables that were placed haphazardly. Most were occupied with groups of people, eating, drinking or just deep in conversation. Most kept their eyes down and did not glance up at the newcomers.

Ellyah noticed that the men and women in the groups were mostly dressed in trousers and shirts suitable for fighting; there were few of the robes and smocks she was familiar with as everyday wear back home in Anish. But, she also saw a solitary dwarf with a short beard and a truculent expression, in conversation with a tall man in leathers. As they passed, the dwarf stood and stomped toward the door, uttering a string of incomprehensible expletives.

A couple of tall figures in grey robes must be elves. Hoods and high collars covered most of their faces, but the small slivers of skin that showed were dark as coal.

Luara remained hooded as she stalked across the floor to the serving hatch. Ellyah remained on her shoulder as she lowered her head to address the barkeep. Then, she froze. The auburn-haired woman behind the hatch stared back, waiting.

'Fion?' stammered Luara. The barkeep continued staring for a moment, then her eyes widened.

'You!' she uttered, surprise across her face. She recovered from her surprise quickly. 'What are you doing here?' Before Luara could reply, she continued, voice brisk and urgent. 'No, it's not safe for you here. Go upstairs. Hurry!'

She motioned toward a narrow staircase at the edge of the room, then turned away. As she removed her apron, she called back into the kitchen.

'Rhyn! Come and mind the bar! I have business to attend to.'

Luara hurried obediently toward the stairs, with Ellyah and Nastja following. Ellyah felt distinctly uneasy. She did not like being led blindly, although she had come to trust Luara over these last weeks. The barkeep's reaction had also been worrying. What had Luara not told them?

At the top of the stairs they passed through a door, and found themselves in a bedroom. A woman's bedroom, thought Ellyah as she looked around. The room was plain, but she noticed a tiny vial of scent from Emrys, and the hem of an embroidered dress peeked out from behind a half-closed wardrobe door.

The barkeep was only moments behind, bustling in and closing the door.

'Fion!' exclaimed Luara, pushing her hood back. 'What are you doing here?'

'I asked first,' replied Fion, with mild petulance. 'But as I have nothing to be ashamed of – I am the landlady here. This is my tavern.'

'Oh!' Luara did not try to hide her surprise. 'Well done! I thought you would have settled in Feorhryc, after what happened.'

'Settled with Holt, you mean?' Ellyah glanced between the faces of the two women, who were of similar ages. There was an atmosphere, and it was not friendly. There must be some history between them.

'We tried,' Fion went on. 'But I never felt at home there. Not after losing Bruk. And as for Holt? He was never truly mine. Not in his heart.' She fixed Luara with a flinty glare. 'Not after he met you.'

'Oh,' repeated Luara. This time her expression was thoughtful. Ellyah recalled Luara mentioning the name of Feorhryc as the village where they had stolen the horses. The mystery around Luara's past was growing.

'Anyway,' continued Fion, briskly. 'What brings you here? Some sort of trouble, I reckon. Knowing you. It's a bad time. City's like a tinderbox. Feels like it could go up at any time.'

'Worse than usual?' asked Luara.

Fion nodded grimly. 'The governor's got no control at all. The Cyfres and the Sticasts have bought the tax collectors, so the governor is broke. He can't pay his militia so they're defecting to the gangs. The law is what the gangs say it is, right now.'

'Who are the Cyfres?' asked Nastja. 'And the Sticasts?'

'The gangs,' replied Luara. 'There are two big gangs, and they run the city. Started out as rival families and they competed for everything— territory, trade, influence…until what they were doing got less legal, and they realised they had become so powerful that the authorities couldn't stop them.'

'They do whatever they want, now,' added Fion. 'Only thing holding them back is each other. Trade is good for them, though, and they take a cut of everything. So, the city can't run without them, but they need the city too. They are like a disease where the medicine will kill you too.'

'And they are who we need to deal with,' said Luara. 'The Cyfres, anyway. I think they are more likely to be able to shift the…merchandise.'

'And the Sticasts do not like you,' said Fion, pointing at Luara accusingly. 'They have not forgotten what you did.'

Luara shrugged. 'I can keep my head down.'

'Where?' Fion put her hands on her broad hips.

'Here?' replied Luara, hopefully.

'Psht. I'm not running an orphanage, or a dosshouse.'

'We can work for our keep,' piped up Nastja. 'We can cook, clean and work behind the bar. Do you need a bard?' Ellyah stared, but once more she had to admit that it was a good idea. They had limited money for lodgings and needed time to make contact with the Cyfres.

'Yea,' she said, adding her voice in agreement. 'If you have a spare room, we can help in the tavern in exchange for lodgings. It will only need to be for a few days and then we'll be gone.'

Gone far away with our new-found riches, she thought.

'Well,' said Fion, slowly and uncertainly. 'I suppose I could do with a couple of extra hands. One week though, and then I want you gone. I need the room. And you—' she pointed at Luara once more. 'Don't show your face. I don't want the Sticasts storming in here hunting you down.'

'Thank you,' said Ellyah.

'Don't thank me yet. You'll need to earn your first night's lodge first, and you can start straight away.' She beckoned them toward the door.

'I'll think about how we can make contact with the Cyfres,' said Luara, as they left the room. She headed up another flight of stairs, narrower still, that led up into the roof space.

'Quiet!' snapped Fion.

Ellyah could not help but wonder about the history between these two women, and who Holt was. The village of Feorhryc seemed to be significant to the three of them. Another puzzle.

'Why do the Sticasts hate Luara?' asked Nastja, as they descended the rickety staircase into the main room.

'What I heard,' began Fion in a low whisper, 'is that the Sticasts hired her to do away with the head of the Cyfres family.'

'To kill them?' asked Ellyah, surprised.

'Yea. You'll learn that what that girl is capable of ain't as pretty as her face, or as sweet as her smile. Anyhow, the story goes that she broke into his house at night, crept past his guards and the rest of his family. Then, when she got to his quarters, knife in hand, she gave him something that nobody expected. Something that made her the Sticasts' enemy for life.'

'What did she give him?'

Fion paused at the kitchen door and turned, eyeballing the two other women.

'Mercy,' she said, and opened the kitchen door. Ellyah followed, full of confusion.

THIRTY FOUR

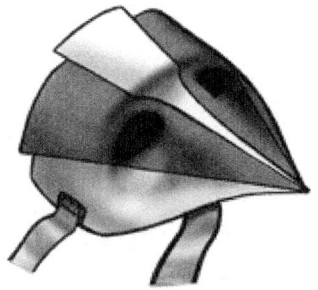

'By the light of the fire I dispel evil spirits. By the purity of the flames shall demons be driven away. By the heat of burning shall the body be healed.'

The cell was bathed in flickering orange light. The flagstones of the floor were covered in candles, with only a narrow aisle left as a route between the door and the bed. Shre Bahram Hilass placed his hand, five fingers splayed, on his upper chest, before pressing it to her chest in turn.

'Blessings of the Five upon you,' he intoned, before adding. 'We will not stint on your care, Sister Claes. Soon, with faith, you shall be recovered.'

Evane Claes closed her eyes, shutting out the unnatural brightness. The ritual and relentless optimism of Hilass's earnest ministrations grated, but were unavoidable. If she pretended to sleep, he would be forced to leave.

She was not ill, but knew that was how it appeared. Her eyes were rimmed with grey darkness and her skin was sallow. Eating had been an effort over these last weeks and her robes hung loose on her bony frame.

'Are you as comfortable as you can be, dear Sister?'

'Yes,' she replied, weakly. 'Your kindness strengthens my soul.'

'The Veil-Flame was yesterday,' he said softly. 'I am sorry you missed it. For a few heartbeats it was like the Five were among us, blessing us with their radiance.' She nodded, weakly. 'There was, sadly, much drinking and carousing, and the High King's militia had to step in.'

'It is ever thus.'

'Sleep now, and I will return in a few hours.' He rose, patting her arm reassuringly. She grimaced with the pain of that gentle touch and resisted the urge to cry out.

Every inch of her skin blazed with fiery agony. It felt as though she had bathed in boiling oil. It felt as though she had been flayed. Yet, there was not a mark on her body.

The other priests had taken this as a symptom of a dire illness, and as she could no longer hide it, she had been forced to go along with their assessment. They could not know the true reason, the true cause.

Him.

While her minions continued to unsuccessfully pursue the jewel and its thieves, he came for her every night. Every night, he took her and in the last weeks she had gained a new understanding of what suffering could be.

In that dark place, that was either deep under the earth or somehow within the confines of her own mind, he had punished her for her failure. The punishment had been severe.

Whips of invisible power and gouts of flame had lashed and scorched her body, and yet, these tortures had been different. He was displeased, but his blows were not driven by rage. They were to set an example.

For, as she writhed and wailed in pain, she was observed.

Desya had summoned the other masked figures and as the punishments were inflicted they were forced to watch, peering through their eye holes in stony silence.

This could be you, was the message to them. *Do not dare fail me.*

Each night, she was summoned. Each night, she was tormented, and afterwards returned to her body with just enough power to continue to order the pursuit. As the other masks faded away, returning through purple portals in the air to wherever the bodies dwelled, he held her back.

His voice was soft, like a thin blade, as he growled a final message; a statement of tantalising hope.

You are still closest to the jewel. You can still be the one who will possess it on my behalf. You can still be redeemed.

She could not give up. The glory of being at Desya's side when he rose once more was all. Everything else was fleeting and inconsequential. Even pain.

The door shut with a thud and a click. Hilass was gone.

Evane Claes closed her eyes gratefully. Sleep was as close as the width of an insect's wing. If she relaxed even slightly, she would be dead to the world. It was tempting. The oblivion, even for a brief time before she was summoned by Desya, would be welcome bliss.

Yet, she could not. She had work to do. Her mask was concealed in a narrow gap between the bed and the wall, and she retrieved it and put it on.

Focus on her faith in Desya came easily. How could it not? After the last few weeks, she could think of little else. The demon was an ever-present reality in her consciousness.

Her breathing deepened and a trickle of power flowed into her. Just a trickle. In her current state, it was all she could manage. It would be enough. It would have to be.

She had a moment to wonder whether the Mackems had done as she had ordered, before the purple portal was around her, and her masked face had passed through.

The squalid surroundings of a grubby room met her eyes. Skane was sitting on the bed, thick fingers clasped, elbows on knees. Jhari leaned against the wall, neck bent so he could fit beneath the low ceiling.

The crate stood in the corner. It was open. As she had instructed. From the way the two men's noses were wrinkled, Claes was glad to be very far away.

'Do you know where the thieves are?' she asked, briskly and with no preamble. She could not let them know how weak she was. They needed to think her all-powerful. They needed to fear her.

'Na,' replied Skane. 'Don't think they went to Annida after all. We thought they might try to fence the jewel there but no-one had seen 'em. They must have got a few days ahead of us.'

'How can you be sure you are still on their trail?' she asked. They had been adamant that the thieves would follow the road west into Kiraband and onto Ben Gedrin, but Claes had not had enough strength yet to obtain confirmation.

'Where else would they go?' replied Skane wearily. 'All roads go through Ben Gedrin. If I wanted to sell something, I'd try to do it there. And if I wanted to escape, I'd go through there and get a boat upriver or across the lake to the Alrean Empire. They'll head for Ben Gedrin.'

'We shall see,' she said, although as the words left her lips she felt a jolt of anxiety, and a flash of pain shot through her frail body.

Desya, she prayed. Please grant me the strength to cast this spell. Grant me the will to control the power.

She directed her paltry flow toward the crate, and its grim contents. It felt like she was trying to wring a cup of water out of a damp cloth, but a trickle passed through her body. Just a trickle.

Would it be enough?

A red glow filled the room as Clayton Moore-that-was opened its eyes. She moulded the power as it flowed, as if squeezing and stretching damp clay.

A dull thump rang out as the creature stepped forward. As it emerged from the crate, the two thugs immediately looked away, faces twisted with disgust. Claes stared.

Moore's skin, where it still clung to his bones, was a sickly, greenish grey. It had rotted away from half the side of his face and one of his crimson eyes stared out from within a circle of bare, yellowing bone. He looked exactly like what he truly was; a corpse, several months dead.

She dismissed his hideous appearance from her thoughts. He was a tool, nothing more.

The jewel. She held the image of the ruby in her mind, concentrating on its form and inner power. Moore's eyes glowed more brightly, and he turned slightly on the spot, raising an arm. A finger that looked like a rotting rib extended, as if pointing through the wall.

'Direction?' She tried to keep her voice even and unaffected by the gruesome scene before her eyes.

Skane glanced up briefly. 'West. Toward Ben Gedrin.' "Like I told you", remained unsaid.

'Good. They will not escape this time. They will be trapped in the city and you will take them, and the jewel.'

Her body shook with the effort but she controlled her voice as she pushed her last reserves of strength into the creature. It stepped back into the crate, and its eyes were dimming back to milky blankness as Jhari moved forward to nail the side of the box back into place.

'This is your last chance,' she continued. 'Fail once more, and it is over for you.'

And me, she thought.

'Understand?' she asked.

'Aye,' grunted Skane, in his strange, nasal voice.

'We'll catch them,' snarled Jhari, his voice like shovelled gravel. 'And they will be finished.'

Claes did not reply. The last of her strength failed and the portal collapsed in on itself. She found herself back on her hard, mean cot. Candles still burned on every surface, the light reflecting in bright waves on the walls and ceiling.

The pain from her skin came crashing back, and she moaned aloud. They must succeed. She could not endure much more of this. The jewel was the only way to make it stop.

She allowed herself to dwell on that. The triumph she would know when she stood before Desya and told him. She pictured that sensation. The knowledge that she would be favoured. That thought was what had motivated her to initiate another meeting this night.

She was loathe to share anything, and yet she was increasingly aware that her strength was failing. An alliance was needed, with one who had the right connections and useful resources.

Even as she considered this anew, there was a purple shimmer in the air and a face covered by a striped mask appeared out of the air.

She smiled grimly as she prepared herself for the inevitable negotiations. She knew though, that together they could set a trap for these jewel thieves. Working together, they could ensure that neither they, nor the jewel, would be able to escape Ben Gedrin.

THIRTY FIVE

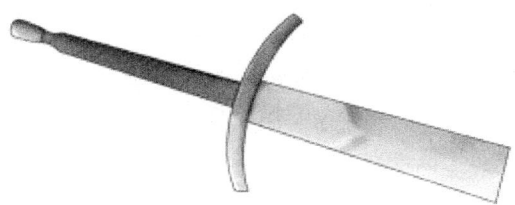

Eain stared at the sword. It was leaning against a rough-barked tree, gleaming coldly in dawn's grey light.

It was a heavy, brutal weapon. The blade itself was three fingers wide at the ricasso, and the quillons curved toward the point like aurochs' horns. It had been forged for a strong warrior, with a hilt as long as his forearm and with a thickness that would suit one with big, powerful hands.

It was not a greatsword. He frowned at it. It was a sword that needed to be wielded two-handed, but it was not a greatsword. Greatswords were forged in Banahgar, and this weapon had not been. He could not wield a greatsword now. He was in exile.

What made his brows crease in thought, though, more than the sword itself, was how holding it had made him feel.

He had not hesitated in reaching for it, back at the inn in Feorhryc. The sound of raised, aggressive voices had roused him abruptly from his sleep, and it had taken him mere moments to decide that he would not let the intruders hurt anyone.

His previous inaction had cost Oke, Reela and the rest their lives. He would not let it happen again.

When the tall bandit had stepped forward to threaten the innkeeper's son Eain had seen a flinty hardness in his eyes that showed that the threat was not an empty one. He would have hurt the boy, just to make a point.

'Be a shield if you cannot be a sword,' Carilton Tann had said. Now, Eain understood. With his presence alone, he had shielded Holt Cookson, the innkeeper, and his family from those who would have hurt them. For the first time since he left Banahgar, he had felt useful. He had felt strong, and full of purpose.

He carried that purpose with him still. He would find out where the bandits were going, and see if they still pursued the three women. If the women were innocent refugees, as he and Holt feared, he would do everything he could to protect them from harm.

He wanted to have the feeling of protecting others again. That is why he needed the sword.

'Here,' Holt had said, passing him a thick leather strap. 'This should work as a baldric.'

They had gone to the village forge. The furnace had been cold, but they had found a whetstone and put a keen edge back on the blade, before polishing it to a reflective grey sheen.

Eain had strapped the weapon across his back, and turned his face west.

'You're serious about going after them?' asked Holt, concern in his voice.

'I told a friend I would try to protect others. This is a chance to do that.'

Holt put his hands to his hips. 'I've half a mind to come with you. But I can't. You know it'll be dangerous?'

Eain had not replied. He could think of nothing worth saying. What did danger matter? What could they possibly do to him, now?

That had been four days ago.

After leaving Feorhryc he had stretched his legs into a loping run. It felt good to feel the ground passing quickly beneath his feet, his lungs sucking in the cool air. He ran until he could see a hazy cloud of dust on the horizon, then carried on until he could make out the outline of the upright crate that confirmed he was on the right trail.

He had continued like that, holding the trundling wagon just within sight, as the days passed. When they entered a town, he skirted around it under the cover of dusk, and made a hasty camp within earshot of the road.

The dull rumble of wagon wheels on the hard-packed road had just disturbed his sleep.

He sat silently for a moment, waiting for the sound to recede into the distance. Then, he stood, rolled his blanket up tightly and stowed it with the rest of his kit.

Slinging his sword around his shoulders, he set off.

Some hours after noon, the walls of Ben Gedrin rose before him.

The road grew busier as the walls loomed closer. Many other travellers walked or rode, both toward the city and away, in various directions. Another road led southward from the city, the junction close to the main gate through the walls. Groups of travellers moved up and down this too; merchants in long robes, warriors in thick leathers, and common labourers in dirt-smeared smocks.

The folk on foot were forced to weave between the steady stream of wagons rolling in every direction. Ben Gedrin was a hub for trade, exotic goods came in and the simple produce of the Riverlands went out; a relentless stream of wares.

And, just visible as it passed beneath the gateway, there was the wagon with the distinctive upright crate. Eain smiled grimly. He had successfully followed them all the way here. Now what?

He upped his pace, stretching his legs to cover the ground to the gateway as quickly as possible.

The walls of Ben Gedrin were built from what looked like a whole forest of tree trunks, thick as a man's waist. Each had been stripped of its bark and planted deeply into the high bank that ringed the city. The tops were sharpened to points, creating a barrier that would be almost impossible to climb, if the gates were closed and the walls defended.

The gates stood open now, beyond an earthen causeway that spanned the deep, defensive ditch. As Eain crossed, just another traveller in the crowd, a putrid smell assailed his nostrils and he glanced down. The ditch was full of rubbish and the bottom held a sump of what looked like raw human waste. He hurried on, trying to keep the swaying wagon in view.

As he approached the wide gateway, a problem occurred to him. The thugs might remember his face, and it was equally likely that they would remember the sword whose hilt stood guard over his right shoulder.

They would not let him near them if they recalled his intervention at the village, and he had no wish to fight them on the streets of Ben Gedrin. Not yet.

His problem was solved in the next couple of steps.

'Hey!' came a voice, and he turned in the direction of the sound. 'Can't take that into the city.' A group of guards stood in the shadow of the gate, clad in black-dyed leather armour and round iron caps. One of them was gesturing at the sword on his back. 'Hand arms only,' the guard continued. 'It can go in the store over there.'

He pointed to a small shack, built in the lee of the wall interior. The rear walls had been cut into the bank and the front was reinforced with a lattice of iron rods, as was the door. A pair of guards stood to either side. They took the sword and one held out their hand. Eain placed copper scraps on his palm until he turned away, satisfied.

'You'll need this to reclaim it,' said the other guard, thrusting a wooden token into Eain's hand, stamped with an angular rune. He nodded and turned away. He could still see the wagon at the end of the street, slowed by the crowds.

He was about to move to follow, when something else caught his eye. For a moment he gaped.

Two tall figures were strolling sedately past, as if the hustle and bustle around them did not exist. They both wore long grey robes, which extended into hoods as well as wrapping around their mouths and noses. Only a narrow strip of dark, shadowed skin around their eyes was visible.

Surely, these were of the Meculvy Dutsch? He had only been able to catch the most fleeting of glimpses when he had attempted his ambush in the hills, but he was almost certain. He felt as though he should call out to them, to try to thank them. But, what would he say?

Then, he noticed that one of them carried a slender tree branch in their hands, with a spray of green leaves at the end. Both bore large, cylindrical knapsacks on their backs of thick, oiled cloth.

By the time Eain had taken in this strange scene and tried to make sense of it, they were gone up the street and into the crowd. But, it had given him an idea. He stepped to the side and ducked into an adjacent alleyway.

Moments later, he stepped out onto the street once more, but this time with a strip cut from his blanket wound around his temples and his mouth. He hoped it would suffice as a makeshift hood. If the Meculvy Dutsch could go about the city masked and hooded, then so could he. It should be enough to disguise his appearance to any unfriendly eyes.

The wagon was still visible at the end of the long, straight street that led from the main gates into the centre of the city, and he hurried after it.

He kept his distance as the wagon weaved its way through the streets. The driver seemed to be searching for something, or else they were just lost. All around the main streets seemed a ramshackle maze of wooden houses. To Eain's eyes, they all appeared to have been built quickly, and not expected to last.

Eventually, with the light fading in the sky as evening neared, they came to a halt in an open space near the city walls. Eain figured that they were on the west side of the city. He paused in the deep shadow of some overhanging eaves, and watched.

Some of the gang rode on the wagon, while others were forced to travel on foot. Once the wagon was still, they gathered and strolled toward a tall building that stood against the walls. They left the tall crate standing atop the wagon, a dark obelisk in the gloom.

It looked more like a large barn than a house. The small group paused for a moment outside a narrow door, before it opened with a brief glow of light, and they filed inside. Eain knew he must follow.

There was a guard at the door. He was a dwarf with a dirty beard, clad in dark leathers. He looked Eain up and down disinterestedly, then held out a thick-fingered hand.

Eain stared for a moment, then reached inside his coat once more. He had salvaged a small pouch of copper rings and silver scraps after the Wild Elf attack. He had no idea of its worth, but so far it had been enough to keep him fed.

He dropped a few scraps of silver into the hovering palm, and the short, burly figure opened the door.

As he stepped inside, he touched his hand to his mouth to make sure the scarf remained firmly in place, and at the same time tried not to show any surprise. As it had appeared like a barn from the outside, so it was also barn-like inside. Thick timber columns, formed from sturdy tree trunks spliced together, rose upward to support the high, slanting ceiling.

Rushlights sputtered along the walls and braziers stood near the columns, bathing the floor in soft, golden light. Smoke drifted through the air. The floor itself teemed with people, crammed in together even more tightly than out on the streets. Here, though, they were not trying to force progress in different directions; most were turned toward a clear space in the centre of the room.

As Eain craned his neck to see over the crowd, he saw a circular dais made of timber planks, elevated a couple of feet above floor level. Currently, it was empty and he looked away, scanning the edges of the room. The atmosphere was boisterous already and he was uncomfortably aware of the people standing in his blind spots.

It was the first time he had been close to so many people in a long while, and the anxiety he felt came as a shock. He glanced back at the door, only a few steps away. He needed to know he could escape quickly.

His eyes flicked around the room, trying to identify hidden threats. Stepping backward, he pressed his back against the wall, making sure that no one could approach him unseen.

There. He noticed the ones he sought as they moved deeper into the shadows of one of the far corners. He recognised the leader by the breadth of his shoulders and his prominent, jug-handle ears. He could not see the half-elf giant.

Eain felt his heart racing in his chest. This could be dangerous. He knew he had to get closer, but without them noticing him. Pushing forward into the press of the crowd, he eased his way through, keeping the group of bandits in the corner of his right eye.

If he approached them directly it would draw far too much attention.

As he forced his way toward the edge of the room, wincing inwardly at the crush of strangers that surrounded him, a bell rang. The voice of the crowd rose in cheers and calls, slapping their hands together in raucous applause. Eain did not look around, despite his surprise, but used the noise as cover to rush through to the wall, leaving space between him and his quarry, but attempting to remain within earshot.

As he turned, resting his back against the rough planks of the wall, two figures jumped up onto the dais.

They were both women, fists bound with white cloth. He remembered Haf's words about the fighting clubs of Ben Gedrin, and as he looked closer he noticed that they both had purple-tinted skin and a slight upsweep to their ears. One had short-cropped hair, the colour of sand, while the other's was longer and dark. They must both be half-elves.

The bout was about to start, and while attention seemed to be toward the centre of the room Eain took another step left, before slouching back into the shadows. It brought him near enough to hear what the bandits were saying.

'I shouldn't be here,' said a voice that he did not recognise. The accent was distinctive, like that of the city guards.

'What? Speak up!' bellowed a voice that he did; the familiar nasal grunt of the leader.

'I shouldn't be here!' repeated the first speaker. 'And you shouldn't either. It's dangerous.'

'We were told to find you here. Heard you owe us a favour.'

'Yes, yes.' The first speaker sounded nervous. 'Keep it down. I'll do what I can, but we need to keep this brief.'

'Tell us what you know.'

'I know you're here looking for a particular…item. I haven't heard that it's here, yet, but word will get around. The Cyfres and the Sticasts will both want to be involved.'

'Who?'

Eain risked a glance across. The burly bandit leader was talking to a slender man who was dressed in a long cloak with a deep hood. Eain could barely see the gleam of his eyes as he glanced nervously around.

'Cyfres and Sticasts are two...families,' he said. He needed to explain but was clearly anxious about being overheard. 'They run this city. The governor is in charge by law...but he doesn't sneeze without the permission of the heads of the families. You must understand that before you do *anything* here.'

'I get the picture. Say on.' The burly man had lowered his voice slightly and Eain strained his ears to hear. 'How can you help?'

'The gangs don't know about your three little friends, yet. They have no interest in them. If the city militia can get to them first, you'll get the item you're looking for and we'll get to keep the criminals. My master has come to an understanding with your master on this. If we let the...families get hold of them, we won't be able to touch them.'

'We?' The bandit leader had noticed the hooded man's slip immediately. He sighed in resignation.

Before he could answer, a roar went up from the crowd. The bout was intensifying, and one of the half-elves had just landed a solid blow. A red weal had bloomed on the other's cheek, but she bore it stoically. She raised her fists and continued.

They were both more than accomplished fighters, Eain could tell. Their balance was astounding and they moved around the dais with liquid grace. It was a very even contest.

The hooded man still had not responded, so the leader hazarded a guess.

'You're in the militia?' There was an uncomfortable, shuffling shrug. 'You're one of the militia leaders? You're *the* leader?' He was laughing.

'I am the Captain of the Ben Gedrin city militia,' hissed the hooded man, stiffly. 'But no-one can know! I shouldn't be here.'

The leader ignored the captain's unease. 'So, the militia aren't in the pay of…the families?'

'It's not possible. If word got out we were in the pay of one of the gangs, we'd be killed by the other. It's why I'm losing militia to the gangs, it's safer for them.'

'Makes sense to me. But you have a good idea what the gangs are up to, right?' There was a pause, filled with tension. 'You can't take silver from either openly…so you must be taking it from both, but secretly!'

'Quiet!' The desperate fury in his voice told Eain that the southerner had hit the mark.

The bandit leader was chuckling. 'Your secret is safe with me! As long as we can work together to find the item, that's all that matters.'

'Yes,' the militia captain agreed, nodding fervently. 'We must get it, and quickly. And the ones who have it now?'

The other man said nothing, but drew one of his thick fingers slowly across his throat.

A gasp from the crowd pulled their attention back to the stage. One of the fighters was swaying drunkenly. Her nose bled freely. The other, the dark-haired half-elf, raised her fists to the crowd, encouraging them to cheer for her. They obliged.

'Kaluva the Queen!' they roared. 'Queen of the mongrels! Finish her, Kaluva!'

Casually, elegantly, Kaluva spun on her heel. Her other foot swung high, kicking out to hit the other fighter square in the chest. She tumbled backward off the dais and a bell rang exuberantly. The fight was over.

As Eain looked out over the crowd he saw copper and silver rings changing hands. Wagers made, now lost or won.

He thought about what he had just heard. The bandits wanted to continue their pursuit of the three women without catching the attention of the two crime gangs, that much was clear. Eain knew what he had to do. How could he go about it, though?

'I must go,' said the hooded militia captain, when the raucous cheering following the conclusion of the bout had died away. 'Do not follow me, it would go ill for both of us.'

'Yes, sir,' said the bandit leader, mockery in his voice. 'How will we contact you, or you us, when the thieves are found?'

There was the soft scuffle of fabric. 'Go to the house at this address. Leave a mark on the wall if you have news, and I will do the same. If we need to meet, leave two marks. Go outside the main gate at dusk on the same day. It's not safe to meet here again.'

With that, he was gone, and Eain used the distraction of his departure to move away himself. He ducked his head and shouldered his way back into the crowd. Before he had got far, another roar rose from the throats of all of those around him and he stopped. Another bout?

The tone was different, though. Jeers, and hoots of derision rang out, rather than shouts and calls of excitement and encouragement.

Eain looked up to see several figures struggling toward the dais. Two were dragging another, who was resisting ineffectually.

'A thief!' bellowed a new voice. A grandly dressed young woman had stepped up onto the dais. She wore a long, embroidered robe and her golden hair hung loose. 'A thief who tried to steal from the family. Another one on his way to the mines!' She raised her hands, and there was a ripple of laughter.

'Just War!' came a new voice, with a desperate, pleading tone. 'Just War! I ask for a Just War!'

Eain craned his neck to spot the source, realising quickly that it was the thief himself.

The golden-haired woman put her hands on her hips. 'He calls for a Just War! Shall we accept his challenge?'

'Just War!' roared the crowd. 'Just War!'

She nodded. 'The Just War is accepted. He must fight for his freedom. If he wins the bout, he walks free. Lose? Then it's the mines, to work off the debt he will owe.' More cheers erupted. 'Bring in our champion!'

There was movement in the crowd on the other side of the dais as they were forced aside by someone new moving forward. Moments later, a figure hauled themselves up onto the dais, and Eain gaped.

'The Mule! The Mule!' yelled the crowd.

'Look at that big half-breed bastard,' muttered a man to Eain's left.

The Mule was short, the top of his head barely reaching the shoulders of the guards who stood holding the prisoner. But, he was the broadest man that Eain had ever seen. He was naked to the waist and his chest, shoulders and arms were almost grotesquely huge; swollen with thick, corded muscle.

He swung his arms casually, and fists like boulders circled his body, fore and back. He was a terrifying sight.

The bell rang and the bout started. It finished mere moments later, the Mule's fist crashing into the thief's face and sending him flying backwards off the dais. He had landed a couple of punches first, but the Mule had not even bothered to raise his arms. The blows had landed as if on a rock, or aged timber.

They dragged the thief away to serve his punishment, the guards pulling the sagging form toward the back of the room. As Eain followed their progress, he noticed that a balcony overhung that part of the great hall. As he watched, the richly dressed woman from the dais climbed a set of narrow stairs up to the higher level. At the top, she bowed her head before a figure in an equally elaborate robe.

It was another woman, but with silver hair.

The foot of the stairs was well guarded, a handful of rough men and women with sturdy staves in their hands. The crowd kept their distance, and the guards' eyes darted around, looking for potential trouble.

An idea formed in Eain's mind. He would need to return to this place tomorrow.

He pushed back through the crowd and out through the door, before strolling away into the night.

As he strode past the wagon bearing the crate, he was unaware that a pair of eyes regarded him from the deep shadows behind.

THIRTY SIX

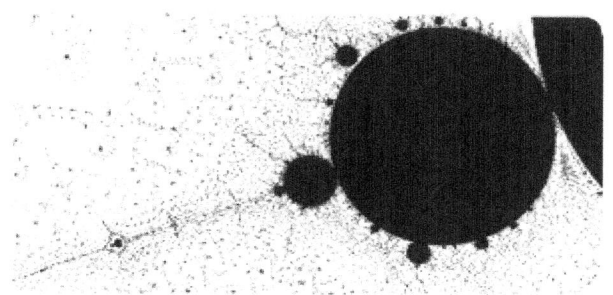

Nastja tried to push away her worries, a hot stone in her stomach, and concentrated on what she needed to do.

She knew that she had upset Ellyah, but although she had replayed the conversation in her head several times, she was still not sure how.

'I can't go out in the city,' Luara had said. 'I'll be recognised and then the game will be up.'

'I'll go,' replied Ellyah, immediately. 'I can blend in. No-one will notice me.'

'But whoever goes will need to pay attention to what they see. We don't know exactly what we're looking for, yet.' As the words left Nastja's mouth, Ellyah's face hardened, her brows lowering, lips compressing.

'And?' Her voice was quiet.

'And I'm better at that. You are more likely to miss things.'

There was a pause. 'Fine. If that's what you really think.'

Nastja was relieved. 'Yes,' she said. 'I think that's the best plan.'

Ellyah folded her arms. 'Fine,' she repeated.

She had withdrawn to the chair in the corner of the cramped attic room that Fion had let them use. Ellyah had not said another word as Nastja had dressed and left the tavern.

Over the last week, while they stayed at Fion's tavern and worked as serving girls, Nastja had been observing people and getting an idea of what fashions were like in Ben Gedrin, and what would enable her to blend in.

So, as she strolled casually through the streets the next day, she wore an uncomfortably snug tunic which was a very different cut to the peasant smocks of Anish. It seemed common to wear them short, regardless of class; rich or poor. Her legs were clad in baggy trousers, tucked into her boots. Instead of a hat she had tied a broad scarf of pale linen over her brow and around the back of her head.

She felt odd, but no-one spared her a second glance.

A basket woven from thick reeds was perched on her hip as she strolled between shops and stalls as if she had no plan and was in no hurry. In truth, she knew exactly what she was looking for, but could not rush to find it.

She kept her eyes and ears open, and tried to take in all that she could as the time passed.

It was mid-afternoon, and she still had not found what she sought. The sun glared down brightly, peering over the west wall on its way toward sunset, but it gave little warmth. The occasional gust was chilling, and she wished she had thought of gloves.

Outside of the city walls, it would be very cold.

Nastja had already noticed that the day had seemed to pass more quickly than she would have expected. Winter was coming, and they were much further north. The climate here was different to Anish. The high towers of the Derufin Mountains gathered the clouds that swelled over the Southern Ocean before sweeping northward, trapping them over the southern countries. They were warm, and wet.

Up here, it rained much less often, and winters were harsh and dry. Most people depended on the harvest months to see them through the coldest season, when nothing grew, and the soil was like stone.

The last month of autumn held special significance, and rituals and celebrations marked the days. It all began with Demonsnight, when sacred fires would be lit to drive away evil spirits and ensure a prosperous harvest. That was only a few nights from today.

Nastja had gathered all of this from snatches of overheard conversations. There were people chattering everywhere, about mostly inconsequential things, and they barely noticed her listening in. This was why she was the right one to be out this day. If it had been Ellyah, she would have ignored any conversations that were not about silver or gold.

The rattle and rumble of cartwheels on the street behind her made her step to one side, and her eyes widened with surprise as she did.

The unmistakable shape of the Mackems' wagon rolled past. Several of them rode on the cart, including the square-shouldered leader and the very tall half-elf thug. That odd, upright crate had been repaired and lashed on the wagon's bed once more.

Her heart raced but she kept her breathing even as they trundled away up the street.

The three of them had all clutched onto the slender hope that the Mackems had been left far behind. That hope was now dashed.

Nastja wondered if they would recognise her. She could not think of an occasion when any one of them had got more than a fleeting glimpse. She smiled grimly. The tall one might remember the feel of her fist.

There was now even more reason for Ellyah to stay hidden.

While she paused, letting the Mackems recede into the distance, another pair of figures walked past. Her attention was caught immediately.

Both were tall, taller than an average human. They were clad in long, grey robes with deep hoods but despite the shapelessness of their garb, Nastja could tell they both had extremely slender hips. It was something about the way that they walked.

These two, then, were elves.

During their travels, they had been told stories of a mysterious tribe who lived an isolated existence in the northern foothills of the Derufin. The rumours went that they moved like grey-clad ghosts, whistling to each other to speak, and only ventured into civilisation to trade.

One carried a leafy branch. This was an archaic sign for peace, so would make sense for those seeking trade. Nastja found this very interesting and watched them intently as they moved serenely up the street.

Hard on their heels was another tall figure. Not quite elf height, he was nevertheless imposing as he pushed hurriedly through the crowds.

His obvious haste drew Nastja's attention, and she studied him. The breadth of his shoulders in a snug goatskin jacket made her certain that it was a man, although she could not see his face. He was masked and hooded, but as she looked closer the hood appeared to be made from a strip cut from a woollen blanket.

This seemed odd, but before she could ponder any further on the reasons for this, the thing she had been looking for hove into view.

Two men, walking in the opposite direction to the hurrying, hooded man. Both were dressed in baked leather breastplates, dyed black, strapped over plain tunics. Both had small silver *pentangs* emblazoned on their armour, and wore round iron caps on their heads.

City militia. Small round shields were slung over their shoulders, and they swung short-hafted spears in time with their casual gait. Despite the arms and armour, they did not look comfortable or confident.

Their eyes darted and their mouths were tight. Nastja watched them with interest as they passed, then moved to follow. Ellyah was better at this part, she admitted to herself, but the streets were so busy she could weave through the crowds easily without attracting any undue attention.

With luck, they would lead her to their guard house.

It took some time.

The pair meandered through the streets throughout the remainder of the afternoon, and Nastja shadowed them carefully. She noted that they stuck to the biggest and busiest streets, not setting foot in the warren of narrow alleyways that ran between them. It suggested to Nastja they were doing their best to avoid trouble.

They disappeared so abruptly that Nastja was forced to scurry along the street to check where they had gone.

A nondescript door in a simple, if reasonably sized, wooden house. The militia were clearly not the holders of the power in this city. She leaned against a nearby wall as if waiting for someone, affecting a posture of boredom, and began to look around.

'The Cyfres hate the city militia,' Luara had said, when planning how to find the drop site. 'They always used to take every opportunity to get one over on them. It would be just their style to do gang business right under their noses.'

Right under their noses, she thought.

And, there it was.

The house opposite had low eaves, extending down to overhang the street. She saw a potential hiding place right away. But, she needed to be sure.

Retracing her steps back up the street, she drew a small, flat piece of wood from a pocket and hid it in her palm. She kept her movements casual and natural, as tension and visible wariness were a sure way to draw unwelcome attention. She had to seem like just another nondescript face in the crowd. She crossed the street, moving swiftly from shadow to shadow as the light faded in the evening sky.

Maintaining a relaxed gait, she walked back toward the anonymous guard house. Opposite the door, she reached up and—there. She found a small hollow space beneath the shingles of the roof overhang.

Without breaking stride, she walked on, leaving the wooden plate with its cryptic markings in the high, hidden space.

Now, she had to wait, and hope that she had found the correct location. She strolled off, at an ambling pace.

'Where have you been?'

Nastja jumped, startled. She had just opened the door of the attic room, and Ellyah was already on her feet. Her brow was furrowed and her face was tight with anger.

'It's so late!' she stormed. 'We've been sat here for hours waiting for you!'

Luara's eyes widened slightly, but she said nothing. She was curled up in a blanket on the bed, and looked quite comfortable and relaxed.

Nastja shut the door and turned to face Ellyah. The taller woman had her hands on her hips, as if waiting for a response.

'I don't know why you're angry,' replied Nastja, eventually.

Ellyah stared at her, dark eyes locked with Nastja's own. Then, she sagged.

'I'm not angry,' she said, quietly. 'I was just worried.'

Nastja searched Ellyah's face. She did not look worried, she appeared angry. There was tension in her face and body. Ellyah could be very confusing, at times.

'I've got some news,' said Nastja, remembering why she had hurried back. She reached into her pocket once more and pulled out a different wooden plaque. It was branded with a series of marks, that were not letters.

She could not read them. But Luara could.

'It could be a meeting,' she said, handing it over to the older woman.

She had killed a couple of hours waiting as evening gathered, then had returned to the street of the militia guard house. Striving to remain inconspicuous, she walked past and reached into the space beneath the opposite building's eaves. She had taken a subtle glance as she hurried away, keen to be off the streets before full dark, and what she saw gave her a thrill.

This was not the scrap of wood that she had left. Hers had been removed, and replaced with a different one. It was a reply.

'That's great, Nas!' Ellyah beamed, her face lighting up as though her scowl had never been there. 'You've done brilliantly, hen.' Nastja kept her face blank, but her insides danced and squirmed with pleasure.

'Yea, it's a meeting!'

Luara was sat up on the bed, studying the coded message.

'They want to meet. They will only send a broker, at first, to assess the value of the…goods. They won't want to lose this opportunity so they won't play any games, but we'll still need to be wary. We don't want to walk into a trap.

'When?' Ellyah's excitement was clear.

Luara looked up. 'Tomorrow night.'

THIRTY SEVEN

The next night seemed to take forever to come. Eain fretted about what he was going to do, wondering constantly if it would work.

The idea had come to him while he was at the fighting club, and he worked through the details in his mind as he looked for somewhere to spend the night. He would need all his strength. In the meantime he needed to find food, and somewhere safe to sleep.

The murmur of talk and the higher tones of voices singing together had led him to a long, low building near the walls. A barrel hung above the door. Jolly orange light flickered through half-closed shutters as Eain approached.

He pushed his makeshift headscarf down to his neck and entered the tavern.

The people nearest the door turned to look as he entered, but otherwise his appearance stirred no noticeable interest.

The intertwining smells of woodsmoke, unwashed bodies and something savoury cooking assailed his nostrils. He wrinkled his nose, but his stomach rumbled. It was a while since he had eaten.

As was common in these lands, the barkeep was no blacksmith. She was a dark haired, pale skinned woman of middle years, and she eyed Eain with mild curiosity as he approached.

'Be you well,' he said, trying the local greeting. She stared at him blankly, without giving a response.

'Do you have food?' he asked, after a moment of silence.

'Bean stew,' she replied, indicating a cauldron beside one of the hearths. 'Two coppers.'

'Yes.' Eain did not care what the food was, he just needed to eat. 'And something to drink. Please.'

She nodded, and after wandering away she returned a moment later with a wooden bowl containing a watery, steaming soup. He set to eating as she placed a cup of foaming brown liquid at his elbow.

'Ale,' she said, in response to his questioning look.

He lifted the cup and took a wary sip. It was bitter and yeasty. Glancing around, he noticed the other customers sucking thirstily at their cups. Maybe this was all they had. He ate and drank.

Suppressing a yawn, he pushed his empty cup and bowl away. Now that his stomach was full, he needed to rest.

'You have rooms? Somewhere to sleep?'

'You want to swing, or to hang?' she asked.

Eain thought he must have misheard. 'What?'

She rolled her eyes. 'We've got a swinging room and a hanging room. Unless you're rich enough to afford a bed. Got a couple of those. Cost silver though.'

He still must have looked bewildered, because she reluctantly moved out from behind the bar and led him to the end of the room. Two doors were set in the wall, side by side.

She opened one and gestured for him to look inside. The room was strung with many narrow hammocks. They were spaced barely two feet apart, in every direction. The room might sleep twenty if all the hammocks were full.

'Swing,' she said, before opening the other door. 'Hang.'

The next room was crossed by thick ropes. Eain was still confused, until he noticed a man in one corner, slumped over the rope with his hands hanging toward the floor. It looked desperately uncomfortable.

'For the drunks,' she said, by way of explanation.

'I will swing please,' said Eain.

It was not the best night's sleep he had ever had, but as he swung gently in the hammock with the buzzing of snoring all around him, he had time to think.

To think about the challenge ahead of him.

Without realising it, his guilt and pain had been forgotten. Now, he had a purpose.

He spent the day in the tavern's common room. It seemed the safest place to wait for the evening to come.

'Got nowhere to go?' asked the barkeep as she plonked a small, round loaf and a yellow cheese with a thick rind before him around noon.

He handed her a single copper section. 'No,' he said, and she ignored him for the rest of the afternoon. The room gradually filled up as the hours went by. By dusk the main hall was close to full, mostly of labourers with muddy hands and miners with dirty faces.

As the noise level increased, Eain stood and headed for the door. He had left his blanket headscarf off this time. Whichever way this evening went, he would not have to worry about being recognised again.

He swallowed down his fear and stepped out onto the street.

The light was dusky as he arrived back at the large building that held the fighting club. Nerves fluttered in his belly as he strode through the doorway and into the open space inside. It was gloomy within, and not yet crowded with people.

He supposed that this club was illegal, but with the same thought realised that the illegality was irrelevant. From what the militia captain had explained, the only thing that mattered was whether the Cyfres or the Sticasts allowed it to happen. And, the Cyfres ran this place. His plan relied on that fact.

He moved across the room, which seemed bigger now it was not full. Finding a dark corner where he would not be noticed, he leaned back to observe the room.

The central dais looked prominent, and he found his gaze unavoidably drawn to it. It was made of rough planks, with thick canvas stretched over the top. Eain could see brownish stains on the surface that must be old blood. He swallowed, and turned away.

At the far end of the room, he noticed a roped off area beneath the looming balcony. Benches were set up, side by side, for the fighters to prepare for their bouts. He could see a few now, stretching, talking to one another, or just sitting in readiness.

Armed and armoured guards stood around the base of the narrow staircase that led up to the balcony. Their posture and attitude made it clear that none would pass them without permission. Getting that permission was what he hoped to achieve this night.

Guards watched the door, and more were clustered around the tables where the bookmakers plied their trade. They all had iron-shod cudgels at their belts and looked ready to use them at the slightest hint of trouble.

Movement on the stairs caught Eain's eye. He watched carefully. A group had entered through a rear door, and were filing up towards the balcony. Most were dressed plainly, in dark tunics, but the two women he had seen last night were at the head of the line. One was younger, one older, but both wore fine, richly embroidered long tunics as before. Their faces were so similar that they must be related, probably mother and daughter.

Eain knew that he needed to speak to the older of the pair.

Then, on the heels of the group, he came. The Mule. He looked as broad as a doorway. The pale skin of his bald head shone in the lamplight. Eain looked down and saw those massive fists once more. He moved aside and took a seat on one of the fighters' benches.

Eain gulped. Maybe there was another way.

Attempting to remain unobtrusive, he skirted the perimeter of the room and headed toward the base of the staircase. The room was filling up and he was forced to dodge around people as they walked across his path. He kept his eyes down. The last thing he wanted was too much attention, too soon.

He had barely got within ten paces of the foot of the stairs when one of the guards, a broad dwarf, stepped forward.

'That's near enough, friend,' he said, holding out a thick-fingered hand. Eain noticed that his other hand was already gripping the haft of his cudgel.

'I need to talk—' Eain began, but was cut off.

'Get back.' He noted that there was no "friend" this time.

'What if I offered you silver to let me pass?'

'Me and my good friends,' he glanced around to indicate the other guards, 'would persuade you that it was not a good idea. Back off, now.'

Eain held his hands up, palms outwards in a placating gesture and backed away. Being beaten senseless for trying to bribe his way to a meeting with the gang leader would not be helpful. He needed to be able to talk.

Ducking through the crowd once more, he slipped away from the foot of the staircase and headed for the fighters' roped off area. He knew the reaction he needed and had planned out what he was going to say.

It would be just like before the unarmed sparring sessions he had as a Sverlaegga and Claihedehle, throwing barbs and insults at each other to induce an angry reaction. He had found out the hard way that taunting Callan Fraevar was a mistake. The taller boy gave no visible reaction, but his reach was long and his fists were hard.

He stepped from the crowd, the dais behind him, and moved toward the rope. Fighters of all shapes and sizes sat on the benches, alone or in small groups. Blocky, muscular humans were next to purple-cheeked half-elves and round-shouldered dwarves, all dressed in simple skirts and vests. Eain noticed a couple of looming, dark-skinned elves and suppressed a shudder as they reminded him of the Wild Elves.

And there, in the middle of them all sat the Mule. He was alone, bare-chested and with his huge fists unwrapped. The pale skin of his broad shoulders glistened in the flickering torchlight.

Eain gathered his courage. This could still go very wrong.

'Hey, Mule,' he called. That round head came up, piggy eyes glaring in his direction. 'I heard they called Kaluva the Queen of the Mongrels. Does that make you the King of the Half-men?' The Mule's thin lips twisted into a grimace. It was not much of an insult but it was enough to get his attention. Eain went on. 'You don't look much like a king though. You look more like something a cow dropped in a field.'

The Mule stood. His jowls and his belly shook as he approached the rope with hasty steps, a furious snarl growing across his face. His fists bunched. It had worked.

The shorter man stepped over the rope and grabbed the front of Eain's coat. His strength was terrifying, and he pushed Eain backwards with ease. He felt people behind him being shoved out of the way, and heard angry voices rising in protest. They were close to the dais, now.

Eain dropped. He let his knees buckle and toppled backwards. With the resistance removed, the Mule also fell. Eain managed to roll away to avoid being crushed, before looking up to see a cluster of confused faces glaring down. It was time to declare his challenge, before the Mule exacted his revenge.

'The Mule attacked me,' he yelled, projecting his voice so as many people could hear as possible. 'I demand a Just War! I will fight to settle the score, in a Just War.'

'What is this?' another voice rang out, and the crowd parted to let the owner through. 'What is the meaning of this?'

It was the golden-haired Cyfres woman. She was dressed in a silken tunic in rich blue, and she glared at him as the Mule slowly clambered to his feet. Her eyes were pale, but hard and narrow, and while her features were fine, the scowl of distrust twisted her face into something unattractive.

'You ask for a Just War?' she said, a slight tone of surprise in her voice. 'Against the Mule? You would choose this?'

'Yes,' replied Eain. 'It is the fair way to settle our dispute.'

'Lose and you will owe the family,' she said, fixing her eyes on his. 'You understand this? You will have to work off your debt.'

'I understand this,' replied Eain. 'And if I win?'

She shrugged, spreading her arms. 'And if you win?'

'A favour. That is all I ask.'

'These terms are acceptable. Mule, do you accept?'

The Mule said nothing but nodded eagerly, bunching his fists as if to strike Eain there and then.

The Cyfres woman raised her voice, crying out to the crowd. 'A Just War is declared!' Cheers rose, a roaring wall of noise. 'It will be settled by fists! Now!'

While they had been speaking, guards had gathered around them and now they grabbed Eain roughly and pushed him around to the rear of the dais. There would be no backing out now. The Cyfres woman turned.

'This one will make a good worker,' she said after looking Eain up and down. 'Get him up there.'

The guards grabbed him roughly and many hands held him. Hands went to his belt and removed his seax, and then quickly stripped him of his coat and shirt. He was thrust, bare-chested, onto the dais. Eain could already feel the unfriendly stares of the crowd as a hostile force. He knew was taking a huge risk.

He felt sick.

'A fool has challenged the Mule!' announced the woman, after climbing up onto the dais behind him. He stood. 'And a big one,' she added. 'The Just War will settle his challenge. The Mule will teach him a lesson. Yes?'

The crowd bayed and roared their approval.

'Call forth the Mule!'

'Mule! Mule! Mule!' they shouted. 'Smash his face, half-breed!' The noise reached a crescendo as he hauled his massive bulk up onto the dais from the other side.

Up close, Eain became even more aware of the contrast between the Mule's abundance of girth and his lack of height. The top of his head barely reached Eain's chest, but his shoulders were massive. His face was jowly and his gut bulged, but he moved in a way that suggested brutal strength.

'Fist on fist!' yelled the Cyfres woman. 'Fight now!'

The bell rang, and the Mule advanced.

His head was large, round and almost childlike in its hairless softness. The irises of his eyes were very pale, nearly white, and his pupils glared out as small, angry pinpricks of darkness.

Eain took a step back, tearing his gaze from his opponent's strange eyes and concentrating instead on his massive fists. They swung menacingly as he moved forward, and Eain knew he had to do his utmost to avoid them.

'Don't get hit, don't get hurt.'

Morgan Blane's voice rang out inside his head, and he was transported back to the Claidah and their training in fighting unarmed. Blane had stood before a group of them when they were young Hniffare, his height and self-possession intimidating.

Eain bunched his fists and raised them in front of his chest, although he had no intention of striking the Mule with them.

'Fists are for fools!' Morgan Blane, again. 'Your opponent will be delighted when you break your own fingers by hitting them.' He had reached out then, taking Eain's hand in his own. His hands were rough, and he had long fingers. He forced Eain's into a fist and wrapped the fingers of one hand around it.

'Hands are too fragile,' he said, beginning to squeeze Eain's fist. 'Too many small bones.' The grip got firmer. Eain felt pain and bit his lip. 'And with your hands out of use,' he continued, as Eain grimaced. 'The fight is lost.' Eain cried out, finally, and Blane let go. His grip had been like iron.

He had never forgotten that lesson. His fists would be useless against the Mule, apart from as a distraction. They were tiny in comparison to his huge bulk. He needed to think of another way.

The Mule growled as he lunged, his right shoulder twisting and sending his fist swinging in a wild haymaker. Eain leaned back and it whistled in front of his face.

Before the Mule could regain his balance, Eain stepped left and took a long stride while lashing out with his elbow. It caught the Mule just above his right ear, but even as he felt the impact something hit him in his ribs, and he staggered forward.

The Mule had spun, faster than Eain had thought possible, and swung his left fist into Eain's exposed right side. Fortunately, he had been moving away so the blow was only glancing. It still drove air from his lungs, and he knew it would be bruised tomorrow. He needed to be more careful.

'Elbows, knees, even your head,' Blane had said. 'Land a strike to an opponent's vitals and they'll go down. Doesn't matter how good they are, or how big, or how strong. Nose, throat, eyes, or a man's jewels. Hit them there and they'll drop.'

As Eain was thinking about his next attack, the Mule drove suddenly forward, launching a straight jab toward his face. Eain did not have time to move, so braced his arms together before his face. He blocked the blow but was knocked back by the pure force.

The Mule kept coming, lashing out again with a left-handed blow. This time Eain was not quick enough, and a hammer-like fist thumped into his ribs. A right cross caught him a glancing blow across the face as he flinched back, and Eain felt his cheek split. He rolled with the punch as well as he could, but it still knocked him down.

The boards of the dais were unforgivingly hard beneath his body, and the roar of the crowd as he fell was feral. It could not end like this.

'Up, Connow!' Morgan Blane's voice rang out from his memory. Callan had just floored him with a right hook and his face glowed with pain even as the stones of the Claidah chilled his body. 'You're not done. On your feet.'

Back in the present, he looked up as the Mule loomed over him. He rolled away as his stocky adversary lunged down with a double-fisted blow, like he was swinging a great axe.

Eain came near to the edge of the platform, but pushed down hard with both hands and leapt to his feet once more.

'The time to strike, Connow, is when your enemy thinks they are about to land the winning blow.'

More of Blane's advice. He had climbed to his feet and ducked an overconfident jab from Callan before knocking the taller boy down with a rapid uppercut.

The Mule lunged forward. Eain dropped his weight onto bent knees, extending his left elbow and leaning into it. The Mule did not see it coming and though the point of Eain's elbow missed his throat, it cracked hard and painfully into the top of his sternum.

It stopped him in his tracks, his hands rising involuntarily to where he had been struck. Eain did not wait. Swivelling from the hips, his right elbow whipped around, power from his shoulders driving it on.

The Mule barely had time to flinch before it hit him, just above the right eye. He cried out, a grating, gravelly sound, and staggered.

That had hurt him, big as he was.

Eain had put all the strength of his shoulders into the blow. The Claihed insisted on all its members undertaking strength training several times a week. Eain could recall the dull, empty ache after sessions swinging stone *holters* and wooden *cabers*. It had been a point of pride to try to lift the most.

He knew that he still carried that strength in his body, even after his long journey.

The Mule was backing away now, and Eain followed.

Eain could see his deep chest heaving as they circled each other around the dais. He was not used to bouts that lasted this long, or opponents who were able to hit back so hard. The crowd was quiet now, and tense.

In a rush, Eain surged forward and threw a blow. It thumped into the Mule's ribs, but he barely seemed to notice the impact. Eain had overextended and suddenly found two huge hands wrapping around his throat.

Eain saw dancing stars before his eyes as the Mule exerted that crushing force, trying to end this fight quickly. It was terrifying.

His training came back instantly this time. He had no time to think, only to react.

He twisted to the right, sweeping his left elbow across the Mule's meaty forearms and breaking his strangling grip. With a whiplash force, he swivelled back to the left, smashing his right elbow into his opponent's cheekbone. It shuddered beneath the impact and the Mule's head snapped round.

Without hesitation, Eain reached out and grabbed the back of the Mule's head with both hands. He brought his knee up hard as he pulled down.

His kneecap exploded into the Mule's piggy nose and Eain felt it break and flatten. The Mule staggered back, blood oozing between his fingers as he raised them to his face, chest heaving.

Eain was barely breathing as he advanced on his opponent for the final time. He was used to walking all day, and he had years of training behind each of his strikes. He was the sum of his parts, the culmination of his experiences, and the knowledge of his victory bubbled through his body in a thrill of emotions.

'That is what the Claidah is about, boy,' Blane had said, as Callan began picking himself up off the ground. 'Defeat. Victory. Humility. Learning. The Claidah is where we strive for perfection. When you understand this truth, you will realise that the Claidah is everywhere you go.'

Eain had left the Claidah behind, but he was about to taste victory.

He moved past the Mule and to the side, hooking his arm around his throat. He thrust his opponent backward, and he could not resist as he was driven backward across the dais and over the edge. He landed on his back in the dirt with a heavy, final thump.

The bell rang.

He had done it.

There were surprised mutters around the crowd, but some cheered and a few put their hands together in a soft patter of applause. The golden haired Cyfres woman climbed back onto the dais.

'The Just War has been decided!' More noise rang out from the crowd, a mix of cheers and boos. 'The challenger was the victor. He has earned his favour.'

This was the moment he had waited for. Planned for. He stepped closer.

'My favour is a request,' he said, the words pitched so that only she could hear. She raised one eyebrow in an arch of surprise. 'I only want one thing.'

'Speak,' she said. Eain's mind flew back to the distant past.

'Do you understand the lesson yet?' Morgan Blane had asked.

Eain had been sprawled on the ground, looking up at the tall, lean Seeker. Blane's tone was flat but to Eain's ears it was a taunt. He could not try any harder. He had launched every wrestling trick he knew but could not get near the stick that Blane held.

Eain shook his head.

'Anyone else?' Blane asked, pointing around the circle of gathered youths with the stick. 'You.' He singled out Eain's friend Arin. 'How would you try to get the stick?'

Arin pulled a face. 'Can I have the stick, please?' he said, with a shrug.

Blane passed him the stick.

'The lesson is simple,' he said, addressing the crowd but looking at Eain. 'Think.'

Eain glared back at the Cyfres woman. 'I have information to share with you. Valuable information. The favour I ask is an audience.' He paused, then fixed her with a determined stare. 'I want to meet your mother.'

THIRTY EIGHT

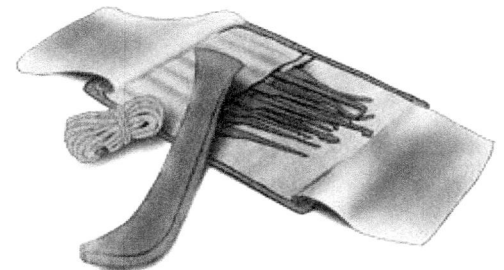

Tonight was the night.

Ellyah fizzed with excitement. By the end of this night she would have done the deal that would line her pockets with enough gold and silver to go wherever she wanted, and live however she liked.

The message from the Cyfres had specified a darkened, deserted shop as the place, and one hour after sundown as the time. The day had dragged while they waited for the hour to come, but now it was almost here.

She had not decided where she would go afterward but was considering northern Buren. It was quiet there, based on the stories she had heard, no-one knew her, and they made excellent wine. She could pass the long, warm summers and short, cool winters in comfort.

'Anything yet?'

Luara leaned forward from where she sat on the grimy floor of the covered market building. Thick logs stood upright around them, holding up a broad roof. At this hour, it was deserted although the noise of conversation and revelry filtered over to them from nearby taverns. It was a handy place to observe the designated shop without standing out.

'No-one has moved near the shop,' replied Ellyah. 'And Nastja will signal if she sees anything. We just need to be patient.'

She said the words but found it hard to mean them in her heart. She kept picturing the moment she would grasp payment for the ruby, and walk from this noisy, dirty city. That moment would be one of elation. Of freedom.

Nastja was stood in the shadows on the other side of the street, keeping an eye on the shop from a different direction. They wanted to be absolutely sure there was no chance of being double-crossed before they went inside.

'If they are going to cheat you, it won't be tonight,' said Luara, repeating the advice she had already dispensed several times. 'They've not seen the merchandise yet, don't know if it's worth the bother. They know if they spook you, you'll vanish and they might lose the opportunity. You've got to be sure the fish is on the hook before you reel it in, right?'

'If they want to double-cross us they'll do it the night we make the trade,' agreed Ellyah. 'I know, I know. We'll deal with that problem later.'

In truth, she was not worried. She had dealt with trickier situations, many times.

'We will, Ell,' said Luara. 'I have confidence in you.'

Luara paused. She licked her lips and her brow wrinkled, as it did when she was thinking.

'I'm curious,' she said, hesitantly. 'And now seems as good a time as any to ask. How did you end up here? Living like this, I mean?'

'I told you,' replied Ellyah. 'My parents died.'

'Lots of people's parents die,' said Luara bluntly, but with kindness in her voice. And they don't end up in your profession.'

Ellyah sighed. 'My parents were killed in a robbery. I hid away so the robbers didn't know I was there. Someone else found me instead.

'Savfa was a trickster and a conman. But a professional. He saw the door to my house hanging open and came in to investigate. Found me curled up in bed. I never knew why, but he decided to take me with him. Took me in. He raised me, like a little sister. Taught me.'

'An apprentice?' Luara raised an eyebrow.

'He taught me to survive,' Ellyah's voice was fiercer. 'Taught me to do what was necessary. He never called it crime and I never saw it that way either. We took what we needed from those that didn't. They had plenty, we had little. It seemed fair. It felt like justice.'

'You will find no argument from me. And no judgement.'

Ellyah reached out to Luara and took the older woman's hand. Luara's skin was smooth, but her grip was strong.

'It was exciting. And sometimes scary, But I mostly remember being content through those years. I realise now that he had been sheltering me from the worst. The gang feuds, the violence, the honour debts. Occasionally, a friend would just vanish, and he'd tell me they had gone on a journey.' She smiled weakly.

Luara squeezed her hand. 'So, what happened to him?'

Ellyah closed her eyes. The pain of it was still vivid. She generally tried to avoid thinking about what had happened, all those years ago, because of how it made her feel, and she rarely had any desire to talk about it. To say the words out loud. But, she felt she needed to tell someone, and believed Luara would understand.

'When I was about sixteen, he went out on a job. Him and a bunch of others. They had spotted an opportunity to hit a merchant's caravan carrying spice from Kotev. There was gold to be made, a lot of it. But, it was risky. Heavily guarded.

'He forbade me to come, said it was too dangerous. I had to wait in Kereva.' Ellyah sniffed. 'Well, I waited. I waited for a long time. In the end I had to admit the truth. He was never coming back.'

'What went wrong?' asked Luara, eyes wide.

Ellyah pulled her hand away, and twisted it awkwardly with the other, fingers tangling on her lap.

'Nothing,' she replied, with heavy reluctance. 'The news spread a week or so later. The raid went perfectly. They all made a fortune, and got away with it. The merchant's guild put a huge bounty on them.' She looked up at Luara, their eyes meeting and understanding passing between the two of them. 'He never came back.'

'Oh.' Luara's voice was as soft as a sigh. 'I'm so sorry, Ellyah.'

Ellyah smiled weakly and turned away. Across the street, she saw a hand raising, a pale patch moving in the gloom. Nastja.

She stood, smoothing her trousers against her thighs, and tucking a couple of loose strands of hair behind her ears. 'It's time,' she said. 'Stay alert.'

Luara nodded, and Ellyah slung the leather bag containing her hopes and dreams across her shoulder once more, before slinking through the shadows to reach the shopfront.

Nastja had her back to the door, her attitude casual and unconcerned. As Ellyah approached though, she noticed Nastja's hands working behind her back. Moments later, the door clicked open and Nastja ducked through. Ellyah followed.

I could have done that too, she thought.

She shut the door behind her, and joined Nastja in the darkened shop.

'I saw someone going around the back,' said Nastja, voice low.

Ellyah peered into the darkness. A faint glow filtered in from outside through the ill-fitting shutters. The planes and angles of pieces of wooden furniture were hard silhouettes in the gloom.

She tried to fill herself with confidence, tried to think about the offer they were about to receive. They were in a strong position to negotiate, after all. She could not avoid worrying, though. Her heart was hammering in her chest. She dropped her hand to her waist, curling her fingers around the polished bone handle of her belt knife.

A glow had appeared beyond the room where they stood. It grew, illuminating a passageway which led toward the rear of the building. As it came gradually closer, a yellow triangle of light shone brightly down onto the floorboards.

Ellyah reached out with her spare hand, grasping Nastja's arm. Her own breathing sounded loud in her ears.

The yellow pool expanded as the point of light rose, and suddenly a face was before them. A figure stood in the doorway, holding a lantern. The bright light cast their face into deep relief.

'Be you well, be you well,' they said, in a croaky voice. 'And, be at ease. 'Tis just me alone, as was promised. We are here to arrange a fair deal, not a robbery.'

The man turned and lifted his arm. He hung the shrouded lantern high on an unseen nail, high on the doorpost. Suddenly, the room was bathed in light.

Ellyah and Nastja blinked.

Around them were the shopkeeper's wares; the polished wood of tables and chairs, ready to sell. Ellyah supposed people who had the money to buy things like tables and chairs had to buy them somewhere.

The man who stood before them was in his middle years, but his hair was still dark. He was clean-shaven and wore a pleasant, calm smile. He had narrow shoulders and clever, long-fingered hands which he laced together at the front of his plain but well-cut tunic.

'Here we are then,' he said. 'You have our attention. You have made a proposition, and I am here to prove our good faith and to set out the terms of our business.'

He had a strong accent. He spoke a little like Luara, but his voice was harsher.

'Do we have an understanding?'

'Yes,' said Nastja. And added nothing else.

How had she got this far through life without being stabbed? Ellyah wondered.

'We understand you perfectly,' added Ellyah quickly. 'We know that you appreciate how unusual this offer is, and the value it offers.'

'Quite,' he replied. 'Curious to see what you have got to show me. Also somewhat curious how you found our dead-drop sight and understood our code. Because you ain't local. But I'm going to guess you wouldn't tell so I won't ask. We need to get to business.'

Ellyah was glad about that. Hopefully, they would forget that part in their eagerness to obtain the jewel. They needed to protect Luara. They also had to make sure they got a good price for the ruby.

'So,' he continued before either of them could speak. 'Can I see it?'

Ellyah did not reply, not trusting herself to say anything without betraying her nervous excitement. She unslung the leather bag from her shoulder and set it down on the floor. Reaching inside, she withdrew the wooden box and placed it lightly on the nearest table.

'Intriguing indeed,' murmured the Cyfres broker, edging closer.

Taking a deep breath, Ellyah released the catches. Then, slowly, she lifted the lid and folded it back.

The room was bathed in eerie crimson light. The inside of the ruby danced with red fire, and its facets refracted and cast the shimmering glow in waves onto the walls and the ceiling. The room felt suddenly otherworldly and mysterious.

Ellyah felt her stomach lurch as she looked across at the Cyfres broker's face. His eyes were wide and his pupils mere dots of red as they reflected the light of the jewel. Shock, delight and greed all warred to take control.

He gathered himself a moment later, but Ellyah had played dice many times. The look on his face had revealed much. He had showed his hand. It told her that they possessed something truly valuable, and that this man would pay dearly to have it.

He stepped closer, gazing down into the simple wooden box.

'I need to take a closer look,' he said, a slight catch in his voice. 'To assess the quality of the jewel and to check for any… imperfections.'

Ellyah gestured for him to do as he wished. She held her breath as he extended a hand and reached toward the box. His fingers wrapped around the fist-sized ruby, and he lifted it reverently from the box.

Shafts of red light glared out into the dark corners of the room, radiating warmly between his fingers. He stared down, his whole face bathed in the ethereal crimson glow. His eyes were wide with wonder, his mouth hanging open.

He lifted his eyes from where they had been staring, rapt, into the heart of the jewel and opened his mouth to speak. But no words came out.

His face twisted, and in a heartbeat it was filled with an expression of horrified agony. Staring down at his hand, he turned it over as if trying to drop the jewel. But, he could not let it go.

His fingers were locked around the jewel, like a claw. The rest of his body was stiff with agony as he suffered. The smell of burning flesh filled the room.

'Shit!' The word burst from Ellyah's mouth as she was gripped by horror. Nastja dashed across to the stricken Cyfres man and rapped him hard on the knuckles with the handle of her own belt knife. Nothing happened.

'Don't touch it!' called Ellyah, as Nastja moved closer.

At that moment his knees collapsed and he sank down. His eyes rolled back in his head and his mouth dropped open before he tipped limply backward to lie prone on the floor.

The jewel was held up in a hand that was twisted like a sinewy talon. The heat coming from the ruby was palpable, even from a few feet away. Ellyah could see that apart from his hand, tensed in unstoppably agony, the rest of his body was sagging, and fading. Dying.

Ellyah stared as Nastja seized the lidded, wooden box from the table and knelt next to the man. She unsheathed her belt knife. Licking her lips once, she went quickly to work. With deft strokes, she sliced the keen blade across the front and back of his wrist. The fingers relaxed as the tendons were severed. As the jewel fell from his slackening hand, Nastja caught it in the box and slammed the lid.

She cast it onto the floor and it skittered across the boards to land a few feet away. Ellyah staggered sideways and sank gratefully into a nearby chair.

'Shit and demon's shitting blood,' she swore. What had just happened? How could this be?

'That is what we've been carrying around for these past weeks?' Nastja's voice was high. 'What if one of us had touched it? That would be us!' She gestured to the limp shape of the Cyfres broker.

'How is he?'

'He's dead, Ell. Very dead.'

Ellyah stared around the room, eyes shifting from the jewel's box, to the body on the floor and then to Nastja. Her face was blank but Ellyah could tell from the stiffness in her body that she was scared.

It was terrifying to think that they had been completely unaware of the power of that beautiful, precious object. They could have lost their lives, to horrifying agony, from a mere touch. How many times had they been close to holding it? Too many.

It just showed that it must be truly special, and probably unique.

'What are we going to do now?' asked Nastja. She seemed to be frozen to the spot.

Ellyah did not reply immediately. Instead, she moved across to the table, and carefully lifted the box. Aware of Nastja's eyes on her, she bent and picked up the leather bag, before slipping the box inside. She slung it over her shoulder and turned.

'Well,' she said. 'We need to move the body.'

'And the jewel?'

Ellyah paused. 'Next time', she began, choosing her words carefully. 'We'll have to make sure they don't touch it until they have handed over the gold.'

Nastja wore an expression of aghast horror. 'Haven't you noticed it just killed someone?'

'Yes, of course,' replied Ellyah, with forced patience. 'But there are two gangs in town. We have another chance, yet. We'll have to put the word out that the Cyfres could not make a reasonable offer, and that we are open to an approach from the Sticasts.'

'How can you still think about selling it?' blurted Nastja. 'We shouldn't have any more to do with it. We should just get rid of it and get out of here!'

Ellyah forced down her own fear and mastered her frustration. She took a step closer to Nastja, and leaned forward.

'We could do that. We could just throw it away. And, if we did then everything we have been through to get here will have been for nothing. Everything we have risked, everything we have suffered, will have been completely pointless. We will walk away with our hands empty.'

And my dream of escaping from all of this for good will be dead, she added to herself.

'This is just getting more and more dangerous, Ell,' said Nastja, shaking her head. 'What about when the Cyfres find out we've killed their broker?'

'We never thought it would be easy, hen. But we're so close. We can do this. These people are common criminals who are used to having it their own way, but we can beat them, because we are smarter, and stronger than they know. We can live with them as our enemies.'

She sensed that Nastja was wavering, and decided to push her over the edge.

'You and me together, hen,' she said, softly. 'We can do anything when we work together. There's no-one better than us. And, once our purses are full we can escape, together.' She reached out and lightly touched Nastja's arm. 'You and me,' she repeated.

Nastja stared back blankly for a moment.

'We need a blanket to wrap around the body,' she said, abruptly. 'We just need to get it far enough away that it isn't found quickly. They'll be hunting us as soon as they realise he hasn't come back.'

'I know. But they don't know where to find us. And it'll take them a while to find out. We have a little time. Enough to do what we need to do.'

'What are we going to tell Luara?' asked Nastja. Ellyah cursed, inwardly. She had not thought of that.

'We'll say he double-crossed us. Tell her he attacked us, and tried to steal the jewel. We just defended ourselves against him. Right?' Nastja just nodded.

'Then what?' she asked, after a moment's thought.

'We lie low, and find out how to meet the Sticasts. We move fast and make it clear they need to make us an offer quickly or we leave and take the jewel with us.'

And when they do, thought Ellyah, *we will take their gold and then get away from this stinking city as fast as we can. Nothing else can get in our way.*

THIRTY NINE

Eain was still waiting.

'I want to meet your mother,' he had stated boldly, after defeating the Mule.

'You want what?' The golden-haired woman had asked, as they both climbed down from the dais and were immediately surrounded by guards. Her expression was incredulous. 'My mother does not meet with just anyone.'

'I won the Just War!' insisted Eain. 'But, I insulted the Mule to start the fight. I needed to get your attention.'

She stared at him. 'Are you trying to tell me that you did that for the opportunity to declare a Just War? You fought the Mule by choice?'

'Yes.'

Her face did not change from the sarcastic sneer, but her eyes widened slightly. Eain pressed on.

'I have some information that your mother will want to hear. Information about valuable goods being smuggled through the city. That is, if you and your mother are the real power in Ben Gedrin...?'

'What sort of valuable goods?' she asked, interested. 'And who is smuggling? The Sticasts?'

'Not here,' said Eain, glancing around to indicate that where they stood they could be overheard by anyone.

She hesitated, but he could see that she realised the opportunity that bringing this news to her mother presented. And the risk that it could be brought by someone else. She had nodded to the guards and then gestured toward the staircase at the rear of the room. They had given him back his shirt and coat, but not his seax, and escorted him to the stairs. At the top though, they left him to wait.

And they had made him wait a good while.

The room beyond the edge of the balcony was a stark contrast to the bare, barn-like hall below that held the fighting club. The plain wooden walls were hidden behind wall hangings and tapestries, and the soft light of oil and candle lanterns replaced the sputtering and smoking of rushlights and braziers.

The air was nonetheless still hazy, and fragrant with the rich scent of pipe smoke which wafted toward Eain's face from a corner where several figures sprawled in low chairs. Like the mother and daughter he had seen at the front, they were all dressed in fine tunics, albeit these were less colourful.

They were huddled around a table, rolling dice, and they paid Eain no attention as he entered and stood at the top of the stairs. There was nowhere to sit that was not with that group, so he remained standing.

He had stood and waited for many hours during his training as Hniffare and then Sverlaeggare, and found it no hardship. He simply let his hands drop to his sides, with his eyes staring straight ahead, and stood still. The wait gave him time to think.

What was he even trying to achieve? He found it hard to pin it down, but he knew that if he did nothing then the bandits from Feorhyrc would hunt down those girls, with the assistance of the militia, and they would be lucky to survive. If he could get one of the gangs interested, maybe they could get a fair deal for the item they carried and perhaps some measure of protection.

To him, that felt fair.

He was still wondering what he should say, when footsteps sounded on the stairs and several guards muscled their way onto the balcony. Eain turned to face them, taking a step back to leave more room.

The fair-haired young woman led the way, with her mother, silver-haired, on her shoulder. They both moved with the same smooth, arrogant grace. Their hair hung loose to their shoulders and seemed to shine like polished metal in the room's soft light.

'The lady Eacnung Cyfres comes!' announced the younger woman, in strident tones.

As one, the others in the room got to their feet. They all raised their right hands to their breasts, before drawing a single finger sideways across their hearts.

'A knife to my flesh for the family,' they intoned in unison.

'Sit,' she said, with a dismissive gesture. Her voice was deep and melodious. Eain heard the scrape and rustle as they took their seats, but he kept his eyes on her. She turned to him next, regarding him imperiously. Her face was narrow and her cheekbones were prominent. Thin, delicate lines creased the corners of her eyes but her gaze was eagle-sharp. Her eyes gleamed with a fierce intelligence.

'Now,' she said. 'What is this?'

'He challenged the Mule, and won.'

'This, was foolish. Why does he stand here?'

'It was his favour for the victory in the Just War. He claims he has some information to share.'

'Claims.' Eacnung Cyfres' voice was cold.

'It is true,' said Eain. He could feel all eyes in the room moving to focus on him as he spoke. It was an uncomfortable sensation, but he pressed on.

'I followed some outlander bandits to the city. I think they are from the south, and they were tracking three women here, who carry something very valuable.'

'This is known to me,' said Eacnung.

Eain's heart fell. He swallowed. 'They are in league with the city militia to try to obtain it before you can. They have already met with the militia captain.'

'This,' she said, after a pause, 'I did not know.'

'They have pursued it across the Riverlands, from near Annida. From the way they talked, it was a very valuable object. They wanted to keep the truth about it from you. They intend to steal the item and kill the bearers.'

'Styth!' she called, and one of the men at the gambling table stood and hurried over. She leaned her mouth to his ear and whispered something that Eain could not hear.

'A knife to my flesh for the family,' he murmured, putting his finger to his chest and repeating that unusual gesture, before hurrying from the room.

'You have come before me with news of value,' she said, when Styth had gone, stepping closer to Eain. 'A question burns within me, though, and it is a simple one.' She looked up at him. 'Why?'

Because I want you to stop those bandits from getting what they want, he thought. *They are without honour, and would threaten and kill innocent people. I want them stopped and I know I cannot do it myself.*

He thought this, but knew he could not say it. He could only think of one thing to say that would make sense.

'I would join,' he said. 'I would become part of the Cyfres…family. I came with this knowledge to share so that you would know you could trust me.'

She smiled wryly. 'Interesting indeed! I do not think we have accepted an outlander as one of us before. And yet, one who could best the Mule with fists could prove useful indeed.

'Will you take the oath? Will you be loyal? Do you understand the consequences of breaking faith?'

'Consequences?' asked Eain, before he could stop himself.

'Anyeei! Nkhono! Fetch the prisoner!'

Two of the guards, both dwarves, scurried off, darting behind a screen toward the rear of the balcony. They reappeared a moment later dragging a limp, pale shape. They dropped it to lie on the floor between Eain and the Cyfres gang leader. Eain glanced down, and swallowed nervously.

It was a young man, or had been, with short cropped fair hair. He was naked, his slender body deflated and pathetic. A large, livid brand had seared the skin away from the middle of his chest.

'I see that our guest has finally perished,' said Eacnung. 'I can assure you that it took some time. The brand is the rune "C" for Cyfres. This man was a member of the militia who thought he could get away with taking the Sticasts' filthy money.

She took a step closer. 'I can promise that the punishment for a gang traitor is worse.'

Eain kept his face blank, but his stomach churned in revulsion at the thought of the agony this man must have suffered before the end. These people were no better than bandits. But he could not turn back now. He was certain that they would not let him leave alive if he tried.

'I will swear,' he said, in a voice that croaked slightly.

'Give him his blade,' she ordered. Eain grasped his seax as it was passed to him. Eacnung looked at him pointedly and waited.

'Doff your shirt, lanky,' grunted one of the dwarves. Eain quickly pulled his shirt over his head, and as he looked around noticed that the other gang members had all pulled back their tunics to expose the top of their chests. Each had a single scarred line just above their hearts. They pointed it at it with their fingertips.

'When you become one of us,' said Eacnung, her hand pointing to her own chest as she bared it. 'You become free. What matters now, is what you can do, and what you will do.

Nothing else is important. Confidence in our abilities, and strength of will, are what lets us control our destiny.' She looked down at his chest.

Eain looked down too, at the knife in his hand. It was clear what he had to do.

'A knife to my flesh for the family,' they chanted.

He set the sharp blade to his skin. It nicked his flesh with a mere touch, and a trickle of blood ran down his chest. It hurt already.

'A knife to my flesh for the family,' he repeated, before clenching his teeth. With a rapid motion he drew the keen blade across, cutting a deep gash in his own chest.

The cut stung as Eain waited nervously in the shadows. They had smeared the wound with honey and bandaged it with clean linen, but it still hurt, a line of fire across his chest.

He forced himself to ignore the pain. At this moment, it was unimportant.

A full day had passed. Eain had been sent away after the cutting ritual with strict orders to return the following morning. He was told he would need to do a job for them, to prove his loyalty.

The Cyfres base during the daytime was a sprawling tavern beside the docks. Eain had approached the building warily, all stained timber planks and heavy beams, the cold of dawn around him like the grip of an icy hand.

A road of packed earth led past the wide doorway of the tavern and down a shallow slope toward the city docks. Eain took a few more steps and then and beheld the broad, shimmering expanse of Lake Gedrin for the first time.

It was a cloudy morning and the light was dull and flat. The lake's surface gleamed like polished pewter, but it was the sheer scale of the expanse of water that took Eain's breath away.

He had run beside the broad Osturfjord many times, where the river Ostur flowed through a high-sided valley that cleaved the mountains, but the breadth of Lake Gedrin made even that seem like a mere stream.

Small boats with high prows could be seen in the water near the city, and yet more crossed the water further out, dwindling into the distance to become little more than darks specks on the shining grey. Grains of sand on a woollen blanket.

The opposite shore was visible only as a dark, hazy smudge on the far horizon. So much water.

He had turned away and entered through the door as instructed, finding himself in a deserted common room. Cyfres were not early risers.

He waited patiently, as he knew how, and more people began to arrive from mid-morning. Most wore a coloured tunic and many made the cutting finger salute across their chests as they met.

Eain took a seat in the corner where he could see the door and was generally ignored throughout the day. He sat uncomfortably, knowing now that he had thrown in his lot with people who were no better than the bandits he was trying to thwart.

But, what choice did he have?

It was early evening when Eacnung Cyfres and her daughter entered the room. They came from a different door, as if they had been in another part of the inn. Everyone stood and saluted. Eacnung gazed around silently while her daughter spoke.

'Tonight, is a night of action!' She paused while the cheers died down. 'At dusk, a shipment will be unloaded. A shipment of fine Bureno wine for the governor Ceolbaght's Demonsnight celebrations. We feel it would be better for his health if he did not receive those barrels, and instead they came to us.' More cheers, and a ripple of laugher. 'I expect the governor will send some of his militia as guards, but we are the Cyfres! We will sweep them away!' The cheers grew louder still, men and women stomping feet and banging tables.

Now, Eacnung spoke. 'No mercy for the militia. We will teach them the cost of taking dirty Sticast money. Now, go!'

He had followed the other gang fighters, loosening his seax in its sheath as they filtered silently through the dark city, down toward the docks. They stuck to the smaller alleyways and the gathering gloom of the night hid their advance.

Torches flickered on the docks. Some were still, while others bobbed and swayed with the unmistakeable motion of a boat on water. The lake was black, and the lights reflected in the rippling surface like tongues of fire.

'Soon,' whispered a woman's voice near Eain's elbow. She had introduced herself as Heafrid and had told him she intended to stay at his side. 'You look strong enough to take on the whole militia by yourself!'

He cursed himself for ending up in this situation. Why had it seemed like a good idea?

I won't kill, Eain told himself. *I won't kill any of the militia unless there is no other choice.*

He could see a cordon of militia guards, standing in a line across the top of the wharf. A well-tended brazier burning on each side cast their grim faces into deep shadow and reflected brightly from their polished leather armour and the points of their spears.

'Ready?' asked Heafrid, drawing a wickedly curved knife. Eain nodded. 'Now!'

From alley mouths and darkened doorways, figures emerged and stalked across the open ground toward the wharf. The militia line stiffened and set their spears. They made a solid barricade, but were heavily outnumbered.

The Cyfres surged forward, men and women armed with knives, cudgels and staffs. They were silent. Eain was with them but hung back behind the front line. Weapons clashed, metal on metal and wood on wood. Voices full of anguish and pain cried out in the first moments, splitting the stillness of the night.

The darkness, the fight quickly descended into a chaotic brawl.

Heafrid staggered back past him, hand clasped to a dark patch that bloomed on the side of her tunic.

'Get in there, big man!' she grunted, shoving him toward the action. Her hand left a bloody print on his coat. He knew he could not stay out of the fighting completely, so he drew a deep breath and stepped forward into the melee.

Immediately, a broad, leaf-shaped spear point flew at his chest. He swivelled, palming it away and lunged at the spearman. He caught a glimpse of a pair of wide, frightened eyes as he swung the hand holding his seax. At the last moment, Eain turned his wrist and hit the man with the side of his fist instead of his blade. He went down, poleaxed.

The militia were falling back, those that were still standing in defence. The Cyfres pressed forward and crowded in close, preventing them bringing their shields up properly. The militia looked desperate.

There was a cry, and a splash. They were over water now, out on the wharf, and one of the burly Cyfres men had grappled one of the militia fighters off the edge to tumble into the inky lake below.

The Cyfres had nearly fought their way to the precious cargo.

At that moment a shout came from the rear.

'Hey. Hey! Turn! Cyfres, turn and fight!'

Eain turned to see the shouting figure, one of the wounded Cyfres fighters, standing at the head of the wharf and pointing north. Pointing into the shadows of the dockyards, where another group of figures had emerged and were rapidly approaching.

'Sticasts!' cried the same voice.

At the same time, the echoing clatter of feet on wooden boards sounded from the lakeward end of the wharf. The militia were suddenly reinforced by new numbers, fighters who had been hidden in the boats.

Sticasts to the rear, resurgent militia massing in front; the Cyfres were suddenly in trouble.

'Flee!' rang out an authoritative voice. 'We are betrayed! Cyfres! Flee now!'

All around Eain figures were panting and jostling, trying to get away. Everyone was desperate to be clear of the wharf before the Sticasts closed in and cut off their escape. Panic was in the air.

As Eain moved to follow the surging crowd of fleeing Cyfres fighters, a younger gang member tripped and fell at his feet. Eain stumbled in turn, only just managing to hurdle the sprawling figure. Sensing the Sticasts on their heels, Eain stretched out his hand to the other Cyfres.

'Get up!' he shouted. 'Hurry!'

The clasped hands, and Eain hauled him to his feet. But, it was too late.

The Sticasts had spread out to surround them, moving swiftly to cut off any escape. The rest of the Cyfres had vanished into the night, leaving Eain and the younger fighter to face the Sticasts. Men and women alike were dressed in snug leathers, as if ready to ride. Or to fight. In the dim, orange light they were a threatening sight.

The other Cyfres cowered next to Eain but gripped his spiked cudgel tightly. Eain thought fast. They would not fight their way out of this, and while it might be possible to break through and outrun them through the maze of dark streets, another course of action had occurred.

He threw down his seax. It clattered to the earth as he raised his hands, palms outwards.

'I surrender,' he said, the eyes of the Sticasts boring into him as he waited for their response.

'Kill 'em.'

Eain's eyes widened at the words, and he took a step back as several gang members loomed forward, blades bared.

The speaker was a heavy-shouldered young man with a shock of very fair hair. Eain caught the Sticast's eyes with his own, noticing they were pale grey and burned with a sharp intellect.

'Wait,' called Eain, in a tone he hoped sounded confident. He grabbed the arm of the other Cyfres and pulled him close. 'I have information. Valuable information. Spare us now and take us to your leader, and I'll tell you what I know.'

The Sticasts' killers paused, and the leader moved forward. There was curiosity in his face.

'What sort of information?' he asked. His voice was surprisingly soft, like a breeze across dead leaves.

Eain glanced to his left and right warily. 'I can't say here. But, give me the chance to bring it to your leaders. I swear they will be grateful.'

'And if they are not?'

'If I have spoken false, you may slay me then. You will have lost nothing. But if I do not, then your leaders will be pleased with you.'

The blond Sticast pursed his lips in thought, but only for a moment. 'Bind them. Bring them,' he ordered.

Eain forced himself to remain still as a pair of leather clad Sticasts bound his wrists with a long strip of hide cord. Every sense screamed at him to resist, or to run. To hide. He knew he would not survive if he tried.

More torches were lit, and Eain saw that the ground nearby was littered with Cyfres dead. They had paid heavily for blundering into this trap. Others had been pursued into the nearby alleys; many would not escape.

They are not my people, thought Eain. *They are common criminals. I owe them no grief.*

The blood still sickened him, though. If has hands had not been bound, they would have been shaking. A pair of Sticasts moved along the wharf, rolling Cyfres bodies unceremoniously into the water. They bobbed away into the dark lake.

'Fetch the barrels,' ordered the blond-haired leader. At his words, a handful of Sticasts stalked down to the wharf, stopping by the stack of cargo sitting by one of the boats. The remaining militia force shrank back, spears raised.

Each of the Sticasts grabbed a barrel and carried it back along the wharf, before heading off into the night. The leader raised his hand in an ironic salute toward the militia, and then turned and followed.

Eain's wrists were jerked forward as his guard tugged on the cord. He found his footing and walked along behind the crowd. The other Cyfres captive was at his side.

'Traitor!' he hissed. Eain shrugged. What did he care? He had no allegiance to any of these people.

The night had deepened by the time the group arrived at another tavern, this one ramshackle and dimly lit. The Sticasts bearing barrels disappeared through a narrow door at ground level, with most of the other gang members filtering off through a wider entrance.

The leader stepped onto a staircase, seemingly cobbled together from scrap lumber. It led up to a doorway beneath the tavern's broad, pitched roof.

'Come!' he barked, beckoning with a single finger. Eain and the other Cyfres followed, the guards' treads heavy on the steps behind. The structure groaned uncomfortably beneath their weight.

The leader thrust the door open and ducked beneath the lintel. Eain followed behind and they all squeezed into the cramped space.

'Well?'

The new voice was gruff, and impatient. Eain peered around the bulk of the blond Sticast to look toward the speaker.

A man with short, dark hair that was streaked with silver sat in an extravagant, throne-like chair. His shoulders and arms were heavy and broad, those of a warrior or a fighter, and his face was jowly but hard. He wore the same close-fitting fighting leathers as the other Sticasts, as did the woman sat at his side.

She was slender where her husband was bulky, and blonde-white hair cascaded in wild curls down to her ears. She was fine-featured, with high, elegant cheekbones, but her eyes were cold.

The room in which they sat was small, the height limited by the slope of the roof above, but it was opulently decorated. A thick rug of red wool was beneath Eain's feet, the walls and ceiling were hung with embroidered cloth and the room was well lit by the glow of many gilded candlesticks.

'We surprised the Cyfres,' replied the blond leader of the raid. 'As we planned. The barrels are being put in the storeroom as we speak.'

'Good. Any losses?'

'None of ours. We threw two fistfuls of Cyfres dogs into the Gedrin, though.'

'Too good for them,' put in the woman.

'You've done well, son,' said the seated man. 'But what is this?' He gestured toward Eain and the other Cyfres.

'Prisoners.'

The older man spat on the floor. 'Why? Slit their throats and be done.'

'The tall one says he's got some useful information. Would only share it with you.'

'Well, he's got brass balls, at least.' He fixed Eain with an unfriendly stare. 'Out with it, then. And quickly.'

Eain drew a breath.

He had been a fool to ally himself with the Cyfres. He had thought that they might have some honour, some decency, but they were little more then a group of bandits and robbers. Murderers. His actions had probably put the fleeing women in greater danger than before. He had to try to put it right, and could only see one option.

'I have no true allegiance to Cyfres,' he began. 'They gave me no choice but to join them, and I hate them for it.' He put his hand to his chest, where the wound still burned and throbbed.

'Traitor!' shouted the other Cyfres, but a backhanded swipe from one of the guards stilled him to silence.

Eain continued.

'Cyfres are trying to get their hands on a valuable item. It has just arrived in the city. I do not know exactly what it is, but Cyfres are trying to get it before an outlander gang can.'

'I heard about these outlanders,' put in the woman. 'Southerners. We've been watching, but have not moved against them yet.'

'They are in league with the militia,' said Eain. Mutters rumbled around the room. 'If you move fast, you may be able to get it for yourself. It would bring much wealth to you, and would be a victory over Cyfres.'

'Do not advise me!' snapped the Sticasts leader, but his face was thoughtful. 'Take them down and tie them up in the storeroom,' he said, after a moment.

The guards steered Eain and the other prisoner toward the door. As they reached the threshold, he spoke again.

'If there is truth to your words, we will speak again. But,' his voice hardened. 'If they are false, you will die.'

FORTY

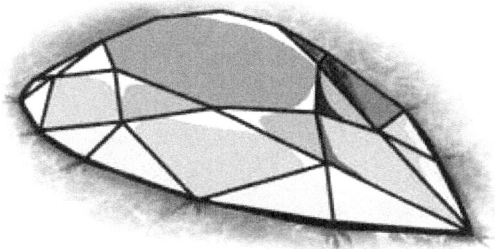

A red glow filled the space. The warehouse roof was high above them but the shock of crimson light reached all but the deepest shadows as Ellyah opened the box.

This time, thought Nastja. *They would be more careful.*

Luara had accepted their version of the events of the previous night without surprise.

'He threatened us with a knife, and tried to steal the jewel,' Ellyah had lied after beckoning Luara over to join them in the dingy furniture shop.

Luara shrugged. 'Sounds about right for Cyfres.'

They found a dark woollen blanket out in the back of the shop and wrapped the corpse tightly in it, before dragging the heavy bundle out into the night. He had not been a big man, fortunately, and between the three of them they were able to manage his weight quite easily.

Luara navigated them through dark back alleys, so that they could avoid bumping into anyone. Getting caught while carrying a dead body through the streets of Ben Gedrin had never been part of their plans.

She bade them pause where a narrow passage opened out onto a lane that was wider and better lit.

'We need to cross this lane to get out to the walls,' hissed Luara. 'Can't avoid it. Move fast, keep your eyes open.'

They edged out onto the street, the long bundle tucked under their arms, but froze as two militia men appeared from another alleyway further away. Their backs were turned but they paused in conversation, as if deciding which way to go.

'Down!' whispered Luara, and they hastily dropped the wrapped-up body and shoved it into the gutter. By the time the two militia turned, the three women had lunged to the other side of the street and were leaning against a wall as if engaged in casual conversation.

'Evening, ladies,' said one of the men as they passed.

'Piss off,' retorted Ellyah. Luara smirked but Nastja was aghast. What if they were arrested? But the militia men just shook their heads and walked away, without another word.

'What did you go and say that for?' asked Nastja, angrily when they had moved out of earshot.

Ellyah was defensive. 'I didn't want them to think we were whores.'

Luara laughed out loud. 'Dressed like this?' she gestured to Ellyah's dusty leathers. 'No, no danger of them thinking that.'

She was still chuckling as they picked up the body and continued their grisly journey.

It was deep into the night when the city wall loomed before them. The city was ringed by a high bank, and the upright logs which formed the wall had been driven deep into this to form a sheer barrier from the outside. From the inside, it was possible to scramble up the bank and look over the wall.

Quickly and smoothly, the three women hurried up the bank and tipped the grey bundle over the top. There was a distant thud and slither as it rolled down into the deep ditch which surrounded the city. Nastja looked along the wall and started as she saw someone else leaning over the pointed logs. They too hefted something over to fall into the ditch, before turning away.

'Everyone dumps their shit over the wall,' said Luara, noticing Nastja's concern. 'No one will remember seeing us here.'

Without another word, they fled down the bank and back into the sanctuary of the city. Being seen was one thing, but now they needed to ensure they were not followed.

As they reached the dark doorway of Fion's tavern, the door opened and three figures emerged. Two were half-elves, with purple-tinted cheeks; one he- and one she-*helf*. The third was female but squat, and broad. Nastja immediately thought that she looked like a mix of human and dwarf. Half-dwarf? Nastja had never seen one before, but it made sense.

All three wore long and elaborately embroidered robes in eye-watering colours, and boots with tall, built-up soles. Their faces were painted, with dark lines around their eyes and red outlines to their lips.

'Now,' said Luara, pausing at the door. 'That's how to dress if you fancy a career lying on your back.' She had smirked as if at a private joke, before ducking inside.

Nastja spent the following day walking the streets of Ben Gedrin once more. She had tied a couple of strips of pale linen around her head as a headscarf, making sure her fair hair was tucked in and out of sight. She was unlikely to be recognised, but her hair was distinctive.

Once more, Luara had given her a good idea of what to look for. Once more, she had no idea where to find it.

She heard it after strolling through the streets and alleyways for several hours.

Close to the central square she passed enclosures where bullocks were being kept. Each had a strange device attached to their sweeping horns. It looked something like a brazier, and though the young bulls tossed their heads in rage, they could not knock them off.

It was as she moved away from the cattle pens, the grunts and lows of the beasts fading into the distance, that she heard the sound she had been searching for.

A plaintive, staccato melody drifted through the air between the densely packed buildings. It was the sound of plucked strings, playing a local tune, and it was what Luara had told Nastja to listen out for.

She increased her pace as she followed the sound, and as she rounded a corner, Nastja saw her. She had long, braided fair hair and was plucking at a boxy wooden instrument with three narrow strings. As Luara had suggested, she was wearing a leather coat. She was a Sticast, or at least paid by them to watch the streets and take messages.

Nastja approached and carelessly threw a handful of copper scraps into the player's upturned hat. Except that one of them was not copper, it was a small piece of wood, cut in the shape of a knife. The player reached out, palmed it, and hid it away, barely missing a note of her tune.

Immediately, her tune changed. Nastja began to stroll away but was listening intently. The busker began to sing:

> *Come back to me, my love, when the night do fall*
> *Return this way again, when darkness covers all*
> *Come back, my love, and I'll tell you true*
> *Where we shall meet, just me and you*

The song continued but Nastja walked away. She had understood the code in the song and would return after dusk.

She whiled away the time around the streets of Ben Gedrin, listening to rumours flying about the governor's Demonsnight party and how he hoarded his wealth so jealously. Some said he was ill, and barely left his chambers. Most were preparing for a night of revelry and cared little for the governor's troubles.

There was a bustle around the cattle pens as she walked back that way, and she stopped to listen in to the chatter.

'I'm going to bring one down,' boasted a broad-shouldered young man in a dirty work tunic. 'I'm going to eat beef on Demonsnight, and drink the *torro*.'

The *torro* was bull's blood, Nastja had gathered. Drained from a vein while the furious bullock's heart beat its last, and drunk by the one who had brought it down, it was believed to grant strength, health and fortune.

'You'll never catch them!' laughed another in response. 'You should see how these beasts move when the fires are lit! It's more likely that your blood will flow.'

'Fate decides who catches a fire-bull on Demonsnight,' stated a tall woman wrapped in thick furs and skins. She grasped a cattle-handler's prod like a sceptre of office. 'The Five will be watching when we open the pens, and the fire will drive the demons hence. That is all that matters.'

As well as your fee for providing the cattle, thought Nastja. She turned away.

Dusk had fallen when she returned to the street. The busker was not there. Nastja panicked for a moment. Did this mean they would not get a meeting with the Sticasts? They must. Ellyah was desperate to sell the jewel, and this was their last chance.

As she strolled along, trying to look unconcerned, a hiss came from an alley mouth to her left. She half turned, slowing her stride. She saw a flash of pale, braided hair. The busker.

Her voice was clipped. 'Grain store. Street of Crows,' she whispered. 'Midnight.'

It was the address of this building.

Luara had stayed outside again as they had entered the dark warehouse. Nastja had glanced back as they crossed the open ground to the door, but even knowing where Luara must be hiding, she could not pick her out of the shadows.

Luara was very useful to have around. She moved quickly and silently when she needed to, and when she stayed still she could become almost invisible. Nastja truly believed that she and Ellyah, and the jewel, would have been captured by now, without Luara's strength and deadly grace.

The Sticasts broker was dressed in dark and shining leathers. He was older than they, his dark hair streaked with silver, but his shoulders were broad and his fists were heavy. Nastja would not want to fight this man.

'Let's see,' was all that he said as an introduction, and Ellyah had opened the box.

The red glow was unearthly and disquieting, especially now that Nastja had seen what it could do with a mere touch. The man's tanned face was bathed in that vivid crimson light, but he reacted with impassive stoicism.

'Interesting,' he said, slowly. Nastja fidgeted impatiently but kept her mouth shut. It was a redundant thing to say. They already knew how interested the Sticasts were from how eager they had been to arrange a meeting.

'Not common, that's for sure,' he continued. 'And we'd be interested in taking it off your hands. Five gold marks.'

Ellyah made a hissing sound. Then, she shut the box abruptly, plunging the dingy interior into sudden darkness.

'Come on, let's go,' she said, her voice hard. 'I didn't come all the way here to listen to a clown telling bad jokes.' She turned to leave, but the Sticasts' broker just laughed.

'Going to play that game, are we?'

Ellyah turned back. 'I'm not playing. I'm serious, and this is a serious merchandise. I know what it's worth, something this rare. And so do you.'

'How much?'

'Twelve gold marks,' said Ellyah, face blank and emotionless.

'Planning on buying the city afterwards?' scoffed the broker. 'Or buying out Ceolbaght and becoming governor?'

'No, but you could, if you wanted. I know how this place works. Where the power lies. And the wealth. You need this, even if it's to stop the...others getting it.'

The man frowned, but shrugged. 'Six marks, two pounds of silver.'

'Oh dear,' said Ellyah. 'Seems like you'd prefer that we made an offer to the Cyfres. Let's get out of here.'

She beckoned to Nastja and turned toward the door once more. Nastja was bewildered. If they left now, there was no-one else to turn to. They could not approach the Cyfres again.

Surely Ellyah must know that.

'Wait.' The broker's voice was a low growl in that darkened, quiet place. 'Eight gold, two silver.'

Ellyah swivelled her head, fixing the man with an icy stare. 'Ten gold marks or we walk away now.'

He shifted uneasily, jaw jutting.

'Do you want to go back to the rest of your rabble and tell them you're the reason the Cyfres have the ruby and you don't?' Her voice was dangerously sweet.

'Nine,' he said.

'Nine,' repeated Ellyah. 'And five pounds in silver rings. I need spending money for my journey away from this shithole.'

'Done,' he replied.

'And done,' agreed Ellyah. She put the box back in her bag. 'When?'

'Tomorrow night. Here. You two and the jewel. If we see, hear, or smell anyone else then the deal is off.'

Ellyah nodded. 'And if you Sticasts even think about trying to swindle us, we'll vanish forever, and us with it. Maybe you'll see it in the hands of the governor.'

Without waiting for a reply, Ellyah turned and strode toward the door. As she put her hand to the handle, he spoke again.

'Has anyone ever told you,' said the broker, 'That you're a really annoying bitch.'

Ellyah's smile was like cinnamon. 'Frequently.'

Then she breezed through the door and out into the night, with Nastja following.

'I don't trust them, Ell,' said Nastja once they had put a few streets between them and the warehouse. 'They will try something.'

'Of course they will,' replied Ellyah. 'I'd be amazed if they didn't. But who is smarter, Nas? Us, or them?'

'I don't know—' began Nastja, but Ellyah cut her off.

'It's us! We've been through worse and come out on top. We outwitted the Mackems all the way from Carhinn to here. We've avoided having our lives sucked out by that jewel, and are about to make our fortune from it. Right?'

Nastja felt that a lot of what they had done between Carhinn and here had needed a healthy portion of luck, and they could have very easily have ended up captured on a number of occasions. But she sensed that was not what Ellyah wanted to hear, at that moment. She nodded.

We're so close, Nas,' said Ellyah, and her voice was softer, warmer. 'One more night on the tips of our toes. One more night expecting a knife in our back, and we'll be free. We can vanish and they won't ever find us. Don't you want that?'

'Of course I want that,' replied Nastja. 'I'm just worried that we're going to walk into a trap.'

Ellyah nodded before throwing an arm around her shoulder. It was sudden and unexpected, and Nastja could not help flinching at the contact. Ellyah felt warm, and soft though. The scent of her body was difficult to ignore.

'I know,' Ellyah agreed. 'And we'll keep worrying until we walk away with our purses full of gold.'

Nastja twisted her face into what she hoped was an easy smile, and Ellyah took her hand. Together, they strolled through the shadowy streets.

At the intersection of two narrow alleyways, Ellyah paused. Something ahead seemed to have caught her eye. Stealthily, she moved forward and stared out into the open area beyond. Nastja joined her, and her eyes widened at what she saw beyond.

Before them was the city's central square. Other streets and alleys opened into the square from every direction, and an area of about a bowshot on all sides had been kept clear of buildings. During the day, it would be filled with barrows and temporary stalls as a bustling marketplace. At night, as it was surrounded by taverns and liquor-houses, it became an open-air temple to drinking, fighting and debauchery.

But, not tonight.

Tonight, the centre of the square was cordoned off with fences of pale, raw pine. Members of the militia stood around the perimeter, eyeing the nearby revellers with nervous vigilance. Behind them, craftsmen laboured on despite the lateness of the hour and the lack of light. Beneath their thudding hammers, structures were emerging.

Nastja gazed curiously at what was being built. Lightweight timber framing formed the shapes of a whole village of houses.

Thin, pale linen was being stretched over these frames and tacked into place. A new settlement, in bright white. Each of the houses stood on a platform with staves that protruded front and back, as if they were intended to be carried like a litter.

'I've heard of this,' whispered Nastja, mouth close to Ellyah's ear as they both observed the strange scene. 'It's part of the Demonsnight festival. They build these houses and tomorrow they are going to set them on fire.'

'What? Why?'

Nastja shrugged. 'Fire and flame to scare the demons away. I think they used to put torches to houses they thought were cursed. I guess that gets a bit expensive, especially as all the other houses here are in dry wood.'

Ellyah laughed, but Nastja had not been joking.

'Maybe once we've sold the jewel tomorrow we can spend some of our new money on a good feed and a jug of fine wine, then watch the show.'

Nastja smiled once more, weakly, but she had a feeling that their work tomorrow night would not be so straightforward.

The door of Fion's tavern had barely closed behind them when Fion herself grabbed Ellyah by the arm.

'You,' she commanded, without preamble. 'Get an apron. I need you cleaning tables and carrying drinks. Now.' Ellyah's face hardened but Fion ruled her place with an iron fist, so none of them dared to speak against her. Besides, they still owed her. Ellyah scurried away.

'And you,' added Fion, turning briskly toward Nastja. 'I'll need you in a few hours. Don't go anywhere. And I'll need you both all night tomorrow. Demonsnight is one of the busiest of the year. They'll be packed in tight before the fire run.'

We can't work tomorrow night. The words formed on Nastja's lips, but she thought of how Ellyah would react, and merely nodded. She hurried across the bustling, rowdy saloon of the tavern and her boots tapped a rapid rhythm on the steep stairs.

Luara looked up as she entered the poky garret room. She let out a deep breath and smiled broadly.

'Here you are then!' she said, standing and moving toward Nastja. She opened her arms slightly, as if contemplating an embrace, but stopped short. 'How did it go? Where's Ell?'

'We got an offer. Nine gold marks and five pounds of silver.' Nastja sat and began to wriggle her sore feet from her boots. 'Fion collared Ell downstairs. Got her at work already.'

'She drives herself and everyone around her so hard. It's her way of forgetting.'

Nastja slumped back in her seat. Did she mean Fion, or Ellyah? 'Forgetting what?'

Luara wrinkled her nose, as if thinking. 'Her life didn't turn out the way she thought it would,' she said, after a thoughtful pause. 'She always believed she'd have a settled, stable life, with a husband and children. That was stolen from her, and she still grieves.'

'Oh.' Nastja digested this information. 'Like you?' she asked, and Luara's head snapped around.

'What?' Her eyes were wide, a shocked expression on her face.

'You said that Fion wanted a family,' explained Nastja. 'And I think things might be similar for you.'

Nastja was not sure how she knew, but she had been thinking about Luara during their journey, and wondering why she was the way she was. Why she was with them at all. She had clearly suffered loss, and known sadness in her past, and the way she had described Fion had been with deep understanding.

'How could you know that?' asked Luara. Nastja was surprised to see that her face had crumpled and that her eyes were swimming with tears.

'The way you talk about Fion is as if you know how she feels. You don't like being alone, and you like to keep busy. You're distracting yourself from sadness, just like Fion.'

Luara looked like she had just been slapped. Her mouth was open as if about to argue, or shout, or simply break down in tears. Instead, after a few moments, she sighed.

'Maybe you're right,' she said, her voice full of resignation. 'But, I don't know another way. Being with you two on this journey seemed to push all the memories away…the thought of being alone again…I couldn't bear it, Nastja.'

Nastja got the feeling that there was something that Luara wanted to say. Needed to say. Sometimes people skirted around their problems, but what they really wanted was the opportunity to speak of them, and have someone listen.

'What happened?' she asked. Luara dabbed her eyes with the hem of her vest.

'I met someone. A man. Gods! He was handsome. And honest—a silk merchant. Not like us.' She laughed. 'It all seemed to happen really quickly. I put away my swords and moved into his fine house, overlooking the lake. I didn't miss this life at all, Nas. I was suddenly happy. Truly happy. We both were.'

She tailed off, eyes dropping to stare down at the floor. Nastja sensed that she needed one more push to say what she needed to say. The painful part was still unsaid.

'What happened?' she repeated.

'I fell pregnant,' said Luara, matter-of-factly. 'It was what I had secretly hoped for, and as I grew I felt more and more complete. We were both so full of joy. There was suddenly more love in my life than I knew could exist. But…' She tailed off.

Nastja stayed silent this time. She could see now that the secret grief that Luara bore was near the surface. This was her story to tell, in her own way.

'Near the end, something went wrong. I could feel it, but I pretended I couldn't. I just kept smiling to him, and trying to fool myself. The babe in my belly had kicked and wriggled, but when it was nearly his time he slowed…and stopped.

'He was born sleeping, Nastja,' said Luara, in an artificially calm tone. 'My beautiful boy never woke up. I never got to meet him. Never got to watch him grow.'

'I'm so sorry,' said Nastja, and truly meant it. To bear a child for all that time and then to find out that they had died before birth must be the saddest thing. 'Didn't you try again?'

Luara laughed, a short bitter bark.

'I was damaged goods, Nas. He said he still loved me, and that we would try again. That we would always have each other. But he did what all men do when they can't get what they want. He went somewhere else.'

'Another woman?'

'Of course. A younger version with broad hips and a ripe belly. I didn't wait around to see them together. I left and did not look back. Walked away. That's how I ended up in Anish.'

'That's very sad,' said Nastja, making her voice soft so that Luara would know she was sincere. 'I'm happy we met you though.'

'Me too,' Luara smiled again. 'The past is part of my story, but it made me realise that I couldn't wait for my idea of a perfect life just to come along. I needed to make the most of now.'

'You have been really useful to us.'

'I do my best,' said Luara, inclining her head. 'It's been a good adventure. I can't wait to see what happens next.'

Nastja frowned. 'I'm worried. I'm scared we're going to walk into a trap.'

'Probably. But if anyone can spring a trap and walk away with the cheese, it's you two. When?'

'Tomorrow night.'

Luara raised an eyebrow. 'Demonsnight.'

'Yes,' replied Nastja.

Everything would be decided on Demonsnight.

FORTY ONE

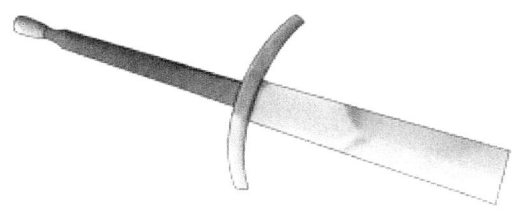

It must have been past midnight. The light had faded away, leaving the storeroom in pitch darkness. Pale slivers crept around the gaps between the ill-fitting door and the frame but only deepened the shadows within.

The other Cyfres had spat abuse at Eain for a while but had gradually tailed off when Eain refused to respond. He seemed to be sleeping now.

The wait made Eain worry. What if he had been wrong? He would die.

There was no way of knowing if the Sticasts would let him live, though, even if they found his information of use. Eain felt his chances of surviving the night slipping away with each moment that passed. He fretted as time crawled.

When the door eventually opened, the brightness was a dazzling shock. Eain raised his bound hands to shield his eyes, while the sleeping man beside him grunted as he stirred.

The broad, blond-haired Sticast was framed in the doorway.

'Up,' he said. 'Come.'

Eain nudged the other Cyfres in the ribs, nodding his head toward the doorway when they grumbled sleepily. They both staggered to their feet and shuffled through.

The room beyond was much larger, and well lit. Despite the late hour, it was full of people and Eain glimpsed leering, sneering faces as they were ushered through and toward one of the far corners.

This room was sparsely furnished, bare wooden floorboards and uncovered walls glowing a rusty orange in the flicker of the rushlights. Simple benches and chairs were strewn haphazardly across the floor and held Sticasts drinking, dicing and arm wrestling. Wine flowed from barrels stood on rickety trestle tables. The barrels from the docks.

The blond leader led them to a table, and a few other gang members stood up as guards for Eain and the other Cyfres. Eain shifted uneasily as the man stared at them. Was he about to be killed, right here?

Eventually, he spoke. 'Seems it's your lucky day. Your information was good. It's going to let us get ahead of the Cyfres and this outlander gang.'

'I spoke true,' said Eain. 'I have no love for Cyfres, or the outlanders.'

'So you say,' said the Sticast, looking from Eain to the other Cyfres, then back. 'Question is…what do we do with you now? I can't let you go, not knowing what you do. But, I can't trust you. See my problem?'

'Can you trust anyone?' asked Eain, bitterly.

The Sticast laughed. 'True. But I hold the longer knife here. You're the one in the worse position.'

Eain stared at him. His bonds were tied tightly. The chances of him fighting his way out were non-existent. He truly believed that this Sticast would kill him rather than let him escape.

He could only see one option.

'Let me join you,' he said, speaking quickly. 'I'll prove I care nothing for Cyfres, and join the Sticasts. I'll swear any oaths. I can be useful to you.'

The Sticast glared at him for a few moments more, then his face broke into a sneering grin.

'I'll give you the chance to prove yourself,' he said, with undisguised glee. 'But Sticasts don't swear oaths, right?' He lifted his head and looked around at the gathering crowd, who responded with chuckling disdain. 'Sticasts are fighters,' he went on. 'To earn the right to join us you've got to fight. You've got to fight, and kill.'

'Fight? Kill?' Eain was surprised. 'Who?'

The leader did not reply, but turned his gaze to the other Cyfres.

'Two Cyfres enter the square. The one who lives will have earned our trust.'

Eain kept his face blank, but his insides churned. He knew he should have expected this. Bloodshed and death seemed second nature to these people. There was no honour in this dirty city. Once more he had no choice, and told himself that if he survived he would do everything he could to disrupt their plans.

'When?' he asked.

'Right now,' replied the blond Sticast. 'Clear a space! Mark the square!'

Eain was shoved out of the way as the gathered Sticasts moved quickly to push the benches and chairs to the edges of the room. A pale white rock was dragged along the floor in four straight lines to mark a wide square on the floorboards.

It was all done with practised ease. Soon, an eager crowd was gathered, and the guards were loosening the cords that bound Eain and the other Cyfres'.

'Give 'em their weapons,' said the leader, before striding forward into the square. 'We all know the way,' he cried to the crowd, pacing around in the cleared space like a feral dog patrolling its territory. 'Two step in, one walks out. The other will be carried away. The way of the blade!'

The crowd called back. 'The way of the blade!'

Eain found his hands free, and the hilt of his seax was thrust into one of them. He wriggled his fingers and rolled his wrists, trying to ease the stiffness. The Cyfres clutched a broad, straight knife and eyed Eain as he licked his lips.

The leader turned to face them. 'Once you step into the square, the only way out is to win. To lose means death. To try to escape, like a coward, means death. It's simple. Bring them in!' he called to the guards.

One of the guards shoved Eain hard in the back, and he resisted the urge to lash out in retribution. Instead, he stepped forward and crossed the daubed line. He had entered the square. Now, there was no turning back.

The other Cyfres had stepped inside too, backing away toward the other side. He seemed oblivious to the spitting and jeering crowd that surrounded him on all sides. His brutal, heavy knife was held close to his forearm, and his blue eyes were fixed on Eain's face.

Eain suddenly felt nervous. Fighting short blade against short blade was not something he had spent much time training. His seax was intended as a backup weapon, and for fighting in spaces too constricted to swing a greatsword.

What if he lost?

He danced back as his opponent lashed out, a horizontal cut toward Eain's chest. A backhanded thrust followed and Eain swivelled out of the way. He struck back, but his opponent had already dodged.

Their build was compact and wiry, and Eain knew not to underestimate their skill and speed. He circled while thinking hard, staying out of range while he planned his own attack. What were his advantages? He was used to being able to use the reach and deceptive speed of a greatsword against any other armed opponent. He did not have that advantage here.

The Cyfres rushed in, blade moving rapidly as he tested Eain's defence. Eain swayed, raising his forearm to bat the attack away. At the same time, he swung his longer, slimmer seax toward his opponent.

He aimed low, trying to beat any parry, but the man dropped his left arm and blocked the strike. For a moment they remained in that position, locked together. Eain could smell the Cyfres' sour breath in his face, and feel the desperate strength in his arms.

They sprang away from each other in synchrony. Stepping back, Eain made sure he was out of the reach of that flashing blade.

'Stick him!' bellowed a man stood at Eain's right shoulder. 'Stick the Cyfres scum!' Eain was not sure which of them he was shouting at.

'Bite him! Bite him!' shouted another, with rabid enthusiasm.

The Cyfres attacked again, catching Eain by surprise. He ducked one way, then the other. Not quickly enough. A sharp, red sting of pain tore across his left bicep. The keen edge of the Cyfres knife sliced through his coat and into his flesh.

He ground his teeth. The cut was not deep. He could fight on, but he needed to be more careful. He was taller, and his arms were longer. He spread them wide, the seax held outstretched. Now, any attack the Cyfres made would meet the point of a blade first.

They circled warily. The Cyfres had drawn first blood, but could see the threat Eain posed. It was a well-matched contest.

The crowd was jeering and stamping their feet as Eain lunged forward again. The Cyfres batted it away and countered. Eain barely managed to dodge, stepping backward rapidly.

The Cyfres fighter followed. He slashed, left and right, not aiming to cut but to force Eain to retreat. In a moment, Eain's heels were at the white line on the floor. Wine-stinking breath hissed in his ear, and the points of the Sticasts' knives pricked at his back.

He could not go back any further. The leader had said that to leave the circle was to die, and Eain believed it.

He rolled his shoulders down, ducking, twisting and flinging himself to the side. This was desperation. He shouldered past the Cyfres, trying to push him aside with pure strength, but as he surged away he felt another sharp lash of pain across his back.

He grunted as he staggered to the other side of the square. He was losing. He could die here. He needed a new plan, and quickly.

Turning, he gathered his resolve and faced the Cyfres. He needed to concentrate absolutely to make this work.

Warding away retaliatory blows with his left hand, he slashed and stabbed at his opponent. They dodged, parried and evaded his attacks, but stepped back toward the edge of the square.

As Eain expected, that was the point where his opponent turned defence into attack. His blade whistled out, scything through the air close to Eain's nose. Eain's head snapped back as he stepped away, but then he…tripped.

His shoulders twisted as he staggered, almost falling as he headed for the line on the other side of the square. His arms were spread, waving madly as he sought balance.

The Cyfres' footsteps grew louder as he approached, rushing in to deal the killing blow to Eain's unprotected back. Eain could almost feel the cruel point of the knife as it cleaved the air.

At the last moment, Eain recovered from his feigned stumble. He shifted his body to the side and as he glanced down, the cold, grey length of the knife slid past his ribs. The Cyfres' hand followed and Eain clamped down with his left arm, trapping it in his armpit.

He half turned, and the Cyfres could not resist as his body was twisted. Eain's seax felt heavy in his hand.

'Stick him! Stick him!' roared the crowd. The moment stretched as Eain continued to turn. 'No mercy in the square! Stick him good!' Even as Eain raised his blade, the bloodlust of the crowd sickened him.

The words of Morgan Blane haunted him once more, echoing from the past. 'Strength of will is a man's greatest ally. Never accept defeat without a fight.'

He had fought. Had he the strength of will to take the victory?

The Cyfres' eyes were wide as he watched the blade moving closer.

'What matters now,' the Cyfres leader had said. 'Is what you can do, and what you will do. Nothing else is important.'

Stick him! Stick him! Stick him!

'You'll never be hard enough. You'll never be strong enough.' Morgan Blane's voice rang in Eain's mind once more. 'You will hesitate in the moments when you need to act without mercy. You will fail.'

The words of the Eacnung Cyfres and Morgan Blane seemed to twist into one another, mingling in the depths of his mind. They mocked him, belittled him. He hated them.

Eain's lip curled and he thrust the blade forward. He felt a slightly resistance as the tip pierced his opponent's tunic, but then he drove it home into the Cyfres' heart.

His mouth gaped soundlessly and his eyes bulged. Eain withdrew the blade and let his opponent fall. He stared down, dispassionately, as the Cyfres' movements slowed, and then stopped as bright blood darkened the floorboards around his body.

Maybe now, he was the man Morgan Blane wanted him to be. One who did what was necessary and did not fear the consequences. A warrior. A survivor. A killer.

The cheers and roars continued, an animalistic, wordless drone that assaulted Eain's ears. He hated them all.

'A winner!' proclaimed the blond leader, strutting into the ring. He paused beside Eain and reached out a hand, as if to clap him on the shoulder, before glimpsing Eain's expression and pulling his hand back.

'The way of the blade!' he cried, and the crowd bawled the words back drunkenly. 'A new Sticast is born. We honour his blade and the blood he has spilled. Let's drink!'

As the room whirled with a chaos of noise and movement, a new figure approached Eain and the blond leader. It was the dark-haired older man that Eain had met the earlier that night. The man he assumed to be the blond Sticast's father.

'You,' he said, moving to stand close. 'You fought well. Cleverly. The way of the blade.'

He was a big, broad man, only a couple of inches shorter than Eain. He was carrying a little fat around his middle but looked very strong.

He leaned in close. 'Your information was sound. Useful. It's going to put us in a good spot. Glad to have you on our side.'

Eain had nothing to say, so simply nodded.

'The deal will happen tomorrow night. Demonsnight. Should be plenty of distractions around, so we can move easily through the streets. I want you to help.'

He lowered his voice so that he was not overheard.

'We'll do the deal, and take the merchandise, but when our two little girls have taken the money we'll jump them and take it back. I want you there to make sure it's done. A big lad like you will scare them into accepting whatever we offer them. They can't escape.'

Eain ground his teeth. Inside, his guts roiled with sickness and fear. How had he ended up in this desperate place, surrounded by those with no honour? The blond man mimed drawing a knife across his throat.

'The way of the blade,' he said, gleefully.

'The way of the blade,' repeated his father.

Evane Claes woke. She blinked uncertainly, wanting to be sure she was truly awake. Her recent dreams had been full of fear and pain, and she was often uncertain which were punishments inflicted by her demonic master, and which were tortures created by her own mind.

She could not go on like this.

Lifting her head slightly, she shivered as waves of fatigue scoured her body. She knew she was on the very brink of collapse.

The Mackems had been in Ben Gedrin for a couple of weeks since she had last made contact. There had been no choice but to trust them to search for the jewel using their own stealth and discretion; she did not have the strength to intervene. Her power had been drained and it was taking longer and longer to recover.

Tomorrow, however, she would try once more. Tomorrow was Demonsnight in Ben Gedrin and so it seemed an apt time to put the last of her energy into obtaining the jewel. Clayton Moore would walk again, and would point the way.

At the thought of Moore, something repeated in her memory. Last night, as she lay on her cot in a state of exhaustion… something had happened. Something undefinable had tugged on the edge of her consciousness. Something…new.

She could not find enough focus to pin down what it was. Perhaps nothing. Her mind was foggy these days.

She slumped back onto her meagre pillows and prayed to Desya that her sleep would be restorative. She would need all her strength tomorrow night.

For Demonsnight.

FORTY TWO

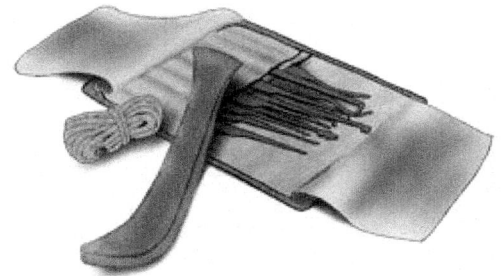

The flicker of flames cast shifting shadows onto the walls of the alleyway. Ellyah hurried along toward the warehouse, Nastja and Luara bustling along in her wake.

Tonight. They would finally escape Ben Gedrin, weighed down by a new fortune. And they would do it tonight.

Bonfires had been lit all through the city as the night fell, the streets busy with people bearing torches, lanterns and candles. Drummers hammered out crazy rhythms. The flames would scare away with demons and guarantee a good harvest. This was the reason for Demonsnight.

Ellyah would like to see the model houses go up in flames and the fire-bulls chased through the streets, but they had no time to stand around and watch. They had got the Sticasts interest and had to close the deal before the Mackems or the Cyfres interfered.

She strode confidently down a narrow passage, the last alley before a strip of open ground in front of the warehouse. Excitement bubbled through her. She had known, from the moment that she heard the rumour in Carhinn about the Mackems' valuable acquisition, that it could be the job that defined her.

And she was so nearly there. She had outwitted the Mackems repeatedly and was about to outwit two other bunches of crooks.

Crooks who thought they controlled everything. She would defeat them all.

Fear fluttered within her too, but she ignored it. Worry was no use, this plan just had to work.

A small hand tapped her shoulder lightly. She turned.

'We should check we aren't walking into a trap,' said Nastja, in an urgent whisper. Her face showed worry. 'There could be an army hidden around these alleys.' She indicted the many dark voids, opening onto the area before the warehouse. Gaping mouths. Sightless eyes.

'And we could waste a lot of time checking them all,' replied Ellyah, with patience, although they had been over this many times already. 'Luara will be watching out. She knows what to do.'

Luara nodded. 'Go well, hens,' she said, with a tight smile, before slipping off into some deeper shadows. Clothed in dark colours and hooded, she was almost invisible.

Ellyah reached out and found Nastja's hand with her own. She gave it a brief squeeze. 'Together, hen,' she said, and was rewarded with a quick smile.

Ellyah led the way across to the solid, squat warehouse, with Nastja following. The uncomfortable sensation of watching eyes prickled between her shoulder blades, but she dismissed it. She was just on edge.

Pushing the door open, she edged inside.

The interior of the storage space was pitch black. She stepped forward carefully, navigating between piled boxes and barrels from memory. There was a rustling noise behind her, and a few moments later a warm glow shone out, casting the edges of the room into deeper gloom.

She turned to see Nastja holding a lit candle lantern. She only carried a small pack, but it seemed to fit an astonishing array of useful things inside.

'They are already late,' she said, face bathed in flickering light.

'They'll be here,' replied Ellyah. 'We have what they want. Be patient.'

They waited.

Moments passed, uncounted heartbeats of anxious stillness. Would they come?

There was the sound of scratching near the door, and after sharing a glance with Nastja, Ellyah shrank back into the shadows. She would be gone out of the rear door at the first sign of trickery.

Ducking her head, she watched carefully.

The door opened and the broad, dark haired Sticast leader entered. Following behind was another man in the same fighting leathers, but with very fair hair that shone white in the lamplight.

One, two. Two was fine and did not signify a double-cross. Then, another figure entered, stooping beneath the low lintel.

Ellyah gazed at him. His skin was an unusual golden hue, but his eyes were pale and gleamed coldly as he gazed impassively around the room. Ellyah was tall for a woman, but this man would overtop her by half a foot or more, and the breadth of his shoulders made him seem to loom over the scene. The long hilt of a sword protruded over his shoulder.

Nastja's eyes must have betrayed her surprise at his entrance, as the broker turned to her.

'He is just our guard,' he said, motioning for the tall man to stand back. 'You don't have to worry about him. Now,' he said, peering around the room expectantly. 'Where's the jewel?'

'Where's the payment?' Nastja's voice was shrill, but emotionless. The leader tapped the blond Sticast on the arm, and he set a heavy sack down on the nearest crate. The unmistakeable clink of money was crisp and loud in the quiet of the warehouse.

'It's all there,' said the broker, belligerently. 'Now, your turn.'

Her eyes fixed on the bulging sacks, Ellyah stepped forward into the light. She could feel their stares on her, and on the bag she carried.

'Let's see.' The elder Sticast's voice was croaky, expectant.

Not trusting herself to speak, Ellyah peeled the strap from her shoulder and set the pack down. She made sure to stay a few paces away from the men, standing behind Nastja's left shoulder.

Willing her hands to remain steady, she dipped into the pack and slowly withdrew the wooden box. Such a simple box. The basic carpentry betrayed nothing of the mysterious and valuable item that lay within.

Her fingers felt clumsy as they undid the latches. Then, tenderly as peeling away a lover's clothing, she opened the lid.

As before, eldritch crimson light bathed the room. The Sticasts' avaricious faces were cast into stark, scarlet relief and their eyes glowed with reflected red. Ellyah noticed that the tall guard was also staring, but with curious interest and perhaps…fear?

She shut the lid. The moment passed. The Sticasts' eyes were hard and considering once more.

'The deal is done?' said the broker, the hint of a question in his voice. Ellyah was suddenly reluctant. She had carried that precious cargo for so long, she was saddened by the thought of surrendering it. The ruby had been her great secret, valuable knowledge that only she possessed.

The weighty bulk of the sacks caught her eye once more. Escape. That was all that she had ever wanted, and it was what those bags promised. She stepped forward.

'You have been wise,' she said, as she handed the box across. It was always best to leave the other feeling they had got the best end of any deal. You never knew when your paths might cross again. She could not hold back a smile.

She moved toward the sacks, but a soft noise from toward the door caught her attention.

The blond Sticast was sinking to his knees. His eyes bulged, and his broad hands were at his throat. Bright blood oozed between his fingers and ran slickly down to his chest. The tall guard stood behind him, a long and bloody knife in his hand.

'No!' gasped the leader, turning. His hand was dropping to the knife at his waist. He had time to do no more than turn before the guard was on him too. He thrust forward, stabbing the bulky broker through the heart. He collapsed bloodily to the floor, with barely a sound.

Nastja was backing away, and Ellyah stared in horror as the huge killer now turned toward them.

'Do not worry,' he said. 'I won't hurt you. This was a trap.' His voice was surprisingly soft, and tinted with an accent that Ellyah could not place. His consonants were clipped, and his vowels were elongated. His words were clear enough, though.

'They planned to kill you once you handed over the jewel,' he continued. 'They just wanted to check it was not a fake first. These were bad men. Bad people are everywhere, in this city.'

'We had this under control—' began Ellyah. This was not how she planned this, and now she did not know what to think.

'No,' he interrupted. 'You did not. They have many fighters nearby. Even if you had escaped this building, you would not get away.'

'And you're going to save the day?' Ellyah's stomach fluttered, and she felt her annoyance growing.

'Go out the back. I will go out the front and distract them. I'll say you're already dead. I can show them the box for proof. Take the money and go. Get far from here, quickly!'

Ellyah said nothing, but inside she was fuming. This was all wrong.

'Ell, he's right,' put in Nastja. 'He saved our lives and he's giving us a way to escape. Let's go.'

Nastja did not mention that she had repeatedly warned of this being a trap, and for that Ellyah was grudgingly grateful.

'Fine,' she said, eventually. She reached out and lifted the heavy sacks, stuffing them into her pack where the box had been.

'We need to find Luara too,' added Nastja.

Luara, of course. They needed to find Luara on the way. They would probably need her help again this night, if they were to escape.

As they turned to dash toward the back door, the tall stranger was opening the front door. In the rush, Ellyah had barely noticed him picking up the jewel's box and stowing it in his own pack.

Luara Orsini was on edge.

She had spent most of the last few months on high alert. She had tried not to show any of her concerns to the two girls, and it had mostly been exciting. The feeling that the unknown was around every corner had been a welcome distraction.

This was suddenly different. This felt dangerous.

She had tucked herself into a dark and overshadowed corner as Ellyah and Nastja entered the warehouse. Still hidden, she had watched the three Sticasts follow them in. One of them towered over the others and was openly carrying a long sword across his back. That was interesting.

Otherwise, so far this was all going according to plan.

Then, something worrying happened. The gentle patter of creeping feet reached her ears through the still evening air. A group of people were moving, and they were nearby. As she watched, barely daring to breathe, a number of figures in tunics moved across her vision to hide themselves in alley mouths around the warehouse. Cyfres. Were Ellyah and Nastja about to walk out into an ambush?

She thought fast. She could not fight so many. Maybe she could sneak around and get into the building from the rear? She had to warn them somehow. They would walk out into a thicket of knives if she did nothing.

She had to try.

The Cyfres had moved into positions overlooking the warehouse, around the perimeter of the open ground. She should be able to go backwards and then move around behind them. She would need to be absolutely silent.

Inch by careful inch, she eased herself from her hiding place beneath the low, overhanging eaves of a closed-up workshop. With light, silent steps she crept backwards until she was out in the alley. Now, she had to find a way to work around to the rear of the darkened building where Ellyah and Nastja would be trapped.

She turned. She stopped, dead.

Plodding steadily toward her with mechanical, ponderous steps, was a vision of nightmare. She stepped back in involuntary disgust.

Clothes that were torn, and in some places rotten, flapped loosely around a man-shaped frame. Rents in the dirty fabric revealed skin that was a greyish-green and putrid; the flesh of a long-dead corpse.

The creature's face was a ruin. Skin sloughed away from the pale bones of its skull in several places, and its lack of lips twisted its expression into a morbid grin.

Every instinct told her to run, and yet she was transfixed by its eyes. They burned with an unworldly red gleam.

She thought back to the same colour light glaring from the crate in Kereva, and before that, in the attic room in Carhinn…the jewel.

This thing was following the jewel.

She did not understand how, but suddenly it made sense. The jewel was calling to it, somehow. And if it interrupted the negotiations at the warehouse, everything could be ruined.

She reached her decision in a heartbeat. Her swords were already drawn, hissing from their sheaths in a blur. She lunged at the beast.

A thrust to its chest hit home. The creature did not make any attempt to block or dodge the strike, and the blade slipped between its ribs to the hilt. The creature did not slow its ponderous march, but raised one of its rotting fists to swipe at her.

Luara withdrew the blade and leapt back, evading the clumsy blow. Surely, it could be killed. The red, glowing eyes. That had to be it.

Lunging forward once more, she slashed one of her swords across its decaying throat. The blade cut deeply, but no blood spilled, and she felt it bite into the beast's spine. She swung the other, putting all her strength into the blow. There was a soft, metallic jolt as the blades touched. Greenish slime oozed across the gleaming metal.

The creature's head leered to one side, then toppled from its shoulders, flesh and bone both cleaved through. Luara looked down as the head rolled to a stop. The vivid red glow in its eyes faded, and was gone. The street darkened as those crimson lights went out.

A moment later, the gangrenous body also slumped sideways and fell to the street with a dull, wet thump.

As she looked up, she noticed for the first time that the other end of the alley was filled with people. They had been following that creature, and were looking straight at her, frozen in shock.

She opened her eyes wide, gazing into the darkness as she wondered how much they had seen. She noticed that one of them was freakishly tall. He must have been nearly seven feet in height, and Luara recognised him instantly. She recognised them all. It was the Mackems.

This could turn into a disaster...unless. An idea sprang into Luara's mind, and she turned and fled. The Mackems followed, as she had thought they would, chasing her out toward the warehouse.

Once she was halfway across the open space, she turned. Flinging out an arm, she pointed with one of her swords.

'It's a trap!' she shouted at the top of her lungs. 'You are surrounded! Look around!'

It made no sense, really. The Cyfres were not there for the Mackems, but her words were enough to make the Mackems pause their pursuit and turn. Likewise, the Cyfres saw the threat and began to melt from the shadows and out into the open.

Weapons were drawn. The two gangs glared at each other. The light was dim but the moons and stars shone down. The two groups slowed.

Luara turned and ran again. If she could get to the back door of the warehouse, maybe she could help Luara and Nastja.

As she reached the corner of the building, the front door opened. Luara kept running but glanced toward the door. A tall figure was emerging, with a long sword and a bulging pack strapped across his back. The same fighter she had seen going on, only now he was alone.

As he emerged, many other eyes turned toward him.

Luara kept running.

FORTY THREE

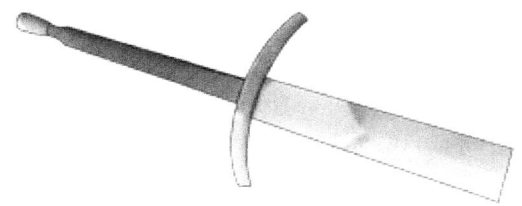

Eain Connow ran.

It had taken him a few confused moments to get the measure of what he was seeing when he stepped out of the warehouse door, but as his eyes adjusted he had picked out the distinctive tunics of the Cyfres.

They seemed to be facing off with another group, but Eain did not take the time to identify them. He just needed to escape.

He did something that he knew that he could still do better than most; he ran. He ran as though the wolves of winter were at his heels.

The Sticasts had planned for something like this, though, and the rest of the gang were nearby. The district to the east, near the central square, was home to many low taverns and they had set themselves up in one of the lowest. All were armed, and ready to fight if the jewel trade turned out to be a trap.

They would have no idea that it was Eain himself who had set up and sprung the trap.

His boots slapped on the packed dirt of the narrow street as he ran east in the direction of the square. He could hear the pursuit behind him, but they would not catch him.

His sword was a comforting weight on his back. He knew that if the militia caught him with such a weapon in the city, he would be fined or imprisoned. But they would not catch him this night.

The blond Sticast, Roodwin, had been delighted by the idea of retrieving Eain's sword, when he had suggested it.

'Yes!' he had cried. 'Our guardsman should be properly armed. The way of the blade!'

They had bribed the guards of the weapons store near the gate, and smuggled the long blade away wrapped in a bundle of firewood.

He did not admit to the real reason for recovering his sword, which was that he knew he would need to escape the city quickly, whichever way his plan went.

He sprinted out onto a broader street, looking ahead to where he knew the tavern lay.

The central square was at the end of the street, and Eain could see the glow of bonfires lighting up the night sky. The sounds of celebration reached his ears, with pounding of drums and the sound of voices singing a loud counterpoint to the thrum of many people talking. Even this street, away from the focus of the festivities, was thronged with people.

Snatches of song and loud conversation were all around him as he pushed through the crowds. The stink of unwashed bodies and the bitter tang of spilled ale and wine made him feel dizzy. His chest heaved with the exertion of the run.

Raised voices behind him told of the Cyfres forces driving through the same crowds as they sought to catch him. He had to reach the Sticasts.

Then, there they were. The open front of a bawdy tavern was suddenly before him, and a host of leather-clad fighters were gathered around the door. Most seemed deep in drink already.

One of them looked up as Eain approached.

'Where are Roodwalaed and Roodwin?' he asked, naming the leader and his son. In response, Eain simply shook his head. At the same moment, shouts of alarm and shock split the air. The Cyfres were closing in.

'Let's make these posh bastards pay!' roared the Sticast as he drew a long, serrated knife. 'The way of the blade!'

They surged out of the tavern and down the street, the crowd parting fearfully before them.

Eain followed a step behind, noticing how quickly the street had emptied. The lawful people of Ben Gedrin had seen fights between Cyfres and Sticasts before and wanted no part in it this night.

Then, the air was split anew with grunts and cries as the charging lines of the two gangs met. Both had been ready for violence and had brought as many of their best and most savage fighters as they could muster. In the burnished, flickering half-light, the fighting was brutal.

Two fighters collided and went down at Eain's feet. Hands bearing cruel blades rose and fell mercilessly. Both grunted in pain as the steel pierced the flesh, over and over. Blood ran, thick and black, and soon both lay still.

A Sticast grappled with a struggling Cyfres, nearby. As Eain watched, the Sticast pivoted the Cyfres on his arm, before reaching around to slit his throat. The gore was like crimson rain. So red, so dark.

Eain was determined that he would not die here. He was certain that the jewel did not belong in the hands of any of these people.

He drew his sword.

The grip was thick, made for big or very strong hands, and while it did not have a greatsword's length or reach it was a heavy and powerful weapon. He lifted it up.

He just needed to survive this nightmare.

Without conscious though, he raised the sword high above his head. Kell's stance. A ready stance. His eyes darted, watching for the threats. There were many.

A slender Cyfres in a dark tunic charged forward. They swung a short-hafted wood axe, but before they had covered half the distance, Eain stepped forward. His blade dropped down behind his back and swung back up in front of him swiftly; Rule One. The simple attack caught his opponent completely by surprise and they were run through on the broad blade before they were close enough to bring their axe to bear.

Eain tipped the blade to let the body slide off and turned, moving smoothly into the position of Rule Two. His blade moved in a blurring figure-of-eight, chopping down another Cyfres that he had barely noticed approaching. Not with his conscious mind, in any case. Blood spurted, dark in the dim light.

He felt nothing. These people were nothing. They had exerted their strength on the innocent of this city for too long, and they deserved this retribution.

All around, Sticasts and Cyfres were fighting and dying, and he could not find any way to care.

Something was wrong, however.

The Demonsnight revellers had flooded from the street, but as Eain looked in that direction, over his shoulder, he noticed that where it led into the main square was now lined with dark shapes.

He stepped back from the fighting and looked closer. He could make out the dull gleam of black leather armour, and each figure wore a round iron cap and bore a short spear. It was the militia.

Another Cyfres lunged at him with a club, and Eain dodged aside, almost absent-mindedly, before striking down with the powerful diagonal cuts of Rule Three. At the other end of the street, behind the Cyfres, Eain noticed another line of militia, shoulder to shoulder, and next to them he recognised the huge, dark-skinned bandit from Feorhryc.

He stared in incomprehension, but suddenly it all made sense. The militia captain must have learned that both the Cyfres and Sticasts would be out in force this night and had allied his militia with the outlander bandits to trap them all. And destroy them.

The realisation filled Eain with fear.

It did not matter how many Cyfres he killed, if the militia would just sweep in afterwards. He could see that they were many, and were in strong defensive positions, blocking the escape routes. He could not fight his way through alone.

He would be trapped with the rest, and even if he survived he would be treated like any other gang criminal. The jewel would be taken away with his freedom.

Another Cyfres attacked him, wielding a short, stabbing sword. Rule Five had his broad, weighty sword stabbing out in a powerful thrust that took his attacker's throat. He fell, clapping his hand to the gaping wound as his lifeblood cascaded over his pale fingers.

He needed to get out of here.

The rear of the warehouse was even darker than the front. Sheds and storehouses loomed on all sides, blocky, featureless and black.

The sky was a deep shade of indigo blue, decorated with an uncountable multitude of cold, glittering jewels. The twin crescents of the moons hovered, low on the horizon. Demonseye moons. Ellyah looked up and shuddered. It was an evil omen to be in the sky on Demonsnight.

Nastja's face was full of worry in the pale, milky light cast by the thin slices of the moons. Her eyes darted.

'We've got to get away, quickly,' she gasped. 'They will be looking for us. They'll look here soon, I know it.' Ellyah ignored her frantic fretting as she peered around, trying to decide on the best direction.

At that moment, she heard running feet, getting closer. Ellyah drew her belt knife. A dark shape flew around the corner, a long blade flashing in each hand.

'It's me! It's me!' panted Luara, before they could sink their knives into her. 'We have to go. Now. We have to run.'

Her usually bright and cheerful face was drawn and lined with worry. She darted past them, toward the other end of the warehouse. They followed.

'What's happening?' demanded Ellyah, in a forceful hiss.

'No time to explain,' called Luara over her shoulder. 'Keep your eyes open. Follow me.'

Ellyah had to hurry to keep up as Luara strode out from the behind the building and into the open. She pointed straight ahead, and started striding away in that direction, but Ellyah's attention was drawn to the open ground in front of the warehouse, away to their left.

Two groups of fighters were facing off, their stances showing that violence was near. As she looked closer, she recognised the tall, looming figure of Jhari, the giant Mackems half-elf. The other group, in dark leathers, must be the Cyfres.

Before blows could be struck, a tall figure ran from the front door of the warehouse and away toward the city square. He ran with an easy, long-legged stride, and the long hilt of a two-handed sword stuck up over one shoulder.

Angry shouts split the air as both groups, Mackems and Cyfres, turned to give chase. Luara kept running, leading Nastja and Ellyah away in a different direction.

The nearest alley mouth beckoned, but as they closed in on its dark shelter a Cyfres in a gold-hemmed tunic dashed out, as if running to join the pursuit.

Luara moved without hesitation, drawing one of her short, slender swords and barely breaking stride. She stepped smoothly to one side and the Cyfres ran onto her slicing blade. The fabric of their tunic parted and blood flowed.

Even as they slapped their hands to the long wound, face a mask of horrified pain, Luara was spinning on her heel. The point of her blade burst from his chest. She turned away as the body fell and did not look back.

'Come on!' she urged, slamming the sword back into the sheath with an air of finality. The narrow, dark streets beckoned, and they hurried in her wake to follow.

A few moments later, the upper reaches of the looming houses were lit by a pulsing, orange glow. It was noisy ahead, and with each step the volume increased. It sounded like the pounding of many drums. At the end of the alley, they paused and peered out, and were greeted by a scene of chaos.

They were looking out into the central square of Ben Gedrin. It was filled with people. They wore dark clothing, and their eyes were bound with pale cloth, streaked with black. Many of them were moving slowly around the square in a procession, and Ellyah's eyes widened as to see what they carried.

Bearing the ends of long wooden staves, they carried broad wooden platforms between them. Each of the platforms was topped with a towering burning structure. Ellyah realised that they were the houses she had seen under construction the previous day but set afire and carried aloft.

All around the lurching, fiery plinths, revellers danced as red-clad drummers hammered out a pounding rhythm with their curved sticks. This was Demonsnight, at the peak of the festivities.

Urgent bellows and grunts rang out from a wide, fenced enclosure at the centre of the square. A small herd of bullocks ran around inside, colliding with each other and shaking the fence as they barged into it. Ellyah goggled. Each animal was crowned with fire. They wore a brazier atop their wide, curved horns and a roaring, smoking fire burned in each. Occasional sparks dropped onto their heads and backs, increasing the noise and the apparent rage of the herd.

Around this enclosure, bonfires dotted the square and people gathered beside them as they spilled out from the surrounding taverns and liquor-houses. The very air was thick with the fumes of drink as people staggered everywhere. None of them were paying the three women any attention. They could pass across the square and easily slip away.

'Let's go!' urged Luara. Her brows were heavy with worry, her hands twisting anxiously. Ellyah had never seen her like this before. She turned and began striding away, without looking back to see that they followed. Ellyah knew that it was not far from there to the city gates.

She was ready to follow Luara across the square when a different noise caught her attention. It was the sound of steel clashing against steel, alongside a cacophony of screams and yells. The sounds of fighting.

'What's going on?' she asked, almost to herself.

'A gang fight?' replied Nastja from behind her shoulder. Ellyah stepped a little closer. Something drew her.

Before Ellyah could do anything else, she was hit by a solid force and knocked off her feet. The packed earth was hard beneath her body as she tumbled to the ground. Looking up, she was surrounded by the milling, uncertain shapes of a crowd. The revellers in the square had noticed the fight and were trying to escape.

Crouching to her feet and moving with the crowd, she weaved her way through, trying to find some calm, some respite. Where was Nastja?

Her eyes darted, taking in the streaming tide of people moving across the square. Then, she saw the reason.

A dark mass was bunched where a broad street opened into the square, and as she looked closer she realised that they were a line of black-clad militia. They had their spears set and were slowly advancing, moving further down the street.

Another line was advancing across the square, herding the revellers away. The Demonsnight party was becoming a chaotic brawl, but the spearpoints of the militia were keen enough to deter any attacks, and people were fleeing in fear instead. The square was clearing. The fiery platforms were still held aloft, the flames twisting and dancing into the night, but space was growing around them.

Down the street to her left, Ellyah could see a twisting mass surging against the militia line. Fighters in leather trousers and jackets clutching long knives. Sticasts.

One figure stood out from the crowd. It was a tall, fair-haired fighter who gripped a long and broad bladed sword. It was the guard from the warehouse. The one who had slain the two Sticasts. She did not have time to worry about him now. She needed to find Nastja.

Looking right, she saw her. Another bunch of militia had a crowd of revellers pinned in a corner. Nastja's shock of fair hair was just visible at shoulder height against the surrounding men. Ellyah could not make out her face but could imagine it tight and drawn with fear. This was no good. They needed to escape, and quickly. If they were caught by any of the gangs again, they would lose everything.

What could she do against so many?

Glancing in the other direction, she watched the crowds being herded towards the south of the square. The way had been cleared by the militia and people were pouring down the streets and away from the fighting. She could go that way, easily, and be gone into the night. The bag holding the gold and silver was heavy on her back. She had what she had come here for.

But, Nastja remained trapped.

Taking a step to her right, her hip collided with something solid. She turned. It was the pen of the fire bulls. A bullock bearing a flaming head-dress charged past, close enough for her to feel the wind of it, and she stepped back. The other bulls stamped and barged each other. Their small, dark eyes reflected each other's flames, and they lowed urgently in fear and rage.

Ellyah made her decision.

FORTY FOUR

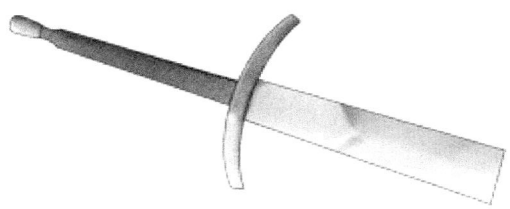

The bonfires cast the bloodied fighters with a demonic glow. As the militia stepped forward in their tight ranks, the Cyfres and Sticast had broken away from their fight with each other, turning to face their common enemy.

'Some bastard has betrayed us!' growled a nearby Sticast.

'Good chance to kill some of these black-vests,' said another, raising a jagged knife and advancing.

'Yea, let's hurt them. The way of the blade!'

'The way of the blade.'

Eain followed, staying a few paces back from the front line. He needed room to swing his sword, although once again he was not sure he could bring himself to kill any of the militia. They were not his enemy. They were just doing their job.

He cursed under his breath. He knew that the only alternative might be to surrender and be taken.

There was a clash of weapons behind him. Eain turned toward the sound to see the Cyfres trying to break out at the far end of the street. The militia were standing shoulder to shoulder, spears set firmly. Their line was strong and there were reinforcements in more ranks behind. It looked hopeless.

Ahead, the Sticasts were also charging into battle. The desperation of the attack, and the shudder and shock of many impacts were loud, and visceral.

Eain knew he would need to fight if he wanted to survive. In the chaos, he risked a spear or knife to the chest if he did not defend himself. He stepped forward, raising his sword reluctantly.

Then, something happened. The determined faces of the militia had been lit by the dull orange glow from the bonfires but were plunged into silhouette as a more intense firelight grew behind them.

Shrieks and shouts rose from the street, and the previously solid line began to break and split as individual militia fighters turned and shrank back. Eain stared. Fanned by a growing breeze, flames were licking up the nearby buildings.

The timber was dry, and the fire spread quickly. The militia were driven back by the heat and the Sticasts surged forward, stabbing and killing.

Before Eain could move, there came an intense drumming sound which rapidly grew louder. With a howl of horror, the leading Sticasts either jumped back, or were flung back by the force of a sudden impact. Several huge shapes charged down the street and Eain barely evaded them. As they passed, he watched in amazement as he realised that it was a small herd of bullocks, and each of them bearing a flaming brazier above their heads.

The terror of their brutal horns and the ferocity of their charge turned the fight into a press of people suddenly desperate to get out of the way. Eain saw several, Sticasts, Cyfres and militia alike, trampled or gored. The bullocks were followed by a sheet of flame, sweeping along the street like a force of malice.

Eain saw his chance. Blade held upright, he loped forward and dashed through to where the street opened out into the square. All resemblance to an organised battle line had been shattered by the charge of the bulls and the threat of the flames, and it had degenerated into a running battle through the surrounding streets.

The fight was far from over, but now Eain could escape.

As he dashed across the square, he noticed that a blackened structure of slender timbers was learning drunkenly against the front of a nearby tavern. Fragment of burning fabric rose into the night sky like feathers from a downed game bird.

He disregarded it as unimportant and ran on, sheathing his sword across his back and drawing his seax.

In every direction, the streets were a churning chaos. They were filled with a mix of gang members and militia, still engaged in bloody combat, and drunken revellers trying clumsily to escape the fighting, the bulls, and the flames. He ignored them all, and they barely saw him.

Moments later, the tall portal of the main gate was about him, and then he was striding across the causeway, toward the southern road and freedom.

Ellyah and Nastja hurried out of the city's east gate. Ellyah had her hand clamped firmly around Nastja's wrist. She was determined that they would not be separated again.

'No sign of Luara,' said Nastja, as they crossed the narrow causeway and followed the road that circled the city toward the south. 'I hope she got out.'

Ellyah glanced back. The underside of the low clouds was lit a throbbing orange as the flames spread through the city. Her doing.

She had opened the gate and shooed the fire-bulls out into the square. They had caused instant mayhem. Enraged by the spots of burning oil that dripped onto their heads and necks, they charged about furiously. Revellers, militia, gang fighters; all fled from their brutal horns.

As Ellyah had dashed across to where Nastja stood within a loose circle of panicked militia, one of the bulls had collided with a burning house-structure. The platform had toppled over and into the front of a tavern. Moments later, flames were licking up the dry wood, lighting up the sky a coruscating orange.

The distraction had been enough. Ellyah had grabbed Nastja, heedless of her shock and resistance, and dragged her away. Before they had left the square, though, something caught her eye. A tall figure moving purposefully in their direction.

It was the guard from the jewel trade, and as Ellyah watched he sheathed his long sword and drew a knife before striding away into the chaos of the streets.

So, he had escaped too.

'I'm fairly sure she got out ahead of us,' replied Ellyah, thinking of Luara. She had seen the horror in the older woman's eyes as they had darted through the dark streets. Luara had seen enough. She had bolted, Ellyah was sure of it. 'She knows how to keep herself safe.'

Nastja nodded.

'Look,' she said, pointing. 'That's where we left our horses.' She meant horses they had stolen, but was right. They had tied them up in a lean-to structure just outside the city walls. It was empty.

'Luara,' said Ellyah. She had said she intended to return them. Maybe she had. 'So, we're walking. I don't know about you, hen, but I want to get as far away from this city as possible.'

Nastja nodded again.

'I've heard Buren is a nice place to spend autumn,' Ellyah continued. 'We just need to follow the road south.'

She took Nastja's hand and they set off, walking away into the night as Ben Gedrin burned at their backs.

Eain had no idea where he would go, he just knew he must get away from this city. He had the urge to be somewhere different, and to leave this place far behind. The air was cold. Winter was close.

Eain had not taken more than a few steps onto the southward road when a charnel stink reached his nose, and he gagged.

Turning in the direction of the smell, he saw a figure approaching from the banks of the deep-cut ditch that ringed the city. It was wearing a tunic that had once been fine, but now looked as though it had spent a week in a midden.

It approached him with a stiff, awkward gait, arms outstretched, fingers grasping at the air. The face was of a middle-aged, dark-haired man but its skin was grey with the pallor of death.

'Stay back, friend' ordered Eain, dropping into a fighting crouch. Then he noticed the eyes. The eyes were fixed on him and glowed with an unnatural, red light.

He did not hesitate. The sense of wrongness exuding from this creature was almost overpowering. His sword hissed out of the baldric on his back and scythed down into the first back foot strike of Rule Three. The figure did not raise a hand, or even flinch.

It hit home, carving down from where its neck and shoulder met to cut deeply into its chest. The head lolled gruesomely, and blood oozed. Not enough blood. It barely bled from the wound. It came on, stepping forward undeterred despite the horrific, gaping wound.

Eain took a step away as the sharp smells of death, dirt and excrement assaulted his senses.

He withdrew the blade and lashed out again, a high horizontal strike powered by his fear and confusion. The heavy blade slashed through the thin strip of flesh and bone that remained, and the head tumbled to the ground, cleaved from its shoulders.

The body came on for another step, then the knees gave way and it toppled over. Eain looked down to where the head had come to rest in time to see the red light fading away. The cold, glassy eyes of a corpse long dead gazed out sightlessly.

The night was still once more. Eain could hear his own ragged, frightened breathing in his ears.

Eain could not explain what had just happened, but it was just one more horror to add to the rest of the night. He looked up, and back toward the city. Smoke billowed into the starry sky above Ben Gedrin. Beneath, the throbbing red of the spreading blaze lit up the skyline. The whole city could soon be afire.

It should be a shocking thought, but Eain could not make himself care. He could happily watch it burn as if it might burn away all his pain. He did not have the capacity for any more guilt.

He sheathed his blade once more and turned away. It did not matter. None of this mattered. All that mattered was what he could do, and what he would do. From now on, he would do whatever he needed. To survive. To carry on.

Eain Connow walked away as the flames rose higher in the sky. The jewel buried deep in his pack was forgotten. He did not look back.

EPILOGUE

It was snowing again. It had come down heavily in the night, drifting against the sides of the round tents of the camp. Dusk was near, the light fading from a low and heavy sky.

Cerla stamped the snow down in a circle around her. It would keep her boots dry. She had an hour or so yet until her watch was complete, and she had no intention of voicing a word of complaint about cold or wet feet.

Her right hand gripped the smooth, pale wood of her spear's haft proudly. This weapon felt as much a part of her as her own arms and legs did. It had saved her life and spilled the blood of Banahgar's enemies. She knew both were an honour, and a privilege.

The darkness was deepening. Vetundaeghur had been and gone and the days would get shorter for a few weeks yet. She imagined the wolves of winter, black furred and red-eyed as they raced across the darkened land with the *garmhounds* beside them. She shook her head. It was just a story to scare children.

Boots crunched behind her in the crisp snow, but she kept her gaze trained on the curve of the road, a mile away down the hillside. She was a soldier on duty.

The looming presence was right beside her before she allowed her eyes to drift to the side.

'Be at ease,' said a deep voice, and she stiffened. Her commander stood beside her. 'There will be no danger now.'

She turned to look at him, craning her neck to look up at his face. Callan Fraevar stared out through the swirling, dancing flakes to where snow was piling even more deeply on the road.

He was the Claihedehmore in charge of this camp, and although he was a brave and inspiring leader, he made her feel uncomfortable.

His Sword-Name was Dusk Wolf, and in battle he hunted his enemies and slayed them like a wild beast. The horror of battle touched him not, and he flung himself fearlessly wherever the fighting was fiercest. He spoke softly but was capable of ruthless violence. It was disquieting.

'Master?' she responded, questioningly.

'They won't come now,' he explained. 'Not unless their captains are morons. Even if they are, the Kotevari armies will freeze before they get this far north.

'The war is over for winter. They will make camp in the lowlands, and try to survive. So, we need to spend the winter getting stronger. They will come again in the spring.'

'Yes, master,' she nodded.

Since the Skjilde had been called upon to strengthen the lines, the tide of the war had been turned. The extra numbers had helped to halt Kotevari advance. It had slowed still further as autumn chilled into winter, and if Fraevar was right then the snow would halt them completely.

It had been bought dearly. Her friends Aidtha and Freaga had already fallen in battle. The tears she had shed for them had been hot and bitter.

But, Cerla still stood, and would defend Banahgar while she still drew breath.

'Roll on spring then, Master,' she said, with a slight smile.

Fraevar laughed loudly, clapping her on the shoulder with one of his huge, heavy hands.

'Aye!' he agreed. 'Roll on spring!'

Holt was awake. He stared blankly into the darkness, halfway between full wakening and his usual fitful sleep.

His nights had been disturbed recently, with restful sleep elusive, and it seemed to him that it had begun when those outlanders had come through Feorhryc.

He could not have clearly explained why, but he felt like the strange events of that day had been the start of something. Like a herald of change.

This night, though, something had disturbed him. What? There had been a sound.

It came again, and this time he knew it for the soft click of his front door being gently closed. His heart beat faster with fear as he lifted his furs, swinging his feet out of bed and down onto the floorboards.

He could not bring himself to speak as he stood and moved toward the noise. All he had was his bare hands. If it was a robber they would be able to take everything.

Then, a shadowy figure stepped away from the door and into the centre of the room. The pale moonlight gleamed onto a cloaked and hooded shape.

His breathing was deep and anxious. His fists were clenched.

The figure raised their hands, pushing back the hood that obscured their face. The room was still dark, but the pale silvery light from the sky outside was enough to illuminate their face.

That face, that he knew as well as his own two hands. That face, that he saw in his dreams as well as in quiet moments each day.

'Luara…' he breathed.

As she moved forward, she said nothing. He was silent. There were no words needed.

The final stage of their journey was beneath crystalline starlight.

'We should make camp for the night. Here. Now.'

Cerle Connow had tried to assert himself, a couple of hours previously.

'My wife is tired.'

The light was fading, the bleak featureless plains of the eastern extent of the Lands of the Great River washing out from sandy ochre to gloomy grey as dusk closed about the travellers.

The wagon driver had shaken her head, firmly.

'Not far to the farm. Not far. Safer, warmer, if we keep going. Not far.'

Cerle had clenched his jaw, ready to continue the argument but Indaella had laid a cool, calming hand on his.

'She speaks true, husband mine,' she said. 'It will be better if we rest indoors. The next stage of our journey will be harder.'

Cerle had pressed his fingernails into his palms with frustration and worry, but sat back silently in the swaying wagon. His eyes darted as he scanned the bleak horizon for any signs of lights or life.

They had taken their journey from Anish steadily. Both had left their middle years behind, and while Cerle remained fit and strong he found that the cold got into his bones more easily these days. His muscles took longer to recover from exertion, and his back stabbed him with knives if he had to sleep on the ground, or on a hard bed.

Indaella found travel harder still. She had never been strong and grew more frail with each year. Decades of disturbed sleep had sapped her endurance.

Still, they had managed to keep moving.

They knew about the Dry Leagues east of Annida and had paid a travelling merchant handsomely to take them as passengers on her wagon, with enough supplies, water and warm furs to make the journey safe and bearable.

She was a dark-skinned trader who had come from Tayo with oils and vinegars, and planned to travel to one of the most easterly farms in the Riverlands to trade.

'It is here,' she said, suddenly, pointing out into the blue-black darkness ahead.

Warm lights glimmered through chinks in shuttered windows, and the farmhouse building was discernible as a low block of deeper shadow.

Cerle was relieved. 'Now, we just have to hope that this farmer will welcome us.'

'Yes, yes,' she said, waving away Cerle's concern. 'Everyone welcome.'

Cerle prepared himself for the formal greeting and introduction that he knew would be required. He prepared himself to be humble, patient and polite.

'Remind me of the name of this farmer,' he requested.

'Tann,' she replied. 'He is called Tann.'

Evane Claes floated in darkness. Sometimes she woke, staring uncomprehendingly at the ceiling of her cell. Other times, she drifted in dark and haunted dreams. Always, her body was wracked with pain. And fear. Desperate fear.

For she had failed.

She had gathered her strength, praying fervently to Desya, and channelled it into the rotting body of Clayton Moore. It had been torture.

She had felt her energy draining away, moment by moment, as the former thief plodded through Ben Gedrin, drawn inexorably toward the ruby.

A slight increase in her strength had told her that it was close at hand, when a dark figure wielding two shining blades had leapt from the shadows. The swords lashed out, left and right, and the magical link had been abruptly severed.

She had fallen back, hands rising to her throat. Pain lashed across her, as if it was her own body that the swords had defiled. Fatigue had overcome her then, and she had slumped down and lost consciousness.

Some time later, she had been jerked into wakefulness once more. Something drew her, as though she was a fish caught on a hook. She managed to draw a trickle of power from within her deepest self, and suddenly she was seeing through another's eyes once more.

It had taken her some moments to realise what was happening, but eventually she managed to force the limbs to lift the lifeless body from the foul, dark ditch where it lay.

Without being able to express how, she knew that once again the jewel was nearby. Its mere presence was a beacon, and it lent her power. Power that she needed.

Climbing awkwardly up the bank, the eyes of the other beheld a tall man, striding along the nearby road. She could sense that he had the jewel as though it were a burning torch on his back. She bade the once-living body to approach.

Before it had taken no more than two or three clumsy steps, the man turned, drawing a long and gleaming sword.

No! she wanted to cry. *I am so close this time!*

But, the blade had lashed out in blurring arcs, and once more the connection was severed as the body was broken.

After that, she drifted into exhausted delirium. Hours and days passed uncounted as her mind and soul travelled outside her body, along paths of pain and terror.

Agony lashed her body, and whether it was sent as punishment from Desya, or whether her own guilt and fear conjured the torment; she could not tell.

Until all the sensations of moving ceased.

His presence beat upon her consciousness, and she quailed. The very weight of his might filled her with enough dread to make her scream, had she dared.

'My Lord Desya,' she began. 'I have failed you and I am sorry—'

Be silent.

His unearthly voice rang loudly in her mind. She was silent.

I have deemed that it is not your fate to hold the Demon's Tear.

Fate drives the jewel's path, and it will come to the right one to hold it, at a time that I cannot foresee.

They will serve our purpose at that time.

There was silence. Claes was surprised at the sudden change in the demon's ambition for the jewel, but held her tongue.

I have summoned you to give you a new mission.

She inhaled a shocked, eager breath. A new mission must mean that she had not lost all favour with the demon. Not yet.

You must find this.

A shimmer in the air coalesced into an image.

Claes watched it as it became clear.

It was a sword. An old-fashioned, short bladed single-handed sword, with gilding to the lumpy pommel and hilt. What drew her eye were the twisting, rippling patterns in the complex weld.

They writhed and squirmed as if the sword held a nest of serpents within the blade. It glowed darkly. It projected ancient, dark power.

The sword must be found, and one who can wield it.

Ancient blood must be in their veins, and might in their hand.

With its power at the head of my army, they will sweep the world in my name.

I will walk the world once more. I will be reborn.

Claes shivered, but she knew not whether it was from excitement, or fear. The only thing she could be certain of, is that Desya, and the forces he commanded, were about to darken the world.

THE END
OF
BOOK ONE
OF THE
JANTAKAI SAGA

GLOSSARY

ANISH – Country in the confederacy of Re'Emsser

ANNDRA CO JORTO – Traveller, apparently from Kiraband

ARALL RATHVEDD – Soldier of the Claihedehmore and instructor. Sword-Name – The Hound's Tooth

BANAGHAR – Country in the north-east, isolated and encircled by mountains

BEN GEDRIN – Capital and only city of Kiraband

BESNIK VO PUSHTO – Kotevari noble. Aristo and member of the Tecati

BRIN GALLIT – Leader of the Mackems in Carhinn

BUREN – Most powerful country in Re'Emsser

CAIVANE – Former swindler from Anish, now living on Tann's farm

CALLAN FRAEVAR – Banahgarian, member of the Claihedehlar

CANNIS "BUTCHER" FLETT – Deputy leader of the Mackems in Carhinn

CARHINN – Capital city of Anish

CARILTON TANN – Farmer and smallholder in the Lands of the Great River

CERLA – Banahgarian, member of the Skjilde

CERLE CONNOW – Banahgarian, disgraced former member of the Claihedehmore and Eain's grandfather.

CLAIDAH – Claihed training area (lit. 'place of the Claihed')

CLAIHED, The – The professional standing army of the country of Banahgar

CLAIHEDEHLAR – the rank of the Claihed below the Claihedehmore

CLAIHEDEHMORE – the upper rank of the Claihed

CLAYTON MOORE – Master thief and adventurer

CONFERAN - One of the Five gods of the world, the god of heroes

CYFRES – A criminal gang based in Ben Gedrin

DEMON'S TEAR, The – A mythical fist-sized teardrop-shaped ruby

DEMONSNIGHT - Autumn fire festival, celebrated in the Lands of the Great River, Alrean Empire and Tayo

DERUFIN MOUNTAINS - The biggest mountain range in the world, running east to west and dividing The Lands of the Great River from Buren, Anish and Kotev

DESYA – Mythical creature and demon

EAIN CONNOW – Banahgarian, member of the Claihedehlar

EDICH IANSSON – Banahgarian, member of the Sverlaeggare

ELLYAH JERIM – Anise thief and entrepreneur

EVANE CLAES – High priest of the Veil, title "Shre"

FORDON – Ancient fortified town in Northern Anish

GRAIGOR FARGUSON – Banahgarian, Master of the Claihed. Blind. Sword-Name – Eyes of the Sword

HAFIOH –The peasant levies in the army of Kotev

HELDEN HARADSSON – Banahgarian, Grandmaster of the Claihed. Sword-Name – Death's Face

HIERAAD – the Kotevari ruling council

HNIFFARE – the lowest rank of the Claihed

HOLT COOKSON – Village elder of Feorhryc in the Lands of the Great River

INDAELLA CONNOW – Banahgarian, wife of Cerle Connow and grandmother of Eain

JHARI – Member of the Mackems criminal gang in Anish. Half-elf

KALED - One of the Five gods of the world, the god of fate

KELL LEOWRACSON – Youngest of the Twelve Brothers of Banahgarian myth and founder of the Claihed

KEREVA – City in central Anish

KIRABAND – Frontier region between the Lands of the Great River and northern Tayo and Buren

KOTEV – Country in the east of the continent. Member of the confederacy of Re'Emsser

LANDS OF THE GREAT RIVER, The - A great land to the north and south of the Great River, in the north of the world. Also known as the Riverlands

LEOWRAC - Last king of Banahgar

LUARA ORSINI – Mercenary fighter from the Lands of the Great River

MACKEMS, The – Criminal gang in Anish, based in Carhinn

MAICHEN MUNRAE – Banahgarian, Master of the Claihed. Sword-Name – The Bear's Claws

MANEG – Eagle-headed god of wisdom. Foremost of the gods of Banahgar

MARA VA PUSHTO - Kotevari noble. Aristo and member of the Tecati. Wife of Besnik

MECULVY DUTSCH - A mysterious tribe of the Lands of the Great River. Also known as the Walking Birds

MORDEA - One of the Five gods of the world, the "Mother"

MORGAN BLANE – Banahgarian, Master of the Claihed. Sword-Name – The River in Flood

MZINDA BISANI – A mythical dwarven city lost in the Lands of the Great River. Known as "The Hidden City"

NASTJA MJETTE – Anise polymath and entrepreneur

OME - One of the Five gods of the world, the god of death

OSTURBROST – Capital city of Banahgar

PENTANG – Five-pointed symbol of the Five gods

PRATHIN PRA MITHRIN- An ancient legend about the forging of the Twin Swords

ROYAL SENTINELS, The – A military organisation based in the southwest of Anish

SEVERED CITY, The - The dwarf city between Buren and Anish

SJONACAIDHAN, The – Banahgarian organisation of bards, historians and musicians.

SKANE - Member of the Mackems criminal gang in Anish. Deaf, former prize-fighter

SKJILDE, The – Organisation comprising young female Banahgarians

SKYLE BURNS – Banahgarian, Master of the Claihed. Sword-Name – The Centre

STEYFAN JUKEEV – Anise historic figure. Former Duke of Fordon

STICASTS – A criminal gang based in Ben Gedrin

SUDVIRKE – The southernmost fortress and garrison of the Claihed in Banahgar

SVERLAEGGARE– the rank of the Claihed above Hniffare

TAYO – Country in the southwest of the world

TECATI – The noble elite and fighting knights of Kotev

TORRO – Bull's blood, drunk for luck as part of the Demonsnight celebrations

TUREANK - One of the Five gods of the world, the god of unity

TRESSIN OKE – Wagon train leader in the Lands of the Great River

VEKWICC – The northern fortress and garrison of the Claihed in Banahgar

WÖLFIN – Dwarf wolf-god

AUTHOR'S STATEMENT

I am an independent author. I am not represented by an agent or a publishing house. This means that I am free of any pressure to hit sales targets or to write to market. I am free to tell my stories in the way I choose.

Being independent also means that I have very little support for my writing. I carry out nearly every stage of the creative process myself, and the task of turning the story into a book also rests entirely on me.

I have no budget to hire professional help for development, editing, formatting or proofreading so I have had to do most of it myself, and rely on the generosity of friends from time to time.

I should also declare again at this point that I do not, and will not, use generative AI in any way during the writing and publishing process.

By reading this far you have already done a huge amount to encourage me to keep writing. I hope you enjoyed this book, and if you did, please tell people about it.

As an independent author my marketing budget is close to zero, but you can help me by leaving a review somewhere, or blogging about the book, or telling a reading group. These small things are huge for indie authors, and do more to spread the word about our stories than we can do ourselves.

Choose indie, and tell the world about it.

THANK YOU

A number of people have volunteered their time and attention to help me take this story from an idea to a finished novel.

Firstly I need to thank my initial readers; Rich P, Claire S and Julia M. Your patience with me messing around with the story as you're trying to read it is infinitely appreciated, as is your insight and feedback.

Thank you also to my fellow indie authors who have offered support and sympathy while I've been slowly losing my mind; Eryn McConnell, Seán O'Boyle, Hannya Kay, P.K. Dawning, Andrew D. Meredith, Morgen Christensen and Tea Spangsberg (among others). All fabulous author that you should check out.

Credit is also due to Paul B, who was a co-creator of the original concept for the setting and the story, whose fabulous artwork can be seen throughout the book as chapter headings, and who is always enthusiastic to offer martial arts and swordwork choreography advice.

Lastly, I must thank my wife Claire, who has to put up with me living in an alternative world a lot of the time, and my son Jim who has endless curiosity for stories.

Thank you all.

R.E. Sanders – Spring 2024

SECRET SCRIBES

The Secret Scribes are an affiliation of independent fantasy authors. If you have enjoyed this book, why not check out some of the great authors and titles below?

Dave Lawson - The Envoys of War

Bella Dunn - The Dreams Thief

R.A. Sandpiper - A Pocket of Lies

Bill Adams - The Tenacious Tale of Tanna the Tendersword.

T.G. Terral - Bloodwoven.

Sean O'Boyle - The Ballad of Sprikit The Bard (And Company).

L.M. Douglas - Gharantia's Guardian

Damien Francis - The Tome of Haren

Alex Scheuermann - The Odyllic Stone

Printed in Dunstable, United Kingdom